**Anne O'Brien** was born in the West Riding of Yorkshire. After gaining a BA Honours degree at Manchester University and a Master's at Hull, she lived in the East Riding for many years as a teacher of history. After leaving teaching, Anne decided to turn to novel writing and give voice to the women in history who fascinated her the most. Today Anne lives in an eighteenth-century cottage in Herefordshire, an area full of inspiration for her work.

Visit Anne online at www.anneobrienbooks.com. Find Anne on Facebook and follow her on Twitter @anne_obrien

ANNE O'BRIEN

The
SCANDALOUS
DUCHESS

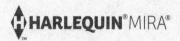

This edition published in Great Britain 2015
by Harlequin MIRA, an imprint of Harlequin (UK) Limited,
Eton House, 18-24 Paradise Road,
Richmond, Surrey, TW9 1SR

© 2014 Anne O'Brien

ISBN 978-1-848-45385-2

56-0115

Harlequin (UK) Limited's policy is to use papers that are natural, renewable and recyclable products and made from wood grown in sustainable forests. The logging and manufacturing processes conform to the legal environmental regulations of the country of origin.

Printed and bound by
CPI Group (UK) Ltd, Croydon, CR0 4YY

To George, who for a whole year tolerated having
to play second fiddle to John of Lancaster,
but knows that he always remains my hero.

Families of de Roet, Swynford and Chaucer

Sir Gilles (Paon) de Roet = wife/wives unknown

Elizabeth
c.1335 - 1368

Walter
c.1338 - 1356

Katherine
c.1350 - 1403

= 1. Sir Hugh Swynford
1340 - 1371

= 2. John, Duke
of Lancaster
1340 - 1399

Philippa
c.1351 - 1387

= Geoffrey Chaucer
c.1340 - 1400

Elizabeth
c.1365 - ?

Thomas
c.1367 - 1434

Blanche
c.1364 - 1376?

Margaret
c.1365 - 1433

Thomas
1367 - 1342

Lancaster and Beaufort and Tudor descendants of John, Duke of Lancaster

King Edward III = Philippa of Hainault
1312 - 1377   c.1314 - 1369

1. Blanche   = John, Duke   = 2. Constanza   = 3. Katherine
of Lancaster   of Lancaster   of Castile   Swynford
1342 - 1368   1340 - 1399   1354 - 1394   c. 1350 - 1403

Philippa   Elizabeth   HENRY IV   Katalina
1360 - 1435   1363 - 1426   1367 - 1413   1372 - 1418

John Beaufort   Henry Beaufort   Joan Beaufort   Thomas Beaufort
c.1373 - 1410   1375 - 1447   1377 - 1446   1381 - 1426

Margaret Holland = John Beaufort, Duke of
                     Somerset 1404 - 1444

John Beaufort, Duke of   =   Margaret
Somerset 1404 - 1444   Beauchamp

Margaret Beaufort   =   Edmund Tudor,
1443 - 1509   Earl of Richmond
                          c.1430 - 1456

HENRY VII   =   Elizabeth of York
1457 - 1509   1466 - 1503

HOUSE OF TUDOR

'… he [John, Duke of Lancaster] was blinded by desire, fearing neither God nor shame amongst men.'

Knighton's Chronicle 1337-1396

'… a she-devil and enchantress…'

The Anonimalle Chronicle 1333-1381

'… an unspeakable concubine…'

Thomas Walsingham's *Chronicon Angliae*

Prologue

January 1372: The Manor of Kettlethorpe, Lincolnshire

The water that had swamped the courtyard overnight, thanks to a sudden storm, soaked into my shoes. And then my stockings. I hitched my skirts, scowling at the floating debris around me. Even the chickens, isolated on a pile of wood in the corner, looked morose.

'Who left that harness out?' I demanded, seeing the coils of leather black and dripping on the hook beside the stable door. My servants, few as they were, had gone to ground, and since nothing could be done until the rain actually stopped, I squelched under cover again.

Kettlethorpe. My young son's inheritance, and a poor one at that. The burden of it, since my husband's recent death and the administration of the estate not yet settled, fell on my shoulders. I flexed them, my sodden, mud-daubed cloak lying unpleasantly around my throat. The shadow of a lively rodent caught my eye as it vanished behind the buttery screen.

'What do I do?' I asked aloud, then winced at the crack of despair in my voice.

There was no one to give me advice.

I imagined what Queen Philippa might have said to me. Raised by her, educated by her at the English court, the wife of King Edward the Third had been my model of perfect womanhood: a woman without physical comeliness, but with a beauty of soul that outmatched any I knew.

'Duty, Katherine!' she would have said. 'It is for you to carry the burdens. You are twenty-two years old and Lady of Kettlethorpe. When you wed Sir Hugh Swynford you took on the responsibility of your position. You will not abandon it when your feet are wet and rats scurry around your ankles. That is not how I raised you. You have the tenacity to make something of Kettlethorpe, and you will.'

I sighed, the tenacity at a low ebb, even though I admitted the truth of her knowledge of me. No, of course I would not abandon it. That was not my way, for the Queen's principles had been lodged firmly in my heart. What I did not have was the financial resource to improve my lot.

Despondent, I stepped to the centre of my hall where a fire burned with smouldering reluctance, and turned slowly round, pushing my hood back to my shoulders. The walls were running wet in places. The haze of smoke that never cleared tainted everything with acrid stench, for which there was no remedy that I could afford. I could not even think of installing a wall chimney.

'God will give you his grace, and the Virgin her compassion. Go to your prie-dieu, Katherine.' Queen Philippa again, framing my face with her hands as she imparted to me her own rigorous strength.

Certainly I would go to my knees before this day was out—was not the Blessed Virgin my solace in all adversity?

But on this occasion I needed coin as much as the Virgin's blessings. I rubbed my hands together, regretting the abrasions, the ugly burn on my wrist where one of the torches, flaring, had caught me unawares. Once my hands had been soft, my nails perfectly pared. Once my gown pleased me with the soft rustle of silk damask rather than the roughness of this coarse wool, the only cloth fit for the tasks that fell to me. Silk skirts did not sit well with wringing the neck of a scrawny fowl for dinner.

I sighed a little.

Once I had been honoured, chosen as a damsel in Duchess Blanche of Lancaster's household. I covered my face with my hands, shutting out the images of that pampered life of luxury at The Savoy Palace, for here, around me, was the reality of my present existence. At The Savoy I never had to sweep up the evidence left by a pair of doves roosting in the rafters overnight and now shuffling into wakefulness. Now I clapped my hands, frightening them into flight and further fouling of the floor.

There was one remedy, of course, to all this destitution. Duchess Blanche was dead these past three years, but the Duke had a new wife. Would there not be a place for me there, where I might earn enough to put all to rights? Where I might, in ducal employ once again, acquire sufficient money to ensure a better home for my son to inherit?

Why not? Why should I not return to the world I knew and loved? Surely, given my previous experience, there was some role that I could fulfil. Queen Philippa would have sanctioned it as an eminently practical decision for me to make in the circumstances.

I flapped my hands to disperse the smoke and a few downy feathers that still hung in the air and marched across to the stairs, to climb to my private chamber where I cast aside the heavy cloak. Lifting the lid of my coffer, I sifted through the layers of court dress, the fragile cloth sadly marked with moth and mildew however careful my attention with lavender and sage leaves, and lifted out a much treasured mirror. Opening the ivory case, dull with disuse, I wiped the moisture from the glass on my bodice and looked.

I pursed my lips.

'Who are you, Katherine de Roet?' I asked.

Katherine de Swynford now, of course, married and widowed. Suddenly distracted, I turned my head. Children's voices, raised in sharp complaint, sliced through the silence, but then dissolved into laughter, and I returned to my critical survey. I considered my hair, tightly braided and pinned, dark gold with damp, and dishevelled where the pins had come adrift under my hood. Darker brows took my eye. Once I might have plucked them into perfection, but no more. A rounded face, with soft cheeks and soft lips, a little indented at the corners with my present excess of emotion. A generous mouth, quick to smile, yet any softness there was belied by a direct stare. I raised my brows a little. No one would accuse me of shyness nor, brought up as I was in the strictest canons of propriety, of frivolity, yet I enjoyed all the comfort that wealth and consequence could bring, and to which I no longer had access.

And I wished with all my heart that I enjoyed that consequence again.

It was not a plain face that looked back at me. True, such enhancements as I might have worn at court were entirely absent. Indeed, it could have been, I decided, the face of one of my kitchen maids with that suspicion of dust along the edge of my jaw where I had rubbed at it with my sleeve. The mirror was misted again, and I polished it on my hip. They said I was beautiful. That I had the look of my late mother whom I had never known. Perhaps I was, although I thought my sister had more claims to beauty than I.

What was I looking for? What had driven me to resort to my mirror? Not the symmetry of my features, but to discover the woman behind them. I tilted my chin, considering what I might see.

Honesty, I hoped. Courage, to seize the opportunity to make more of my life. Not least a determination to live as I had been raised, with integrity and good judgement. That was what I hoped to see.

And perhaps I did see it, as well as the duty to my family name and honour to the Blessed Virgin that had marked every step of my life.

So I would go to The Savoy. I would petition the Duke in the name of my previous service to Duchess Blanche, accepting that I must relinquish my pride for I had a goodly measure of it—but I would do it, for my own sake as well as that of my children. If honesty was strong in me, I must accept that life in a desolate fastness, stretching out changelessly to the end of my days, filled me with dismay, whereas life within the royal court and ducal household with friends from the past beckoned with seductive fingers.

I smiled at the prospect, yet felt my pleasure fade. Replacing the mirror in my coffer, sifting through the words that had slipped through my mind, my heart fell a little at the sheer weight of them. Integrity. Restraint. Respectability. That was to be my life. That was what I knew. I would conduct myself as a respectable widow, unless I was fortunate, one day, to wed again. Queen Philippa would be proud of my strength of will to accomplish it.

My hands, in the act of closing my coffer, paused on the open lid of it, as if reluctant to shut away that reflection of the woman behind the familiar features. How dull, how colourless my chosen life sounded, as even-textured and familiarly unexciting as a line of plainchant. And how prim and prudish the woman who would live it. Was this me? Was this really what I wanted? It was as if I had decided to exist in shades of black and grey and religious observance, when energy, with sly enthusiasm, was surging though my whole body, opening up pictures in my mind of how it would be to sing and dance again, to be courted, to flirt, to exchange kisses in the company of a handsome man who desired me.

Perhaps this was the real Katherine de Swynford, lively and frivolous, thoroughly pleasure-loving, rather than a staid widow who looked for nothing in life but allowing the beads of her rosary to slide through her fingers as she petitioned the Virgin's grace for herself and her children. The sheer thrill of returning to The Savoy, to a position in the Lancaster household, glowed even brighter in my mind.

And then, as if summoned by my delight, there was the image of the Duke of Lancaster himself, standing in my chamber with the light behind him, as clear as if he were really there, as the sun creates a fantasy when shining through raindrops.

Impressively tall. Impressively proud. Impressively everything.

I considered him in my mind's eye: Duke John of Lancaster, a man I had known all my life, a man whom I admired. Admired. Yes—that was it, for was it not admiration? A man of wealth and power and striking appearance, the Duke attracted high regard and vilification in equal measure from those who crossed his path. Would I wish to live once again within his forceful presence? Well, why should I not? I might be overawed, overwhelmed by the extent of his authority and the sheer magnetism of his charisma, but I knew him for a man of unfailing chivalry too. He would not cast me adrift. Returning to The Savoy held no fears for me.

Opening my eyes, finding the bright image dispelled, I closed the coffer and locked it, before walking to my open door with a light heart despite my wet stockings, and called down the stairs to my steward.

'Master Ingoldsby! A moment of your time, if you will.'

And enjoyed a shiver of excitement, such as I had not experienced for too long. I had more important tasks for my steward to supervise than sweeping up after my doves. I was going to The Savoy.

I realised that I was smiling again.

Chapter One

January 1372: The Savoy Palace, London

It was like a proclamation of royal decree. A command complete with banners, heralds and fanfare. Every muscle in my body tightened, my breath whistled in my throat on a sharp inhalation, and I was no longer smiling. I was not smiling at all.

His voice was impeccably courteous, but the words he uttered sliced through all the bother that had occupied my mind for the past two months with the precision of a rapier. I could not believe what he had just said to me. This Plantagenet prince, so unconsciously dramatic on this winter's morning, had just carelessly shaken the ground on which I stood.

Yet was he carelessly unthinking? I looked at his face, to find his gaze direct and deliberate, enough to cause an awareness to run along my spine. No, he was not thoughtless at all. He had uttered exactly the notion that had come into his mind.

For my part, I had not foreseen any outcome of this nature. How would I?

And no, it was not like a rapier thrust at all, which would be clean and sharp and precise. This was more like a blast of hellfire. All my previous worries, trivial and domestic as they were now presented to me, all my confidence in my ability to cloak my thoughts in careful restraint, paled into insignificance beside the inherent danger in those chosen words, cast at my feet like a handful of baleful gems.

Cast there by John Plantagenet, royal prince, Duke of Lancaster.

My audience with the Duke, until this verbal cataclysm, had been much as I expected, as I had hoped. He welcomed me with all his customary grace. Had we not been acquainted for many years, since I had been raised from my days as a very youthful Katherine de Roet in the household of Queen Philippa, his lady mother? Our paths had crossed; we had shared meals and festivities. I had been a member of the royal household, held in high regard and affection, both as a child and as damsel to the Duke's wife, Duchess Blanche. I was assured that whatever the outcome of my plea, the Duke would put me at my ease.

I rose from that first deeply formal curtsy when he had entered his audience chamber. Eyes downcast, breath shallow with nerves—for however well regarded I might be, if he refused I did not know where I would apply for succour— I made my request. It was hard to ask for charity, however gracious and generous the reputation of the benefactor.

'Lady Katherine.'

'Yes, my lord. I am grateful.'

His soft boots, the edge, gold-embroidered and exquisitely dagged, of his thigh-length robe, appropriate for some court function in heavily figured damask, came within the range of my vision, and I glanced up, momentarily alerted by a rough timbre in his speaking my name. Nor was the Duke's expression any more encouraging. His straight brows were level, hinting at a frown, his lips tight-pressed, causing my heart to flutter against my ribs. He was going to refuse me after all. There was no position for me here. By tomorrow I would be back on the road to the fasts of Lincolnshire with nothing to show for my long journey. He would tell me kindly, but he would refuse me.

But then, as he caught some anxiety in my expression, he was smiling.

'Don't look so anxious, Lady Katherine. You never used to. Did you think I would turn you from my door?'

The roughness was smoothed away as he touched my arm, a fleeting pressure. My heart's flutter became a thud.

'Thank you, my lord,' I murmured.

'I cannot express my sadness for your husband's death.'

'Thank you, my lord,' I repeated.

There was nothing else for me to say that would not over-whelm me with one difficult emotion or another. My husband was dead a mere two months, somewhere in the battlefields of Aquitaine.

'I valued Sir Hugh's services greatly.' The Duke paused. 'And yours have been inestimable. For you, Katherine,' he lapsed into the more familiar, abandoning the title that had come with my marriage, 'there will always be a position here.' And then, with gentleness: 'Your place in the Duchess Blanche's household earned you great merit. You must come to us again.'

Relief spread through me, sweet as honey. I sighed imper-ceptibly. All the fears that had pinioned my mind in recent weeks so that I could not think, could not plan, could not

envisage the future, fell away. I would no longer be dependent on the limited revenues from the Swynford estates at
Kettlethorpe and Coleby. I would have money to spend on
critical refurbishments. My children would lack for nothing.

'Thank you, my lord,' I said for the third time in as many
minutes. I seemed to have lost the capacity to form any
other response, and for a moment I was touched with a pale
amusement. I had not been known for lack of conversation.
'Forgive me,' I said. 'I cannot tell you how much that will
mean to me.'

'Is Kettlethorpe very bad?' he asked. He knew my situation.

'You have no idea, my lord.'

And with the relief I raised my eyes to his, to discover that
he was watching me closely, so that I felt the blood rise to
heat my cheeks, and my relief became overlaid with a layer
of uncertainty. Perhaps he was waiting for a more effusive
sign of my gratitude. After all, I had no claim on him, no tie
of duty or blood. Some would say he had done quite enough
for me and my family.

Could it be that he thought me unfit for the position I
sought? Damsels in royal households were chosen for their
elegance and beauty as much as for their practical skills,
women worthy in appearance and demeanour to serve the
lady. I had done my best. My dark robes were as fine as I
could make them, with no remnant of Lincolnshire mud.
As for my hands and face, all that could be seen in the all-
enveloping shrouding, I had applied the contents of my stillroom with fervour to remedy the effect of Kettlethorpe's
demands. I did not think the Duke would judge me too
harshly, knowing my circumstances. And yet his eye had
the fierce focus of a raptor.

To deflect the appraisal I launched into what I thought he wanted from me.

'I cannot express my thanks enough, my lord. I feared for my children, living in hardship. I thought I should not come to you, because although I no longer have a claim on your generosity, Hugh was in your service, and you were good enough to stand godfather to my daughter Blanche. I knew that you would want Hugh's son, Thomas, to do well in the world, and before God, there is little to give him anything but the most slender of incomes from the Swynford estates. Thomas is still so young and I have not the experience to manage the land well—or the money to do it, of course...'

My words dried. A minute ago I had been impossibly tongue-tied: now I was ridiculously garrulous. Had he not said that he would employ me? My problems were at an end and I could be at peace, but my heart continued to bound like a squirrel caught in a trap as the huntsman approached with a predatory gleam in his eye.

I thought that there might be such a gleam in the royal Duke's eye, then chided myself. Most likely it was nothing but a shaft of light through the glazed windows, or simply amusement at my lapse into trivialities.

'Forgive me, my lord,' I found myself saying yet again.

His reply was plain. 'You have asked pardon enough, my lady. You did right to come to me. I will arrange that you take up a position as damsel in my wife's household.'

He hesitated, the pause drawing out to fill the room. There was no doubt that he was frowning. Apprehension built again, a wad of sheep's wool to dry my throat.

'No,' he said. The harshness of his tone unnerved me. 'That is not what I want...' And stretching out a hand towards me, he added: 'I had forgotten how very beautiful you are. Your face has a grace, a translucent loveliness beyond my recall. And if you deigned to smile at me once in a while, it would illuminate every corner of the room.'

Which robbed me of the ability either to smile or to make any coherent response at all. Not understanding why the Duke should flatter me so highly—or was it flattery?—simply hearing the denial of what he had offered barely a minute ago, I took an uneasy step back, rejecting the thought that he might actually expect me to place my hand in his, and replied to the least shocking part of his speech.

'Forgive me for being importunate, my lord.' I forced my voice to remain uninflected. 'I should leave. Until you have decided where I might be of service. Perhaps at some point in the future. I am sure that with the coming of drier weather in spring the problems of Kettlethorpe will not seem so overwhelming.'

I closed my lips, angry that I had been drawn into such a show of weakness. I would not beg. I would not make more excuses. It not being in my nature to ask again where I had been refused, I curtsied, a brisk farewell. 'I am grateful that you received me, my lord.' I turned to walk towards the door, pondering at this strange outcome. The Duke did not have the name for being a man who played fast and loose with the sensibilities of his dependents.

'Don't leave, Katherine.'

It was not a request. Suddenly it was very personal, and I halted.

'Don't go.'

I looked back over my shoulder but did not turn, my sole thought to depart from that room and the humiliating refusal he had just handed to me.

'But you said that you did not wish to arrange a position for me, my lord.'

'No, I don't.'

'Then what do you want, my lord?'

An inappropriately peremptory question perhaps, but by now I admitted to profound irritation. His dark hair might lay feathered against brow and cheek, curling immaculately against his neck; his elegant figure might express the epitome of earthly authority; he might be the proudest man I knew; yet he was still a man, prone to strange moments of inconsistency. And, as if to prove me right, he spoke the words that undermined every tenet I had been raised to honour.

'I don't want you as governess to my children. I don't want you as damsel for my wife. *I* want you. I want you for my own.'

He did not attempt to moderate his voice to any degree, a voice used to issuing commands on a battlefield, in the cut and thrust of Parliament or in fiery debate with merchants over the extortionate level of taxes. The words reached me, with perfect clarity in their meaning.

'I want you, Lady Katherine de Swynford.'

Now, slowly, every sense suspended in shock, I turned to face him, unable to lower my gaze from his.

'I want you.' He strode forward, and before I could thrust them behind my back he had clasped my hands in his. 'Do you understand what I am saying? I want to kiss you, and I don't mean a formal salute to your undoubtedly pretty fingertips.' Which he instantly executed with neat precision. 'I want to take you to my bed.'

Those fingertips lay nerveless in his clasp, my lips parted, but no words issued. Every sense, every feeling, seemed to be frozen in shock. In outrage when he raised one hand as if he would touch my cheek. I stiffened, anticipating what must surely be a caress. Then he simply ran his fingers along the edge of my veil, putting to rights its elegant fall. And I exhaled slowly, until he demanded:

'I think you are not averse to me?' He made of it a question. 'Katherine…' There was the exhalation, the familiar impatience that I recognised so well, but his voice and face were as smooth as the silk I had once worn, as I had hoped to wear again. 'Will you come to me? You are a widow, owing loyalty to no man. You are without a protector. Will you give yourself into my keeping and allow me the honour of being your lover?'

Now I looked at him in sheer disbelief. John of Lancaster, the perfect knight, the most honourable and chivalrous of King Edward the Third's sons, newly wed to Constanza of Castile a matter of months ago. And I, at twenty-two years widowed and of good repute, raised by his royal mother to uphold all the precepts of piety and virtuous dignity. And he was asking me if I would be his leman.

'You stir my loins, Katherine de Swynford.'

Well, that pronouncement I could not mistake. The words slammed into my understanding. Was the Duke exerting some *droit de seigneur*, demanding my compliance? I did not wait the length of a breath to consider and select a reply; there was only one word I could say.

'No.' It was as flat a denial as I could summon.

'Is that a considered refusal?'

'Yes. My answer is no.'

'Why not?'

I flushed. His brows indicated that he was surprised. 'No,' I repeated. 'I don't need to consider it.' And bracing myself, for John of Lancaster had a chancy temper, I added, in case he had not taken my meaning: 'My answer is without qualification. No, my lord, I will not. How could you ask it of me?' I tugged my hands from his, thinking that perhaps I should escape before the torrent was released.

It was too late.

The Plantagenet prince lifted his chin as if he could not envisage a refusal, and then as I tensed against the verbal assault that would assuredly fall on my head, he gave a shout of laughter that reverberated from the walls.

Which was inexplicable. Was he mocking me? I bridled.

'I see nothing to laugh at,' I remarked coldly.

On which he stopped to draw in a breath, his eyes still gleaming with whatever it was that had moved him to a show of mirth.

'You have a way with words, Lady Katherine.'

'Because I said no?'

'Exactly. I could not possibly mistake your sentiments, could I?' He seized my hand again, and before I could stop him, saluted my fingers with a perfect propriety, at the same time as he executed a courtly bow.

'I will have to make do with that after all,' he observed, running his thumb across my fingertips.

'And that is all I will offer you, my lord,' I responded. That my hand tingled was not to be considered.

The Duke laughed again, but briefly. Whatever humour he had discovered in my predicament, or his own, had fled.

'It seems that I have been too previous in my request. Now it is my turn to ask pardon. Forgive my insensitivity.' He paused, his expression grave, the tendons of his jaw stark. And then a gleam appeared in his eye as he added: 'But I should warn you, Lady Katherine. I will not be denied. It is not in my nature to accept so determined a rebuttal.'

And as he strode from the audience chamber, as his footsteps faded, as he crossed the antechamber beyond and took the stairs to the upper floor, I was left to wonder if I had imagined the whole unnerving incident. But when I heard his final parting shot, delivered to me and echoing from the well of the stairs, there could be no denying his meaning.

There was no misinterpretation on my part of the whole of that inexplicable episode. His final words, which had floated back to me as clearly as if he had been standing in the room, had been quite as unambiguous as all the rest.

I sank down where he had left me, onto a stool that had been pushed with its companion against one of the walls. Hands clasped together, so tightly that my knuckles showed white against my dark skirts, I stared at the tapestry on the facing wall, a masterpiece in silk and wool.

Of all the tapestries in the superbly appointed Savoy palace, why did it have to be this one, with its frivolous portrayal of courtly love, a lady and her lover languishing in a field of blossoms beneath a flowering tree, while silky rabbits frolicked at their feet. He held a hawk on his fist; her arms were entwined around his neck, her hair mingling with his as he reclined in her arms. His stitched eyes were admiring; her red lips were full of longing. I imagined they were not wed, or in any way concerned about the sinfulness of their relationship. They looked untrammelled by any pious demands on their virtuous behaviour.

'I wager you would share your lover's bed without any holy water sprinkled over you,' I informed the red-haired wanton, crossly.

I thought that she smirked as I imagined her reply. 'And would *you* be prepared to languish in the arms of a lover, Katherine de Swynford?'

I most certainly would not. I was no Alice Perrers, infamous royal mistress, who shared the King's bed with bold impunity, careless of the vilification. My behaviour must be beyond criticism. I must be able to kneel at my prie-dieu or before my priest with a clean heart. How could the Duke

have so demeaned himself, and me, to offer me such an outrageous position? I was no wanton.

I want to kiss you.

He had had the temerity to make such a request of me,
clad as I was in full widow's weeds from chin to toe to in-
dicate my deepest mourning. If my dark robes had not her-
alded my state to the whole world, the all-enclosing wimple
and long veil should have been as obvious as a slap in the
face to any man with ulterior motives. I was no loose harlot, willing to accept any position offered at court to secure
my future comforts.

Flexing my fingers, I smoothed the black cloth over my
knees. Hugh had been dead so short a time, struck down in
the Duke's own service in Aquitaine. Did the Duke think I
would soil my husband's memory by leaping into his bed—
or that of any man—at the first opportunity? I could not
comprehend any action of mine in the past to give him the
opinion that I would care so little for my reputation, or for
God's judgement on what would be a blatant act of adultery.

Adultery.

The harsh judgement shivered over me and as my outrage built, I pondered all I knew of the Duke. A prince with
a reputation for high-minded courtesy and chivalry, he had
adored his first wife, Blanche, and was plunged into desolation by her untimely death three years before. He would
never have strayed from her side. And now he had a new
wife, a marriage of three months' standing, and the prospect
of a new child and a new kingdom to rule if he could enforce
Constanza's claim to Castile in his own right. A man of ambition, the Duke would do nothing to jeopardise the authority
in that distant kingdom if he wore its crown. He would not
take a mistress within three months of bedding a new wife.

It was all beyond sense. The Duke of Lancaster was not the mindlessly pretty, disreputable young man of the tapestry whose sole concern was dalliance.

And yet, at the same time I was forced to acknowledge that the puissant Duke of Lancaster, raised in royal indulgence from his cradle, was the possessor of a will as strong as cold steel. *I will not be denied*, he had said. *It is not in my nature to accept so determined a rebuttal.*

It was an uncomfortable thought.

And my next proved to be an even more disconcerting companion.

Was the fault mine? Had I, however inadvertently, however cleverly cautious I had considered myself to be, encouraged the Duke to think that I would welcome so impious a request? I could not imagine that I had dropped so careless a word, made so flirtatious a gesture, just as I was certain that I had never led him to believe that I would step so far beyond seemly behaviour. Inappropriate desires and longings, even if I had them, were to be held under restraint and confessed only before the priest.

I cast my mind back over the three years since I had left the household on Duchess Blanche's death, when we had all been deluged in mourning black, overwrought with grief. The only occasion on which I had seen the Duke was two years ago at the interment of Queen Philippa in Westminster Abbey, when he had pinned a mourning brooch to my bodice. Hardly an occasion for unseemly flirtation.

So perhaps I had misconstrued the whole of the past hour, making my present tumbling concerns entirely irrelevant. But of course, I had not misconstrued it. I would have been witless to put a wrong interpretation on his parting shot

And I don't like you in widow's weeds, he had informed

me from a distance. *They don't become you. If I were your lover I would clothe you in silk and cloth of gold.*

No, I was under no delusion about that: so intimate, so personal a comment on how I looked, what I wore and how he would remedy it. What right had he, when custom demanded that I wear mourning for a year? Vanity—assuredly a sin—lit a little flame of anger, as I spread out my skirts, disliking the weight of them in the voluminous amount of material, fretting that my wimple and veils leached colour from my skin. I knew I did not look my best, and was woman enough to regret it.

But how dare he remark on it?

And why had he laughed at my refusal?

I was furiously unsettled, for my future was still dependent on the Duke. He had not yet made an answer to my request. Had he changed his mind entirely in the face of my flat rejection?

With a swish of my hated widow's weeds I turned my back on the couple deliriously in love, wishing the smug lover buried under his blossoms, and strode off to return to normality and the company of those I knew, a household for whom I had a deep affection. A good bout of common sense and feminine gossip would do the trick. As for the lovers, the cunning rabbits would soon eat up the blossoms—and then where would they be?

I made my way to the royal nurseries.

Feeling an urge to knock on a door that I would once have walked through without a second thought, I resisted. Opening it, I walked through. How familiar the scene was: nurse and chambermaid, governess and damsel and sempstress, all intent on the burden of care of the three precious Lancaster children. Once as damsel to Duchess Blanche I had been one of this number, and would wish to be so again. There, at their lessons, were three little girls, two of them with royal blood, all much grown since I last set eyes on them: the ducal daughters, Philippa and Elizabeth at eleven and eight years, eyes trained seriously on their psalters— although it had to be said that Philippa showed more concentration than her sister who cradled a tabby kitten on her lap—while Henry—how he had grown!—all of four years old now, stood at the side of a lady who was engaged in explaining to him the illustrations in a book. And then there was the third little girl, whose age I knew precisely...

For a moment I simply stood and watched the scene in all its busyness, my heart so overburdened with love that tears welled. It had been an emotional day, one way or another. I swallowed and took another step.

'Good day, my lady.'

I curtsied.

The lady with the book looked up, expression arrested between irritation and then gradual recognition. The book was slowly closed and placed out of Henry's reach. The lady exhaled slowly.

'Katherine, as I live and breathe...'

Which caused me to smile, it being a well-recognised expression on Lady Alice's lips, whilst Alyne, wife of Edward Gerberge, one of the Duke's squires, surged across the room towards me. It brought all eyes to my face in a mix of pleasure and curiosity. Philippa smiled. Elizabeth barely remembered me, Henry certainly did not. As for the other child...

My eyes on the little girl's bright face, I curtsied again to Lady Alice. 'My lady, forgive my intrusion.'

'Nonsense!'

Lady Alice was on her feet, and then I was enclosed in female arms, patted and fussed over, Alyne relieving me of my cloak and gloves, before both found the words to commiserate.

'I recall the day you were wed,' Lady Alice said and sighed. 'Hugh was a good man—and I expect a good husband to you. But for the wife of a professional soldier, life can be very difficult.'

And I found that, prompted by such solicitous expressions, I was weeping at last, for Hugh and for myself.

'Forgive me, Lady Alice…' I could not seem to stop the tears falling endlessly, all the tears I had been unable to shed.

Alice FitzAlan, Lady Wake, merely poured a cup of ale and, as Alyne wiped away my tears, pushed me to sit in her own chair, handed me the ale and dissuaded Henry, gently but deliberately, from climbing into my lap.

At last I laughed and sniffed, but my eyes were for the third little girl who had come to stand at my knee, her hand now grasping my skirts. She was seven years old, almost eight now. I knew exactly, for this was Blanche, my eldest daughter, honoured with the position of damsel to the Duke's daughters. My lovely Blanche, named for the Duchess in whose service I had been when she was born.

Abandoning the cup of ale, I swept her up in my arms and kissed her.

'My daughter,' I said, touching her face. 'My little Blanche—not so little now. Have you forgotten me?'

For a moment she hesitated, as if reflecting on the matter in her solemn way, then Blanche buried her face against my neck. My tears threatened to begin all over again.

'She is a credit to you,' Lady Alice remarked in her cool manner.

'One day she will marry well,' Alyne added. 'She is very pretty, like her mother.'

I took Blanche's face between my hands, kissing her

cheeks, tucking away her curls beneath her linen cap. It was true she looked like me. Her hair was the same rich burnished gold as mine, the colour of autumn wheat ripened under a hot sun, but her features still had the soft unformed edges of childhood.

'And can you read and write yet?' I asked her.

'Yes, madam,' she replied with quaint confidence. Then reached up to whisper in my ear: 'Better than the Lady Elizabeth. She does not try. She likes the kitten more.'

For a moment it surprised me, that Hugh's death seemed not to have touched her to any degree, but then she has seen so little of him in her short life. She would barely recall him, and on this day of our happy reunion I would not burden her with his death.

'Damsels should not tell tales about their mistresses,' I whispered back.

'I know that!' she replied, her clear voice ringing out. 'But it is true. It is not a secret.'

I hid my smile

'Is that true, Elizabeth?' I asked. 'That you do not work hard at your lessons?'

Elizabeth considered me. 'Sometimes I do. I have learned to dance and sing.' There was a roguish twinkle in her eye— when had she acquired that? And she promptly demonstrated by tucking the kitten under her arm and executing a succession of childishly uncoordinated steps across the room to my side. But one day she would be elegant.

'And you, Philippa?' I asked.

'I always do my best,' she assured me, smiling so that her face lit as if with a candle within. She would be beautiful one day. 'You are right welcome, Lady Katherine. We have missed you here. If you returned to us, Elizabeth would mind her books again.'

I laughed, all my tears and previous anger forgotten. I had come home. It was good to laugh again

'Will you return to us?' Alyne asked. 'Now that you are alone?'

'I had hoped so,' I replied uncertainly.

'Have you spoken with Lord John?' Lady Alice asked.

'Yes.' I could feel my cheeks heat, and attempted to hide it by kissing Blanche's still-escaping curls.

'The income from Kettlethorpe was never great,' Lady Alice mused.

'No, and it's no better now,' I admitted with a sigh. 'And without Hugh's soldiering…'

'Lord John will be generous.' Lady Alice patted my hand as if I were one of her charges.

I was not so sure. I had refused what he had offered me, out of hand, generous or no. And if my present companions knew what that offer had been, they would not now be welcoming me back like a long-lost sister. Lady Alice, governess to the ducal children, was cousin to the Duke and a lady of high principle, strong on morality, firm on good manners. I suspected that she would banish me from the room, if not from The Savoy.

It behoved me to keep my own council.

Chapter Two

There was a commotion at the door, an exchange of words in male accents, and then the Duke entered the chamber where, on the morning following my arrival at The Savoy, the children learned their catechism, Lady Alice cast her eagle eye over all and I stitched at a length of linen in the window embrasure. His immediate awareness of me, conspicuous in his glance alighting on my face, made my belly clench and my heart thump beneath the mourning black that he did not like. It was in my cowardly mind to keep my eye on my work, as if stitching the border of an altar cloth would save me from humiliation.

Would he offer me the position I needed? Or would he continue to pursue the startling proposal of the previous day?

Not in public, he won't, I castigated myself. *You are a fool, Katherine!*

And indeed there was no need for my fears for it became self-evident, as his regard moved rapidly on from me to the other occupants of the room, that my worries were not his priority.

This morning there were matters of higher business to attend to. The Duke was uncharacteristically brusque, with a line between his brows, even though he found time to smile at the children, kiss the cheek of Philippa and Elizabeth and brush his hand over Henry's already tousled hair. The smile was, it had to be said, a bleak affair. I rose to my feet, putting aside the sewing, and, with Lady Alice and Alyne, made the requisite curtsy.

'I will be away.' His attention was for Lady Alice. 'I leave the children in your care, Alice, as ever.'

He was dressed for travel in wool and leather, the metal plates of his brigandine masked in fine velvet. In such a garment he was not travelling far.

'Is it bad news, John?' Lady Alice asked.

'It could be better.' It was impossible to mistake the grimace. 'My brother Edward's health does not improve and the King is…' The Duke shrugged.

We all knew of this terrible cause for concern. The Prince, heir to the throne and with a reputation second to none on the battlefield, was come home from affairs in Aquitaine, gravely ill, and his son, Richard, no older than Henry. Lionel, the King's second son, was dead in Antwerp these last three years. King Edward's own powers had waned in the months since Queen Philippa's death. Suddenly the smooth security of the royal inheritance was under attack: it was not a good prospect for England to have both King and heir ailing and the future king so small a child. Which left the Duke in a delicate situation.

Some said he had his own ambitions for the English crown, for no man of sense would place a wager on the longevity of either the King or the Prince. If the worse came to the worst, better an able man at thirty-two years and in his prime to wear the crown than a child of fewer years than fingers of one hand.

Looking at him now, at the authority inherent in his stance from his ordered hair to the fine leather of his boots, I wondered where his ambitions did lie. I did not know.

'The situation in Aquitaine and Gascony rests on a knife-edge,' he continued, as if picking up my thoughts. 'The progress of the English troops, without direct leadership—it's not good. I'm going to Kennington to talk with the Prince. I'll need to stay if it's decided that I lead an expedition. We badly need a victory against France, and it may be that Parliament must be summoned to finance such a lengthy campaign. It will not be popular, even though a victory's in everyone's mind...'

He was already moving towards the door, as if the burden of these decisions was driving him into action.

'I'll send word when I know my future movements.'

So, after shaking my world into disorder, he would leave without making any decision about me. My mind leaped crossly with indecision.

I really need to know where I stand.

It is not appropriate for you to trouble him with your inconsequential needs when the government of England rests on his shoulders.

I followed him to the door.

'My lord?'

He turned his head, his hand on the latch.

'Lady Katherine.' Impatient to be gone, yet as he took in my appearance not without a glint in his eye. 'Still garbed like a winter raven, I see.'

'And, as a widow, will continue to be until the year of my mourning is ended,' I replied tartly.

'As you will, lady.'

Oh, he was preoccupied, and I bristled beneath my widow's black. If the royal duke had been suffering yesterday from a blast of inappropriate lust for my person, it had been a remarkably short-lived one. Which was hardly flattering to me.

'Lady Katherine...?' His brows flattened. 'My time is precious.'

So I asked him one question. The one question that had troubled me, to which I needed to have the answer. Not why he had impugned my honour. Not if he would consider a position for me—a respectable position—in the household of his new duchess, or even an inferior position in one of his other establishments. But the question that had teased my female interest.

'My lord, why did you laugh at me yesterday? Was it all a piece of mockery?'

For if he had been amused, perhaps his intent had been to disconcert me, simply to see what a respectable widow, given the chance to become an unrespectable whore, would say. I could not believe him guilty of such dishonour, yet there had to be a reason that I could not see.

'Did my discomfiture amuse you?' I repeated.

He seemed to consider this for an inordinate length of time. Then, when his stare had disconcerted me so that my cheeks were flushed the pink of summer eglantine: 'Amuse me?' He shook his head, his mouth settling in a wry twist. 'I was not amused at all.' There was no laughter in him today, rather a lick of temper.

'You laughed at me, my lord.'

'Then I must ask your pardon, Lady Katherine.' It did not sound like an apology. 'If it was laughter, it was because it seemed to me impossible that it should happen twice in a lifetime.'

'What should? What should not happen twice?' I asked,

as confused as ever, refusing to be intimidated by that penetrating regard.

His hand fell from the latch and he turned to face me fully as he lowered his voice. At least he had the consideration to do that.

'That the woman at whose feet I would kneel in knightly adoration should refuse me outright.'

'My lord…!'

I simply did not know how to respond as, cursed with fair skin, my face flamed even brighter. I was saved from further embarrassment only when William Parr pushed open the door to appear behind the Duke's shoulder.

'Your escort is ready, my lord,' the squire advised.

'One moment, if you will.'

But Will Parr, well used to the Duke's manner, persisted. 'Forgive me, my lord. A message has just been delivered, that the King too will travel to Kennington. He requests that you accompany him.'

'Of course. I'll come now.'

He held out his hand to me, the jewels stitched on the cuff of his glove glinting, leaving me with no response but to put my hand there on the costly leather. With a curt little bow, he touched his lips to my fingers.

'It would be unforgivable of me to make you an object of mockery, Madame de Swynford. What it would please me to do is to put the light back into your eyes.'

And then I was left staring at his back.

He had made no decision on my future at all, and I had not asked him. How could I when he had clearly pushed me to the back of his busy mind? It might be a superbly romantic conception to serve me unto death, but only when the Duke considered that he had the time to encompass it.

We took the children to watch the departure from the steps that led down from the Great Hall into the inner courtyard. Since the Duke would travel by road to Westminster and then on from there to the Prince's palace at Kennington south of the Thames, rather than travelling by river the whole way, the great portcullis had been raised. The gates were opened and the courtyard thronged with horses and liveried servants in the Lancaster colours of blue and white. I lifted Henry in my arms so that he could see the Duke swing into the saddle of his favourite bay stallion. The escort fell into formation.

Without doubt, even his critics must acknowledge that he was superb, that he wore the power that had been his from birth with smooth ownership, as elegantly as he wore the livery chain on his breast, and just as arrogantly, as now, when he raised his chin, lifting his hand in a peremptory gesture to summon one of his henchmen who moved smartly to obey. Too arrogant for many. The Duke made as many enemies as friends.

'Did Duchess Blanche refuse to wed Lord John?' I asked Lady Alice. It was time that I sought enlightenment from the best source. She would know, as a cousin to both the Duke and Blanche of Lancaster. I thought my query innocuous enough.

'So they say.' Lady Alice glanced in my direction but without suspicion.

'I did not know. I was too young, I suppose.'

I had been sent, by Queen Philippa, to take up a position in Duchess Blanche's household in the months following her marriage to the Duke, when I was barely ten years old. If there had been gossip, I had not understood the implications.

A blast of the horn from John Tyas, the herald suitably puffed-up in Lancaster livery, a nod from the Duke and they rode out, stillness finally settling round us. So Blanche had initially repulsed him. But the Duke had obviously refused to take no for an answer from the woman he had loved. He had persisted, wooed her and won her.

But why had he placed me beside Duchess Blanche? He clearly did not love me in the same overwhelming manner. Lust, perhaps. Were not all men subject to bouts of uncontrolled desire?

'Why would any woman refuse to wed him?' Lady Alice mused, picking up the conversation as if there had been no hiatus—something she often did. 'It seems to me that he has every prerequisite for a husband. Exceptional features, grace, nobility, courtesy…as well as wealth and royal blood and all that implies.' There appeared the faintest sneer on her lips. 'Constanza of Castile was quick to take up the offer.'

'So why did she?'

'Because Constanza wants the Duke to win back Castile for her and—'

'Not Constanza. Why did Lady Blanche refuse?'

'Who's to say?' Lady Alice grasped Elizabeth's hand, to prevent an attempt at escape. 'It's said the Duke fell in love with her when they were both children, and he remained true until the day she died.'

I knew that. I remembered her death, with the Duke at her bedside, stricken with grief. I remembered him at her lying-in-state in St Albans Abbey when he could do nothing but stare blindly at the seated wooden effigy of the Duchess, clad in robes of state, the painted face uncannily lifelike.

'It was a day of heartbreak for everyone,' I murmured. I had adored Duchess Blanche. Did not everyone who knew her?

'I think perhaps Blanche did not believe him, when he first declared his love,' Lady Alice continued. 'She thought it was no more than a comfortable childhood friendship on his part, and she wanted more. She made him wait, and woo her in style. And then, when she was certain of his affections, she said yes, for she loved him, without any doubt...'

'Is it useful to make a man wait?' Alyne asked.

'Why not? If his love is true...' Lady Alice said.

'I have no experience of it.' Alyne sighed dolefully.

'Nor I.' Like Alyne's, my own marriage had been arranged. I had not had the choice to refuse or keep Hugh dangling on a bodice-lace as Blanche had done with the Duke. How empowering it must be to be so certain of the love of the man held close in your own heart. So certain that not even a self-imposed absence could destroy it.

If I had loved Duchess Blanche, I had envied her too.

Lady Alice sighed, nostalgia making lines across her brow. 'They were the perfect couple. How tragic that she should die so young.' The lines deepened. 'We'll see what Constanza of Castile is made of. Will she be able to win his affection, do you suppose?'

'Perhaps she already has,' I suggested. 'She carries his child.'

'We'll see...'

I looked round, counting the number of nursemaids who hovered in the background, ready for any demand on their services should Lady Alice or Alyne call on them. The children were well served, well educated under Lady Alice's hand. The new Duchess would bring her own women from Castile. How could I possibly think there would be a place for me here? And as things stood it would be better for me if I were not...

I made my decision. I would return to Kettlethorpe, a most sensible course of action that would shield me from any future enticement. The Duke would build a new marriage with

his foreign bride, he would forget me—had he not already
done so?—and I would be free to oversee the construction
of the best memorial I could accomplish for Hugh. I would
administer his estates to the best of my ability so that my
son might inherit a property of some value.

I nodded, my mind made up. It was a good end to my
visit. An entirely suitable end.

I wished I felt more enthusiastic about it. I wished I could
tear those words from my thoughts but they clung there, like
stubborn autumn leaves resisting all the efforts of a winter
gale to scatter them.

... the woman at whose feet I would kneel...

Such sentiments might be those the Duke recalled from
the initial days of his wooing of lovely Blanche to be his
wife. He had loved Blanche. He did not love me. Such sentiments had nothing to do with me, who would be no better
than a court whore if I complied.

I took the first opportunity offered to travel north—
running away, if I were honest. With my maid, my groom
and a manservant from Kettlethorpe who served as protection, I joined up with a group of hardy pilgrims intent on
journeying to pray at the tomb of St John of Beverley. It was
not the season for pilgrimages, the winter days being short
and the weather chancy, but the air was clear and crisp, the
ground hard with frost and the road surfaces better than the
soft mire of spring.

I was pleased to be on the move. Lady Alice begged me
to stay, not understanding my determination, but to what
end? I thought it best to be absent when the Duke returned
and his new lady was ensconced at The Savoy.

We travelled slowly and steadily, putting up at inns as we
followed the straight line of Ermine Street, the old Roman

road, before turning east at Newark along Fosse Way. Now the scenery, the flat open expanses, became familiar to me, and when we crossed the Trent—looking innocent between its icy banks but the cause of many of my problems at Kettlethorpe—I knew that I was almost home. And there was the vast bulk of the cathedral at Lincoln, the two magnificent towers emerging out of the distance like a ship looming out of mist at sea.

Not far now. I ought to be making a stop at Coleby but the depredations of winter made me keep to my track. Kettlethorpe would not be much better, but the state of Coleby would utterly depress my spirits. Suddenly I could not reach home quickly enough.

On that final morning, before I turned north from Lincoln, I fell in with one of the pilgrims who urged her horse alongside mine. I had taken note of her, although she preferred to converse with the menfolk. Loud and lively, her good humour was infectious on the long days and she was quick to sing and laugh. Broad of hip and shoulder, broad of feature too, her colourful garments proclaimed her perennial optimism, as did her hat, round and large as a serving platter to shelter her from sun and rain. I envied her confidence, her high spirits.

Mistress Saxby, a cheerful flirt and incorrigible gossip.

She settled beside me, the pilgrim's badges, mementoes of her many travels, jangling where they had been pinned to her cloak. I smiled warily. Her talk could be bawdy and she was not quick to take the hint to go away, but surprising me, her voice was low and respectful of my mood. She bent her head to look at me, her sharp eyes, grey as quartz, darting over my face. She made me uncommonly nervous.

'You look sad, mistress.'

It interested me that she had noticed. 'Not inordinately,'

I replied. I did not want to converse about my worries with this worldly woman.

'In fact, you have looked in poor humour since we left London,' she remarked, in no manner put off. 'Why is that?'

And so, since I must: 'I have just left my daughter—in London. It was hard to say farewell. She's seven years old.'

It had been hard indeed, but I had kept a smile in place, pinning memories of her farewell kisses in my mind.

'It's young to leave a child. A girl child...'

I detected a hint of criticism, and was quick to respond. 'She's in the Lancaster household. A damsel to the two daughters. I was there too until the death of Duchess Blanche.'

Mistress Saxby nodded comfortably. 'Then she'll not lack for aught. You should give thanks, mistress.'

She made me feel ungrateful of the blessings that had fallen on me.

'Are you a widow?' she asked, gesturing to my black skirts.

'Yes. Almost three months ago. He was fighting in Aquitaine for the Duke.'

'Ah. A soldier.'

'I don't know whether he was killed in battle or brought low by disease.' My companion did not need to know that he was a knight and a landowner.

'Disease is a terrible thing,' she mused solemnly. 'Last year my own husband took sick and died within the week. Look at the Prince, God save him. He's not long for this world, you mark my words. We'll say a rosary for him at Lincoln.' Her squirrel-gaze held mine. 'You're young to be a widow, mistress. How old did you say you were?'

I hadn't, but I recognised a practised talent for acquiring

information. 'Twenty-two years,' I said, smiling at the success of the technique.

'You'll wed again. Or perhaps you have a sweetheart already? Unless it was a love match between the pair of you and you're still in mourning.' I flushed at the implication that my emotions were so flighty. Mistress Saxby chuckled. 'I see you have!'

'No. I have no time for such things. Nor will I.' My reply was as sharp as her stare. 'I have two children at home who need my care. And my husband's estates…'

Mistress Saxby tossed her head, the veil attached to her hat dislodged from its neat folds. 'Your children will grow and move away. Your land will bring cold comfort. You need a man in your bed.'

I took a breath. 'That's the last thing I need,' I remarked.

It was as if I had not spoken. 'Your youth will be gone and forgotten before you know it. Without your pretty face, how will you attract a husband? You'll be a lonely old woman.'

'Do you speak from experience?' I retorted, but she took no ill-humour from my sharpness.

'Not so. I have had three husbands. And more than one… *admirer*, shall we say. I am a widow at present, but I have my eye on a likely man.' Mistress Saxby pursed her lips at the prospect of the man in question. 'Are you courted?'

Was I?

I would like to put the light back into your eyes…

'Yes,' I said, lured into indiscretion before I could stop myself.

'Is he a worthy man?'

'Too good for me.'

'Nonsense. No man is too good for a good woman.' She slid a glance over me, her smile widening. 'Do I suppose it is not marriage he offers?'

And I found myself replying to her catechism. 'No.'

'Is he wed?'

'Yes.'

'Do they live together?'

'They spent Christmas together in Dorset at Kingston Lacy.' That much I knew. 'She travels to London to join him. She carries their first child.'

Mistress Saxby's ample lips became a thin line as she contemplated. 'It doesn't sound too hopeful. I'd be wary of him, if I were you. Conflicting loyalties make for difficulties. But the question is: do you like him?'

I shook my head, turned my face away.

'If you wish to keep your own counsel, it's your choice.'

This made me feel churlish. 'How do I know if I can trust him?' I asked this worldly woman.

'Has he given you a gift?' I shook my head. 'If he does it shows he has designs on your respectability.'

'Oh.' I thought about this. Not that any gift had been offered. 'So I should refuse any such gift?'

Her eye gleamed. 'I'd not say that. I'd say accept any gift he makes you.' The gleam brightened to a twinkle as if she had been the recipient of many gifts in her past life. 'It may well be that it is the sign of a true regard, if he is willing to spend money on you and he matches the gift well to your inclination. And before you argue that it is too particular, the great Capellanus says—have you read Capellanus?—well, he says that a woman who is loved may freely accept from her lover a mirror or a girdle or a pair of gloves.'

'So if he gives me a gift of a mirror he loves me true?' I found myself smiling.

'Of course.' But her answering smile was sly. 'Unless he merely wishes to lure you into his bed. Only you can tell. You need to balance the good against the bad in any relationship, mistress. But I'd say take him, if you would. I have taken a lover, and enjoyed the experience.'

I thought about this too. I could well imagine, as I took in the expanse of her comfortable figure, assessing the quality of her enveloping cloak and her stocky grey palfrey. She was not without means.

'And sin?' I asked bluntly, startling even myself. 'What about sin? What about adultery, if I take this man to my bed?'

'Sin!' She brushed the word away as if it were a troublesome gnat. 'Will God punish us for snatching at happiness in a world that brings a woman precious little of it? I say not. I live a good life, I give charity to the starving, I confess my sins and find absolution. Would God begrudge me a kiss or the warm arms of a man on a cold night? I'm too old to look for marriage, I think. Now you'll be an object of admiration and desire. You're comely, and doubtless fertile, mistress.'

And Mistress Saxby raised her harsh voice—much like the raucous jays that hopped along the hedgerows—in song.

'Love is soft and love is sweet, and speaks in accents fair;
Love is mighty agony, and love is mighty care:
Love is utmost ecstasy and love is keen to dare,
Love is wretched misery: to live with, it's despair...'

She leaned to nudge me with a knowing elbow.

'But to live without it is even worse,' she added in an aside accompanied by an arch look.

I was sorry to see her go at Lincoln.

'I need to offer a prayer for inflammation of the knees,' she said with a roguish wink. 'And other bits of me. I'll not be able to go on pilgrimages for ever.' The badges on her cloak glinted in the cold light. 'Make the most of your youth, my girl. You'll regret it if you don't.' With broad fingers, surprisingly agile, she unpinned one of her badges showing the Virgin seated in Majesty under a canopy, with the Christ child in her arms. 'Take this. One of my better ones—pewter rather than lead—can't afford the silver. From Our Lady's Shrine at Walsingham. She'll keep you safe.'

Mistress Saxby patted my hand as her face grew sombre. 'If you do take this man, what I would say is: beware of the wife. It's easy to be carried away by the glamour of stolen kisses, but a wife can make your life a misery. Take my word for it.'

'I have no intention of crossing the path of his wife.'

Mistress Saxby's sharply cynical smile returned.

'As you wish, mistress, as you wish. Depends how fervent his kisses are, I'd say. Or how bottomless his purse!'

A hitch of her broad shoulders and she was gone, but her advice occupied my mind, all the way to Kettlethorpe. And then I abandoned it, because what Mistress Saxby might choose to do with her life was not for the Lady of Kettlethorpe. Besides, there was no choice for me to make. The Duke, in typical Plantagenet manner, had swept me aside as if I were no more than a young hound under his feet. Something much desired in one instance could become a matter for boredom in the blink of an eye.

Chapter Three

The rank poverty of Kettlethorpe settled over me in a desolation, as thick and dark as one of the boiled blood puddings that my cook was too keen on stirring up. Three thousand acres my son held here, and all of it either sand or stone or thick forest. Of good soil there was none; the land was incapable of producing anything other than a poor yield of hay, flax or hemp, and the meadows flooded regularly. Ruinous was the only word to come to mind as the mean houses came into view. The village looked run down, grim with deprivation, and so did my manor.

No surprise then that Hugh had sold his soldiering skills. Not that life as a soldier was anything but his first preference. If it was a choice of riding off to war or tilling the land, farming came a long way second, even if it meant being absent from me for most of our short married life. I considered, not for the first time, how I had managed to conceive three children. But I had, and they were my blessing.

For a moment the hall was silent except from the drip of water into a wooden bucket and the distant irritable bark of a dog. Then a rush of feet, followed by an authoritarian voice. I opened my arms, and into them fell Margaret, growing awkwardly at six years, and Thomas who at four had more noisy energy than he could control. I kissed Margaret, as self-contained as Blanche, and hugged Thomas until he squirmed for release. Hugh's heir. Hugh's pride and joy and hope for the future.

And there was Agnes Bonsergeant, my own nurse, who had come with me to Kettlethorpe, and did not mince her words as she clasped her hands on my shoulders and kissed my cheeks.

'I thought we might not see you for a little while yet. You were not offered a position with the new Duchess then?'

'No.' Stripping off my gloves enabled me to hide my expression.

'Why not?'

I sighed silently, hoping she did not notice. 'The Duke was busy. The Prince is ill, the King fading.'

'Nothing new in that. I thought that he might have valued your service—his wife carrying a child and all. Nothing like a mother with healthy children to give good advice. I'd have snapped you up.'

'So I hoped. Her own childhood nurse attends her. And her sister travels with her. Why would she need more?'

I did not want to answer any more questions.

'Still…you look pale, Katherine.'

'Tired, that's all,' I admitted, allowing Margaret to pull me into the private chamber.

'And Blanche? How is my little Blanche?' Agnes asked, collecting up Thomas with an experienced arm.

'Well. They are all well. Lady Alice sends her best wishes to you and wishes a fine husband on you.' I sank onto a settle by the fire. 'It's good to be home.'

Agnes grunted at the suggestion of a husband, fine of otherwise. 'We have some problems.'

I raised my brows. 'Some wine first, I think. Then the bad news.'

And while I drank, Agnes told me of the leaking roof, the pest that had affected the chickens, the poor quality wood, and lack of it, set aside for burning. We were short of ale, the last delivery being sour. A request that the road over towards Coleby should be improved at my expense—the list went on.

'It's not good,' I said.

'Nor is this place good for your health. Or the children's. You could go into Lincoln. Hire a house there for the winter.'

'I have no money to be spent on hiring houses. If I have no money to mend the roof, or pay to bring Hugh's body home, I have no right to squander what I have where it is not necessary.' I watched Thomas. We had given him a wooden sword for a New Year gift, which he wielded with dangerous vigour. Would he choose to be a soldier like Hugh? 'How would I forgive myself if I had nothing to give Thomas but a worn-down inheritance, and me sitting in luxury in Lincoln?'

'Hardly in luxury...'

'We must do what we can. I suppose the roof is the first priority.'

'A position at court would have solved the problem.'

'But I haven't got one,' I snapped, then immediately regretted it when Agnes scowled as if I were an ill-mannered child. 'I ask pardon, Agnes. I am more weary than I thought.' Then on impulse: 'Mistress Saxby said I should take a man to my bed.'

'Did she now. And who is Mistress Saxby?'

'A pilgrim with a practical turn of mind.'

'A man would double your problems, some would say!'

And at last I laughed. She was doubtless right. Agnes had never married nor ever would. Her opinion of Hugh had not been high.

'I have not come home empty-handed,' I announced before Agnes could consider asking me if I had any particular man in mind. And from my saddle bag I brought sweetmeats for Margaret and Thomas, a length of fine wool of a serviceable dark blue, well wrapped in leather for Agnes.

'From Lady Alice. She thinks we live in dire penury. I think she assessed the value of the clothes on my back and found them wanting.'

'She would be right. Did she give you anything?'

'No.'

I kept the pilgrim's badge in my scrip, even when I had considered pinning it to Margaret's bodice. I would keep it for myself, a memento of a very female heart-to-heart.

'And how was Lord John?' Agnes asked as, much later, we sat at supper, an unappetising array of pottage and beans and a brace of duck. 'Apart from being busy.'

'Why?' I was immediately on guard.

'Because he is the only member of the household you have not talked of.'

It was a jolt, but I forced myself to smile, my muscles to relax as I considered my reply, finding a need to dissemble. Agnes of the suspicious mind was watching me. With an arm around her shoulders, I hugged her close. She was very dear to me.

'Conspicuous,' I remarked. A word that barely did justice to the Duke's eye-catching quality, but it would satisfy Agnes. 'When is he ever not?'

And just as enigmatic, I could have added, but didn't. Agnes's eye would have become even more searching.

Meanwhile, the Duke's disturbing assertions continued to echo in my mind like the clang of the passing bell.

'Visitors, my lady. And by the look of them, they've travelled far.'

'It's not the Duke of Lancaster, is it?' I asked caustically.

Master Ingoldsby looked puzzled. 'Why no, mistress. I'd not say so. Did we expect his lordship?'

I squeezed his arm, sorry to have taken advantage of his limitations. Grey of hair, his face deeply lined, Master Ingoldsby's years were catching up with him. 'No, we did not. I doubt he'll find a path to my door.'

The Duke's carnal desire for me had died a permanent death. It must be something of a relief to both of us.

I was in the cellars, bewailing the contaminated hams—the roof leaked here also—and assessing the barrels of inferior ale, when Master Ingoldsby came to hover at my shoulder. I left the hams and ale willingly, and went out into the courtyard, tucking the loose strands of my hair beneath my hood, considering whether it might be my sister Philippa. I did not think so. Life in the country did not suit my sister, a town mouse, born and bred.

And no it was not. The sound of horses' hooves greeted me and the lumbering creak and groan of a heavy wagon on the road, and as I walked out past the gatehouse, I saw that the wagon had an escort of men, without armour or livery to help my identification, but well-mounted with an impressive array of weapons. As Lady of Kettlethorpe I would have to offer them hospitality. I wondered if my cook could stretch our supper of mutton collops and a dish of salt cod to accommodate another half-dozen mouths. Something, I supposed, could be achieved with bread, eggs and a hearty pottage, as I walked towards the man who had already dismounted and was pulling off his hood as he bowed. His expression was severe, his carriage upright, and I thought he had the look of a soldier despite his advancing years.

'Lady Katherine de Swynford...'

'Sir?'

The man inclined his head. 'I am instructed to deliver this to you.' He raised his chin in the direction of the wagon. 'I am Nicholas Graves, my lady. A soldier by profession.'

The ever-present nerves in my belly settled, assuaged by his courtesy. 'What is it?' I asked.

Intrigued, I walked to the wagon, expecting I knew not what as he drew back the heavy canvas cover.

'Oh!'

It took me a moment to acknowledge what I saw. A large linen-wrapped bundle of what would be pieces of armour and mail, another swathed roll of knightly weapons. A worn travelling coffer. A smaller box with a lock. And over all was draped a banner. A sea of silver, divided by the slash of a black chevron, three snarling boars heads in gold, teeth and tongues gleaming through the wear and tear of warfare.

The possessions and accoutrements of a knight on military service.

My attention was drawn back to the box with the locked lid. Someone had carved a chevron and three boars' heads on it, rough but recognisable. It was the small size of it... and as truth struck home at last, my knees buckled and I found myself clinging to the side of the wagon. Then Agnes was beside me, an arm around my shoulder, and Master Ingoldsby had a grip of my arm.

'I was ordered to arrange to conduct Sir Hugh's possessions home, my lady,' the soldier said.

'Hugh...' I whispered.

'Yes, my lady.' He looked at me as if he expected me to collapse at his feet, but I was made of sterner stuff than that.

'How did he die?' I asked as the driver climbed from his seat and began to unload the wrapped pieces of armour. My voice seemed faint to my ears and far away. I was shivering uncontrollably, but it was not the cold of the little wind that had picked up.

'Dysentery, my lady,' he replied laconically. 'He was too ill to travel home in September. We thought he was growing stronger—but he failed. In November.'

'Yes, I knew it was November. I was told.' I frowned at the fiercely grinning boars' heads, hating their vigour. 'But I did not arrange this. I cannot pay.' Now I heard the panic in my voice. I had visions of these sad remnants being taken away from me, because I did not have the coin to pay the driver of the wagon or the escort. Where would I find the money for this? I felt Agnes shift her grip and her hands closed tighter on my shoulders.

'There is no need for your concern. It is all paid for, my lady.'

'Who paid for it? Who arranged it?'

'My lord arranged it.'

I shook my head. I could not seem to take my eyes from the battered gauntlet that had slid from its wrapping and lay, fingers curled upwards.

'The Duke arranged it all. I serve him, my lady. The Duke of Lancaster.' As if he was addressing a want-wit. 'And I am instructed to give you these.' He pushed into my hand two leather bags, one large and one small, and two folded letters.

I blinked as I exhaled slowly. So this was the Duke's doing.

'Sir Hugh's body was too…' Master Graves began, then

bit off his words. 'Given the circumstances—well, it was decided to bring only his heart back here to England.'

'Yes…'

'My lady…?' I became aware of my steward looking to me for orders. I must think about the Duke of Lancaster's gift to me, but not now. Not yet.

'If one of your men could take the…the heart to the church, sir,' I said, pointing to where the tower of the little church of St Peter and St Paul could be seen behind a stand of trees. And to Master Ingoldsby: 'And these men need ale, if we can find any fit to drink. Then food.'

How superbly practical I had become as a warmth bloomed in my belly that Hugh's heart had been brought home. It was enough, and what he would have wanted. Later I would open the other packages brought by Master Graves. Later I would read the two letters. Then I would supervise the cleaning, repair and storing of Hugh's armour, which would one day belong to Thomas.

And I would, of necessity, consider the implications of such generosity from the Duke, for it was no light matter. Such open-handedness would put me under an obligation.

For no reason that I could fathom, Mistress Saxby of the wide hips and wider hat swayed flirtatiously into my mind. A lady might accept a mirror or a girdle from her lover. Or even a pair of gloves, for they were symbols of a true affection.

What if the impatient lover gave the gift of the husband's heart? The Duke had restored the only remnant of my dead husband to me, with the money to assure a tomb of some magnificence. The Duke had given far more than a passing thought to what I would most desire. Where did a dead husband's heart weigh in Mistress Saxby's assessment?

I had no idea. For a moment I wished she was there in her jingling pilgrim's garb to advise me.

I knew that would not serve. Any decision I made must be on my own conscience.

The larger leather purse hardly needed investigation. I could tell by its weight that it contained a sum of money sufficient to inter Hugh with honour. I pushed it aside. It meant much to me to be able to pay for an effigy on Hugh's tomb at the hand of a true craftsman, but it was the demands of the living, not the dead, that drew my eye. Lingering in the hall, I addressed the letter that I considered to be the more innocent of the pair, carrying it to a cresset, my nose wrinkling at the stench of hot fat. The wick needed trimming. It was all a far cry from the fine wax candles of The Savoy.

And there it was. What I had hoped for.

To Lady Katherine de Swynford,

Monseigneur de Lancaster has expressed a wish for your attendance and future service at The Savoy. It is expected that the Duchess of Lancaster, Constanza, Queen of Castile, will make her entry into London in the second week in February. As a valued member of Duchess Blanche's household, and in recognition of Sir Hugh Swynford's valuable contribution in Aquitaine as Monseigneur de Lancaster's retainer, a place is offered to you in the household of the Duchess Constanza. Your remuneration will be generous.

We expect to see you forthwith.

It had the pompous tone of a demand rather than a request, much as I would expect from Sir Thomas Hungerford, the Lancaster steward who exercised his authority over all the ducal properties in the south, but my heart leaped, and I was smiling as my eye ran down to the less formal hand, added at the bottom. Lady Alice had applied her own brand of entreaty.

Do come, Katherine. With your knowledge of the dangers of childbirth and your experience in the rearing of young children, you will be invaluable to the new Duchess who seems to be fragile in her pregnancy. Her journey from Dorset has been uncommonly slow. We will judge her calibre when she arrives.

It is expected that your sister Philippa will also return as part of the household since her husband has been dispatched abroad.

It is anticipated that you will bring your children with you. We expect to be settled at Hertford.

I look to you and your sister to support me against the influx of Castilians. Do you by any chance speak Castilian?

Quite like old times, I think. I look forward to your coming...

Alice had signed her name.

I folded the page and pushed it into the bodice of my overgown, my face warm with pleasure. A position again. A welcome. A generous income to bolster the rents from Kettlethorpe. Perhaps the ever-flooding Fossdyke would be put to rights at last and my neighbours would not glower as I rode past.

I would see Blanche, reunite all my children, install myself with Alyne and Lady Alice. I swept Thomas up into my arms, already on my way to my inner chamber, but then my steps slowed and reality checked my delight. Here was

danger. I had made my refusal of the Duke's demand suc-
cinctly clear, but if I returned to The Savoy, into Duchess
Constanza's household, was that not my being complicit in
placing myself back within the Duke's power? Was I not
opening myself to a situation that would be a moral insult
to both myself and his new wife?

I had wanted this position so badly, yet now all was
changed, all my initial naïve pleasure dimmed. I came to
a halt halfway up the stairs, furious with the absent Duke,
who, I suspected, had answered to no one since the day of
his birth. I was not responsible for his arrogant invitation. I
was the innocent party, I was not complicit. I had said no.
The Duke was under no illusions about my thoughts on this.
He might have a claim on my loyalty, he might pay me for
service to his wife, but there it would end.

I was perfectly entitled to make my dignified return to
The Savoy, on my own terms.

But there was the other folded page and a soft leather bag,
small enough to fit into my palm, with a seal on the parchment that was the Duke's own with the leopards of England
quartered with the fleur-de-lis of France.

Open it! I ordered. *You are making more of this than need
be. It cannot possibly make your obligation to him greater
than it already is. Read it!*

Instead, I tucked both items into my bodice, where the
letter proceeded to burn a hole against my breast and the
pouch nestled until it seemed to be a weight on my soul. I
could barely resist opening it, even though I knew with certainty that if I did, if I read what must be a personal missive from the Duke, then it would be opening a dangerous
window. Better that I consign them both to the flames in
my bedchamber.

But I destroyed neither. Instead, dispatching Thomas to

Agnes's care, I wrapped a cloak around me, strapped on a pair of patterns and made my way to the church, squelching through the puddles and wondering if I had lost my senses. Once there I walked down the aisle towards the final resting place of the earthly remains of Hugh Swynford.

Replenishing the candles, re-lighting them, I knelt by the little casket, where one day a fine effigy would stand, and prayed first for the repose of Hugh's soul. He would have been thirty-two years old, the same age as the Duke.

Looking over my shoulder to ensure that I was alone, I began to explain.

'I am going to Hertford. I am to have a place in Duchess Constanza's household. She is the Duke's new wife, the Castilian Queen. You would not have known about this alliance with Castile—or perhaps you did before you…well!' I took a breath. Speaking to the dead was foolish perhaps, but I felt a need to do it. 'I know that is what you would want for me. Have we not always served the royal family? I will take the children with me. But I will not neglect my role here. They already call me the Lady of Kettlethorpe, did you know? I am proud of that and I hope you are too.' I paused for a moment, trying hard to concentrate. 'I swear I will preserve your inheritance for your son. Thomas is growing well. His education under Lady Alice's eye will be of the best. I expect he will become a page and learn all he needs to know about being a good knight. I give thanks for it.'

The letter against my heart almost vibrated with an urgency.

'I am grateful to the Duke for his generosity. He remembers you with affection.'

I closed my fingers over the cloth of my bodice so that the parchment of the letter crackled. The package felt hard and uneven, its composite parts moving one against the other.

'It will be good to reunite the children,' I said. 'I have missed Blanche.'

I retrieved the letter.

'Master Ingoldsby will look after everything while I am away. The meadows have flooded again.'

I broke the seal and opened it, smoothing the creases.

'I don't have the money to clear out the Fossdyke. Not yet—but perhaps I can do it when I am remunerated. I will try to do my best…'

My words dried and I sank back on my heels and read. Strikingly formal, it was not of any great length. My heart beating in my ears, I read, my eye skimming over the first brief paragraph. It was as if he were standing beside me, with a similar irritation to my own, colouring his choice of words, which were abrupt.

To Madame Katherine de Swynford,
I had hoped that you would remain at The Savoy until my return from Kennington but you found a need to re-turn to Lincolnshire. Perhaps the fault was mine, that circumstances prevented me from making your situation clear. I remedy that now, by the hand of Sir Thomas.

That was good, was it not? Rather sharp and caustic, even a thread of criticism that my precipitate departure had ne-cessitated this letter. My heart steadied.

There was a space on the single page and then:

As for the rest that stands between us, I have no re-gret in voicing it. The matter is not closed. I live in hope that you will reconsider your refusal. I should warn you that it will be my life's quest to win you for my own. Your anxieties reached out to my notions of chivalry and honour, demanding that I come to your aid, but it was your infinite beauty, finely drawn through grief and the burden you carry, that smote at my senses. Your image remains with me still, even in your absence, as if I carried a painted icon against my heart. It is beyond my fathoming, but you are ever present, instilling me with your radiance. I need to see you again.

I send you this trifle as a symbol of my regard for your welfare, of both body and soul.

I am, and will always be, despite your expressed qualms, yours to command.

My future happiness, for good or ill, rests with you.

There was another little space. And then:

It is my wish that you will leave your widow's weeds in Lincolnshire. I wish to see you clad as befits your status in my household. Apart from my own wishes, why would a felicitous bride desire a damsel dressed like storm-crow?

There was no signature. There did not need to be, for the owner of the flamboyant wording and forceful command was without doubt the Duke. As I took in what was imperiously issued with no consideration that I might actually refuse, I scowled at the final comment, and was aware of making a little mew of distress as my heart once again thudded against my ribs. I looked up—surely a sign of guilt—as if Hugh might be aware and would ask what tormented me.

But the church was settled into its habitual silence around me.

So what had the importunate Duke sent me?

I laid the letter down, loosed the draw-string of the little pouch, but, before I could catch it, out slithered a rosary, a string of simple beads threaded on a length of silk, to fall to the floor at my side. But not simple at all, I saw as I scooped them up. The *aves* in their little groups of ten were of coral, the softest pink, as seductively smooth as a baby's palm, richly interposed by the larger paternosters of carved jet with gilded flowers.

This was no trifle. I breathed out slowly, lifting the gift so that the candlelight glimmered along its length. I looked again at the letter and the lovely beads, which I allowed to slide again from my hand to be caught by the fullness of my skirts.

And there was Mistress Saxby beside me, with her world-weary smile.

Has he given you a gift? If he does it shows he had designs on your respectability.

So I should refuse any such gift?

I'd say accept any gift he makes you. It may well be that it is the sign of a true regard, if he is willing to spend money on you and he has matched the gift well to your inclination.

He had given me a rosary. He knew that such a gift would be close to my heart.

Unless he merely wishes to lure you into his bed. Mistress Saxby was still needling with her observations.

But a rosary, with its exquisitely carved silver crucifix. Did he make light of my strong faith, which would make the position of mistress, no matter how important the lover, anathema? Were these gifts, a string of beads, a purse of coin and a preserved heart, nothing more than lures to buy my compliance?

Or was he concerned merely to give me what I needed? What would please me?

How could I discover the answers to such impossible

questions? For the briefest of moments I covered my face with my hands, then knelt upright and squared my shoulders.

'Dear Hugh, I want you to know. I honoured you. I was loyal to you in thought and deed through all the years of our marriage. But…forgive me.' I stuffed the letter and beads back into my overgown and placed my hand flat on the carved coffer lid. 'I was never unfaithful to you. I was a good wife. But now…'

And because I could no longer stay there in that holy place with my thoughts in such wanton turmoil I stood, genuflected and hurried out.

Will God punish us for snatching at happiness in a world that brings a woman precious little of it?

I pushed Mistress Saxby's questionable wisdom aside, but shame and desire kept joint pace with me. Returned to the manor, I made excuses—I knew not what—to Agnes and Master Ingoldsby and took refuge behind the closed door of my chamber.

And there, for the first time for almost eight years I allowed thoughts of John of Lancaster to flood in without restraint, and take possession. This was the man. This was what he meant to me.

I stood by the head of my bed, in the shadow of the thick damask hangings, once a lustrous blue, worn and faded now into a uniform greyness. I stood as if I were an onlooker, for the walls of my chamber grew dim in my sight, to be replaced with the rich severity of the chapel at The Savoy where I had been wed to Hugh.

How powerful memory could be. Instead of the dusty silence of my chamber, broken only by occasional rustles and cheeps from the singing finches in their cage, bright little birds that I had bought for Margaret's amusement, the scene was peopled with faces and figures from the past that I knew well, a little gathering to celebrate an old and sacred rite. The candles were bright, the high quality wax perfumed with incense, the altar heavy with gold, but it was a quiet, intimate scene, without display as was fitting. I, fourteen years old and newly delivered of my daughter, stood with the child in my arms.

It was as if I had stepped into the ceremony already underway with prayers said and promises made. With the appropriate words, the priest lifted the infant from me, allowing the linen covering to fall to the floor, before lowering her into the font where the shock of the cold water caused her to drag in a breath and expel it in a cry of pure anguish. Her hands beat on the water, her dark eyes wide and staring with distress, and I, new mother as I was, was stricken.

It was the Duke, standing as my child's godfather—was I not highly favoured in the household in those days?—who lifted the baby from the font, wrapping her slippery body with astonishing deftness, in a pearl-encrusted chrysom robe handed to him by Duchess Blanche herself, for whom my baby was called. His cradling of her was sure, confident. I could not imagine Hugh doing as much with his soldier's hands, rough with old scars and abrasions even though the two men were of an age.

'Hush then,' the Duchess murmured, touching her namesake's cheek while, cupping her head with his hand, the Duke smiled ruefully.

'There's no need for all this, Mistress Blanche Swynford,' he said. 'You are named in the sight of God and much loved. Look at all here-present, who will care for you. Why would you weep?'

The unexpected words struck hard at my heart, the unbelievable tenderness of them, and my infant's cries instantly subsided to whimpers, before ceasing on a sob and a hic-cup. Everyone laughed, the domestic replacing, for that one instant, the sacred. As if entranced, little Blanche's myopic gaze fixed on the face above her.

Entranced? If my daughter was caught up in the Duke's glamour, then so was I.

It is his hands, I thought, trying to swallow against the lump in my throat. Broad palmed, long fingered, eminently capable, whether lifting a child or wielding a sword. Fine boned and beautiful, they transfixed me.

'Will you take her, Hugh? The first of your line?'

'I'm more likely to drop her,' Hugh admitted. 'Katherine has a safer pair of hands.'

'You have a comely daughter, and I foresee a clutch of strong sons.' The Duke stepped to hand her to me, and in doing so his fingers brushed against mine. The rock in my throat hardened and my breath shuddered between my lips, catching a little as it never did when Hugh touched me far more intimately. When I felt my heart tremble, I clutched little Blanche so tightly that she whimpered again.

'Gently,' Duchess Blanche advised, as if it was my inex-perience that was the problem.

I loosed my grip, turning my face away, as the priest of-fered his blessing on the little gathering.

What had happened here? It was the only question in my mind as my daughter settled to sleep against my breast.

I looked at the priest who was smiling benignly. At Hugh, who was every inch the proud husband and father, hoping that indeed next time it would be a son. At Duchess Blanche who, already mother of two fine daughters and despite the loss of her baby son, John, was carrying another ducal child high beneath her jewelled girdle.

And the Duke?

I had known him for ever. What was different today? I had seen him in full royal splendour, all gold and jewels and Plantagenet lions. In gleaming armour, the sun illuminating his tall stature as if resplendent with God's heavenly blessing. I had seen him walk into the Hall at Kenilworth, at Hertford, at Tutbury, hot and sweaty with effort in the tilt-yard, dishevelled and dust-ridden but his face alive with the expending of energy. I had heard him in furious argument with his brothers. In flirtatious laughter and tender mood with Duchess Blanche. Had seen him short-tempered with a clumsy servant, furious as a youth when his will was thwarted, repentant when taken to task by Queen Philippa.

This was nothing more than a domestic scene, the Duke and Duchess seeing fit to lavish an unexpected honour on two of their dependents, and it should not have moved my heart in this manner. His tunic and hose were plain for a prince, his sleeves wet from the font, the breast of his tunic dark with water. No jewels, no weapons, no armour. No heraldic motif to advertise his power. Nothing here to force a reaction from my nerves that continued to ripple beneath my skin.

And then as I raised my eyes from his hands to his face, I saw the Duke look over at his wife, a glance of such heartfelt compassion, of such gentle understanding for her, for the recent loss of their son. He too longed for a son to be heir to the Lancaster inheritance. The Duke's love for his wife was a thing of wonder. Such utter devotion, equally returned by his Duchess. A blinding love that I wished was for me.

Before I could be observed, I gave my attention to my child, ordering my thoughts into acceptability. Much, I decided, like pounding herbs and spices through a sieve in a stillroom. This is an infatuation, I remonstrated, from a young girl for her lord who has the glamour and handsome features that a troubadour might sing of, a foolish longing that would fade and die within the time it took for my little Blanche to find her feet and walk unaided.

But it was not. It was a longing that would not leave me.

Why Lord John of Lancaster? I demanded. Why him? It was not his position, his wealth, or his power. It was not his royal blood. As part of Duchess Blanche's household my path had crossed those of the other royal sons. I did not shiver at the splendid proximity of Prince Edward. Nor was I seduced by the easy charm of the tragically dead Lionel. Or enjoy the easy wit of my lord of Gloucester. It was John of Lancaster who made my blood race. It was that dangerous indefinable allure that moved my heart.

Did I try to douse that flare of desire?

Yes, I tried. Of course I did. Did I not know that the Duke of Lancaster was not for such as I? His royal blood placed him so far above me, while he, oblivious to my youthful yearnings, had eyes only for his beautiful wife, which was as it should be. And so I learned to live with the terrifying discomfort. I was free to admire his glamour and worship silently at his feet. That he had no feelings for me other than honour and duty and a light affection was in some sense a safety net, for he would never look at me and suspect the tenor of the feelings that stalked me.

And Hugh? Did that make me a disloyal wife to my husband? As an arranged marriage between a girl of good birth but no substance and a young man from a solid knightly family, it was a perfect arrangement to suit us both. On a personal level I seemed to please him well enough, for he was briskly considerate and I was of a practical turn of mind. I gave him my loyalty and the duty of my body. I was to bear him another daughter, Margaret, and his precious son and heir, Thomas.

I did not think that I was disloyal.

Except when my mind evaded my conscience.

The scene from the past winked out as a movement, perhaps the hopping of one of the finches from one perch to another, brought my mind back to the here and now so that I once more stood beside my marriage bed, the bed curtain clenched tight in my right hand. As I released it, smoothing out the creases I had made, my thoughts turned inwards. I had been a gracious and well-mannered wife who served the Duchess and administered the Kettlethorpe estates if need arose.

Duty, honour, loyalty. Hard words to cling to when my thoughts were with a man who could wield the power, with the faintest smile, the most innocuous of requests, to make my heart lurch. But I swore that I would go to my death without his knowing how the hand of desire touched me that day with such fervour that the need still growled in my belly. Nor would Duchess Blanche ever guess, for my disloyalty to her was unthinkable.

And yet sometimes when the Duke laced his fingers with Blanche's, kissed her lips with his, the longing was a raging fire in my veins.

I had never spoken of it, nor would I. Some sins were best kept between the sinner and God. I had been the perfect damsel, and I learned to keep my distance, to hide my thoughts. I was not without intelligence or the ability to dissemble when the need arose and I saw the right sense of it. It was a relief when the Duke went to France to fight at the side of his brother Prince Edward.

But what now?

I sank to the edge of the bed.

As a widow, as a mother with a duty to her children, duty and honour still guided my steps. Acting on the stark awareness that beat beneath my bodice was still not a choice I could ever contemplate. My respectability was assured and inviolable. It was bearable for had I not been the perfect mistress of self-command for more years than I wished to count? I knew what was expected of me and what was due to me and to my family name. I would never follow my chosen path in life with anything but propriety and courtly dignity.

Easy to say. I found that once again I had clutched the hangings, for now all was changed. The Duke's statement of intent had made it unbearable, and if he would trifle with my emotions, it would undermine all I had done to keep my thoughts under strict discipline. I did not understand how a man of such erstwhile integrity could place this burden at my feet. I did not need this complication. I did not want it.

But he wanted me.

I want you. I want you for my own.

My feelings for him were so complex as to defy definition, my heart and mind in severe conflict: to take care, or to throw care and discretion to the wind. To refuse a priceless gift, or seize it with both hands. To condemn what was a gross sin, or claim it as my heart's desire. How I wished that he had not spoken, yet when I closed my eyes, the words were written on the darkness of my vision, shimmering there in gold, and horribly seductive.

A light knock, the click of the latch that encouraged the finches to trill briefly, and there was Agnes at the door. 'We have a problem, Katherine.'

'Not another.' I stood, banishing the Duke to where he properly belonged, waiting at The Savoy for the arrival of Duchess Constanza. I had enough to worry about without malingering in the past.

'The reed thatch on the stable block has collapsed in the

inner corner. It's brought down a portion of the hay loft. Master Ingoldsby says the rest is sure to follow if this rain continues, so we must move the horses to dry accommodations. He says do we send to our neighbours? Then there's the little matter of water seeping into the well in the courtyard…'

'And I need the funds to put it all right. I know.' I must have succumbed to dismay, for Agnes approached, eyes narrowed on my face, but I essayed a laugh to deflect her concern. 'The Duke's offer could not have come at a more opportune moment. Do you suppose that he foresaw our thatching difficulties?'

Agnes snorted at my levity. 'A pretty thing.' She nodded at the rosary clutched in my hand.

Lifting it, I allowed the light to play along its length, picking out the carving on the crucifix. 'Yes. It's beautiful.'

Beautiful, but the implications of its giving were dangerous.

'A gift?' Agnes probed.

She knew I could not afford to purchase an item of such value.

'Yes.' How easy it was to be drawn into deception. 'From Lady Alice.' And as if to hide my guilt I closed my hand over the beads.

'Nice if you have the money,' Agnes sniffed. 'Did I see coral there? And gold?'

'Yes.' It was as I knew, too valuable even for Lady Alice's giving.

'I thought you said Lady Alice gave you nothing.'

'Did I?' Beware, those who lie. I tried a rueful smile. 'I forgot.'

'Heaven knows you could forget that!' I squirmed with discomfort but just shook my head. 'You could sell it and re-roof the stables. Unless you are absolutely fixed on joining the new Duchess?'

I returned her puzzled stare for a moment, suddenly calmly assured, quite certain in my own mind.

'Yes, I am fixed on it. I will earn enough from my position with Duchess Constanza to re-roof the whole house,' I said. 'What possible reason would there be for me to refuse such open-handed generosity?' I began to slide the paternosters into their leather pouch.

'It's a very costly gift,' Agnes remarked, looking at me rather than at the beads.

'Then I must be sure to be worthy of my hire.'

Tucking the rosary into a coffer, with unwarranted impatience I cast a cloth over the finches whose singing had picked up in volume.

'And you'd better take those with you,' Agnes continued in the same sceptical tone, as if she did not believe one word I had said, 'or Margaret will never forgive us. I don't suppose the Duke will mind.'

'No, I don't suppose he will,' I responded briskly.

And since there was so much to organise, I extinguished the scene I had just conjured up as efficiently as if I had used a candle snuffer, yet there remained with me a complicated interweaving of thoughts, lingering like a final wisp of smoke.

What would I say to the Duke when our paths next crossed? Would it not be for me like stepping into a hornets' nest? If he demanded again that I be more than a lady-in-waiting to his wife, as he surely would, what would I say?

So many questions. I knew the answer to none of them, but my mind was resolved to go to The Savoy, whatever fate might hold in store for me.

I refused to admit what was in my heart.

Chapter Four

My first impression, as she was helped to dismount from the gloriously swagged and curtained palanquin, was how young and insubstantial she was. Or perhaps it was just that she resembled nothing more than a drowned rat. The heavens had inconveniently deposited a torrential downpour of sleety rain on the crowds of gawping bystanders as she was welcomed into the city of London by Prince Edward of Woodstock, struggling from sick-bed to horseback for the occasion. She was not so very young for a royal bride. The noble lady, Constanza of Castile, was after all only five years younger than I, and hardly some protected, pampered child with no mind of her own.

There we all stood in the Great Hall to receive our new mistress, with freedom for me to appreciate the impression the Duke intended to make, with his tunic blazing in red and black and gold, proclaiming his new status, the royal arms of Castile with its castle and lions quartered with those of England, the gold stitching shimmering as he moved restlessly from foot to foot. It sat well on his tall slenderness:

not one of the Castilian entourage could question the presence of this royal duke. I tried to read his expression. Impatience, above all, for we had been waiting for three hours.

I smoothed my hand down the silk damask of my skirts. When the Duke's stern eye swept over his assembled household, he had registered with the barest glance the quality and condition of my garments, taking note of my obedience to his demand that I clothe myself with appropriate richness in honour of my new position. So my trailing skirts were in Lancaster blue, the close-fitting bodice, exquisitely fur edged, patterned in blue and white. Out of some female caprice, I had chosen to wear the coral rosary, ostentatiously looped over my girdle.

Now, waywardly volatile, strangely defiant, I wished I had not.

He had not even found the time to speak to me. I was merely one of many in the household. How could I have expected more?

Duchess Constanza trod the shallow steps to the Great Hall, her furs trailing and spiked with wet, her robes plastered to her body. Her pleated hair clung to her head and neck beneath her sodden veiling, the ruffles on her cap sadly limp. I could only imagine her discomfort in spite of her being tucked back into her litter after the welcome. But in spite of it all, yes, I acknowledged, she was beautiful. Not like Blanche, fair and so very English, smooth and pale as a pearl. This young woman was as sharp as a pin. Magnificent eyes, dark and secretive as beryls, were turned on her new surroundings and were not uncritical, and there was a pride in the thin nose, the arched brows. Perhaps her pride was to be expected, given the difficulties of her birth and young life.

Lady Alice had sniffed her disgust of gossip but Alyne

had answered my curiosity as we completed the stitching on that same altar cloth that would be used for the Mass to give thanks for Duchess Constanza's safe arrival amongst us.

'Constanza is illegitimate, to all intents and purposes...' she whispered. 'Her father got three daughters and a son on a whore whilst his wife was still alive.'

'But he claimed to have married her—the whore, that is,' interposed Lady Alice who, in the end, could not resist the delectable lure of scandal.

And so, between them, I received the strangely horrifying history of my new mistress whose father King Pedro of Castile had imprisoned his rightfully wedded wife in a dungeon, while he continued his disreputable liaison with Maria de Padilla, whom he claimed to have wed before his marriage to the ill-fated legal wife Blanche of Bourbon. He was a man of persuasive tongue and his children by Maria had been recognised as legitimate by the Castilian Cortes, and so were heirs to the throne.

'Pedro had his wife poisoned, so they say. Died in mysterious circumstances,' Lady Alice stated with extravagantly raised brows.

Alyne added in counterpoint: 'Constanza's father is also dead, so she is Queen of Castile by right.'

'Except that the Crown has been usurped by King Pedro's bastard half-brother Enrique.'

'Which means that Queen Constanza has no kingdom to rule over.'

'Only a claim that Enrique will never honour.'

So there was the skeleton of Constanza's lineage. It was an unenviable position for the young woman, whom I now assessed as, chin lifted, she approached the Duke. No wonder she held to her pride like a mouse to the last ear of corn during a bad harvest. She had little else. Owning the title of

Queen of Castile certainly gave her a presence, despite the outmoded gown of red velvet with its strangely fashioned blue kirtle. The creation of veils and frills and buckram that covered her hair was a monstrosity.

'Castilian fashion!' Lady Alice murmured. 'I doubt it will catch on.'

The Duke bowed low. We all made appropriate obeisance.

'You are right welcome, my lady.'

When the Duke held out his hand, she placed hers there, her stark gaze at last come to rest. He smiled, saluted her fingers and then her cheek, her lips. I noticed that although there was no reticence in her response, she did not return the smile. Perhaps she was overawed by the splendour of her new home. Compared with the hovel rumour said she had been reduced to occupying in a village in Bayonne—even worse than Kettlethorpe, Lady Alice had informed me with a wry smile—this palace in the very heart of London must seem to her like paradise.

'You will never be in danger again,' the Duke assured her. 'Nor will you ever again live in poverty. This is your home.' Then turning to the ranks of his household: 'I would introduce to you my wife. Queen Constanza of Castile.'

We bowed, curtsied.

The Queen of Castile sneezed.

The Duke was immediately solicitous, for though it was undetectable, we all knew that beneath those voluminous robes the lady carried his child. 'Your hands are cold. Forgive my thoughtlessness.' He beckoned to Lady Alice: 'My wife needs our consideration. The English winter has not been kind today. I'll leave her in your efficient hands.'

The welcome was thus cut short out of concern for her health and that of her child, and she was handed over to her new household. To me. I found myself directed by Lady

Alice, since I had not yet settled into any routine of duties for my new mistress, to conduct the lady to her accommodations, help her disrobe, organise her bathing and then put her to bed with a pan of hot coals and a cup of warm spiced wine. And to instruct her handful of Castilian ladies who were looking apprehensive and as wet as she.

'You know how we go about things here. None better,' Lady Alice murmured. 'And next week, God willing, your sister can take over when she has wished her husband farewell. She can soothe the Castilian fears, and you can concentrate on the welfare of the coming child—as well as giving me a hand with the clutch of growing children in my care.' She sighed as she observed the Castilian retinue and clicked her tongue. 'They look frightened to death. Do they think we will eat them?'

I curtsied to the new Duchess, who glanced rather wildly at the Duke, but she followed as I led the way, lingering in every antechamber, every room, to take in the furnishings, the painted ceilings, the glowing tapestries. Even though she shivered with cold, she found a need to take in every aspect of her new home, until I decided that enough was enough when she sneezed again.

'To take a chill, my lady, would not be good for your child,' I advised firmly. Subtle deference, I sensed, would not pay with this young woman. 'It would be better for you and the baby if you were out of those clothes immediately.'

She blinked as if she had not expected me to speak, or did not understand. Perhaps that was it, I realised. How good was her understanding of the French that we habitually spoke at court?

'You are cold,' I said clearly, slowly. 'You need to be dry and warm.'

She nodded and quickened her steps.

'Ah! Good!' she said at last. For as we arrived at her private chamber, a wooden bath, the staves held in place by brass mounts carved with fish and dragons, had been manoeuvred before the fire to accommodate the water, steaming and fragrant with herbs. It was, I realised, the first word she had spoken since her arrival.

I stood back to allow her to enter, then, closing the door on the last empty bucket, followed her as the Castilian ladies stood around helplessly.

'Find your mistress's garments,' I chivvied, seeing that some of her coffers had already been placed in the room. 'A shift, a robe. Some soft shoes…' I pointed at the bath. 'Now you must bathe, my lady.'

And under my eye the maidservant I had brought with me began to strip the fur and matted velvet from the Castilian queen's slight body, releasing her hair from its confinement so that it snaked, damp and tangled, over her shoulders. The Duchess simply stood and allowed it to happen.

'Clothes for your mistress,' I snapped again at the damsels, thinking that my sister Philippa, with all her experience in Duchess Blanche's household, would find it a hard task to help me beat these women into some sort of order. They had clearly not served in a noble household before. Then I addressed the Duchess, who was standing shivering in her embroidered under-gown. 'How do I address you, my lady?'

She regarded me steadily, looking far younger than her seventeen years. 'I am Queen of Castile,' she pronounced carefully.

Which did not help. She was also Duchess of Lancaster. Since she had not objected, I continued as I had called her.

'A poor welcome for you, my lady.'

'Yes. This is my sister, the Lady Isabella.'

She gestured casually with her hand towards the young

unsmiling woman at her side, before handing to me, without looking at it, the brooch that had been pinned to the bosom of her gown. Making the requisite curtsy to the Lady Isabella, I placed the brooch on the coffer beside me. It was heavy with gold, depicting St George and a flamboyant dragon, all picked out in sapphires, diamonds and pearls. The dragon's eyes were ruby-red. Much discussed, it was a gift from Prince Edward to acknowledge the Queen of Castile's arrival, and was indeed worthy of royalty. I was surprised that she treated it with such indifference, for it was a remarkable jewel. Perhaps she was merely tired, yet I did not think so, despite the shadows beneath her eyes and the obvious strain on her aquiline features. I did not think it meant anything to her, and wondered what would move her to true emotion. As I turned back to her, she spoke, carefully:

'Who are you?'

'Katherine de Swynford, my lady.'

'You are part of this…?' She sought for the word. I had been right. Her French, heavily accented, was not good.

'Household,' I supplied. 'I am part of the Duke's household. And of yours. I am appointed to be one of your damsels.'

She stared at me. 'One of my ladies?' she repeated.

'Yes, my lady.'

'Do you also care for the Duke's children?'

'Yes, my lady. When it is necessary.'

'I have not met the children yet.' She frowned. 'My lord has told me of them.'

'Tomorrow you will see them.'

She lifted her arms to allow her under-gown to be removed, then stood in her shift as the maid unrolled her stockings, obediently lifting one foot, then the other. 'I will have a son of my own,' she announced. 'You served Duchess Blanche?'

'Yes, my lady.'

The shift removed, I saw how undeveloped her body was at hip and breast. Childbearing would not be easy for her. The pregnancy showed barely a roundness of her belly. I offered my hand to help her step into the tub and lower herself into the water, where she sighed with pleasure and closed her eyes.

'Are you married?' she asked.

'A widow, my lady.'

'What is that?'

'Una viuda,' murmured one of the women who seemed to have more French than her mistress.

'I understand. Your husband is dead. Do you have children?'

She had so many questions.

'Yes. I have three. My daughter Blanche is the Duke's godchild. What is that?' I looked at the woman who had replied before.

'Un ahijado,' she supplied.

The Duchess's eyes opened, focused on me, then narrowed. 'He—the Duke—has a regard for you.' There was no friendliness there and I sensed a jealousy in what was obviously a question. Who should recognise it better than I?

'For me, a little, for the service I gave to his wife. And for my husband, much more,' I explained. 'He died in Aquitaine last year, in the Duke's employ. Sir Hugh was a soldier in his retinue.'

'I see.' She understood enough, and what was most pertinent. The resentment in her eyes cooled. 'Your husband was a man of title.'

'Yes. He was a knight.'

'Ah!' She smiled, her face suddenly lit with an inner beauty. 'So you are Lady Katherine de Swynford.'

'Yes, my lady.' Status also meant something to her. I wondered how fluent the Duke was in Castilian. He would need to be, to pick his way through all these conflicting impulses.

'Then I have decided. I want you to be my damsel,' she stated with all the imperiousness of the house of Castile.

'As I will be. The Duke has appointed me.' I explained, slowly: 'My sister, Mistress Chaucer, will also come to care for you.'

'Is she like you?'

'She is very capable. She knows about children.'

The new wife stretched out her arm for the maid to wash with a soft cloth. Her glance to me was suddenly sharp. 'I fear this…' She spread her free hand over her belly. 'It makes me feel ill.'

'There is no need to fear, my lady. You are young and strong.'

'Still I fear.' She shrugged. 'Were you with Duchess Blanche? When she was with child?'

'Yes, my lady.'

'She lost some of her babies, did she not?'

'Yes, my lady.' I could not lie, but I poured her a cup of warm wine and offered it, hoping to distract her. It would do no good to speak of the three little boys who had not seen the first anniversary of their birth. Or the girl, Isabella, who had barely breathed.

'How many?' the Duchess insisted.

'Four,' I admitted. 'But she carried three who are now grown.'

She waved aside the wine. 'Have you lost any babies?'

'No, my lady.'

'Then you will stay with me. You will give me your advice.' A demand again, not a request. 'It is…it is *imperativo* that I carry *un heredero* for Castile.'

I caught the gist. 'Of course,' I soothed. The Duchess Constanza needed an heir.

'My lord will get my kingdom back for me. I will not live in England long. My lord will drive my *vicioso* uncle Enrique from Castile. He will kill him for me. And I will take back what is mine.'

It sounded as if she had learned the phrases. So confident. So driven. Her eyes were aflame, her hands fisted on the edge of the bath. Then she looked at me, gaze narrowed again on my face.

'You are beautiful.'

Which surprised me. 'Thank you, my lady.'

'I am said to be beautiful too.'

'Yes, my lady. The people of London filled the streets to look at you.'

Her frown deepened into a scowl. 'Was Blanche beautiful?'

'Yes, my lady. But fair. Not dark like you.'

'My lord likes beautiful things.'

'Yes, my lady. You will lack for nothing here at The Savoy.'

My soothing comment elicited a torrent of Castilian.

'A excepción de la tierra de mi nacimiento—y la venganza.'

I looked helplessly at the Castilian damsel who had hovered at my side throughout.

'The Duchess says: "Except for the land of my birth. And vengeance."'

'Vengeance for what, my lady?'

Which was answered by a flash of eye and another stream of invective, carefully translated for me:

'My father—King Pedro—his murderers live on, unpunished. He was ambushed by assassins, paid for by my uncle Enrique. He was decapitated and left unburied to his great dishonour. His head was sent to Seville for public exhibition. *Dios mio!* It is my life's ambition to have my father interred in Castilian soil with all honour and his murderers slain. That I will do before I die.'

'Of course, my lady.'

Her flat chest heaving, extreme vexation in every gesture, Constanza surged to her feet, splashing water, the evidence of the forthcoming child clearer as she arched her body.

'My lord will take Castile from the deplorable Enrique. We will rule it together as King and Queen. This child—this son—will rule in his own time. I will have fulfilled my destiny—and my new husband's too. What more could he desire, than to be King of Castile?'

What more could the Duke desire? There was no path for his ambitions in England, but Castile might just provide them. A kingdom of his own, to rule in his own name, answerable to no one. For the first time I understood the importance of this marriage for him. This marriage, the promise of this kingdom, would give him his heart's desire.

'I am tired,' she announced. 'I will go to bed.'

We dried her with soft linen, combed her hair. Wrapped in an embroidered chamber robe, feet in fur-lined slippers, she was soon propped against the pillows on her bed.

'Do you think the Duke cares for me?' she asked.

How could he not love her? She was beautiful and well-born, an heiress with a kingdom for the taking by a courageous man. Obvious to all, the Duke was chivalrous and caring in his first meeting with her. Of course he loved her.

'The Duke chose you before all other ladies who wished

to wed a Plantagenet prince,' I replied, for was that not the truth? 'How could he not care for you?'

'*Bien!* I hope it is so.' She nodded, seeming to understand.

Do you care for him? I felt an urge to ask. I had no idea. She gave nothing away. She was shrewd and sharp, and I knew it was my duty to hope that the Duke would be happy with her and she with him.

Jealousy, bitter as aloes, coated my mouth as I left her to sleep, but then the erratic leap of my thoughts forced me into a wry smile.

Beware of the wife, Mistress Saxby had warned. *It's easy to be carried away by the glamour of stolen kisses, but a wife can make your life a misery. Take my word for it.*

I would indeed beware, if ever such kisses came my way. It seemed, on my first steps as a damsel to Duchess Constanza, an unlikely eventuality.

So this marriage to the Queen of Castile was of vast importance to the Duke. It was brought home to me just how critical a step it was for him when a messenger arrived from the King as the household, without the new Duchess, sat at supper in the sumptuous splendour of the Great Hall. He bowed and handed over a sealed document.

'His Grace the King asks that you consider the contents, *Monseigneur d'Espaigne.* He would value *Monseigneur's* advice at the earliest possible moment.'

The Duke took the packet, inviting the messenger to sit with us while he read.

Monseigneur d'Espaigne.

Already he was recognised as King of Castile in his wife's name. I would never see him as that—to me he would always be the Duke—even if courtesy and etiquette determined that I comply, but without doubt it would colour the direction of his future life. Would *Monseigneur d'Espaigne* not forget everything but the road to the throne of Castile, paved with gold and bloodshed, which lay stretching in a glittering seam before him, with the bride at his side? He would take an army and begin a re-conquest of the kingdom—and then he would live there, far from England, far from me, with his wife and new family.

An excellent outcome for all concerned. All my concerns should be allayed.

But they were not.

I offered up a silent prayer for forgiveness as the Duke perused the King's letter, and my spoon congealed in a rich dish of *mammenye ryal*, the minced poultry redolent of almond milk and sweet wine, while I listed my sins in silent petition before the Blessed Virgin. Lust for a man who was bound to another. Avarice, the sin of deadly excess, as evidenced by my uncontrolled emotion. Greed that made me wish for an affection that was not mine to take. Envy against the Duchess, beautiful and regal, in her rightful place at the Duke's side and in his bed. Pride that blinded me to my own unworthiness.

All of those. The tally of them horrified me.

Can you not find evidence of Sloth, Wrath and Gluttony as well? I asked bitterly.

I was sure I could. I put my spoon down, determined to eat no more that night. I should never have come back. It was an unforgivable mistake. I should not have allowed myself to be drawn into dreams of what could never be. I had allowed myself to live, however briefly, in a magical scene in which my love was no longer unrequited. One day spent at The Savoy, absorbing the high politics of the occasion and the determination of the new Duchess, had shown me the futility of it all. The Duke would assuredly have other fish to fry.

'Has my wife found her chamber to her liking?' the Duke asked Lady Alice as we rose at last at the end of the meal.

'Yes, my lord, so I understand. Lady Katherine waited on her.'

Since I was standing within earshot, he could do no other than look to me for clarification.

'I trust she has suffered no ill effects from the journey, Lady Katherine?'

'None, my lord,' I replied, coolly informative and nothing more. 'The Duchess is weary, of course. She will be strong again by the morning. I am honoured to be appointed as her damsel, my lord,' I added.

'I can think of none better.'

He moved on beside Lady Alice, head bent, absorbed in some household problem.

Well, that had been entirely impersonal, completely centred on the well-being of the Castilian Queen, as it should be. His smile was such that he would bestow on any one of his retinue from his most eminent physician to Nichol, the gardener at The Savoy. That briefest of conversations had made everything crystal clear. All my worrying had been futile.

Now it must be for me to put it right in my mind, to return to the calm existence of my previous service at The Savoy. It would be just like before. It would be like stepping back into my old skin, before all the upheaval. Before the Duke had said what he said, and torn my world apart.

Why did he have to do that, when it was obviously an aberration? Why were men sometimes as insensitive as a wild boar's charge when faced with a huntsman's lance? And there he was, entirely oblivious to the disturbance he had created, presumably concerned for nothing more than the perfect lie of the damask along his shoulders, the dramatic gleam of the gold chain against the red and black and gold of the cloth.

A little bubble of anger in my belly made me wish I had not eaten those final spoonfuls of the highly spiced dish. I regretted it even more when the Duke abandoned Lady Alice and awaited me by the door. My heart leaped, then plummeted as he raised a hand to stop my progress.

'Lady Katherine.'

'My lord?'

'Are you angry?' he asked abruptly.

We were, for that one moment, alone.

'No, my lord,' I reassured him quickly, smiling lightly, as I smoothed what I thought must be a particularly unyielding expression from my face. How well Queen Philippa had schooled me. 'There is nothing to disturb me except gratitude for your kindness.'

'I will send for you,' he said with a shadow of a frown.

I was not to be allowed to slip into my old skin after all. His appraisal, agate-bright, was direct and uncompromising. I met it the same way, until he gestured for me to precede him from the hall, adding imperiously:

'You will come to me.'

I opened my mouth, to refuse, or so I thought, until, fleetingly, he touched my arm. My adroitly composed refusal promptly fled, my willpower compromised by the slightest pressure of his fingers against my tight-buttoned sleeve. I think I looked at him in horror.

'You give me no peace. Why should that be?' he demanded.

I could find no reply at all to that.

I walked on, conscious that the Duke's footsteps did not follow me, until a prickle of awareness snatched at my attention. I was being observed from the little knot of newcomers just arrived at the outer door.

There, muffled in furs, eyes cool and searching on my

face, a cage of singing finches much like my own in her hand, was Philippa. My sister. I smiled, and kept my smile lively, even though I did not enjoy the judgemental quality of her expression. Philippa was not smiling.

In my own chamber, before she could descend on me, I put the rosary away in my coffer. Caught between sister Philippa and the Duke, I must tread carefully.

'Where is he then, Philippa?'

'I have no idea. Picardy, the last I heard.'

As I seated myself on my bed, my sister began to divest herself of her furs, placing them carefully over a polished settle, sweeping her hand down over the lustrous skins. She was not without means, but she took care of her possessions with a neat exactitude I recognised from our shared child-hood. Her voice now, in maturity, was clipped with displea-sure. 'A military expedition, so I'm led to believe, but why he should feel the need to go when…' She hissed her irritation. 'I am, as usual, kept in the dark. He gave me the finches to keep me company and sweeten my mood.'

'Very poetic,' I observed, not daring to laugh.

'Poetic, but useless,' she remarked, uncharitably I thought. But then, I was not wed to Geoffrey Chaucer. I did not think that it was an experience I would enjoy, despite his erudition and clever way with words.

Philippa had arrived eventually at my chamber, leaving me much relieved that what I had thought to be a censori-ous stare had proved to be nothing of the sort, when she had laughed and fallen into my arms. Or perhaps she was keep-ing the censure for later. I knew my sister well.

'I am so very pleased to be back here,' she announced. After Duchess Blanche's death, when her household was disbanded and I had gone to Kettlethorpe, my sister had taken up residence in the Chaucer family property in Thames Street. 'It was becoming very cramped. I've brought the children too, as you saw.'

As I had. Elizabeth and another Thomas, their ages matching with Margaret and my own son.

Philippa's eyes glinted. 'Are you pleased to see me?'

'Delighted. I'll happily hand the Duchess over to you, and all her starchy women, while I lurk in the background. Do you speak Castilian?'

'No.'

'A pity.'

'Is she like Blanche?'

'She is nothing like Blanche.'

'So I presume we're going to Tutbury. Or Hertford.'

'If Queen Constanza can be persuaded that that is where she wishes to go.'

'So it's like that, is it? Do you come too?'

'I am appointed as a damsel with you. Just like old times.'

Except that it was not, and never would be, no matter what the outcome of the promised conversation with the Duke.

Philippa must have seen some shadow of my torment. 'What's wrong?' she demanded.

'Nothing.'

'Missing Hugh?'

'Yes.'

'I saw the Duke being very solicitous.'

'The Duke is always solicitous,' I replied, more quickly than was perhaps wise.

'To have a *tête-à-tête* in the Great Hall, with his wife's damsel?'

So I had been right about the censure. Philippa had been saving her well-sharpened arrows. Perhaps, divorced from court, dissatisfied with the restrictions on her life because of her perennially absent husband, she had been storing them up for such an occasion as this. It behoved me to keep my wits about me. I might be an innocent party in this situation, but guilt had a habit of encroaching on the edges. I grimaced at the image that sprang to mind, like fat around a bowl of mutton pottage.

'The Duke is solicitous of everyone, as you well know,' I responded. 'He has my eternal gratitude. Without this position, Kettlethorpe would sink beneath the floods.'

'You look well in the role of Lady of Kettlethorpe.' The sharp assessment was still there in her eyes. 'I envy you.'

'As a widow? With a ruinous estate?'

'No one would know. You look very sleek and smart.'

I laughed, smoothing the rich fur edging. 'I was asked to put aside my widow's weeds.'

'By the Duke?'

'Yes. It would not have been appropriate.'

'I see!'

The twinkle in her eye drove me to employ diversionary tactics. 'Being a widow has its problems.'

'I see none!'

'It has still to be decided who will administer the estates. Since Thomas is a minor, and Hugh a vassal of the crown, they have reverted to the King. The wardship of Thomas could be sold to anyone. Our finances are worse than you can ever imagine. You're lucky to have a husband with a steady income.'

Philippa found my plight of no great importance compared with her own miseries. 'I may as well be a widow, the amount of time I spend without him.'

'But you are financially secure. I had to come begging.'

'Kettlethorpe as bad as ever?'

I recalled Philippa's single brief visit there, her pointed

comments and her rapid departure, and replied sharply, 'Worse. Is Geoffrey as bad as ever?'

'Worse.'

We laughed, not unkindly. It was an old exchange and so we settled into gossip, now that we had established our old relationship: Philippa sharp and brittle, critical of the world, I more tolerant. I was the elder by little more than a year, yet it was not always obvious. Philippa sometimes proved to be the more worldly wise.

I sat and watched her as she told me about the doings of her two children. We were close, neither of us having any memory of our mother, and barely of our father, Sir Gilles de Roet, a knight from Hainault, who had died there when I was three years old, having given us into the tender care of Queen Philippa to whom he owed his service. We had a brother, Walter, taken to soldiering like my father, dying in the retinue of Edward of Woodstock at the battle of Poitiers, and an elder sister, Elizabeth, who, a nun in a monastic house at Mons, had gone from birth to death without my knowing her.

So, to all intents and purposes alone in the world, Philippa and I owed everything to the kindly and maternal Queen: our raising, our education and our position in the household of Duchess Blanche when we were very young, as nothing more than cradle-rockers to the two tiny daughters. Without parents we had clung to each other, and although our lives had taken different directions, the closeness remained. But that did not mean that I was not careful around my sister's caustic tongue.

'Are you happy?' I asked, interrupting a long list of complaints about Agnes, Geoffrey's ageing mother, who still occupied the Thames Street house.

'As much as I ever am. I don't think it is in my nature to

be satisfied. Perhaps if I had wed a handsome knight like you.' A twist of bitterness curved her lips.

'Your husband is a man of great worth.'

'Yes. I know.'

'His writing brings him great fame.'

'True.'

'You have your children.'

'And they are a blessing. But I'll have no more.'

I paused, considering whether to ask why she was so adamant, and decided against it. 'Geoffrey cares for you,' I observed instead.

'Geoffrey is entirely indifferent to me. He has never written a poem to my beauty or my fine eyes. All he does is condemn what he calls the entrapment of marriage.'

I laughed.

'Don't laugh! Do you know? He owns over sixty books. He'd rather spend time with them than with me.' She chuckled as I continued to laugh at her complaint but there was a sadness there that touched my heart. 'I am just dissatisfied. It will be better at Hertford.' She rose and walked to the window to look out over the Thames. 'What about you, Kate? Do you have an eye to another husband?'

'I have only been a widow for a matter of months.'

'A lover then.'

'Philippa!'

'You're too pious for your own good. You had not seen Hugh for—how long before his death?'

'Sixteen months. And I am not pious.'

'I know you better than you know yourself. You would have to say a full decade of paternosters before leaping into a lover's bed.'

'I would not!'

But I would, as I knew only too well, as I was thrown into

a puddle of doubt. My conscience was a strong force within me, and sin was not something to be lightly cast aside, as I was finding to my cost when all my strictly held tenets of living seemed to be hanging by a thread in the face of the Duke's campaign. If I took this step to please him, if I went to him when he summoned me, the thread would be cut as cleanly as if I were finishing the edge of a girdle. I could not hold to any pretence that it would not matter. It would. If I stepped, I must accept the guilt and the condemnation.

'Katherine.' Philippa nudged me. 'Where were you?'

'Nowhere.' I knew my cheeks were flushed. 'You were saying?'

'That I could take a lover…' Philippa mused.

'Geoffrey might mind.'

'Geoffrey might not even notice. So, have you set your eye on anyone?'

Another diversionary tactic was needed. 'Speaking of Geoffrey, does he talk to you about court matters?'

'Sometimes. Why?'

'I'm interested in the Duke's ambitions. He's now addressed as *Monseigneur d'Espaigne*. Does he truly seek the crown of Castile?'

Does he love the Queen? That is what I wanted to know. *Has he wed for love, as he wed Blanche, for the passion that was between them? Or was Constanza a pawn in a foreign alliance, a means to a political end because he saw the crown of Castile as a jewel on his horizon?*

'Geoffrey thinks so,' Philippa replied carelessly. 'The Duke has ambitions. It has always been so for him, to seek power. It was once mooted that he become King of Scotland. Now it's Castile. A chance for a kingdom of his own.' She shrugged, displaying her own lack of interest. 'He's an ambitious man. It's no surprise. Why are you so interested?'

'I am not.'

'Well, he would not remain unwed for long, would he? He only has one son to step into his shoes. Perhaps he fell in love. Love at first sight.'

'Perhaps he did.'

It confirmed only what I had thought.

'Geoffrey says he gave her a magnificent wedding gift. A gold cup fashioned as a rose with a white dove on the lid. Sounds like a lover's gift to me.'

So it did to me. Which made everything so much worse. His invitation to me was the prelude to a mere dalliance, and I would not comply.

You will not comply anyway! My conscience lectured.

'And she is strikingly beautiful, I hear. Enough to entrap the heart of any man.'

'Yes, she is.'

Philippa had convinced me.

'Enough of Constanza.' Philippa stood, looking round appreciatively at the spacious accommodation reserved for me. 'Do I share this room with you, or do I have a Castilian damsel to entertain? Let us go and discover, and find my children. By the by, I have been granted an annuity of ten pounds by the Duke in token of my service.' The slide of her eye was piercing. 'It's good to be appreciated. What are you paid? Are you worth more than I?'

I shook my head, quick to lie. How easily half-truths and deceptions leaped to my lips these days. 'How could I be?'

Another confession that I must make. I was relieved I had packed away the rosary. I would not have liked to explain that gift to her.

Chapter Five

'Robert!' I called out as I turned a corner in the early dusk. 'Robert Rabbas! Where are you, in God's name!'

It was cold enough to turn the Thames to ice.

Shivering, infuriated, fingers so frozen I could barely bend them, I held my hood close beneath my chin. Why was there neither sight nor sound of a squire or a page or even a household servant when one was most needed to carry out a burdensome task? And why had we been blighted by a basket of green wood which did nothing but smoulder and smoke and give out no heat, when the weather was at its bleakest, driven in by March winds from the north?

Our plans to transfer the whole household to Hertford had gone awry, when Henry, the Lancaster heir, was struck down with a fever. Cross and fractious, sometimes weeping with pains in his joints, his little body alternated between burning heat and intense cold. With concerns for the health of her unborn child—for might it not be the plague?—Duchess Constanza was not to be persuaded that this was a childish ailment and expressed the desire to leave London immediately for the Duke's castle at Hertford. Within a day she was packed into a palanquin with her ladies and Philippa in attendance and they departed, the Duke accompanying her before returning to London to re-engage with the King and Prince Edward in planning for the campaign against the French for the New Year. It was expected that the Duke would lead the forces.

He had not sent for me. In the circumstances he might well leave England with nothing resolved between us.

Meanwhile we remained at The Savoy, the young people and their household, expecting the fever to run like wildfire through the rest of the children before it wore itself out. It was agreed that we would follow to Hertford when the danger was passed.

I was not sorry, as I sat and bathed Henry's forehead and heated limbs with common henbane boiled in wine. The large furry leaves might look uninviting but they were of sound reputation in cooling inflammations, I consoled myself. I could hear Constanza's voice raised in Castilian complaint even as the ducal party rode out of the gate, and silently wished my sister well as I decided that it would be a relief to be free of the Duke's presence.

Yet living in such a milieu as The Savoy, in the world of the Duke's own creation of art and wealth, it was hard not to sense his presence, even when he was miles away. At the turn of a stair, there he might be. Kneeling in the chapel, riding his bay stallion into the courtyard, sitting at supper in the Great Hall. Even though he did none of those things, it seemed that I might catch that glimpse of him if I looked carefully enough.

I would not give in to temptation. I would not look.

Better that he is not here! I reprimanded myself.

So now with hoar frost forming on the insides of the glazing and the fire making little impact, we had wrapped the children as warmly as we could in furs and bedcovers and sent for fuel two hours ago, until spurred by righteous anger I had volunteered to chase it up. Thomas Haselden, Controller of the Duke's Household, was nowhere to be found. Sir Thomas Hungerford, our steward, had travelled with the Duke and Constanza to Hertford. Somehow the smooth running of the household had got out of kilter, and approaching the hour for supper as it was, the servants would be busy in the kitchens, but that was no good reason for us to freeze to death. Elizabeth had developed a cough, exacerbated by the acrid smoke, and I suspected Blanche would follow suit. Even Alyne, usually stalwart, had taken to her bed, feeling her age in her bones, she said. Lady Alice was considering the tenor of her complaint to the Duke when she next set eyes on him.

The shadows here in the inner courtyard were thick and deep in the corners, but as I strode on, there was a movement. Emerging from the side door in the far corner came a dark-clad figure with a bundle under his arm. He would do very well for my errand. I raised my hand to draw his attention. I also raised my voice again.

'Robert, is it?' The figure was tall enough to be the lanky page who had brought us the basket of unseasoned logs. 'We have need of fuel in the schoolroom. Would you arrange it?'

He paused. Hesitated. Bowed.

'I have already requested more wood. Four hours ago.' A little exaggeration would not come amiss.

The figure remained motionless. I raised my voice a little more so that it echoed back at me off the dank stones.

'Fetch some if you please. And don't just pass the message to someone else and forget about it. It is too cold for the children. And not unseasoned wood either!' I added, as he disappeared within.

I returned to the schoolroom.

'Any success?' Lady Alice shivered in the draught with the opening of the door.

'It has yet to be seen,' I replied, thinking that the temperature was little different inside than out. The children looked pinched, and yes, Blanche was coughing, her eyes red-rimmed. Only Henry, newly recovering and already beginning to resent the curb on his freedom, looked full of energy. As I stooped to tuck a fur bedspread more firmly around Philippa, the door behind me was shouldered open.

'Fuel, mistress,'

'And about time too!'

'I came as fast as I could, mistress.'

I swung round. There, placing a basket of logs beside the sulky fire, with an impressive flexing of arm and shoulder muscle, was the Duke. Swinging his short cloak back over one shoulder, he applied himself to brushing twigs and dust from his hands, beating the residue from his tunic.

'My lord!' We curtsied hurriedly. The children began to emerge from their wrappings like moths from a cocoon, lured by this timely distraction. I busied myself with some entirely unnecessary task, hiding my flushed cheeks, but not before I had registered the gleam in the ducal eye.

'More's on its way.' He looked round, taking in our beleaguered state, frowning as he pulled his hat from his head and ruffled his hair. 'Before God, it's as cold as Hades in here.'

'What are you doing, John?' Alice asked, walking across to remove more pieces of debris from his sleeve. 'Do we employ no servants?'

'I expect we do.' His eyes were wide and guileless when they slid in my direction. 'But I was instructed to fetch this personally, and not pass the message onto another and then forget about it.'

I felt a flush of heat creep even deeper from chin to hair-line.

Alice laughed. 'When did you return?'

'Just this moment, and not before time, it seems. I'm pleased to be of use.'

'Forgive me, my lord,' I said. I could not meet that apparently innocent stare. 'I would not presume…'

He brushed it aside with a little gesture, much as he had brushed the twigs from the richly figured cloth. 'I'm rarely mistaken for a servant, much less Robert. Some would say it was good for my soul and I should thank God that I am reminded of the humility of Christ.' But there was laughter in his voice as he looked round, taking stock, graciously accepting a psalter from Henry, ruffling his son's hair much as he had ruffled his own. 'It's too cold in here. They'll all come down with the ague.' With a grin he pulled his soft felt hat low onto his son's head so that the fur brim covered the child's eyes, making Henry chortle with delight. 'Take them to my rooms, Alice, and make them comfortable. Lady Katherine and I will arrange to bring books and whatever else she considers we need…'

'An excellent thought…' Without fuss, Alice rounded up and ushered the little party of children and nursemaids out. Leaving me to face my nemesis. There he stood, between me and the door, hands loosely at his sides, his eyes watchful, expression unreadable. There was no escape and he would require an answer from me.

He must have seen me glance at the open door.

'No…' Within a breath, he had taken one stride and possessed himself of my hand, his frown deepening. 'You are frozen.'

And without more ado he seized my other hand, pulled me down to the settle just vacated by his daughters, wrapped my hands in the fur-lined folds of his mantle and held them firmly against the breast of his tunic, tightening his grip when I struggled to release them. Since to continue would be fruitless, and undignified, I gave up the lost cause and simply sat. Beneath my palms I absorbed the beat of his heart, hard and steady, far steadier than mine. All my thoughts were dominated by the one: he was too close, too overpowering, and I did not know what to say to him.

'I did not know that you were returned,' I said, inwardly flinching at the banal comment.

'I had to. I had to see you,' he replied evenly.

His eyes were dark, their usual brilliance muted, the flat planes of his face still.

'This is wrong,' I remonstrated. 'I must not be here with you like this.'

'Do you deny me the right to comfort you?'

'You have no right.' Panic rose in me, because his touch made my blood beat in my ears.

'I am Plantagenet.'

Delivered with a swagger that took my breath with its arrogance.

'So I am yours to command?'

'Yes.'

'I don't know what you want from me, sir.'

'You. I want you.'

And I struggled even more to find a reply. 'Your loyalty is to your wife, my lord.'

Beneath my palms I felt him inhale, and tensed for a blast of Plantagenet irritation. Though his response was lightly made, it was unnerving in that he picked up our conversation as if there had not been a strained hiatus of six weeks.

'You know what I want, Katherine. In God's name, I made myself plain enough. Too plain. I think if I recall correctly I showed a lamentable lack of finesse—but I had hoped you would reconsider. It's been too long. How long is it since you came to me and I offered you my service and bed?'

The simplicity of that statement made my own heart bound. 'Six weeks, my lord.' I knew exactly.

He laughed, making me feel foolish. 'So you have been counting too.'

And suddenly I cast off any thoughts of the difference in our status. We were no longer royal duke and loyal dependent, simply a man and a woman encountering a choice that was no choice, and never could be.

'My answer is no different now,' I said.

'Nor is my desire to have you with me. Are we at stalemate? I wanted you then. I want you now.' His words were low and urgent, forcing me to listen and consider rather than wilfully reject. 'I cannot accept that you are indifferent to me. I can feel the blood raging through my body as I hold you, just as I can feel the beat of yours throbbing in your wrists.'

How horribly true. How could I deny what he could sense through the simple fact of our proximity? My throat was dry, my heart furiously beating against my ribs, as his heart did too with increased vehemence against my palms. I would be a fool to claim indifference when my cheeks were flushed with sudden warmth and my whole body trembled.

'If I kissed you now, this very moment,' the Duke surmised, eyes as keen as one of his goshawks in the mews, 'I wager your lips would be warm and welcoming.'

So did I. I knew they would. Close enough that I could see my own reflection in his eyes, it was impossible to hide the turbulence of my thoughts. Helplessly, I turned my face away.

'If I kissed you, how could you deny the attraction that draws us together?' Lifting our joined hands, he turned my face to his. 'Do you fear me? I don't think you do—and I'll not kiss you without your permission.' And with a smile that hacked at the base of all my convictions: 'Will you be my love, Katherine?'

But I was not so lost to good sense. 'I can't!' Why could he not *see*? 'It was wrong then and it is wrong now.'

'That's what you said last time.'

'And I say it again. You should not ask it of me.'

Formality had fallen away from both of us. His eyes moved over my face, as if absorbing every feature. At first their hard brightness had returned, full of what I could only interpret as displeasure that I refused him. But then they softened, perhaps with regret. 'It is not my intention to distress you.' It had the sound of a benediction as his grip loosened a little. And then, when I had thought he might actually accept my denial of him and leave me, his gaze sharpened as it flicked over my person.

'Why are you not wearing my rosary?' So he had noticed the simple length of wooden beads at my waist, replacing the coral.

'Because it is an unsuitable gift from you to your wife's damsel.'

'Unsuitable? What is unsuitable for the Duke of Lancaster to do?' Arrested, he lifted his chin. 'I thought it most suitable. I thought you would like it, and would find more use for it than a hanap.'

'I do. Of course I do. It is magnificent.' I felt an urge to shake him, as a woman might shake any obtuse man who could not follow her line of reasoning. 'To give me such a gift—a gift of such portent—and then ask me to become your mistress, when I am part of your new wife's establishment…it is too much.'

His brows, previously amused or lightly assured, drew into a flat line. 'A sin, in effect.'

'Yes.' My mouth was dry, my heart as cold as stone, but it must be said. 'It is immoral,' I whispered. 'It goes against all I learned as a child, in my upbringing at your mother's hand. And in your careful raising too, I imagine.'

Nostrils flaring, the royal blood had never been so obvious. 'If a man had said that to me, I would have cleaved his head with my sword. So you accuse me of immorality, Lady de Swynford?'

'Yes. No…' I had, hadn't I? I felt my face flush again as I stumbled over my muddled response.

'Well, that's clear enough.'

'It's not clear at all!' His fingers tightened around the soft wrappings as I tried to pull away again. 'It weights on my conscience.'

'So you reject me because of conscience.'

'Yes. But not only that.' I determined to explain. 'I would never become the mistress of a man who did not respect me, or whom I could not respect to the same degree.' So I asked him. A question I had never asked any man, certainly not a question I could ever envisage presenting to the Duke of Lancaster. 'Can you respect a woman who agreed to give herself, in carnal sin, into a relationship with a man without the blessing of the Church?'

There was no hesitation: 'Yes, I can, if you are that woman. Since I have made my desire for you more than plain, how can you ask it? I am the man who will cherish you, with or without the Church's blessing, and I will stand protection for you against the accusatory world.'

A fine promise that touched my emotions. So he might be that man, but was I the woman to give myself over to that sin? Could I live a life founded on lust, on unholy, unsanctified, physical desire, which would call ignominy down on my head? It would take a strong will to face family and friends as the acknowledged mistress of the Duke of Lancaster and accept their judgement.

'Do you deny my power to accomplish it?' the Duke demanded. 'I will make you my mistress, and as the woman who is chosen by a prince of the Plantagenet line, you will be answerable to no man.'

But I would be answerable to my own conscience and to God. All I could do was retreat to a dilemma that he must understand.

'I cannot. I am too far below you, my lord, a mere daughter of a royal official, a widow of a minor knight. But nor am I a court whore, willing to please any man in exchange for nightly gratification and a handful of jewels, as he sees fit. I know what is due to me, just as I know my place in the ordering of worldly affairs, and that place is not in your bed. I cannot accept your invitation simply because…because…'

'Because I have an itch that is in need of scratching. Is that what you wished to say?'

'Yes.'

My cheeks were on fire from the deliberate crudity, but the Duke laughed.

'Your scruples, madam, are magnificent.'

'I know that you value my service,' I tried to explain despite the sharp irony, for was he not still smiling at me? 'I know that you have a kindness for me and my children. I will serve the house of Lancaster in heartfelt gratitude for all you have done for us. But how do you desire me? You loved Blanche to the depths of your soul. Your love for her shone as a bright halo around you, around the pair of you. I know the pain of your grief when she died.' I held his whole attention now. 'You have a new and beautiful high-born wife who is carrying your child. She brings you a kingdom, a valuable alliance. She is young and vulnerable and would appeal to your chivalry. Would you not love her too? I know you have a care for her—you treat her as if she is made of fine glass. Why would you not adore her?'

Why did I have a need to say all this? It was fruitless, painting a picture that was far more familiar to him than it was to me. But still I would speak out. I took a breath, flattening my hands, still warmly enwrapped, against his chest.

'I will not be the mistress of any man who simply wants me for a casual hour of dalliance and a fast satisfaction between the bedsheets,' I declared, as outspoken as he.

'And a handful of jewels. So you said.' The Duke tilted his chin as his eyes gleamed with something like appreciation. I thought I had surprised him after all. 'That was quite a speech. I knew there was a reason I appointed you as the Duchess's damsel. I am mightily impressed. Have you finished dissecting my morals and my character?' he asked. 'In my own defence then, I worshipped Blanche. Her death near broke my heart. But she is dead three years now, and a flame does not remain alight for ever.'

I thought about this, accepted it. 'Yet now there is Constanza, my lord.' The Queen of Castile stood between us, as formidably as if she had stepped into the room.

'Do you think I dishonour her?' he asked, his brows angling. 'Constanza does not love me, nor I her, if that concerns you. It is a political marriage, to our mutual benefit, and one that could bring me great power. I am a man with ambitions that I will not see fulfilled as my father's third-born son, and so I value Constanza for what she can bring me. I will never show her less than respect. I will do nothing to harm her or cause her distress. I will never hold her up to ridicule or slights in public, but will treat her with every courtesy.'

'I think you might be hypocritical if you invite me to be your mistress within a six-month of your bridal vows, my lord. And no, I was not dissecting your character,' I continued, my words carrying an unmistakable burden of acidity. 'I'll not be any man's mistress, to be enjoyed for a few passing weeks of pleasure when the desire runs strong, only to be cast aside when the appetite palls.'

The Duke grinned. 'I see that you don't think much of my staying power. I think the pleasure we would find together would be of longer duration than that. Do you think I'd cast you adrift after only a few weeks?'

'I don't know.' And to my dismay I felt the sting of tears. I swallowed hard. 'I think you do not understand my dilemma. I have a conscience,' I repeated, feeling that I was fighting a losing battle against his obstinacy.

'And you think I do not, it seems. What a very low opinion you have of me.' He shook his head in mock reproof. 'You have given me a hard task, have you not? I must find a way to prove it to you that an hour or two of dalliance would be most enjoyable.'

'I defy you to try, my lord. I'll not be persuaded.'

The Duke stood, pulling me with him, drawing me into his arms when I tried to step back. So we stood, unmoving, breast to breast, thigh to thigh. I thought for a moment, in which I stopped breathing, that it was in his mind to kiss me. Then footsteps sounded in the distance, approaching briskly, and he raised his head.

'I vow I will do it. Stay in the chapel after Compline.'

'I'll not change my mind.'

'I command you, Katherine. And it will give you time to

think. I can feel your body shivering with the beat of your heart. I swear you feel this strange appeal between us just as strongly as I, and it's in my mind to make you abandon your so carefully constructed arguments and admit it.'

He addressed me with such a note of intractability, forcing me to acknowledge just how ruthless John of Lancaster could be. It chilled me to the bone, if it had not been for the little leap of fire in my heart. He unwrapped his cloak from around my hands, releasing me at last.

'At least I've made your hands warm. Now it is my holy grail to make you smile again. And I will do it.'

He said no more for the footsteps materialised into the form of the absent Robert, but I felt the weight of the Duke's obstinacy, as he ordered the servant to collect up an abandoned lute and drum, pushed books into my hands, tucking others under his arm. I followed him to his rooms where, surrounded by childish voices and blessed warmth, some form of normality returned.

As he opened the door for me he stood for a moment, holding me back.

'I'll woo you and win you, lady. I'll give battle to your conscience and defeat it. I give you fair warning.'

'I will not be won over.'

'Do you say?' His lips were against my ear as he whispered: 'I'll have you yet.'

In a spirit of defiance I knelt for Compline with the household. I would be honest and firm. I would restore myself to God's good grace. I would not be swayed by either specious argument or base desire.

I would refuse the Duke of Lancaster.

As the priest made the sign of the benediction and the service ended, the chapel emptied, but, because I had been so commanded, I remained on my knees, with a brief smile for Lady Alice who presumed that I had a final personal petition to make. Immediately I heard the door close behind me, and there was the Duke moving softly to stand at my side.

Not daring to look at him in all his magnificent smooth elegance, his tunic and jewels gleaming, I fixed my eye on the figure of the suffering Christ on the altar's gold crucifix. This should be a very brief confrontation.

'My answer is still no, my lord.' I could not make it plainer.

Which the Duke ignored.

'You have returned to your doleful black,' he remarked, surveying my widow's weeds from head to foot. There was laughter in his voice.

'Yes, my lord. I have.'

'You have also, it seems, reverted to stiff formality.'

'Yes, my lord. It is for the best.'

'For whom? Don't answer that.' As I opened my mouth to do just that.

'There is nothing more to say between us, my lord,' I said instead.

Which deterred him not at all, offering his hand, persisting when I was slow to take it. 'Perhaps we should discuss my proposal further, and I would rather you were not on your knees, my lady. Did I not vow to persuade you of the rightness of our being together? I will do it, but I would rather contemplate your lovely face than that unflattering veil.'

Colour rushed to my cheeks but I took the offered hand and stood, conscious of nothing but his touch. The altar shimmered with gold, my bones turned to water, my flesh was consumed with heat. I suspected this was going to take longer than I had foreseen.

'This is not an appropriate place, my lord.'

I kept my gaze level on the glittering altar panel of saints and angels surrounding the risen Christ. Every one of them was regarding me with judgement in his face.

'This, my delight, is the only privacy we'll get. Keep your piety under control.' And when I stiffened in outrage, he laughed. 'We'll make the most of the time we have here without interference.' And placing his hands on my shoulders he turned me to face him, taking me entirely by surprise when he leaned to kiss the space between my brows. 'Do you know that your skin has the glow of the most precious pearl I possess? And since this is the only area of skin you allow me to see…' Disturbing the pattern of my heartbeat further, he stroked my cheek from brow to chin with the tips of his fingers. 'It is softer than the finest silk.'

My thoughts were in a tumble of awareness of him. The breadth of his shoulders, the strength of his hands. The striking lines of his features. The brush of his lips against my skin had completely unravelled my certainty, like the mayhem a kitten might have created in a box of embroidery silks.

'You brows are the gold of a summer gilly-flower,' he continued, smiling as if unaware of my chaotic emotions. Of course he was aware. This was quite deliberate. 'You have the grace of one of the iridescent damselflies over the mere at Kenilworth. Your eyes hold a depth of ancient amber. You, Madame de Swynford, are a rare and beautiful woman.'

I trembled in his grasp. I could not prevent it.

'Is this a wooing, my lord?'

'Of course.'

'Or a sophisticated flirtation, to undermine my decision?'

'That too. I always knew that you were an intelligent woman as well as a beautiful one.' He paused, watching every expression on my face. 'Am I succeeding?' His eyes became intent, the flippancy dissipating in an instant, his hands more urgent, but he kept his tone light. 'Do I engage your senses to any degree?' he enquired conversationally, as if asking after my state of health. 'Your veil is shivering with your response to me. But will you admit it?'

What could I say? Honesty had its own dangers. 'Yes, my lord. I admit to feeling an…an attraction to you.'

The intensity deepened. 'Then be with me,' he urged, his fingers flexing. 'Be with me, Madame Katherine, and allow me to open the doors of heaven for you.'

It seemed to me that the angelic throng frowned its disapproval.

'What's wrong?' he asked. 'What have I said now to distress you?'

'The angels disapprove,' I observed.

'The angels are free to make their own judgement. This is not their concern. This is between you and me.'

And before I could speak he had framed my face with his hands and kissed my lips, the gentlest, most tender of kisses, his lips just brushing mine. It took my breath.

'There,' he said. 'I knew that kissing you would be like sipping honeyed wine. And God will forgive me for taking it.'

Which robbed me even more of words. How like him, I thought mutinously. How like the Duke of Lancaster to flout convention and woo me so carnally in this holy place, in the sight of God, and apparently with all due reverence.

'If I recall,' he continued, 'your hair—which you do not allow me to see—would challenge the sun itself in its brightness.' Then: 'Look at me, Katherine.'

And I did. I had no will to resist under the power of his words even if I had not been entranced by that kiss. The Duke's eyes, reflecting the gilding on angel and cherub, were level and clear on mine.

'I saw you in my audience chamber and I wanted you.

You know that. I wanted you to be mine. I still do, and I won't let you go. You were made to belong to me. It is my right to claim you.'

As if there could be no other reason for our being here. Perhaps there was no other for a man such as he. He saw me and wanted me. I simply stared. If the angels were astounded to hear it so forcefully expressed, so was I.

His hands moved slowly down from my shoulders in one long caress, until he was in possession of my hands.

'You came to me because you needed help,' he said. 'There you stood, pale and worn and overwrought with too many sleepless nights and worries, and for the first time since I had known you, you were in need. I had never thought of you as fragile, but on that day I wanted to lift the burden from your shoulders.' His breathing was rather fast, matching mine. 'I still do. And I want more than that. I want to strip that black garment from you and take you to my bed and show you the pleasures that can exist between a man and a woman who have, if you will, an attraction. I will care for you, protect you and bestow every comfort on you. I will respect you and hold you in esteem. You will be my mistress and my heart's desire. All I ask is that you say yes, for I have a powerful need of you.'

He was so close that I thought he would kiss me again. And that if he did not I would drown in longing.

The Duke kissed me. Not a tender embrace, no fleeting moment, no chivalrous brush of mouth against mouth, but a kiss of heat, of passion. Of promise of what might be. And I drowned anyway in the splendour of it.

At last, when I clung to him, the Duke lifted his head. 'Well, Madame de Swynford, my superbly respectable, black-clad widow? What do you say?'

There was the shadow of passion, now well governed.

What could I say to so powerful a declaration, such a heart-stopping invitation? Severe in my widow's black, my thoughts anything but respectable, I regarded him, thinking of what this would mean for me.

'You wish me to be your mistress,' I stated.

'Yes.'

'You wish me to be part of your household.'

'Of course.'

'You will treat me with respect and esteem.'

'Yes. I will revere and honour you as well. Before God, Katherine! Is this a catechism? Here it is, laid out for your appreciation. I cannot give you my name.' As if negotiating a deal between traders, I found myself thinking in a moment of ridiculous levity. 'I cannot give you any recognition in the eyes of the world, but all I am, and all that is within my power to give you happiness, that is what I can give you. That is what I offer you, Katherine de Swynford, if you will only stop prevaricating and step willingly into my arms.'

The candles, now burning low, seemed to leap and shiver, casting an even greater mystery over our surroundings, even more furious reactions on the faces of the angelic throng.

'I can still see your heart beating through the shiver of your veil,' he continued when I remained mute, attempting to encompass all. 'Can you breathe enough to give me a reply? Why can you not simply accept that you and I should be together?'

He wanted me. John of Lancaster desired me. The levity returned in full force.

'If I give myself to you, will you fetch wood for me?' I asked.

His brows rose, his eyes gleamed, but he replied with equanimity.

'I will. And all else you ask of me. I will pour your wine and tie your laces.'

Which made a breath of laughter rise inappropriately to the surface, but I looked away, absorbing the reality of the threshold before which I found myself standing.

'I could not bear to be the object of gossip, my lord.'

'You know the ways of the court.'

'I know that it is impossible to hide anything for long.'

'I would never draw attention to you. To us. Is that what you fear?'

I breathed out slowly. 'Is such discretion possible?'

'I don't know.' He was honest too. 'All I know is that I have a need of you, beyond all good sense.'

His words slid over my flesh like the finest cloth, like the blue and white damask he had given me. How fatally simple it was, after the recent weeks of heart-searching. His assurance had the power of a battle mace against an enemy's helm. His conviction could have carried an army to victory against the most powerful foe.

'Come to me. Allow me to take care of you and worship at your perfect feet.'

He saw no difficulty in my choice, whereas I could count every trap in the path of an unwary woman. And yet in spite of my qualms, all I could do was marvel at the richness of the gift he had placed at my feet. How could I have ever believed that the Duke of Lancaster would invite me to take my place at his side, in his life?

'Do it. Say yes, lovely Katherine.'

'Does nothing at all about this worry you?' I asked instead in bewilderment.

'Not a thing.'

The silence of the chapel around us grew taut, for had we not turned full circle, to face once more the unpardonable sin? The Duke was so assured whereas I wallowed in a puddle of indecision.

'I said I would kneel at your feet. Behold I do.' And still holding my hand he dropped to one knee, looking up at me with all the old glamour in his presence. 'It is this easy, my lady. I want you. Do you want me?'

'My lord...' I studied his handsome features, of which he was very well aware. In a final attempt to combat temptation, I adopted as remote a tone as I was able. 'I would ask one thing of you.'

'And I will grant it.'

'Will you give me one night? To consider my answer.'

'God's Blood, woman! What can you decide in one night, that you haven't managed to decide in six weeks?'

'It is a dangerous step.'

'It is a glorious step!'

Which understandable irritation I ignored, for I would not be rushed into a decision that would have so great an impact on my life. 'And will you agree to abide by the choice I make, my lord?'

'That's two things.' He looked askance.

'Then make it three. I wish to borrow a book from you, my lord.'

'A book?' The irritation was overlaid with bafflement. 'A missal? Come then, if that is your wish. And perhaps you could practise not calling me my lord with every breath. My name is John.'

'As I know, my lord.'

With an appreciative laugh, opening the door, we left the angels in no way the wiser as the Duke escorted me to his library, leaving me there to make my choice. For a moment he stood, watching as I lit a candle from a wall-torch.

'Katherine?'

I looked back at him where he stood by the open door. How had I never realised the caress of his voice on my name, even when the mischief had vanished. The Duke was very serious as he bowed deeply.

'How you intrigue me. You kisses are sensuous yet you are governed with stark piety. Promise me that you will not allow fear of what the world will say to guide your choice. Promise that you will not give power to past sorrows and present fears to chain you to your bleak widowhood. I swear there is more for you in this life than what you are today. And I should tell you: for me it is no mere attraction. It is an overwhelming desire.'

'I promise, my lord.'

Briefly I read naked desire in his face, before courtesy returned and he strode back across the room to kiss my fingers with typical flamboyance.

'When you smile, you are so very beautiful. Don't look so baffled. Sleep well, my dearest one. I would give you happiness and fulfilment, not anguished soul-searching.'

And with a final salute to my fingers he left me to my search.

The decision I was about to make was hazardous indeed: to follow the hard and narrow but entirely respectable path dictated by morality and virtue, or to step aside to snatch at that bright happiness the Duke offered me. I knew full well what I ought to do. My conscience was a lively creature, prompting me into the way of godly righteousness, for how should I live with so great a sin on my soul?

I swore the Duke of Lancaster stood at my shoulder as I selected my book. My mind was all chaos.

I discovered the Duke in his library, where he would be engaged in business affairs after early Mass and breaking his fast. Quietly, only half-opening the door, I paused. Then, entirely certain of what I must do, I pushed it open, the well-greased hinges failing to announce my presence. There, his back to me, the Duke poured over a large expanse of vellum on which I could see was drawn a map of England and France and the northern reaches of Castile.

I stood, watching him as he worked, unaware of his audience, his finger tracing what I thought was a route to Aquitaine, continuing south to Castile, the object of his new ambitions. The success or failure of this new expedition would rest on his shoulders.

I moved inadvertently, my shoe scuffing along the tiles, but he did not respond, probably did not even hear.

'My lord.'

'Leave it over there.'

The Duke was not the only one to be mistaken for a servant.

'I would rather—'

'Go away.' He was more abstracted than I had thought. 'Come back later.'

With a grunt of exasperation he scrubbed his fist along the edge of his chin, much as young Henry had done earlier in the day when reprimanded for cleaning his inky fingers on the front of his tunic, so that I smiled at the similarity.

I was so sure, my decision clear in my mind. So sure that I walked softly forward and placed my hand on his shoulder.

'I will return if it pleases you. I thought you wanted an answer from me. I am here to give it.'

'Ah…have you come to refuse me?' he asked, staring ahead.

Every muscle in that shoulder was tensed beneath my palm as he anticipated my ultimate rejection. His hands clenched into fists on the map.

'So you pre-empt me,' I replied evenly.

'Why not? You would not be the first virtuous woman to find lechery too painful to contemplate,' he replied, his voice harsh, his observation grating against my senses. 'Perhaps you have not the courage to seize what you desire.'

Here was a man who never questioned his own courage, but he would question mine. I lifted my palm and stepped back. Did he think it would not take courage to refuse him?

'I am here to give you my reply,' I said with a calmness that belied by leaping heart. 'Whether I have courage, it is for you to judge.'

Standing, stretching to his full height, quite carefully the Duke placed the pen beside the document, and turned. I remained motionless. I did not say a word: I did not have to. I watched as a smile began, slowly at first, then growing to illuminate his face, enhancing his beauty as he saw what I had done. Fisting his hands on his hips, he tilted his head in contemplation, making me smile again for it was as if he was appreciating some new object in his collection. I remained perfectly still and let him look.

'What have you got behind your back?' he asked softly when, as I knew he would, he had taken in every aspect of my appearance.

With one hand I produced the book I had borrowed, like a wise-woman revealing some mystical source of magic. 'I have this to return.' I placed it on the table next to the map.

'The missal you borrowed to direct your actions into righteous pathways.'

'No missal,' I replied solemnly, for it was not a book of prayer that I had sought for my night of contemplation, with the Duke's kiss still hot on my lips.

The Duke opened the cover page, and looked up quizzically. 'I would not have expected this.'

'Why not?' Its depictions of Love in all its forms in the *Roman de la Rose* had occupied my hours, while the sensuous illustrations had seduced my senses.

'Did it help?' The Duke closed the page, his gaze holding mine. 'Did it persuade you that Divine Love was your ultimate goal in this life?'

'No, my lord.'

'Platonic love, then. Is that what you seek between us?'

'No, my lord.'

He knew I did not. His eyes glittered with a sense of victory, as if he had just overcome an enemy of great power. How could he not know? He knew my answer, as I had intended, without a word being exchanged between us, as he had taken in my appearance from the little round buckram hat that fixed my gold-edged veil, to my gilded slippers. For what had I done? Rejecting the respectable widow for ever, I was dressed as if for a bridal in green and gold, my bodice gleamingly patterned, my oversleeves trimmed with a full meadow of embroidered flowers. As far from my mourning robes as I could make them. And at my belt hung the coral and gold beads of the Duke's gift.

This was no penitential garb.

The Duke gestured with his chin. 'And in your other hand?'

'This is for you.'

Discovered in The Savoy garden almost before dawn, it was a poor apology, frost-bitten and withered, showing the merest tinge of colour within its grey of decomposition.

'One should never plan to express the state of one's heart with a rose in winter,' I said. 'It will shed its petals within the hour.'

'I will not hold its imperfections against you.' He took

the sad corpse from me. And in taking it his fingers, at last, closed over mine.

'I read Jean de Meun's poem,' I said, struggling to keep my voice even, for his handclasp stirred my blood to a shiver of delight. 'How the Lover battled to win the heart of his Beloved. I recognised the enemies he faced. Jealousy. Danger. Shame and fear. I recognised all of those. Do I not see them in my own choices? I see the dangers in what you ask of me, for I am afraid of the shame that others would heap on me. Am I not jealous of every moment you spend with Constanza, away from me?'

His hand wrapped even more strongly round mine, as if to give comfort and strength when my voice caught a little on the emotion of the moment. But I did not need his courage. I had enough of my own. My night had been well spent.

'But you see,' I went on to explain, 'the Lover won his battle, and his tormenters fled. He gained entrance to the walled garden and plucked the precious rosebud for his Love. As I have plucked this for you, from your own garden. My doubts too have fled.'

And they had. I had made my decision for good or ill.

'So I am here. To say yes to you.'

'I think it was supremely difficult for you.' The timbre of his voice was like velvet, to stroke my senses.

'To find a rose? Well nigh impossible. This was the only one…' I smiled when he used his free hand to silence me, his fingers gentle on my lips.

'To make the decision, my dearest girl! My very dear Katherine.'

'Yes. It was,' I admitted, but still I smiled against his fingers for my heart was leaping with joy. 'Do you remember who it was who helped the Lover in his battle?' I knew that he would.

'Oh, yes. All-powerful, all-conquering Venus. The goddess of carnal desire, of all physical delights.' His hand tightening around mine and the suffering rosebud, he drew me closer. 'So, Madame de Swynford, you will give yourself up to me and all the pleasures I can bring to you?'

'I will.'

'For ever?'

'For all time.'

'Then we will be together for all time. And I will extract a promise from you.'

'Only one?'

'One will do for now.' He stroked his knuckles over my embroidered bodice, over the swell of my breasts, in a possessive movement that made me hold my breath. 'Will you promise me that you will never wear black again?'

'I promise.'

He kissed me on the lips, as light and insubstantial as that first kiss, as a butterfly's wing, although I felt the rigid tension of the muscles in his forearms as he tucked the sad rose into the bodice of my gown. It was like feeling the explosive force of a warhorse, held on a tight rein until released into the heat of battle. I was in no doubt of his desire for me. My fingers trembled as I smoothed them over the knap of his sleeve. I needed him to take the next step, for it was beyond me.

Abandoning the map and the forthcoming expedition, he led me to the door.

'Does Lady Alice expect you?'

'No, my lord. I am in your employ.'

'Then I have need of an hour of your time.' For a moment he hesitated, his eyes studying my face, smoothing my lower lip with the pad of his thumb, a more poignant gesture than any other. 'Or a month, a year. Even a lifetime...'

'You must make do with an hour, my lord,' I remarked practically, even as my heart throbbed. 'Lady Alice will ask after me.'

'An hour it shall be,' he agreed, 'for I too, unfortunately, have demands on my time.'

And in that moment of perception I knew that this would always be so. The Duke's duty was to England. Any woman in his life must accept that she would never be pre-eminent, no matter how strong his desire to be with her. I knew that this driving force in him to be pre-eminent, to wield power, would colour all our days together, however long or short our liaison might be. And in that moment, I witnessed the path of my life stretched out before me, with all its shadows, its moments of brilliance.

You can still step back, my conscience whispered in my mind. *Are you indeed brave enough? Do you have the fortitude to take what you want, what you have always dreamed of taking? Or will you step back and preserve the moral high ground? If you take this step, there will never be any moral high ground, ever again, for you.*

There is no marriage in this for you.

If you accept you will be no better than a court harlot, damned as a fallen woman. What will you say to your children? How will you explain to your son when he asks why those at court point and gossip?

There is still time to retreat. To return to your widowhood, your conscience clear as you kneel before the priest with a clean heart.

There will never be the possibility of marriage for you in this relationship.

Go back to Kettlethorpe and take up the reins of the estates.

But I would not. My decision was made, finally and irrevocably, even when my conscience struck a final blow.

The Duke has never said that he loves you.

I would not listen. Had any woman ever refused him? I could not.

Once outside the library, the Duke broke the contact between us but I walked beside him as he opened the door into his private accommodations and dismissed his body servant who was engaged in laying garments in a clothes press. He did not even glance at me, probably thinking—if he even considered it—that I had come to report to the Duke about one of the children. Yet, even so…

'Is this discretion, my lord?' I asked. 'Coming to your rooms in the broad light of day?'

'I will not lurk and skulk.' A vestige of a frown momentarily settled on his brow. He was unused to his actions being questioned. 'It is not in my nature to hide and dissemble. But nor am I lacking in good sense. You have my word. I will not willingly put you or Constanza into the public eye. Enough! This hour is for us. An hour in which I'll turn your beautifully ordered world upside down.'

Strides quickening, he led me through the sumptuous rooms to his bedchamber, where he flung the door wide.

'Welcome, Katherine.'

I stepped over the threshold, entirely of my own volition. I took in the splendour of the furnishings, the polished wood, the silver sconces, the velvet-padded prie-dieu with its heavy silver crucifix, but my mind was not on prayer. And there was the ducal bed.

The Duke shut and barred the door.

'My bed is cold. Who will warm it for me?'

I did not hesitate.

'*I* will, my lord.'

* * *

Desire swept away all discretion when the Duke closed his door against the world. Passion ruled, all the words, all the explanations, the warnings, all the anxieties excoriated in a blaze of heat. If any doubts remained in my heart, they would have been obliterated. But since there were none, I let my senses be seduced. There were no uncertainties to undermine my decision to be with him.

His control was superb. Had he not promised to tie my laces? He was equally proficient at unlacing them, although he growled at the row of buttons that stretched from elbow to little finger on my sleeves. He proved to be just as skilled at removing my intricately latched crispinette and veil and loosing the braids of my hair. I shivered under his hands, under the sway of his marvellous expertise.

'I thought I remembered, but I had forgotten how rich it was,' he murmured as the length of my hair uncoiled to spread over my shoulder, and his, when I leaned against him. 'The sun's burnish…' He buried his face in it as I rested my head against his breast. It was good to rest against a man taller than I.

There was little rest. He needed no help from me to dis-robe, even though I offered to be his squire for the occasion. Nor did he need help to remove my shift.

No restraint, now, he turned my limbs to flame, my heart to breathless excitement, my blood to molten gold. He wak-ened my body to a sensual pleasure where there were no past shades keep us company.

I adored him.

I no longer cared what doubts the heavenly creatures har-boured. It did not trouble me that the Duke never spoke of love. It was enough that he treated me as if, for him, I was the most precious creature in the universe.

An hour was too short to encompass all we wished to say, every emotion that demanded expression.

'It is a taste of a banquet that will last us a lifetime,' he whispered against my throat.

'I must go, my lord,' I said when the minutes fled, as if winged.

'And you must call me John.'

'It is not easy.'

'But you will practise. Soon it will come readily to your lips.'

His assurance never failed to move me. How could I even contemplate the future with fear when the Duke of Lancaster held me in his arms and looked ahead with such confidence? He helped me to dress and hide my hair, he re-tied my laces. He wrapped a plain cloak around me to hide my inexplicable finery until it could be put to rights. How fast we learned the need for ultimate prudence.

'The rose has fallen into pieces,' I said, seeing it on the coffer with my rosary.

'It is a transient thing. But my desire for you is not.' He tucked the tell-tale gold of my veil into the neck of the cloak. 'Do you have regrets?'

'None.'

'Nor I. *You are of my Life and Death the Queen...*'

I sighed as I recognised the beautiful sentiment, the expression of utmost poetic devotion from the Lover to his Lady.

'Your brother-in-law, Master Chaucer, has a masterful way with words.' The Duke kissed me as if he would linger still, although we both knew that good sense dictated that we could not. 'Keep me in your mind, until we can be together again. Promise me that.'

'Yes, John. I will keep you in my mind.'

Collecting up the rosary into the palm of my hand, I walked slowly back to my room.

I was John of Lancaster's mistress.

Back in my chamber I removed my finery, recalling with a smile it being removed with much more alacrity and much less care.

I loved him, I adored him. I would never not love him.

Why had I done it? Why had I turned my back on every rule I had lived by? It shocked me that I had done so, laying aside my principles because a man had asked it of me, as I would lay aside an old gown that I no longer had use for. Now I had a new garment. A glittering cloak made of love, a magical cloak that in my naïve mind would protect me from the slights and condemnations of the society in which I lived. I was wrapped about by happiness. Pickled in it, I decided fancifully with a smile, as I would store beans in brine to last me through the winter.

Why had I done it? Because I loved the Duke and he had offered me the moon and the stars and the sun in one magnificent gesture. The firmament was mine in all its glory.

I searched for a comb beneath Philippa's haphazardly strewn belongings and addressed the tangles in my hair, allowing other truths to step into my mind.

The end is inevitable, as night will follow this bright day. As grey will streak the gold of your hair and a web of lines mar your skin. One day you will be parted.

I was no blind fool. I could see it so clearly. All the insurmountable obstacles to what for many lovers would be a permanent happiness, whatever words of commitment the Duke and I might choose to exchange. Whatever he might vow to me and I to him. Whatever lasting passion our bodies might promise when they fused with desire.

Did the Duke see those obstacles as clearly as I, an impossible bulwark of walls and ditches, not to mention the stalwart portcullis that would one day bring about our separation and stand between. I did not think he did. When did a Plantagenet prince ever have need to question his own worth? His needs and desires were there to be satisfied.

What would it be that intervened, to destroy this idyll— for that is surely what it was—I mused. Family. Political battles. The demands of England's policy abroad. He might desire me but his life was not his own to direct as he chose.

Nor was I his first mistress. Would I be his last? In all honesty I did not think so. He wanted me now, but I might yet be a forgotten name on the list of women who took his appreciative eye. It might be that the Duke would simply fall out of need for me.

This day I had stepped beyond the acceptable. I had crossed a forbidden line, knowing that I would have consequences to face. At some point, on one day in the future, for some reason that I could not quite see, he would have to make a choice—and then what of me? What would be left for me but memories and a reputation that would destroy my good name for ever?

Momentarily I closed my eyes to hide the contempt that I would assuredly read in the eyes of many who knew me. Then opened them as I briskly coiled my hair into its netted confines.

I would not allow such thoughts to cloud my happiness. The memory of the Duke's arms holding me, the heated demand of his kisses—they were more than enough. And indeed they would have to be, for the Duke had not said those stark, simple words: *I love you*. Not once. Desire and longing. Passion and need. But not love.

What did it matter? I would not allow it to matter. His need for me in his life was enough, and I was free to love him without restraint. But I would choose my words with care. The Duke did not talk of love, so I would not burden him with mine. Silently I vowed that he must never be compromised by my adoration, which he could not return.

Chapter Six

June 1372: Hertford Castle

'She'll have a hard time of it, mark my words.' Mistress Elyot, experienced midwife summoned by the Duke to attend his wife, was quick to give her opinion. We were all established at last at Hertford and the important event loomed.

'Narrow hips. And she's not strong. Comes of being Castilian, I expect.'

Tears filled Mistress Elyot's eyes and she sniffed in doleful anticipation.

I did not see that Duchess Constanza being Castilian had any bearing on her ability to grit her teeth, hold onto the hand of one of her Castilian damsels and push hard when instructed to do so, but since Mistress Elyot had the reputation of a wise-woman, and her nature was well-known to me, I did not argue the point. Mistress Elyot had supported Blanche through her pregnancies so her reputation was well-earned and perhaps she was right. The weather was June-sultry, the rooms at Hertford uncomfortably hot, but Constanza insisted on the windows tight shut to ward off malign forces, since she was Queen of Castile and that is how all royal children were born.

'This son,' she panted between groans and heart-rending cries, 'will be King of Castile.'

We suffered with her, for her demands were frequent. At least the nausea that had so afflicted her in the early months had vanished, but now her ankles and feet were so swollen that the skin was as tight as a drum. I drew on all the knowledge I had, bathing the afflicted areas in rose oil and vinegar, encouraging her to eat lightly of chicken. Praising the beneficial properties of quince fruits and pomegranate.

Duchess Constanza was a poor patient but for the sake of the child gave in to my ministrations.

Mistress Elyot nodded curtly, faint but noteworthy praise. Constanza insisted on my remaining at her side, day and night. The little cluster of damsels, useless except to carry carefully learned messages and fetch trays of food that went for the most part uneaten, glowered speechlessly at me. My sister Philippa, dislodged from her place at Constanza's right hand, observed with a caustic shrug that there was no accounting for the strange decisions of pregnant queens.

'This is a great endeavour for me,' Constanza whispered as her strength waned, despite the cups of spiced wine held to her lips. 'I must bear a son for my lord.'

Her final words, before a dark-haired, red-faced, squalling scrap of humanity took its first breath and howled. Strong enough, lively enough, but not received with any great rejoicing. Constanza's great endeavour was a girl.

Washed gently and wrapped in linen, the baby had improved to the eye when Constanza, also restored, held out her arms. I placed the infant there.

'She has the look of my sister Isabella,' Constanza observed, touching the dark hair, before handing her back to me almost immediately. 'Take her. Fetch me new linen for my bed.'

'She is a fine daughter,' I assured her, the light weight of the child in my arms reminding me of my own labours, the joy and relief at the outcome. That the Duchess showed so little concern except for her own discomfort was worrying me. I would not have handed my new daughter to other arms, with barely a glance.

'Better a son,' the Duchess announced.

'Next time, my lady,' Mistress Elyot cooed.

'I suppose I must.' Her brow was furrowed. 'It is my duty. To my country.'

And I knew that she did not mean England. The frown remained heavy on Constanza's brow.

'Your daughter will be of great value in a marriage alliance when she grows, to the glory of Castile,' I said. An angry woman did not make a good mother. 'She will be very beautiful, and much sought after,' I tried.

'Yes.' She was not soothed. 'I will call her Katalina. Katherine, I think you say.'

I felt my whole body tense, my arms tightening around the child who whimpered a little, as the unpalatable incongruity of it struck home. The Duke's child called after the Duke's mistress. As dismay stirred uneasily in my belly, I could only imagine the waspish tongues, stinging at my expense, heaping mockery on all of us, if the truth ever became the talk of the court.

I would not wish that for the Duchess.

'It is not a royal name in England, my lady,' I suggested lightly, keeping my eyes on the child, keeping my mouth in a smile, selecting the only argument that I thought would hold any weight with her. 'Monseigneur might not like it.'

'Why would he not? It is a beautiful name.' She looked directly at me. 'Is it not, Katherine?'

There was a rustle of laughter at this rather laboured attempt at humour. But for me, although I kept the smile intact, dismay turned to horror. Constanza could not know that I had kissed the Duke with more than the respect expected from a damsel of the household. She could not.

'St Katherine is the saint I admire most,' Constanza continued, impervious to my cold fear.

Of course she did not know. And relief flooded through me. I must learn to control my reactions. I could not allow myself to be so vulnerable, so open to every breath of possible scandal, for the rest of my life. The die was cast and I had the audacity to hold my nerve.

'It is an admirable name,' I replied easily now, for I too admired St Katherine, a virgin princess of Alexandria, martyred for her faith by a Roman Emperor.

'I approve of her courage in adversity, holding fast to her faith in the face of death,' Constanza announced. 'As I will hold fast to mine—that my lord will recover Castile for me. And next time I will bear a son. Go to the chapel and give thanks to St Katherine and the Virgin, for my safe delivery,' she directed us. 'And for the child, of course. I expect my lord daily.'

As I handed the babe to the waiting wet nurse, my compassion was stirred a little, for I saw the disappointment swim in Constanza's eyes with the unshed tears. She would not weep. Queens of Castile, she had informed us, did not weep. But that did not mean that she was untouched by what she saw as a failure.

I would see no successful birth of a child of mine as a failure, son or daughter.

And I too looked for the Duke's arrival. He was in London, in attendance on the King. It was almost three months since we had been together for that shortest of hours, a lifetime of absence and longing.

My sister prayed beside me, then kept step with me as we left the chapel.

'Since when did you care what she calls the child?' she asked *sotto voce* since Lady Alice with her sharp hearing was a mere few steps in front of us. Philippa's glance was equally sharp. 'Does it matter?'

My reply was cool. 'I spoke without any real intent.'

'You never speak without intent, Kate. Your cheeks are flushed.'

'Are we not all flushed in this heat?'

'Perhaps…it's having an effect on your temper too.'

'And on my patience!' I responded as my sister's barbs got the better of me.

Lady Alice, falling back to walk with us, clicked her tongue. Philippa stalked off ahead. I sighed.

'I promise to offer up two novenas in penance,' I remarked, but with a wry smile.

Lady Alice laughed. 'But your sister is right. Something is troubling your equanimity.'

'Nothing that a good night's sleep and a cup of warm ale would not cure. If the Duchess can allow me out of her sight for an hour or two.'

'Perhaps she will become less demanding when the Duke arrives. It will be good to see him.'

I lay on my bed, the hangings drawn back to allow even a breath of air. I wished with all my heart that the Duke would come.

'I present to you your daughter, my lord.'
The Duke had arrived at Hertford.

But I did not want this. I did not want to be in this formal audience chamber with the newest royal child in my arms, under the combined eyes of a nursemaid, a servant, a liveried page and William de Burgh, the chaplain, but the office had been given to me. Since Constanza remained secluded in her chambers until she was churched, it was decided that I should be the one to present Katalina, now two weeks old, to her father.

I did not want to do this at all.

I had once shivered at that brutal word hypocrisy. Here it stared me in the face, that I, the mistress, should present the child of the legitimate wife to her lover.

My excuses were ignored, rolled over like a charge of cavalry, my suggestions for one of the Castilian damsels to have the honour swatted away. Mistress Elyot declared herself too busy. And at least, she added, with a jaundiced eye to the damsels, I could speak good French when I conversed with my lord, which was more than…

I pondered the wisdom of handing the child to Philippa, but she would want to know why I was reluctant and I could not say. Philippa had waved me on, although she was not entirely pleased at what was considered an honour for me.

So there I stood in the audience chamber with the babe in my arms. Uncomfortable with the whole situation, I governed my features and acted out the pretence, taking as my pattern Master Ingoldsby's formidable austerity to me when faced with some conundrum.

The Duke entered, having been informed by Robert Swillington, the Chamberlain, that one of the damsels would present the new child. Even though he had the appearance of a man just emerged from an edgy diplomatic bout, he took in the scene with one sweeping survey, and there was no hesitation as he strode in with perfect sangfroid. Yet I spoke immediately to give him fair warning that I was the damsel.

'Your daughter, my lord. She is two weeks old and thrives. Duchess Constanza is in good health and is eager for your visit.'

How well I had learned my announcement.

How well his features had settled into enigmatic lines. I was merely a servant, no different from young Henry Warde, the page at his heel.

He stopped before me, and I offered the swaddled bundle in case he wished to hold her, watching as his gaze dwelt for a moment on the child, then lifted to me. My hands trembled as if the little body weighed heavily, until the Duke took her in his arms, as I knew he would, his face softening as the baby yawned.

'Tell the Duchess that I look for her churching and her return, if you will. Tell her I will send a gift.'

He touched the dark curls that escaped the little linen coif, and bent to press his lips to the infant's forehead.

'The Duchess wishes her to be called Katherine, my lord,' I stated carefully, adding: 'After St Katherine, you understand.'

My words brought a wry twist to his mouth. 'I will not argue against it, although it would not have been my choice.'

'The Duchess calls her Katalina.'

'Which is good. My thanks to you all for the care of my wife.'

The nursery maid curtsied, the chaplain beamed and I continued to stand with my rigidly schooled expression.

Such a multitude of emotions expressed between us, without any evidence on his face or mine, yet his were clear to me. I saw his pleasure, after his initial disappointment, as with any man, that the child was not a male heir for

Castile. The tenderness with which he supported the child. His surprise that the babe should be called Katherine. And a thought touched me to awaken all my insecurities and the green glitter of jealousy that sparkled through my blood. I had no history with this man to call on when uncertainty struck. I had no place in this family. The Duke, with only one son to his name, would desire more children with his wife. They would of necessity continue to share a bed and the intimate act of procreation. Which I must accept, however hard it might be.

Unaware of the lurch of dismay that began to build beneath my sleekly buttoned bodice, the Duke said: 'Tell the Duchess that I send her felicitations on this happy birth of our daughter.' He glanced up. 'But she wishes it was a son, of course.'

'Yes, my lord. She hopes for more children, an heir for Castile.'

He gave the child to the nursery maid, not to me, but it was to me that he spoke. 'Will you talk to me? About the Duchess? Tell me how she has fared.'

All the time that he was speaking he was unpinning a sapphire from the shoulder cape of his hood, dextrously transferring it to his daughter's wrappings.

'Yes, my lord.'

And then the calmly beautiful chamber with its carved hammer-beams and lightly plastered walls was empty, apart from the two of us, and the atmosphere was not calm at all. We simply stood apart, not talking, not touching, the long drawn-out weeks of our separation formidable between us.

It will always be like this, a voice warned in my mind. *It will never get better. How could it when you will live most of your lives apart, snatching moments that are tainted with guilt and anticipation of loss?*

I waited for him to speak first.

'Smile at me.'

I smiled. The muscles of my face felt stiff, unused.

'Speak to me.'

'You are right welcome, my lord.'

'Not like that.' His voice was unexpectedly harsh. He did not smile at me. 'Speak to me as a beloved to her lover.'

The time and space between us had been too long. It had created a chasm in my mind and I was not able to step easily across it, for ranged on the opposite side, standing closely with the Duke was Constanza with the child in her arms. Our love was too new for me to rest on it. I had no safe harbour, no anchorage that would hold me fast and secure. How could I survive without some continuity of touch, of speech? Of shared kisses and soft endearments? I had nothing. It was as if I felt my way blindly through a maze.

'I cannot...' I said, fretfully. 'Not yet.'

'It is not easy, is it?'

So he understood. And his understanding was as soothing as a bowl of hot frumenty on a cold morn. 'No, it is not easy.'

'Be brave, Katherine.'

'I am trying.'

'The child does not stand between us, any more than Constanza does.'

'But sometimes my heart betrays me and I can see no path for my feet to follow.'

'Tell me.'

So I did, as we stood in the centre of that sumptuous room. 'I fear that you will come to love them more than you need me. And that I will be rejected.'

'Katherine...'

I raised my hand in quick denial. 'I know you will say that it isn't so. I know what I must not ask of you...'

'Because it is not so. Have I not proved to you?'

'I cannot bear that we are apart for so long.'

'Yet it must be.'

He took a step and touched me, drawing the back of his forefinger along my throat to where my blood beat heavily. It was the first time that he had touched me, in public or in the privacy of his rooms, since I first shared his bed all those weeks ago at The Savoy.

'You look tired. And paler than I recall.'

'We have all suffered from the heat.'

'How I have missed you…'

'And I you.'

I thought he might have held me, but approaching footsteps made him look up and draw back. By the time the Chamberlain pushed open the door, we were standing a good distance apart, I by the door, the Duke on the dais.

'My lord.' He bowed with the briefest of glances at me. 'Forgive me. A courier from the Prince at Kennington. He says it is urgent.'

'I will come. Ensure that the man has ale and food.'

'Of course, my lord. It has been done.'

The Duke made to follow, but stopped when he drew level with me and, for form's sake, I curtsied with lowered eyes.

'Prudence is a heavy burden,' he said in response.

I looked up, for once not even trying to hide my despair. Did I not know it? It was like balancing on a sword edge suspended over that chasm that I found so difficult to cross. Agonising for the feet to do the walking: fatally agonising to fall into the depths. Yet this was how we must live. I could not show him how gravely I had missed him in all those weeks apart. I could neither speak nor act, but must exist on these crumbs of conversation, when all I wished to do was to announce to the world: 'This is the man I love.'

'What is it?' He searched my face.

'Nothing,' I whispered.

'It is not a sin, Katherine.' It was as if he had read my concerns.

It is a love greater than I can sometimes bear. But I could not speak of it.

'Come with me to London.'

'I cannot.'

'Yes, you can.'

He left me without explanation. Why did he need to explain? Sometimes his conceit unnerved me.

The Duke's plan was a simple one. Far simpler than if he was planning a military campaign, I supposed, and put into operation with all the high-handed self-belief I had come to expect. I, as one of the Duchess Constanza's senior damsels, he decreed, should be given the office of presenting this royal granddaughter to King Edward.

With my court dress and my jewels packed, I was provided with a litter and outriders. A complete household of nurses and servants, so many for so small a person, accompanied the baby Katalina in her own litter, but I travelled in solitary luxury. Nothing was lacking to my comfort, from a welter of cushions to the spiced wine. I knew where the order had originated. On arrival, as Katalina was settled with her entourage into The Savoy nursery, I turned towards the room I had once shared with Philippa.

'No, my lady.' Sir Thomas Hungerford was standing at my shoulder.

Perhaps I was expected to remain nearer the child. There was always Alyne's room.

'If you will accompany me, my lady.' The steward had a certain stern disapproval about him, but he gestured expansively towards the ducal apartments. 'My lord ordered that you should be housed here, in recognition of your service to the Duchess.'

And he pushed open the door into one of the guest chambers.

All I could think of was the contrast. Here all was opulence, luxury, comfort. My manor at Kettlethorpe was a peasant's hovel in comparison.

And so there I was settled, with two servants of my own to answer to any whim, leaving me with no role other than to enjoy the accommodations, for I was made free of the family rooms. I had no responsibilities except to feed my own pleasure. I could walk in the gardens, sit in the Duke's library with his collection of books, venture out into the city with an escort, as I awaited the royal summons to take Katalina to the King.

It was not the only summons I looked for. My blood sang with the anticipation, my heart scurrying like the rat in my undercroft at Kettlethorpe, as if I were some lovelorn girl.

Within a day of my arrival, the Duke came.

I had a week with him, seven whole, endless days that stretched before me, a se'enight of such magical sweetness, my heart was suffused with it. I did not think that I had ever known such untrammelled happiness as in those days, for we were still new lovers, still caught up in the glory of it, still untouched by the outside world.

How did we use it, that precious freedom? Were we discreet?

Without exception, for we both knew the importance of that discretion. In public we were never alone. We met in company. We dined in company. No slight was cast on the position of the Duchess, on my own reputation, nor on the Duke's joy in the birth of a daughter. Any guest who visited in those days was brought to the nursery to admire this child who was heir to the throne of Castile. I curtsied as any good damsel should. The Duke took the child from me as he had done on that first day, to commend her beauty.

'You will know Lady Katherine de Swynford,' he introduced me to his brother Thomas, Duke of Gloucester, and his wife who, a valuable ring glittering on every one of her fine-boned fingers, regarded me as some species of upper servant. 'Her care of my wife is beyond praise.'

'Lady Katherine.' Gloucester saluted my hand. 'I knew of your return to my brother's household.'

'And I am honoured, my lord.'

All seemly and formal, as it should be.

But the nights...

Where was the seemliness, the formality, of my nights? For when I dismissed my maidservant, the Duke came to me. And then he was the Duke no more.

'John...!'

I laughed as he kissed my shoulders, for I could call him by his name, which I could never do in the Great Hall or the public chambers. Even in my thoughts he was the Duke, as he had always been, royal to his fingertips.

'Say that again,' he ordered.

'John.' And I delighted in softening my voice until I made of its single syllable a caress.

'I never thought that I would hear you call me by my given name so effortlessly.'

Which brought to me how few people did so, outside his immediate family. Not even Constanza in my hearing chose to make use of such intimacy.

'I will call you John,' I repeated, for my pleasure and his. I stood at the foot of my bed in my shift, my court robes discarded, and whispered his name again as he drew me into his arms.

'I cannot believe how much I have missed you.' His lips were hot where my blood beat hard at the base of my throat. 'Should I not be able to control my appetites? But with you I cannot.' He cupped my cheeks so that I must meet his eyes. 'Do you suppose Gloucester would have been shocked if I had kissed you at supper?'

'No, but his Duchess might. She would have called for my excommunication at least,' I said.

Before he kissed me, I watched myself reflected in his gaze, saw my smile, the glow in my own eyes. I saw the planes of his face alter, tighten, as he read the desire in mine.

'Will you lie with me? Will you lie with me, that we might—just for this night—and perhaps tomorrow—forget the world beyond these four walls?'

'I will.'

Ah, yes. We forgot the world. Or I did, and I think the Duke did too for those enchanted days when he conducted business from The Savoy yet found time to walk in the gardens when he knew he would meet me there with the child. The presence of the nursemaid who acted as unknowing chaperone could not stem the happiness that filled me from my pleated hair to the soles of my shoes.

'I want you,' the Duke said, his lips against mine when the night was ours again and the pleats were all undone.

And so he proved it with a tenderness that belied his sometime reputation for harsh and impatient judgement, wooing me with soft words and compelling kisses. Until, with an unapologetic slide into male ribaldry, he ordered me to remove my shift:

'Before I fall into pieces with longing.

'I have a gentle cock,
Croweth me day:
He doth me risen early,
My matins for to say...'

And he tumbled me into his bed. The world was ours, to do with as we wished. I was entirely seduced.

At the end, when I must return to Hertford, when an embrace would have been too painful, too indulgent, he simply held my hands.

'Always know, even when we are apart, when time does not allow me to touch your thoughts over the miles that separate us, that you are held close in my mind. Nothing will separate us. We are made to be together.'

Our road stretched out before us without blemish. There were no personal gifts, no public displays of affection. I did not need them. I read his hunger for me in every careful choice he made to give me seven days of perfect delight. This would be my life, cared for and cherished, even in the servant-cushioned silence between us as we rode through the streets of London. The lengthy absences I could tolerate, my uneasy life at Constanza's side I could support. The Duke's ownership, wrapped around me, was a thing of beauty beyond compare.

'Walk with me,' he invited, for those final moments in the garden.

And for me the world stood still, the air hot on my skin, the sun blinding my eyes.

'I will walk with you,' I replied.

That is where it happened, that exact moment where I slid from being captivated by the Duke's unquestionable glamour into the powerful clutches of pure love. I might speak of its intensity, I might read the romance of it, but I had never known it.

Walk with me, he said.

Until that moment, I had been tiptoeing in the safe shallows of love. Now I fell into its depths. I would walk with him until the day I died, of necessity matching my footsteps to his. Yet although the intensity of that moment was hammered into every element of my body, I did not speak of my shattering conversion, for I thought the Duke would not understand. I was content simply to enjoy his proximity amidst the scented shrubs.

When I began my journey back to Hertford, my horizon was cloudless despite the farewell we had been forced to make. I was effortlessly, thoughtlessly, happy.

I curtsied before Duchess Constanza, my hands clasped around the little jewelled casket quite secure. My mind was equally secure in the decision that had been forced on me since my return. My heart had plummeted to somewhere in the region of my gilded court shoes.

'We are pleased to see you, Lady de Swynford.'

How formal she was, even in her confinement, even with my intimate services to her. She had still to be churched and there was an air of restlessness about her slight figure. Her eyes remained fixed on my face, to my discomfort.

'You look strained, Lady de Swynford. I trust you are not ailing? Is there plague in London? I would not wish any harm to come to my daughter.'

My lips curved into what would be interpreted as a smile by those who did not know me. 'Merely the weariness of travel, my lady.'

'Was the King graciously pleased to receive his granddaughter?'

'Yes, my lady. He has sent you this gift, as a token of his pleasure.' I proffered the casket. She made no move to take it.

'So he was in his right mind?'

Duchess Constanza did not mince her words. Even in seclusion as she was, the court gossip had reached her. A cold breath of air shivered along my arms in the heated room, and I swallowed before replying.

'The King was well, my lady. The gift came from his hand. The sentiments were his own.'

'I will thank him when I can travel again. It will be good to have his support for my campaign.'

It was all strikingly familiar. The luxurious setting of her apartments. My sister Philippa standing beside the door to my right, two of the Castilian damsels stitching beside the fire, chattering softly in their own language, a third with a lute in her hands. Mistress Elyot was stitching some small garment in fine lawn. And there was Constanza, quick of action and ever impatient, with the desire for her distant throne uppermost in her mind. Just as it all had been before I left.

But not so. Taking her daughter from the nursemaid, Constanza was standing by the window with the infant in her arms, inspecting her closely. Constanza had rarely held the baby in the days before I left for London.

I lowered my eyes, unable to watch.

'Did you see Monseigneur in London?' she asked, looking back over her shoulder.

'Yes, my lady.'

'Does he come here to me?'

'He has gone to Wallingford, my lady.'

Constanza wrinkled her nose prettily. 'Ah, yes. The wedding. I wish I could be there with my sister.'

For Constanza's younger sister, Isabella, made welcome at the English court, had found a most advantageous match with another son of King Edward: Edmund of Langley, the Duke of York.

But Constanza was not concerned with her sister's marriage. Gilded by the sun that made a halo of her loosely veiled hair, she was smiling down into the face of Katalina. I had never seen her look so beautiful, so maternal and contented. The jewels set in the little domed lid of the casket glittered as my hands around them trembled. Here was reality in all its cruelty. Constanza's pleasure would turn to wrath in the blink of an eye if she could read my mind.

I dragged in a breath.

Constanza looked up as if I had spoken. 'Yes, Lady de Swynford? There is more that I should know from your lengthy sojourn at The Savoy? Is the English army soon to sail to Castile?'

I placed the casket on the coffer at my side, the fine metal clattering a little as I set it down, drawing, as I was aware, a speculative look from Philippa. I was not normally clumsy.

'I know not, my lady.' I felt perspiration clammily unpleasant along my spine as I considered my next words.

Ignoring me the Duchess smiled down at the baby. 'My daughter grows more beautiful every day.' She smoothed the linen coif from the baby's head. 'Look how dark her hair is. A true Castilian princess.' And she bent to caress the fragile curve to the child's ear. 'I had forgotten how blue her eyes…'

Conscience was a slap to my cheek, a clenched fist in my belly, and I flinched, momentarily closing my eyes so that I might not see. I had thought Constanza unmoved by her child, but as she had regained her strength, maternal love had touched her.

Do it. Do it now!

Straightening my spine, firming my knees, I spoke clearly and carefully because there was really no other way.

'I have a request to make, if it please you, my lady.'

Constanza raised her brows in polite interest. Then walked slowly towards me, and placed the child in my arms.

'Whatever you need, Lady de Swynford.'

The baby whimpered and squirmed for a moment until, warm and sleepy, she settled with a sigh. My heart clenched at my awareness of the little body against my breast.

'I wish to leave, my lady,' I said rapidly. 'I wish to leave your service.'

I felt the silence that invaded the room, as I marvelled at the evenness of my request. I felt Mistress Elyot's sudden interest as her needle stilled. I felt Philippa's stare, gouging like a bodkin in an inexperienced hand, between my shoulder blades. Even the Castilian damsels looked over with a cessation to their chatter.

'And why is that, Lady de Swynford?' The line between the Duchess's brows was sharp-etched. 'Has your sojourn in London, the superior accommodations at The Savoy, made you dislike our life here at Hertford?'

'No, my lady…I need to go home to Kettlethorpe. My husband's estates in Lincolnshire,' I added when she appeared not to understand. 'And now my son's.'

'I see.' Her brow wrinkled. 'I understand that there might be matters of business for you to attend to in your son's name. Then of course you must. But will you not return?'

'No, my lady,' I interrupted before she could say any more and my courage disintegrate. It seemed to me to be already in rags. 'I need to leave your service.'

I heard the rustle of Philippa's damask layers as she changed her stance. Mistress Elyot set down the stitching in her lap, making no pretence that she was occupied elsewhere. The damsels exchanged glances as the lute was discarded.

'I wish to live permanently at Kettlethorpe,' I explained.

'It has become imperative that I do so.' My lips were so dry that the words were hard to form.

'Why would you wish to do that? I thought it was a poor way of life.'

'Yes, my lady, but—'

'Are you not satisfied with your position here?' Constanza's voice was suddenly harsh with accusation, and, I thought, astonishment.

'I am more than satisfied, my lady. It is a position that I value.'

'But I need you. To help with the child.' Resentment was building fast and the Duchess flung out her arms as if it must be obvious to any person of sense. 'You have only just settled into my household. I do not see that…'

Her glance suddenly landed on my face, searching, assessing, reminding me that this lady had a good supply of wit.

'I am aware,' she announced with a heavy dose of disapproval, 'of the gift that my lord has made to you, in recognition of your services to me. And that is as it should be—I have no complaint. But such an increase in your annuity—I confess it is a surprise to me.' Her tone had climbed a little higher than was her wont. 'As I understand it, your annuity for service has risen from twenty to fifty marks. Some would say that is more than open-handed. Can you afford to dispense with such a sum? If your estates are so encumbered? I would say that fifty marks a year would make any woman content to remain in service to me. My lord has been extraordinarily generous. Some would say that you owe us your loyalty.'

I had not expected this level of attack, and felt a flush of uncomfortable hot blood mantle my neck as I heard the intake of breath from my sister. And yet I should have anticipated it, if I had not been so caught up in more pressing concerns. I wished with all my heart that Constanza had not seen fit to announce my annuity to the whole room.

'I am grateful, more than I can express,' I replied, mustering an air of acquiescence. 'But I have a need to go to Kettlethorpe, my lady. The estates do not thrive. I had hoped that service in your household would enable me to remedy this.' I took another breath to steady the nerves in my belly. 'The truth is that I am faced with hostile voices from neighbours, and demands that I put into place improvement of the land drains. I am unable to ignore it. It is my son's inheritance, and so it is my duty. It would be deplorable for me to allow him to inherit land of no worth, or with the burden of local opposition raised against him.'

It sounded plausible even to my ears. Behind me Philippa dug the toe of her shoe against the tiles.

'I believe that I need to be there, to answer the complaints, and show that I am not unsympathetic to local problems. An absent landlord can sometimes stir up trouble simply by being absent.'

Constanza stared at me for a long moment. Would she refuse to release me? What would I do if she demanded that I remain? The Duchess raised her chin. I returned her gaze and prayed silently.

'Very well. Perhaps one day you will return to us.' Waving me aside, her displeasure was intense as she retired once more into formality, but all I felt was relief.

'Thank you, my lady.'

My curtsy was heartfelt.

'When is it that you wish to go?'

'Tomorrow, my lady, if it please you.'

Relief was cold on my brow. I had known that to appeal to the importance of inheritance would sway the Duchess if nothing else would.

'Then perhaps you must make arrangements.'

Constanza, gesturing to Mistress Elyot to take the child from my arms as if my hours in her employ were already numbered, walked away from me, her shoulder deliberately turned, to fall into conversation with one of her Castilian damsels. The lute player began to pick out a Castilian love song.

It hurt me.

But it did not hurt me as much as the impending consequences if I remained at Hertford.

I was surreptitiously blotting moisture from my cheeks with my sleeve when footsteps hurrying after me gave me warning, and there was Philippa at my side.

I marched on, even when she caught at my arm, conscious only of the chill rising from the stones that were no colder than my heart. Winter cold, I thought, with shards of ice to hurt and tear. Tears collected in my throat, only to be swallowed. I would not weep. I was free to go. That is what I had wanted, so what point in repining.

'I don't believe you.'

'Why not? You know the problems with Kettlethorpe,' I replied. 'They get no better with time and my distance from them. And now there is a deluge of complaint to be answered...' Which was not untrue. At least there was some element of truth in the whole episode, I thought bitterly.

'I know all about that.' Philippa gripped my sleeve so that I must perforce come to a standstill. 'You came here to seek a position in the first place because you could not live without the money.'

I could not look at her. 'There have been serious inundations on the land, in my absence,' I said.

'And your presence will make a difference?'

'Yes.'

'I don't believe you. Why in heaven's name do you need to go to Kettlethorpe? Why do you need to remain there permanently? You have a steward, don't you?'

'Yes, you know I do. Don't be obtuse, Philippa.' I shrugged her off with as much insouciance as I could muster. 'I simply feel that I should be there. And with the legal settlement of the estate still not made…'

Philippa waved this aside in typical fashion. 'And what about the children? Will you disrupt their lives again? Are you so selfish?'

'Thomas and Margaret will come with me. Blanche will stay here.'

Before I could stop her she grabbed hold of my hands, forcing me to face her when I would rather not.

'To take yourself off to the wilds of Lincolnshire when you fought so hard in the first place to have this position…' She frowned, refusing to be reassured. 'There's something untoward here and you're not telling me.'

'It is nothing. Just the usual matter of a dilapidated estate and a steward who is growing old.'

'So appoint a new one. The Duke will appoint him for you if you lack the confidence to do it yourself.'

'Of course I don't lack confidence. Just the money to pay some bright young man—'

'And you never will have the money unless you stay in the Duke's employ.'

I saw the trench I had dug for myself but by now had no choice but to leap into it, for good or ill. 'Well, I cannot… Now, if you will let me go.'

She released me, but her tone no less amenable. It had acquired an edge. 'By the by. I did not know of your vast importance, Kate! Fifty marks for your annuity, by the Virgin!'

'For my service to Blanche, I expect.'

'Didn't we all serve her? I do not receive fifty marks!'

I pulled away and left her to her ill-temper.

Next day, our belongings packed onto a pair of sumpter horses, Thomas and Margaret ensconced in a borrowed litter while Agnes and I rode, I left Hertford with little in the way of farewells. There was not much to say between us. Constanza was not pleased, Lady Alice regretful and Philippa, lapsed into a furious silence, essentially disbelieving of any explanation I might give.

Of one fact only I was certain as I looked to the north and the towers of Hertford fell away behind. Discovering my absence, precipitate and without warning, the Duke would be hot foot after me, to demand an explanation. I imagined that he would think that I had lost my wits.

He would follow me to Kettlethorpe.

To slight a Plantagenet prince was to play with fire. I might play hazard with the truth for Philippa and the Duchess. I could not lie to the Duke.

Chapter Seven

It took three weeks. And since I had arranged to have fair warning of the Duke's arrival when he and his retinue crossed the Trent, I was there in my hall, dressed with utmost care in a gown more suitable for court appearances than a countrywoman's existence in Lincolnshire, despite the inadvisability of trailing skirts in damp weather. Master Ingoldsby stood on my right, a servant on my left. I felt a need to match like with like, and so I presented myself with all the authority of the Lady of Kettlethorpe, outwardly composed, prepared to knit my mood to his, whatever it might be. Forsooth, I would beg neither pardon nor understanding.

What was it I hoped to achieve? What outcome of this confrontation did I envisage? In all honesty I had no idea. I simply knew that I must show no weakness. My heart raced as the door opened. At the very least I expected the Duke to be marvellously furious. What I did not expect was the freezing, excruciating, perfectly executed politeness.

I should have expected it. I should have known that that is exactly how he would announce himself into my hall. Had I expected him to rant? To demand an answer as soon as his foot struck my threshold? That was not John of Lancaster's way.

He arrived in the middle of a summer rainstorm that seemed to have soaked him to the bone, yet he gave no recognition of discomfort as he strode into my hall followed by two squires and a page, a body-servant and Symkin Simeon, the steward of his lands in Lincolnshire, all impressive if damp in Lancaster livery. When did he ever travel otherwise? I felt Master Ingoldsby stir, saw his eyes widen at the extent of the full Lancaster entourage that faced us, and that was occupying our courtyard, presenting a severe challenge to our kitchen and our stables.

Entirely unaware of the problems he would cause me, sweeping off his rain-sodden cloak, handing it brusquely to his squire, the Duke bowed to me, a magnificent chill courtesy in this man whose face was expressionless, whose spine and shoulders were rigid, while his voice was as flatly controlled as his features.

'Lady de Swynford.'

I curtsied deeply. 'My lord of Lancaster.'

'I trust you are well.'

'I am, my lord.'

He stripped off his gauntlets, thrusting them toward his page. 'I was concerned for your safety, when I learned that you had left my service. It behoved me to discover your situation.'

The superb, lethally insolent formality of it lodged in my throat.

'I am in good heart, my lord.' I kept my voice high and bright. I would not be intimidated in my own home.

'I am surprised to see you here, knowing the limitations of Kettlethorpe.' He cast a quick glance round, before it came to rest on me again, uncomfortably bland, unnervingly smooth. 'I take it that it was a sudden decision?' He bared his teeth, his studied gravity compromised, as my leaking roof caused him to step to one side and brush the drops from his hair.

'Yes, my lord. It was very sudden.'

'And you acted on it with great rapidity.'

'I did, my lord. Once I had informed the Duchess, there was thought to be little need for me to remain. And I apologise for the state of my roof. Perhaps if you step towards the fire…' I gestured, pleased that my hand was firm despite the tremors hidden behind the embroidered inset of my bodice.

The Duke did not move, even when more drops spattered on the shoulder of his brigandine. 'The state of your roof is an irrelevance and does not concern me. On the other hand the reason for your leaving my employ is a matter for my attention, Lady de Swynford. If you have cause for complaint I should know of it. I would be gratified if you would grant me some enlightenment.'

Surprising me, steadying me, a little ripple of amusement developed to diffuse my present anxieties. I was being addressed as if I were a foreign delegation from a hostile state. The Duke was known to be a master at negotiation with enemy forces. Was I now seen as an enemy force? Was this cold blast to be my punishment?

I raised my chin, prepared to take the initiative to deflect the chill.

'Will you be staying long, my lord?' I asked with conspicuous conciliation. 'Do your men require refreshment?'

'Yes. We've ridden far, and out of our way. On what could be a wild-goose chase if I get no sensible explanation from you. My lady,' he added through gritted teeth.

Superb! Punishment indeed, but I would not be swayed

from my role as chatelaine in my own estate. 'Where do you go, my lord?'

'Kenilworth. My ultimate destination would also seem to be an irrelevance.'

I swallowed another urge to laugh. Would the whole of our conversation be conducted in this style? At The Savoy I had shared his bed. At The Savoy those fine hands clenched around his sword belt had caressed my body into delight.

'Our accommodation is limited, my lord, as you see,' I said lightly, 'if you wish to remain here rather than be be-nighted. The stables are the best we can offer to your sol-diery, and this space for your squire and servants and Master Symeon if they can withstand the drips…'

Where we would house the Duke I had no idea. In my chamber, I supposed, while I had a bed set up with Agnes. The Duke was not here in the manner of a lover.

'My thanks. We have slept in worse places on campaign,' he responded, with a nod to his squire who bowed himself out to begin preparations.

'I am pleased to know that my home offers more than a bivouac in Aquitaine, my lord.' I could not resist my tart response.

'As am I, my lady, in the circumstances. But not much better.'

He swept the sheen of drops from his sleeve with an abrupt movement. And as he once again side-stepped a growing puddle, I saw the flash of light in his eye. This superb con-trol, employing this impeccable, heart-wrenching courtesy to mask what I knew to be heated fury, would not hold fast for much longer. It would be a blow to his pride that his mis-tress had left him without a word, and the Duke had more pride than any man I knew. The gems on his hands refracted the light as he clenched and stretched his fingers.

'I will make arrangements immediately, my lord.' I nodded to my steward who shuffled out in his habitual gloom, taking my servant with him. 'Bring wine to my parlour, Master Ingoldsby. If you would care to accompany me, my lord…?' I would have to face him, and sooner would be better than later.

The Duke did not stir. Instead, he inhaled sharply.

'What in God's name are you doing?'

His voice echoed dully off the damp walls from which pieces of mortar showered down.

'I have come to stay here at Kettlethorpe—for a little while,' I responded carefully.

'As I am aware. Before God, Katherine, what sort of game are you playing here?'

'I could not tell you of my intentions. You were not there.'

'I know I was not. So do you—and the reason for it.' And now the anger erupted, spilling over both of us. 'The pressure in France is building like a pot about to boil over to scald us all. Aquitaine is under attack. So is Brittany. My brother Edward's not fit to lead an army. The Castile problem's a running sore with no hope of remedying it in the near future, no matter what Constanza says.' He took a stride forward, then with a snarl thought better of it as the drips pattered down on him. 'I've just promised my father the King that I will serve overseas for a year and what do I find when I get to Hertford? Constanza in a mood of frenzied religious observance to make herself fit to bear a son and you not there to soothe her.'

So he was annoyed merely because I was not in attendance on frenzied Constanza. I did not believe that for one moment. 'That is so,' I replied equably. 'I am sure that my sister is quite capable of reassuring the Duchess.'

'You've resigned your position, so I am told. You did not see fit to tell me yourself.'

I folded my hands quietly at my waist. One of us must preserve some modicum of composure. I merely inclined my head in agreement.

'What is this? Are you dissatisfied? Do I not treat you well? Are my gifts insufficient? Do I not show you due regard, Katherine?'

'You show me every consideration, my lord.'

Now he moved, stalking the length of the hall and back again, exhaling loudly in disgust as he splashed through yet another puddle. Until he spun to challenge me.

'I expect you to be there when I return. Wherever my household resides, I expect you to be there.'

The raw authority in his expectations heated my blood at once.

'I chose not to be there. I chose to be here.'

'Why?' His beautiful voice snapped in anger like the breaking of a bough in a winter storm. Simply his presence in my hall, dominating it, was enough to make my heart shake. There he stood, in wool and leather for peacetime travelling, his heraldic badge emblazoned on his breast beneath the intricate chain of livery, his features alive with temper, as imposing and handsome as I had ever seen him. 'What, in God's name—'

'I could not stay in the Duchess's household,' I broke in.

'Why not? I don't believe you lack the courage. You were never in any doubt as to the difficulties it would present.'

'Yes, I knew,' I admitted.

But perhaps I had not known. Perhaps I had not truly envisaged the pleasure and the pain, the light and the dark of it. I could not tell him how jealousy, thickly laced with guilt, had struck most inopportunely, on seeing his lovely wife holding his daughter, crowned with golden light and with such unexpected maternal love on her face. Now I knew exactly what it would mean for me, the mistress, to live day after day, with the unsuspecting wife, but I could not explain. Nor could I tell him, in this heated atmosphere, what I knew I must.

I considered making a bald statement of it.

'My lord, I have to tell you…'

In this mood I could not predict his response. Was I afraid? I think I was.

Guile, I thought. A touch of very female guile will do it.

'Have you nothing to say?' Whirling round from stirring a sulky log on the fire with his boot, which did nothing to improve the clammy atmosphere, he faced me. Last time we met, being alone at The Savoy, he had swept me into his arms, off my feet, drugging me with his kisses. Now I could barely see his features in the shadows of my hall, and the last thing he wanted to do was sweep me off my feet. 'Answer me, Katherine. Has living in this godforsaken place for longer than a week robbed you of your usual wits?'

I realised that I had been standing there with my guileful plans circling in my mind.

'Come.' I raised my hand in invitation. 'Come to my chapel and pray with me, if you will.' As an invitation it was abrupt.

'For what?' he fired back. 'Absolution from our sins, by God?'

It hurt, but I met his gaze. 'Yes.'

'And are you intending to take the veil in penitence?'

'Now that, my lord, had not crossed my mind.'

Allowing my hand to fall, since he had no intention of taking it, I walked through the outer door, turning right, grateful when his footsteps followed. I did not look back but walked calmly on, along the edge of the courtyard, past the wet doves hunched in their dovecote, lifting the heavy latch to push the door open into the small space of my chapel, rough hewn and undecorated except for the crucifix on the altar but essentially private, and finally I knelt before the altar rail. The Duke halted, then knelt beside me as I looked up at the statue of the Virgin and prayed for guidance and the right choice of words. The Duke made the sign of the cross on his breast. I did the same.

'Well, Madame de Swynford. For whom do we pray? Is that too much to ask, since you seem to be keeping your own counsel. When were you ever so silent? I swear it's like trying to communicate with a stone effigy.' Despite the holy surroundings his anger had not abated.

'We will make petition,' I said.

'Do we need a priest?' he snapped.

'No.' And I shivered a little. A priest was the last thing I needed in my present state of mind.

'Then let us indeed begin. I hate to hurry you along, Katherine, but I'm cold and damp and my temper is not at its best.'

'I would not have guessed,' I said.

'Yes, you would. Begin your petition, Katherine!'

'Holy Mother,' I began, 'I pray for the safety of Lord John, Duke of Lancaster, in the coming wars in France. I commend him to your care.'

Which surprised him, if his intake of breath was proof.

And our voices were joined. 'Amen.'

'I pray for the health of Duchess Constanza and the new infant Katalina.'

'Amen.'

'I pray for the good comfort of the whole household at Hertford.'

'Amen.'

The Duke's hands were clenched, white-fingered, on the altar rail before him.

I continued: 'I lay before you the lives of my children. Blanche and Margaret and Thomas.'

'Amen.'

'Of my sister Philippa, her husband, Geoffrey, overseas, and her family.'

'Amen.'

'I pray—'

'By the Blessed Virgin, Katherine,' now the Duke murmured, 'do we pray for the whole of our acquaintance?'

But I continued. 'I pray for the clarity of mind of the King. And for your mercy on Prince Edward in his great suffering.'

'Amen.'

I took a breath.

'I pray for the health of my unborn child. The child of this man who kneels with me to join with me in this petition. We pray for this child who will need the compassion of the Blessed Virgin.'

The atmosphere in the chapel bore down on us, drenched with the remnants of old incense and a multitude of unconfessed sins. The Duke's hands gripped harder than ever. So did mine.

Until: 'Amen. Amen indeed,' he whispered on a soft exhalation.

I was carrying John of Lancaster's child.

Why had I, with all my much-vaunted experience, not been more cognisant of the dangers? Were there not methods to prevent such eventualities, known to wise women and any wife with a care for preserving her own health? Or known to a mistress intent on preventing a debacle such as this? In the final weeks of Constanza's pregnancy, I was, unknowingly, embarking on the first weeks of my own.

The realisation had travelled with me on the journey from London back to Hertford. I had been a little weary, lacking in energy, but, foolishly, I had never considered that I would fall for a child from that first expression of our love at The Savoy. My reaction was one of wonder. I had spread my fingers over my belly and marvelled at the fact that I carried the child of the man I loved more than I could ever express.

But then, when Constanza had smiled down into the face of her baby, all my marvelling was undone. There we stood in my mind's eye. A deadly triangle of husband, wife and lover. This child born out of wedlock might blemish the Duke's reputation. It would assuredly destroy mine. Could it destroy our love?

What now? What do I do now?

The question had echoed again and again in my mind, without any sensible reply forthcoming. Instead, the repercussions struck home with the force of a lance in the hands of a master at the tourney, transmuting my delight to base dismay. How could I continue to exist in that household? How could I continue to live, a secret mistress to a wife untouched by knowledge, and I bearing a child, my belly growing under her interested gaze.

I did not have the presumption to do that.

Whilst on a practical level, how would I explain away my burgeoning state, with no husband?

Even more unnerving—and I confessed to not knowing the answer—what would the Duke say to my predicament? Would he banish me to some distant castle until after nine months my shame was dealt with and my figure restored? Or would he brazen it out at Hertford, and claim the child as his own, with Constanza destroyed by the humiliation?

I tried to see myself through the Duke's eyes, and I could not, my thoughts awry. Hypocrisy, as I well knew, was a bitter herb. Subterfuge at this despicable level was intolerable. There was only one course of action for me. I must leave before there was even the hint of suspicion about the width of my girdle. I could no longer be damsel to Duchess Constanza, knowing all the time that I was carrying her husband's child.

We would exercise discretion, we had agreed.

Before God, there was no discretion here.

And so I had come to Kettlethorpe as if I were some wild animal going to ground. Never had I felt such shame. Shame for me. Sorrow and shame for Constanza. I had looked at Constanza and her child, at the two Lancaster girls, Philippa and Elizabeth, at young innocent Henry, and it humbled me. How was I fit to give them guidance? We had taken a step beyond decency and rightness—and we were faced with the consequences.

Now I had to face them in the Duke's unpredictable reaction.

'Amen,' I echoed.

I made the sign of the cross.

'Not here,' he said as I stood to face him. Gripping my hand, he pulled me after him from the main body of the chapel into a little side alcove where an old altar had once stood, now bare and dusty, no longer dressed for worship. 'I feel better that we speak of this away from the Virgin's immediate presence.'

'Does it make it any less of a catastrophe where we speak of it?' My confidence was waning fast.

'Katherine...'

I could not read what was in his face. Anger or joy?

Acceptance or repudiation? For the first time I acknowledged the depths of my fear, for this should never have happened. Was I some irresponsible kitchen maid, enjoying
the pleasures of the flesh in her first taste of sexual satisfaction? I knew the dangers. I knew what must not happen
between such lovers as we were, for ever in the public eye.
There were any number of old wives' methods that were
not unknown to me.

How to stimulate the menses to achieve bleeding from the
womb. Take the root of the red willow...

My belly clenched, my hands flattening themselves on
my embroidered belt. I would not. One sin was enough for
the day. I would bear this child.

I bent my head in sudden despair, until I felt the Duke's
fingers, as cold as mine yet light against my face, lifting my
chin so that I must bear the weight of his judgement. Except
that his eyes were gentle, the corners of his lips relaxed as
they were when I kissed them. All the anger, all the impatience, had gone.

'What were you thinking, to run away from me? What
are you thinking now?' He wiped a stray tear—one I had
been unaware of—from my cheek with the back of his hand.

'I am thinking that I do not know what you are thinking.'
I shook my head at how muddled it sounded.

'Very erudite.' He smiled at little. 'Is that all?'

'I am thinking that I will carry this child to full term.'

His hand, smoothing softly against my neck as if I were
a restive mare, paused. 'Did you think I would advise otherwise?'

'No. I know you would not. But it would be a way out for
some women.'

'But not for you.'

'No, not for me.'

'Nor for me. Why did you not tell me?'

'I did not know what you would say. I thought you might condemn me.'

Hands now firmly on my shoulders, he drew me close so that his chin could rest against my confined hair. Although his eyes were closed I sensed a depth of emotion that shuddered through his veins.

'Why would I be? The child is of both our making.'

'But a child born without legitimacy can pose a problem,' I whispered. 'It would not be the first time that a powerful man has chosen to rid himself of a mistress who has inconveniently found herself compromised.'

He raised his head, eyes wide and undoubtedly stern. 'So you thought I would dispatch you and the child to the depths of the country.'

'You might. For Constanza's sake as well as your own.'

'And you pre-empted it by coming here.'

'I had to.'

'Because you could not face me? Or was it that you could not face Constanza, day after day?' he asked with brutal intuition, and did not even wait for my acquiescence. 'It is my guilt too. We will bear it together. Did you think I would abandon you?'

The Duke kissed me thoroughly.

'I thought I must remove a complication...'

'I do not see you as a complication. Nor this child.'

'But you must regret what we have done.' He thought about this, rubbing his fingers over my knuckles. 'John...?'

'No. It is God's will. The child is a consequence of our union, and so we will nurture it. Is that not so?'

'Yes.'

There was no other reply I could make as we stood together in the dusty atmosphere, fingers enmeshed. Until he spread his palm against my waist, and I covered it with mine.

'How far on are you?' he asked, surprising me.

'Three months.'

I could see him calculating. 'You conceived the first time we lay together at The Savoy.' The rich tones of his laughter lifted to the roof-beams. 'How amazingly effective our un-platonic, un-divine coming together proved to be. Perhaps it was the effect of that poor specimen of a rose after all.' Then sliding his arm around my waist he began to lead me to the door. 'Will you stay here?'

'Yes.'

'I'll send you timber to stop the drips in the roof.'

And I laughed with him, in relief and in recognition of a little flame of joy that his acceptance had ignited in me. 'It will be welcome.'

And then we were outside, where the rain had stopped and the low sun had begun to shine, coating every surface in diamond drops, and his arm fell away for form's sake. We walked slowly back, at arm's length, towards the hall, as if discussing the state of the local highways.

'I'll come when I can,' he said as he drew back to allow me to enter before him, managing to brush his hand down the length of my arm, to brush his fingers against mine. 'You know I'm committed to my father's naval campaign against France.'

'I will look for you when you can come.' I must not be selfish.

And then, when we were standing alone in my private chamber, I became thoroughly selfish as the Duke's reassurances, murmured against my temple as he loosed the pins from my hair, held all the power of an oath before the Blessed Virgin.

'Although I may be far away, I will have my people watch over you. You will be constantly in my thoughts. This child will be as precious to me as any child that Constanza bears, even those of Blanche. Even my heir. You will be brave and steadfast. There is a fire in you that astonishes me.'

If I had lacked fire in those insecure days before his arrival, the Duke set it ablaze with a conviction that I loved him enough to face the stigma and the consequences. He spent the night with me in my marital bed, which proved too short for his long limbs, but no detriment to his ardour or his imagination, and then he snatched a second day to spend it riding with me and my steward around the nearer acres of the estate.

Parting was difficult.

'Keep in good health,' I said, with an arm's length between us. 'I will pray for you.'

'And I for you. God keep you, dearest Katherine.'

The Duke in his ineffable wisdom understood that I could not bear an emotional parting. He was going to Aquitaine. His life would be in danger, so there was always that lurking fear beneath my heart: would death on a distant battlefield take him from me? But we would not part in sorrow. After he had kissed my lips and my brow, abjuring me that our child, which would undoubtedly be a son, should be given the name John, making me laugh with his cool certainty about the matter, I set myself to endure the loneliness with fortitude.

I screamed in agony.

'Holy Virgin,' I panted when I could. 'I don't remember such travail as this!'

'You never do, once the pain is past and the child born,' Agnes observed as she pressed a damp cloth to my forehead.

My pains started in January, on a day of winter cold and frost, the usual ripple of discomfort that deepened and lengthened fast becoming a claw of agony. I drank the wine mixed with Agnes's tried-and-tested potion and looked for completion within the day, but this child was different, when nothing seemed to progress except a monstrous pain that gripped my body and held it in thrall. I lost count of the hours, barely noting the change from light to dark beyond my window, conscious of nothing but what seemed to be the tearing apart of my flesh and bone for the sake of this creature that refused to be born.

'I was worried about this,' Agnes muttered as she allowed me to grip her hands, nails digging deep.

'Well, now you're proved right!' I groaned as the appalling clenching ebbed.

As if she had some premonition of my birthing difficulties, Agnes had been careful of me in recent weeks, insisting on a diet of eggs and fowl, broths of fish. She had rubbed my belly with hot goose-grease. All to no avail.

Was this punishment for my sin? For our sin?

'Will I lose this child?' I cried out in another fleeting lull. 'Is this God's will?'

'It may be.' Even in my extremity I heard the worry in her voice. 'But we'll fight for him.'

She pulled me from my bed.

'I cannot walk…' The muscles in my legs would hardly carry me.

'You will, my lady, if you wish to see this child alive. But slowly…'

She led me up and down my hall, up and down the stairs. And then such tortures as Agnes inflicted on me. Frankincense wafted under my nose to make me sneeze again and again. A bitter tincture of mint and wormwood forced on me, even though I resisted.

Finally she looped the coral beads of my rosary round my neck.

'Fetch the snakeskin from my coffer,' Agnes growled at my diary maid. 'We'll need it if this child is born dead.'

'No!' I resisted such a thought, my hand fastening like a claw on Agnes's wrist.

That must not be. The child—living and breathing—might cut my reputation to shreds and beyond all mending, but I would not see it dead.

I struggled to my feet and began to walk again, using the bed hangings, the tapestries, anything for support, as well as Agnes's stalwart shoulder. Conscious only of pain and exhaustion, the cloying fumes that filled the chamber, I wept in my terror. Surely no child could withstand such a process of birth.

What was it that tipped the balance? When all seemed lost, when I could walk no more, when I could withstand no more hurt, the child, my son, was eased from my body by Agnes, her hands slick with linseed and fenugreek. She picked him up and wrapped him in linen as if he were a fine prince, not some small, wizened creature, mewling like a weak kitten.

Then silence.

I looked at her face, from where I had sunk down on the floor beside my bed.

'Agnes...?' Her features were tight.

'Rest awhile...'

'I wish to see him.'

And as she pushed the matted tendrils of hair back from my face, I reached up to take my child in my arms. Here was no fine prince. His face was suffused, eyes screwed tight, lips flaccid and scant black hair plastered to his skull. It seemed that he gasped for air. Despite the sweat and blood that covered both of us, I held him close to my breast.

'He is so small.'

'We should baptise him, my lady.'

She was frowning and I caught the fear, the urgency.

'John. We will call him John.' It was not difficult to decide.

Tears threatened, through weakness and regret, but I swallowed against them. How light he was, and I barely had the strength to hold him close. His eyes, opened now, were blue and without focus, as all babies. His features had no resemblance to John or, I thought, to myself. I spread his hands. So weak. So small. My heart, so full of hope at his birth, fell into a void as black as the wisps of hair that clung to his head.

'Agnes...'

'What is it, my lady?' So full of compassion was her voice that my efforts to quell my tears failed.

'You must tell him.' It was all I could think of. 'You must send a message to the Duke.'

'And say what?'

Tell him to come to me. Tell him I am in despair and in need.

'Tell him that he has a son.' I would say no more.

'And I'll tell him more than that,' she muttered. 'We may not be troubled by this one long. He'd better hurry if he wants to see his son this side of the grave.'

I tried not to listen as the wet nurse, a young woman from the village who had her own healthy babe, took my son from me.

Chapter Eight

It was nearer another month before the Duke rode up to my door. Was it not to be the pattern of our days? I met him in the hall, as I had before when I had first fled Hertford, waiting until he entered even though it was my first thought to run out to the courtyard so that he might hold me in his arms and tell me that all was well. It was six months and more since I had seen him. An endless length of impossible longing, so that I could not imagine what my first words to him would be.

I retreated to courtly formality. I curtsied.

'You are welcome, my lord.'

'I came when I could, my lady.'

'I have sent for refreshment, my lord. If you would come to my parlour—'

All formality was abandoned. The Duke was striding across the room to grip his hands around mine as if we had only parted a matter of days ago.

'My lord!'

I cast a glance at his squire, who stood impassive at the

door. This was hardly ducal behaviour but the Duke simply gestured for him to go, his eyes never leaving my face. Presumably the squire knew all there was to be known.

'Are you well, Katherine? I see that you are.'

'Yes, my lord.' Formality still clung to me like droplets of mist, refusing to be shaken off as I held tightly to his hands, taking in the familiar features that were suddenly far from familiar. I noted the changes, subtle yet clear to my eyes, for the campaign had foundered, the fleet tossed at sea by storms and gales for two whole months, until the remnant struggled home. Those two months at sea with an ageing father and an ailing brother had taken their toll. It was like greeting a distant acquaintance whom I had once known, but whose absence had snipped at the bonds, still so fragile, that had held us.

Then the emotion that touched his eyes smote me hard and shook loose my emotional shackles.

'The child, Katherine. The child. I am so sorry. And that you should have to bear his loss alone...'

My strangely rigid heart instantly melted.

'No, John...' For I had heard the door opening, although he had not. Now I beckoned to Agnes who marched forward with her burden, unable to contain my smile of pure joy.

'He proved us all wrong, John. I would introduce you to your son.'

Every muscle in the Duke's body braced as he looked from me to the animated wrapping. Then gave a bark of startled laughter.

'By God, Katherine! I thought he was too weak to survive.'

'So did we. We feared for him for many days. But see how he thrives.'

'You have called him John.'

'Yes,' I said, delight bubbling up inside me. 'Did you not

leave your royal command? Already I have a sword ordered for him from my blacksmith.'

The Duke took his child in his arms, staring at the baby, who stared back with eyes of similar hue. The blue of babyhood existed no longer.

And I? I watched my lover's expression with a level of concern, that increased as he remained silent. In spite of all his assertions, what did this child mean to him against the legitimacy of Philippa and Elizabeth, the value of his heir Henry, the vital Castilian blood of Katalina? Where would my little son stand in his estimation?

Perhaps he would have no importance. A bastard child of a woman who had no influence.

I found myself skewered with a level stare.

'I see you are troubled by something. What are you thinking?' he asked.

I stared back. 'That I don't know how important this child is to you.'

His brows arched as if my question was not worth the asking. 'He is my son.'

It should have told me all I needed to know.

'But he is illegitimate.'

'He is mine, and he is precious to me. Does that satisfy you?'

A wave of pure happiness washed through me, so vital that I had to blink against the emotion, all my anxieties laid to rest in that briefest of statements. *He is mine.*

'I'll not reject him. Did you fear it?' When I grimaced, his smile became a grin. Then the Duke quickly sobered, leaning across the baby to plant a grave kiss on my lips. 'He is mine, Katherine. He will lack for nothing. For now, I give him into your care, because I must, to raise him for me, until he is older and he can take his place in my household. As my son.'

The tears slid down my cheeks. The baby stretched out a hand to grasp his father's jewelled chain, pulling on it with his tiny strength.

'He is a fine son and will grow up to be a fine knight. He needs a name of recognition.' The Duke gently unfastened the baby's fingers from his chain: they promptly re-curled around his finger, making him laugh. 'Beaufort. He will be known as Beaufort. A castle I once owned in France.'

I wiped the tears away.

John Beaufort. The tenderness in the Duke's face moved me beyond thought as he touched the child's cheek with his finger.

'And now John Beaufort's mother must tell me what is in her heart.'

He handed the child back to Agnes and took me in his arms and kissed me on each cheek.

'Or perhaps we have spoken enough for one day.'

We did speak, of course we did, but there were other ways to express the pleasure of our reunion, the miracle of it, the magnificent heartfelt gratitude of it, that required no words at all, and indeed we had little breath to express them. Engulfed by hunger, we rediscovered all those ways, and more besides, with some energy, to our greatest enjoyment. In recognition of my fragility, he was very gentle.

And then, when all was seemly and we sat in my private chamber with a cup of wine and our garments put to rights to some degree: 'I want you to return with me,' the Duke said.

Which did not seem to me to be as easily accomplished as the saying of it.

'And what of Constanza?' I asked.

His reply was predictably brisk. 'My marriage to Constanza is no different now from what it was a year ago. A political entity. I will fight to restore her kingdom and I will give her the son to inherit if it is God's will. But you will return with me.'

I tilted my chin in contemplation as my sensibilities smacked up against the rock of the Duke's will.

'Is it not what you wish?' The Duke's flat brows expressed a disbelief that I would not immediately issue orders to pack my clothing into my travelling coffers.

'I am considering it.'

'What is there to consider?'

'My reputation,' I stated solemnly, if it was possible to be solemn in my shift with my hair unloosed and my feet unshod. 'If I return to your household, will it not be as a fallen woman?'

'No, it will not!'

'There are many who will be quick to call me whore.'

'They would not do so in my hearing.'

'They would in mine!'

It was not entirely said in jest. If I returned to the Lancaster household I would eventually become the target of gossip as the fever of solar life began to bubble and boil. But, there again, if I returned I would be with the Duke, not marooned in this distant place.

'How long does it take you to decide?' The Duke scrubbed his hands over his unshaven cheeks. He was as ungroomed as I but the power of command sat on him like an ermine cloak. 'I will make the decision for you. I order you to return with me. And we will continue to be circumspect, as we have always been. I will protect your highly prized reputation.'

I smiled under the force of his reassurance. 'I have missed you so very greatly.'

'As I have missed you.' For a moment, looking up at me from where he lay by my side, his gaze was pensive. 'One morning—when we were at sea and the storm at its worst—I felt you with me. As if you had called to me. It was as if, for the length of a heartbeat only, your mind touched on mine. It was as real as you sitting here today. It was moment of great joy, when all around me was despair and defeat. I will never forget it.'

And I looked at him in amazement, for in those days of isolated waiting, when fear for him had dogged my every step, I had sought for him, on the field of conflict, with sword in hand, as if I could sense the direction of his mind, the tenor of his thoughts. I had worn out the steps to the tower room where I could sit and look out over the flat lands of Lincolnshire and imagine what he might be doing, what his thoughts might be.

One morning I could almost see him. He lifted his head as if I had called to him, and perhaps his mind touched mine. A soft warmth, a sharp knowing, an edge of recognition. It lasted only as long as a slow intake of breath: I did not experience it again, and persuaded myself that it was merely my overworked imagination, nothing more than the bright glitter of the sun on the duck pond.

But the Duke had sought me too, and found me. It filled me full of impossible love, and I bent to kiss his lips. I forgave his spending the New Year with Constanza.

The Duke's gaze sharpened. 'So? What's your answer?'

'Do you need to ask it? I will come.'

As plainly said as that.

But not plain at all, in truth. It was not merely my reputation, but what would I do, in the household of the Duke of Lancaster? What role would I have? I could not, in all honesty, return as a damsel to Constanza, the mistress serving the wife. The degradation in such a relationship for her would be beyond forgiveness. But I was sure that I could not live apart from him, even at a very personal cost for me, which transpired fast enough as I made my preparations to follow him to Tutbury.

'You were not planning to take that baby, were you? Have you looked at that child recently?' Agnes demanded a month later when all was arranged.

'Or course I have.' I folded a pair of newly stitched sleeves in anticipation of my return to my lover. 'He is quite strong enough to travel and can join the nursery.'

'And what do you see?' She gestured towards the cradle, rocked gently by the young wet nurse. 'Look at him, Katherine.'

So I did. The baby clenched and unclenched his fists, making me laugh.

'Look at him!' Agnes repeated. 'When you are asked who fathered this child, who will you say?'

The child had changed since his stressful birth. His features might be still rounded and soft but blue eyes had darkened to bright hazel. His skin was fair and his hair was dark…I exhaled slowly. Agnes had seen what I had not. Sunlight flooding the room illuminated my son so that the feathered curls carried a sheen of rich auburn, like the plumage of the pheasants in the orchard. As a cloud scudded past and the sun brightened, the vibrant colour leaped into life.

If I took him to the ducal household, if the sun shone then, as it did now, the gossip would be on every tongue as soon as I lifted him from the travelling litter. My baby's colouring was too pronounced to deny.

'No,' I said sadly, lifting him into my arms. Had I ever

truly believed that I could introduce this child into the ducal nursery? If my cherished reputation as a respectable woman meant so much to me, how could I paint myself as the mother of a bastard child when his father's identity was so patently obvious? I had been fooling myself in thinking it possible. 'No, I cannot, can I? But I don't want to leave him.'

'But you will. And I will care for him.' Agnes was bracing. 'I'll love him like my own. And you can have him with you when…'

Her mouth snapped shut like a trap.

'When the truth is out? Is that what you were going to say? But when the truth is out I'll be summarily dismissed and be back here in Kettlethorpe.'

'Then that will solve all your problems. Or you could, of course, decide not to go. To remain here…'

I kissed my baby's cheek, conscious that tears were not far away. Here was another choice to be made. To go to my lover, to leave my child and hide the circumstances of his birth, or to remain here to raise this Beaufort son who tugged at all my maternal urges with his tiny hands.

I looked up, conscious of Agnes's critical gaze on my face, conscious that for her there was no dilemma. How could any woman abandon her child to be with a man in a relationship cloaked in sin? A woman's duty was to her children and her good name. No woman of integrity would willingly earn the title whore.

But for me there was no choice.

I handed my child to Agnes before I wept openly. He was flesh of my flesh, but his father owned my heart and I would be with him.

There was no frisson of scandal to greet me when I made my return to the household now established in the solid fortress of Tutbury, bringing me respite as I trod the familiar chambers, but when I was announced into one of the more intimate chambers, into what was a scene of family harmony, it took me aback, striking hard at all my newfound strength.

There were Philippa and Elizabeth, their heads together over a book. Henry's eyes were for a new plaything, the model of a little knight on horseback. The baby Katalina slept in a cradle. Lady Alice, looking across the room as I entered with a smile of welcome, had her ever-present Book of Hours to hand.

Nothing unexpected here.

But here was the Duke in the company of Constanza who was seated in the window, with the light flattering the iridescence of her dark hair beneath her light veil. As I stepped across the threshold she was smiling up at the Duke who was expounding in familiar fashion on some idea that took his interest and hers. I heard her reply, the mention of Castile, and his response in the affirmative.

My first thought: I had been away from this household for well nigh a year, in which time things had changed. I had been gone too long. Relationships moved on, could be made or unmade.

And my second: how strikingly beautiful the Duchess was, with motherhood softening her angular features. How fluently she was now able to express herself. How comfortable she looked in this setting. There was a happiness to her, a contentment, a willingness to smile, that I could not recall. When the Duke handed his wife a cup of wine with a smile and a little courtly bow, the Duchess accepted and sipped with a laugh at something he said.

How alike they were. Both handsome, both driven by ambition, both assured in wielding authority. Another impression, even less pleasant, was forced on me. How at ease they were in each other's company, as if they had at last come to some understanding. It was as if I was suddenly cast under a shadow in the face of their brightness.

Constanza could bring the Duke power and a legitimate son.

I could do neither.

These thoughts raced through my mind in the blink of an eye, but hurtful none the less. Why would the Duke not warm to his wife? What might have begun as a political marriage of necessity for both of them, why might it not become more intimate as they grew to know each other? Why should Constanza not be seduced by this embodiment of Plantagenet mystique and power?

Was this the first blossoming of love?

A hard nugget of jealousy settled beneath my heart, when I had been so assured of the rightness of my return. Now, suddenly, I was not so sure.

The Chamberlain stepped beside me. 'Lady Katherine de Swynford, my lord. My lady.'

At last I was announced, bringing to an end the private conversation. I worked at a smile and curtsied, before walking slowly forward.

'We are pleased to see you returned to our household, Lady Katherine.' Constanza smiled thinly. 'We hope that you will stay longer this time.'

'It is my intention, my lady,' I responded carefully, not looking at the Duke.

'It seems that I am not to have the benefit of your company. Unfortunately I am to be relieved of your experience with young children.'

A cold finger drew a line along my spine. I was no longer one of her immediate household. I looked into her lovely face, expecting disgust, horror, hatred even, knowing that

I would react with fury if I, the legitimate wife, was forced to face the brazen mistress in her own chamber. Had she dismissed me? What was I doing here, if she had refused to take me back?

But Constanza's face was smoothly expressionless within the border of her severe crispinette and barbette, as she waved me towards the Duke.

All movement, all expression on his face stilled as I curtsied again, then he was holding out his hand to take mine and draw me into their company.

'As my wife says, we are pleased to see you returned to our household, Lady Katherine, now that your estate matters allow.'

Slowly, not to draw attention, I withdrew my hand from his.

'It is my wish,' the Duke announced with unquestionable propriety, 'that you to take up the post of *magistra* to my children.'

I tried not to allow my face to express my astonishment, and since no one showed any surprise, I must have been successful. *Magistra*. A position of authority, of very public recognition of my talents. I sank into a curtsy, head bowed to hide my glowing cheeks, that little moment of panic dispelled.

Why had he not told me of this plan? Because it was not in his nature to do so, I reminded myself. I must never forget that. The Duke decided and carried out his wishes with recourse to no one. Sometimes I still forgot that he was a man who never questioned the absolute authority instilled in his royal blood. He had decided; thus it would be.

'Such a position is entirely appropriate for one of your standing,' he was explaining. 'You were educated under my mother's aegis. I can think of no one better to take on the responsibility. You will oversee the education of my daughters, and also my son Henry until he is of age to have a tutor and take up military skills. I expect them to read and to write, to master languages, literature. To behave with courtesy as becomes my children. To sing and dance with grace...'

He paused, perhaps expecting a response from me. 'What do you think, Lady Katherine?' he enquired gently when he received none.

'I have no words, my lord,' I managed.

All I could think of was that the Duke had done this for me. He had cushioned my return in every possible way, seeing for himself, the false posturing that my service to Constanza would engender. He had done this, to remove me from the close-knit atmosphere of the solar with all its household politics and gossip and female disparagements. I had been mistaken in thinking that I had no place in this household. Instead, at the Duke's behest, I had been honoured beyond all my hopes and knew that I was made welcome.

'You are unusually lacking in comment, Katherine,' Lady Alice remarked with spiked humour, coming to my side to plant a warm kiss on my cheek.

'I am overcome with the position I have been given,' I responded quickly, nudging myself from astonishment into good manners. 'My thanks, my lord. It will please me to serve you well.'

I was saved from the moral discomfort of rubbing shoulders with Constanza every day. I was protected from my sister Philippa's frequent inquisitions, which would surely follow my reinstatement here.

I had returned and my heart rejoiced.

* * *

When the Duke came to me that night, in the room that I, in my new advancement, no longer had to share with anyone, it was in the spirit of celebration. Within seconds of his closing the door I was swept into his arms, held tight, and my face and lips covered with kisses.

'Do I presume that you are pleased to see me returned?' I asked, when I could.

'How can you doubt it?' the Duke replied, his hands closing around my waist, lifting me to my toes to plant another kiss on my lips. 'I have missed you, Katherine, as a man in a desert misses a draught of ale. I am no more than a dried husk.'

'You look very healthy to me,' I observed.

'You did not see me yesterday!'

'I wish I had. I have been gone too long from you.'

At which the Duke nibbled along my collarbone. 'You are as delicious as a platter of French strawberries. I'll sing to you, my lady fair and woo you back to me with rich sentiments.'

And he did, but it was a strange choice he made. At supper the minstrels had sung, a song of longing with plangent chords and wistful words. Picking up my lute, the Duke sang the words to me again, beautiful, certainly, but entirely ambiguous is their meaning. Did he know? Or was it merely a song that was in his mind? I listened to the words I knew well.

'I will tell you what inordinate love is:
Insanity and frenzy of mind,
Inextinguishable burning, devoid of happiness,
Great hunger that can never be satisfied.

A dulcet sickness, sweetness evil and blind,
A most wonderful sugared sweet error,
Without respite...'

Abruptly he stopped singing as if the mood of the song touched him, head bent to watch his soft fingering on the strings. When he made no comment, I was moved to ask, but keeping my tone light: 'Inordinate love? Is that what it is, John? Is that what afflicts us?'

Slowly, frowning slightly, he put aside the lute, choosing his words with care. 'I know not. All I know is that I lack the will to step away from you. If it is insanity,' he picked up the sentiments of the song, 'it binds me to you.'

But do you love me? Do you not love me as I love you?

I almost asked it, breaking the vow I had made on that first day at The Savoy. But did not, because I feared the answer. Instead, keeping lightly the Duke's theme: 'And if it is a frenzy of mind, then I am frenzied. But I am not blind to the pain it can cause others.'

'Nor am I blind.' His eyes rested on my face and I returned the regard. The regret I read there touched me with sorrow, for it might be a regret that he could not truly love me as I loved him. Always careful with my choice of words, I never burdened him with the depth of my feelings for him. Would not placing such an obligation at his feet undermine the foundations of what we had together? The Duke needed me, and that must be enough. I would play the role allotted to me with grace.

'It is a great hunger,' I offered, returning to the song, and was instantly soothed by the answering smile.

'Agreed. And a sugared sweetness.'

'And there is much inextinguishable burning—that is also

true,' I urged, allowing him with a shiver of anticipation to alight kisses on my wrists.

'I am on fire,' the Duke said, and lunged.

Only after the kisses had worked their way to my elbow, to my shoulder and then my throat, was I abandoned, and the Duke, with a glitter of pure male gallantry, took up the lute again and with a troubadour swagger coupled with a provocative leer broke into a quite different refrain, obliterating any memory of regret:

> *'Your mouth provokes me,*
> *"Kiss me, kiss sweet!"*
> *Each time I see you so it seems to me.*
> *Give me a sweet kiss or two or three!'*

'John!' I remonstrated, as he snatched the requisite kisses between each line of the song.

'Katherine!' the Duke responded with a crow of laughter before he tossed the lute aside and seized my hands in his. 'Whatever the emotion that touches us, it is not devoid of happiness. You are all my happiness.' He lifted my hands in quick succession to his lips. 'Ah, Katherine. Don't repine, dear heart. They're only words after all, troubadour's fripperies. Let us celebrate your return. Come and show me with your kisses that this is no sweet error.'

Only empty words? They were not empty for me, but I placed my hands in his and returned his salute.

'There is no error,' I assured.

'Then come and show me, for I have sorely missed you.'

Our reunion of the flesh, and of spirit, was sweet indeed. Passionate, possessive, demanding, deliciously seductive, the Duke was all of these and I would refuse none of it.

Chapter Nine

My role as *magistra* was one into which I could slide effortlessly. As the Duke had observed, my own tuition at Court had been unstinting. The ducal children, and my own, would benefit from those rigorous demands, and from my own ability to engage in polite conversation, walk gracefully, hold a tune and entertain competently on the strings of a lute. I found myself able to apply my skills with confidence.

There was only one rule to be followed to the exclusion of all else. Reticence must command with an iron hand. Discretion must guide my every action.

I became used to seeing the Duke: at a distance, at close quarters in the midst of his family, but in public always with that careful separation between us. There must be no suspicion, no careless moment of intimacy to cause an in-drawing of breath from a casual observer. No indiscreet comment that presumed knowledge that should not exist. How it kept me on my toes, to dance to this complicated tune. And I learned to tolerate that void between us, knowing that it would be bridged when he could. His awareness of me was a tangible thing, but handled with delicacy.

The pattern of my days was laid down when we went hawking in the marshes across the river: a family party on horseback, a noisy collection of children with servants to accompany and safeguard. Constanza too, who relished the exercise, and her damsels.

He was frequently with Constanza in those days.

Sister Philippa rode at my side as I kept an eye on Elizabeth who was headstrong. Henry and my son Thomas had their heads together in some plotting. Perhaps one day, I thought absently but with no real hope, my son John would participate in such an outing as this with his father. For there in the midst was the Duke, a keen owner of a new pair of goshawks.

We flew them at pigeons and wading water-birds.

When the Duke handed a little merlin to me, our gloved hands touched as they must. How was it possible to experience the heat of another's hand through two layers of stitched leather of the hawking gloves?

Neither of us exhibited any acknowledgement.

But afterwards, when the falconer returned the hawks to their perches, and the children were engaged in their afternoon occupations, when Constanza knelt at her prie-dieu to petition God for a son and Philippa cared for Katalina, he came to me in my chamber and all my yearnings were fulfilled. When he possessed me, I was a willing captive.

The rumours began, as they must. Did we think we could exist on our gilded cloud of secrecy for ever? Only a fool would give any weight to the possibility.

What was it that drew attention?

I knew not.

First the whispering started, the sibilance of words cut off, or almost smothered, when I entered the room. Constanza's damsels, like their mistress, had a better command of French now, and their vocabulary was not always that of gently reared women. Even when the consonants were hissed in pure Castilian, their meaning was clear. A minor inconvenience, I told myself. I was no naïve girl to believe that so physical an affair could remain a secret in the hotbed of the Duchess's household where gossip was the order of the day. They dared not be overtly discourteous, and they were careful not to express their opinions in the Duchess's company.

The observations were predictable, I supposed.

Who was ever to know the source of such rumours? What I did know was that it would only be a matter of time before the torrid Castilian details came to Constanza's ear. And then, would she insist on my dismissal to rid herself of my contaminating presence?

It worried me enough for me to consider: what would the Duke do if caught in a direct line of conflict between wife and mistress? As a man of honour, of known chivalry, he could hardly support his mistress before his royal wife. As a man of ambition, he could not ignore the wishes of a wife who could bring him the crown of Castile for his own.

I set my teeth and applied myself to the raising of my lover's children, trying not to allow my thoughts to linger with my own small son so far away. I had made my bed. Now I must lie in it, with all the confidence and composure I could muster. When the vile accusations reached me, I raised my chin and pretended that I was invulnerable.

But I could not lay claim to a thickness of skin for long. A constant irritant must soon cause an abrasion, like a stone in the heel of a shoe, and the abrasion showed signs of becoming an open wound when my sister heard the rumbling undercurrent from her solar companions. Nor was that the worst of it. For when our paths crossed, as they must in one of our sojourns at The Savoy, there deep in conversation with Philippa was a figure I could not mistake, and who I wished in that moment of recognition far from England's shores.

Short and stout, son of a London Vintner and so not of Philippa's social worth—which always rankled with her— Geoffrey Chaucer was the other half of her arranged marriage and a man of many things. Most dangerously, a man of clever mind and wicked pen. A shame, I thought, as I approached them, that he didn't love my sister as much as he loved his books. They were clearly, audibly arguing. I considered walking smartly past, but then slowed my steps. Argument was a frequent occurrence in that marriage and I was not without sympathy for Philippa. I might rescue her.

'Where are you going?' my sister demanded of him.

'You know better than to ask.' Geoffrey grinned. The world of cynical patience on his lips would have driven a better woman to harsh words.

'So when will you be back? Can you tell me that?'

'When the royal business is done.'

A writer of naughty verses but a sublime wit, a composer of poetry, of songs and ballads under the generous patronage of the Duke, Geoffrey looked ripe for escape.

Hearing me approach, he looked over his shoulder. 'Katherine…'

Our eyes were not quite on a level, and so he had perforce to stretch to kiss my cheek, while his eyes gleamed, sharp as a hunting knife, with some unspoken idea that I thought I might not like.

'Geoffrey,' I replied. I was always careful around him, what I said and did not say. Every mild, insubstantial implication could be caught up like a pike snapping up a summer mayfly in its maw for he had an unrivalled way with words. 'So you are telling us nothing?'

'As usual,' Philippa said, unable to risk rising to the bait.

'Out and about on the King's secret affairs?' I suggested with a smile.

As well as a man of letters, Geoffrey was also a military man. A courier. A spy, some said. I could well believe it.

'Of course.' He made a neat little bow. 'It is my employment. Even if my wife still takes exception to it.'

'I take exception because I am not considered important enough to know of your business dealings,' his wife retaliated.

'What you don't know you can't gossip about. Do you lack for anything?'

'Nothing that you are willing to give me!'

I sighed quietly. How they ever had children together when they spent so little time in each other's company and with so little charity between them I could not guess. Then Geoffrey's eyes slid to fix on mine. Bright as an acquisitive magpie locating something desirable.

'And what of you, Katherine? I'm hearing astonishing things about you.'

'Now what could they be?' My insouciance was marvellous considering the sudden beat of my heart. I had no wish to be portrayed in any manner, good or bad, by his greedy pen.

'I'll not say...Or not yet. I'll consider it. Now I'm off.'

He saluted my cheek again, whispering, 'There are many who will say. Watch your step, Lady de Swynford.' He landed a brief peck on Philippa's cheek and strolled out.

I would have followed.

'Is it true?'

Philippa thrust out a hand to stop me, her brows climbing to her plucked hairline, mine tightening into a straight line that could quickly become a frown. I had anticipated this confrontation almost as much as I feared the one with Constanza.

'Is what true?' I withdrew my sleeve from her clasp, praying that she had not uttered one word of her suspicions to her husband. Who knew where he might turn his agile mind next? Geoffrey, fervent admirer of Duchess Blanche that he was, had been pleased to portray the Duke as the grieving widower in his *Book of the Duchess*. He might equally well turn him into a pariah if he caught any whiff of scandal.

'Whore? Harlot? Is it true?'

And here was Philippa, selecting the most common of the words, as she worked out her fury with Geoffrey on me. My earlier compassion drained fast away.

'Yes.' What use in denying it? The words still echoed in my head from the breaking of our fast, murmured over the ale and bread so that I would hear. 'Although I would not have put it in quite those terms.'

The damsels had, more fluently. *Puta. Hija de Puta. Mujerzuela.* Even in their own tongue, the meaning was ugly. Whore. Slut. Harlot.

'And when were you going to tell me?' Philippa demanded, hard-eyed. 'Or is your sister no longer in your confidence?'

'I'm sorry. I should have told you.' I would apologise for a sin of omission but nothing else. I held her stare as we stepped aside when a maid from the dairy came between us bearing a round of cheese. Philippa picked up her weapons as soon as the cheese was gone.

'You should be ashamed of yourself. But I don't suppose you are, or you would not be back here. You would be holed up at Kettlethorpe.'

I stiffened. I took up the challenge immediately.

'No. I am not ashamed. I love him, and I'll not ask your permission, your approval or your forgiveness. It is not your affair, Philippa.' Yes, it was a curt reply but I could see from her face that there would be no understanding from her. 'Now, if you will let me pass...' The damsels' words had ruffled me more than I had cared to admit.

Philippa stepped again to bar my way.

'And I suppose you do have a son, as the Castilian bitches say?' she murmured. At least she kept her voice down. 'Would you not have found the opportunity to tell me that either? That I have a bastard nephew by the Duke of Lancaster?'

No, I had never told her. I had told no one. And as I sensed a gloss of hurt running over her accusations, I felt a little flicker of regret that my sister should have discovered the truth from cruel gossip. Why had I not told her? Because I did not want to hear those crude words on the lips of my own sister.

'Yes. I do have a son,' I replied, keeping my voice quiet in the confined space as unlooked for emotion struck at me. 'He is called John. He is almost three months old, and bears too much resemblance to the Duke for me to bring him with me. I love him with all my heart. And I miss him.'

Philippa was unmoved. 'And you are a hypocrite, sister Kate. You are here under false pretenses. In her household—or as near as—and she does not know. I pity her, and I condemn you for your cruelty.'

This is what I had dreaded. Philippa's marriage to Geoffrey Chaucer had brought her no joy and had hardened her spirit.

'Oh, Philippa!' Suddenly overwhelmed with remorse for her loveless state, I touched her arm. 'I am sorry for your own squabbles with Geoffrey, but what I do or do not do has no bearing on it. Nor did I steal the Duke's love from Constanza.'

'You don't know that! Is that what he tells you?'

'Yes, he does.'

'Well, he would, wouldn't he?'

'He would not lie to me, I know that. Their marriage was one of political expediency, as she would be the first to admit. I cannot bear guilt for her dissatisfaction, just as I cannot live my life to please you. I am not responsible for the lack of satisfaction in your own marriage.'

Philippa visibly flinched as if I had struck her cheek. We never talked of her unhappiness.

'I do not expect you to live your life to please me.'

'Yet you think I should repudiate the man I love.'

'Yes, I do, when we all live cheek by jowl…'

'Would you?' I asked.

'Would I what?'

'If you loved your husband so much that he occupies your every thought, would you not follow him to the ends of the earth?' She flushed. 'I know there is little between you. But if there were…'

'We are not talking about me.'

'No. You are picking apart my emotions, my morals. My private life.'

'You have no private life.'

'But you do not have the right to hang it out to dry for the damsels to gloat over.'

It silenced her.

'All I ask is that you do not add your own voice to the gossip. And,' I added, trying a smile, 'that you do not entertain Geoffrey with the details. I don't wish to be pilloried in some fashionable song. Will you do that for me?'

'Oh, I'll not talk about it to anyone,' Philippa responded, rejecting my olive branch. 'I am not proud of what my sister is doing, even if she claims to be lost in love. Is that why you received such an astonishing annuity from the Duke? For your offices in his bed?'

'And if it was?' I was severely discomfited, horrified that she should think that.

'Shame on you, Kate. If it matters to you at all, Constanza is unaware.' Her lips sneered, something I had never seen before. 'I don't suppose you care. You will brazen it out, flaunting your pre-eminence.'

Philippa stalked off along the corridor, leaving me prey to all manner of hurt that I had tried so hard to deny. Now I no longer could, when my own sister placed the blame at my door rather than that of the Duke. Was that not always the way of the world? I should have seen it with far more clarity. I had thought that I had seen the quagmire that would lie in wait, but I had not seen its depths. Now I had a taste of it and it was bitter indeed.

Unwilling to go to my own chamber where I might have to bandy words with Philippa again and defend a stance that, on my conscience, was fast becoming indefensible, I took refuge in Constanza's little garden. Sinking to the stone seat beneath a vigorously pruned arbour, I regarded my reflected image in my little mirror.

Who was this woman who looked back at me? Was it the same woman who had looked back at me in that moment, not so very long ago when I had stood in my sodden shoes and decided to return to The Savoy?

Whore. Harlot.

How repulsive the words were, striking at me again and again like well-aimed arrows.

But what I saw was no different from the woman who

looked back at me every morning. A polished, courtly image: smooth hair beneath its restraining filet and veil, immaculately arched brows, a straight nose and firm lips. A hint of delicate enhancement to brows and cheeks. Without doubt a woman who lived in pampered luxury, composed and confident.

Was this the face of a whore?

My confidence as the Duke's beloved shivered under my own questioning, threatening to crumble into the rose petals at my feet, despite the face showing nothing of my inner turmoil. How strange that I had not felt this sense of ignominy, not until the Castilian women had given it a name. Now it was all too real.

Your integrity is undermined. Your reputation is defiled. You should be ashamed.

At what unaccountable cost had I become the Duke's mistress?

You have dishonoured the name of Swynford and de Roet.

I should have seen the destruction of all I had lived by. I was no ignorant girl, seduced into the Duke's bed. How could I have been so very blind?

What would Queen Philippa say to you now?

I dared not even contemplate it. She would address me with the same lash of contempt as my sister had wielded.

I turned my mirror face down on my lap. I could look at it no longer. I did not like the woman I saw looking back at me.

I slept badly.

'We will play a game.'

Constanza's announcement brought a little silence to the room. And then a ripple of laughter. The Duchess was surprisingly fond of games. Perhaps she had not played much as a child in Castile, and certainly there would have been little opportunity in her days of perilous exile. Lady Alice smiled encouragingly at her. The Duchess had been tense and preoccupied all day. Some merriment would bring a smile to her pale features.

We were a family gathering, with Constanza's sister Isabella and her new husband, Edmund of York, making up a convivial group with one of the Duke's young pages singing and another playing the lute. I stitched, as did my sister. Lady Alice had a Book of Hours open on her lap. The Castilian damsels sat in chilly silence. The Duke relaxed at ease, a pile of scrolls which he had readily abandoned beside him.

'Do you wish to dance, my lady?' he asked.

We were enough to make a good showing.

Constanza glanced round her damsels, then caught us all up in a limpid gaze. Did I detect a hint of mischief? Her eyes swept over me to rest on her husband.

'No. Not dancing.'

She rose smoothly to her feet and raised her hand in imperious summons, whereupon the Duke, smiling to see his wife so animated, strolled over to where she waited for him.

'Your wish is my command, my lady. What is it to be?' He led her into the centre of the room.

'I wish to play *The King Who Does Not Lie*.'

Well, now. I felt the muscles along my spine tense a little. A courtly love game, known to all of us, much played under Queen Philippa's aegis, but generally accepted as not one to entertain an audience of children. The questions could become unseemly, the answers even more so. I had not thought its bawdy nature would be to Constanza's refined taste.

Frowning, Lady Alice responded with some force. 'It is inappropriate, my lady.'

'Why is that?' The Duchess smiled round at us. Why did

I imagine that she was not quite as innocent as she seemed? Did her eye, in this traversing over her guests, rest longer on me than was comfortable? 'We used to play it in Castile,' she announced.

'So you might, my lady.' In no manner flustered, Lady Alice addressed the problem. 'We do not when there are young people in the gathering.'

Constanza raised her chin. 'I do not see it. All it needs is for the truth to be told. The Queen asks questions of the King, who is honour-bound not to lie. Is that not so?'

'I see no harm,' added Isabella. 'Let us play.'

The Duke lifted a shoulder in acceptance although I thought the fine skin at his temples was tight-drawn as he addressed Constanza. 'And are we two to play the roles?'

'Of course. Who else?' There was a challenge in her eye.

My heart began to quicken. I did not like this. I did not like it one little bit. I looked round the family group, praying silently that the presence of the children would keep the questions in line. Or that of William de Burgh, our chaplain, so far silent, but with a hunch of his shoulders much like a moulting hawk.

Constanza had some scheme in mind, of that I was in no doubt. I continued with my stitching. Lady Alice continued to frown. Philippa, thoughts elsewhere—probably with her absent husband—remained aloof. Isabella and Edmund were too interested in each other to pay much attention. The Duke relaxed once more in his chair. If he were as anxious as I, there was no sign of it.

I set another careful stitch.

Constanza stood before the Duke and curtsied to him, playing the game.

'Sire. The Queen wishes to know whether your preference is for a dark lady or a fair one?'

Innocent enough, I supposed, breathing out slowly. Except that Constanza was dark and I was very fair. But it could be answered without causing any real upset. Perhaps my own conscience was making me search for problems where they did not exist. This was merely Constanza playing a foolish game.

The Duke was standing at centre stage, completely at ease, hands loosely latched on his belt.

'Well, Lady, the King has to admit to having been known to have a preference for both,' the Duke responded. 'Duchess Blanche had hair the colour of sun-kissed wheat—much like her two daughters.' He bowed, elegantly and chivalrously playful towards the two girls who giggled. 'And Mistress Blanche here is passing fair.' He raised his cup to my own daughter who beamed with pleasure. 'Now Lady Alice has a pale russet cast and I dare not ignore her. She would make my life a misery if she thought I had slighted her. How could I not love them all? But then my wife's hair, sadly covered, is as dark as jet. And she is very beautiful too…So sometimes I have a preference for dark ladies too, Lady.'

There was a general murmur of appreciation for the clever reply. I ran my tongue over dry lips and kept stitching, the leafy tendrils growing rapidly under my needle.

The Duchess swept her skirts. 'Sire. The Queen wishes to know. Have you ever given a lady *not* your wife a *lacs d'amour*? A love knot?'

My heart bumped a little against my ribs. I was wearing one. A simple interlacing of silver threads to form a knot in the shape of a heart. Little more than a simple fairing bought from a pedlar, a mere trifle lacking any fervent inscription, but it was a gift from John on my recent return, chosen because it was innocuous. I deliberately smoothed the girdle I was stitching beneath my fingers.

'Indeed I have, Lady.' John's laughter was supremely confident as he set himself to entertain the group. 'I must have given a score or more in my lifetime. And some here present. To Mistress Chaucer and Lady de Swynford. For services to my late Duchess.'

'Indeed?' Constanza's gaze roved over me and Philippa with sharpened interest.

'Yes, my lady.' I touched my fingers to the little badge.

'And I think Lady Alice might have one in her treasure coffer amongst all the other gems she has amassed over the years at my grateful hand.'

'I think I have three...' Lady Alice smiled despite her misgivings at the whole tenor of the conversation.

'So many...' John expressed admirable surprise. 'How did you manage that?'

'I've been in your household many years, John.'

'I have never had a lover's knot,' proclaimed Elizabeth.

'You are too young for such fripperies,' I said gently, 'but perhaps for your next New Year's gift someone might buy you one.'

'And I suppose that might be me,' the Duke said. 'So to answer your question, as you see, Lady, I have given far too many, and will doubtless give more.'

'The Queen seems to have been neglected!' Constanza raised an arch brow.

'Then it is shame on me. The King will remedy it instantly. But you asked if the King had so awarded a love knot to a lady not his wife,' he reproved.

Constanza flushed but continued with a distinct toss of her head.

'Sire. The Queen wishes to know. Have you ever taken a lady as your mistress?'

The echo of the question hung in the room, like dust

motes suspended in a sunbeam. I swallowed silently, mouth dry. There was no denying the direction of this line of questioning. I could only presume that the gossip had finally reached Constanza's ears and she was intent on retribution. But would she blatantly hold her husband up for public condemnation? My flesh shivered a little.

The Duke's brows had risen marginally, but he replied readily enough, and with enough circumspection. 'Yes. With regret, the King must admit that he has.'

'Then he must tell!' Constanza was avid for detail, her eyes glowing with an unpleasant species of triumph.

'The King was unwise in his youth,' the Duke responded without hesitation. 'The lady was young and beautiful, and I was young and wilful and drawn by the sins of the flesh.'

'Oh!' Constanza appeared shocked. Then more so when she realised that there was no outcry at such a statement.

Lady Alice on my left was nodding. 'Marie. I remember her. She was a lovely girl and you were but seventeen.'

'And I remember you made due recompense, my lord,' the priest added.

It was no surprise to any one of the English adults present. If it had been a ruse to unnerve the Duke and me, it had failed utterly. We all knew of Marie, one of Queen Philippa's damsels when John had been a young prince and had taken her to his enthusiastic bed.

Constanza looked askance. 'My lord appears to have no remorse.'

'Oh, he has. But he was granted absolution and he has tried to make amends. My lord granted a pension,' William de Burgh explained. 'The lady lacks for nothing and is treated with great respect.'

Constanza, drawing herself tall as if addressing the Royal Council, immediately directed another question.

'I wish to know, Sire. Have you ever fathered a child outside of marriage?'

Now here was a far less innocent question, no longer addressed to the King of the game by the Queen, but to the Duke himself. The frivolity of the courtly silliness had been abandoned, yet the Duke's face did not change from its amiable, well-mannered courtesy, although I could sense his anger at such an impertinent question. Lady Alice clicked her tongue against her teeth. The chaplain grunted over his wine.

'That also is true,' John replied, parrying with skill what was an obvious attack. 'And the King will answer it since the Queen sees fit to ask.' A clever return to the structure of the game. 'It is not a matter for comment or scandal. There is no secrecy here. Yes, the King has a daughter. Her name is Blanche. The King will support her and will arrange a good marriage for her. She is Marie's daughter.'

'How old is she now?' Lady Alice asked, pursuing her own role in softening the charged atmosphere.

'Old enough to be married.' He smiled at some memory. 'And she is as lovely and gifted as her mother.'

The moment had passed, any tension subsumed under reminiscences of Marie and her daughter. If Constanza had hoped to embarrass the Duke, and draw me into an unpleasant situation, she had failed. I glanced across at her. There was no disappointment on her sharp features, and seeing this I realised that she had not yet reached the core of her planning. My muscled tensed again. What would she ask next? I thought I knew. I deliberately set another row of stitches that were woefully uneven.

Constanza smiled. 'Sire. The Queen wishes to know. Does the King keep a mistress now?'

'No,' said Lady Alice, closing her book with a snap.

'But yes,' said Constanza. 'The Queen desires to hear the truth.'

Silence fell on the room, like a woollen blanket, hot and stifling.

My breath backed up in my lungs. I looked at no one and stitched on, and then decided that such disinterest in itself would stir suspicion. I dropped my stitching to my lap and waited for the answer. The truth? Would the Duke tell the truth? The truth would damn us both in public.

He did not hesitate. With deliberation, every action controlled, his demeanour the epitome of chivalrous rectitude, the Duke knelt on one knee and took both Constanza's slender hands in his, saluting one then the other.

'Are you so uncertain of my loyalty to you and your cause? You are bound to me by the rite of Holy Mother Church, Constanza. You are my wife and mistress in the eye of God and Man. That cannot be changed. Your supremacy as Duchess of Lancaster and as Queen of Castile is under no threat from anyone here present. There is no need for such games. Your place at my side is sacrosanct.'

Constanza flushed. 'Do you promise that?' she whispered.

I felt cold and pale as the Duke's affirmation sank in.

'You will always be my wife, treated with every respect. We will have a son, if it is God's will. I commit myself to restoring you to Castile. I promised that when I first wed you. I will not break that promise, made in God's presence as we were wed. You must trust me. You must tell me that you trust me.'

'Do you speak the truth?' she asked, a lustrous softness in her face, all her earlier temper smoothed over.

'There is no guile in my promises.'

'Then I believe you.'

She smiled as the Duke leaned to salute her cheeks.

For a moment my heart fluttered with relief. He had done it. Clever, ambiguous, saving everyone's face, the Duke had stated the plain legality of Constanza's position, without putting me in danger. I dared not look at him, and throughout the whole of that masterly performance to comfort Constanza, he had drawn no attention to me. I knew him to have a reputation at the negotiation table for clever dealings. Tonight I had seen his skills in full flow, to rescue us all from rabid scandal.

But then, as I exhaled, the knowledge bit with sharp teeth. In spite of all the Duke's professed need for me to return to his household, reality struck hard, as it had once before, in that one question:

Who is of greater importance to the Duke? You, Katherine de Swynford, or the Castilian Queen?

There was only one answer in my mind. Unworthy it might be, thoroughly selfish, but there before me was the evidence of the Duke kneeling at Constanza's feet, his lips saluting her cheeks, then her lips.

There was no doubting the reply.

Had the Duke's skilful exoneration been to draw attention from me or had it been to put Constanza's jealousies to rest? She was everything to his ambitions, to his hopes, to the lasting inheritance of his family. What could I give him in comparison? She could give him all, and I nothing. The Duke was not protecting me but Constanza because she was central to his life.

My blood cold, all my hopes foundering under this blast of bleak truth, I turned my face away from both of them in that private little tableau. I had thought that my lover had leaped to my defence, but he had assuredly protected his wife, far more effectively than he had protected me.

The Duke had risen now, taking control of the situation simply by his stance, beckoning to the page who came to kneel at the Duchess's feet as any smitten troubadour, launching into a rendering of a fashionable love-ballad that was lively but far less dangerous than Constanza's spiteful intrigue. Keen to see her reaction, I looked across to find her eye on me, and in its gleam I detected what could only be a challenge. I held it for a moment, then calmly folded my stitching as if there were nothing amiss. The Duke had made it impossible for her to say more, nor would she wish to. The Duchess had emerged triumphant.

I, the mistress, had been put firmly in my place.

For she knew. Constanza knew. She had won this battle for his attention, whereas I had been cast adrift in the chilly margins of this relationship, my only consolation that I had not been held up to public disapprobation. My reputation was safe for a little while, but as Lady Alice and I took charge of the children she tilted her head in my direction to murmur:

'Is it worth it, Katherine?'

My breath caught as her hand brushed imperceptibly against my shoulder, in the lightest of warnings.

'Who is to know?' I replied lightly, deliberately obscure. By now I was beyond denying what was clearly the talk of the household. It had been an exhausting evening of disturbing revelation, leaving me with no wish to defend myself yet again; the condemnation of my sister had been quite enough, and now wounded by this new injury, I was beyond explanation.

'I'll not decry true love, if that is what it is between you,' Lady Alice pursued without demur. 'But you must know the risk is great. What will she say when she finds out?' The lady's gaze slid to Constanza, much as mine had done. 'Which she will. In fact, after that dramatic performance,

I think we can safely assume that she has more than an inkling. You must be wary.'

Oh, I was wary. And I was afraid. Even though I knew it would deepen my hurt, I forced myself to watch as the Duke took Constanza's hand and led her from the chamber in the direction of their own accommodations.

'As I live and breathe, Katherine, all I see is doom and gloom in this marriage,' Lady Alice remarked before we parted for the night. 'As well as heartbreak for you.' She looked as if she might have said more, but closed her lips with purpose, for which I was grateful.

My heart shivered as if I felt a grinning manifestation of ruin that loomed at the head of the bed in which it was clear that I must sleep alone that night. How tender the Duke had been towards his wife at the end, how gentle, while she had responded with an affection we rarely saw. As she drew him closer towards her, I was left to acknowledge the increasing vulnerability of my position. The steely challenge in Constanza's cleverly constructed campaign informed me that she knew exactly what she was doing.

My future was suddenly all clouded.

Who was to know what steps the victorious Constanza would demand from the Duke in return for the promised crown of Castile? My banishment could be the first of the coins the Duchess would see fit to demand. A chill breath whispered along my skin as I combed and braided my hair that night. It was not in the character of the Queen of Castile to remain silent and unresponsive for long, and the Duke, in gratitude, might bow in acquiescence.

A choice between me, a woman who provided a brief slaking of lust, and the royal claimant to the might of Castile? Of course the Duke would cleave to his wife. Even if he did love me, such a superficial emotion could hardly weigh in

the balance. In the depths of my heart I acknowledged it.
How could I blame the Duke for pursuing a prince's ambition? A mistress was transitory, easily discarded.

Was the Duke's decision to appoint me *magistra* to shield
me from humiliation in service to Constanza? Or was it to
shield Constanza? Was it marital respect that she roused in
him, or had it indeed become a more fervent emotion?

My mind tripped over the lines sung so aptly by the
Duke's squire:

> *'Love like heat and cold pierces and then is gone;*
> *Jealousy when it strikes sticks in the marrowbone.'*

Jealousy infused my bones. Constanza, I accepted during that long night, was a foe of merit. My decision to
leave my son and return to my lover, that choice with all
its heart-searching, was transformed into dross. I should
never have allowed myself to dream of a future with the
Duke of Lancaster. What fools love can make of us. How
blind it can make us. All I had done was drag closer the
promise of ultimate degradation.

Of course I blamed the Duke—what woman would not,
faced with such evidence of disaffection? And like all women
struck with jealousy, I took my revenge in the only manner
open to a mistress in so public a place as The Savoy.

With all my seeds of doubt blossoming into bitter fruit I
determined that I would not share his bed.

'I cannot. I am unwell.'

I felt that my smile was brittle enough to scratch the surface of my looking glass as I made the excuse of all womanhood.

When, the household sleeping, he came to my chamber,

it was to find my door barred. Tense with dismay that I had been thrown to the wolves, with Constanza's star in the ascendant, it was the only action I could take. That I was standing within, palms flat against the wood, my heart torn with longing as he knocked lightly, he would never know.

How unworthy my thoughts were, how heavy my regret as his footsteps receded.

My conduct from day to day, hour to hour, remained impeccable. I curtsied. I spoke calmly when addressed. I sat at table. I fulfilled my duties to the ducal children. I laughed and sang and played games. I reverted to the epitome of the dignified, composed and dutiful widow, the Lady of Kettlethorpe.

And all the time I shivered with apprehension.

What are you trying to prove? I asked myself more than once as I made very sure that I was never alone in proximity to the Duke, who was beginning to wear the vexed restlessness of King Edward's caged lion at the Tower.

I knew the answer. I wanted to know that the Duke's desire for me was still as vitally alive as when I had given birth to his son. I needed to know from his own lips. If my star was in decline, I must know it, for my own self-respect. How demeaning to remain the ducal mistress in the face of the Duke's flagging interest—for I had been forced to accept that, for him, love was never an issue. I admitted, with clear-eyed despair, that I was pushing our strained relationship to a shattering climax.

Would I regret it? Would it not be better to cling to the crumbs of the Duke's need for me in his life rather than reject the whole banquet?

I did not think so. My deliberate isolation was as much a challenge to the Duke as Constanza's malicious little game had been to me. It was the only manner in which I could express my fear, for to shout it from The Savoy gatehouse might give satisfaction, but was not seemly. I knew full well, as I had always done, that whereas I offered the Duke love's coin of shining gold, his return to me was of a lesser value.

Duchess Constanza smiled often and kept the Duke frequent company.

'Madame de Swynford! A moment of your time!'

The Duke hunted me down in the Great Hall, and stopped me by the simple strategy of announcing my name, giving me no alternative—other than discourteous flight—but to await his approach with the loping stride akin to one of the fit hunting dogs at his side.

'So that we can hold a conversation without undue emotion,' he announced as he halted within feet of me. 'Are we not in the public eye here?' He smiled, but I was not deceived. This might just be the termination that I had precipitated.

'Yes, my lord?' I curtsied neatly, every muscle braced. There would be no hiding for me here, as he well knew.

'Yes, my lady,' he returned with languid grace as he handed me a fine leather-bound volume, as if that might be the reason for our meeting. I tried to read his expression, and failed, but the tightly pressed lips were not friendly.

'Let us talk siege warfare, Lady Katherine,' he suggested, launching into an unnervingly smooth discourse. 'Tell me what it is that has lowered the portcullis between us. I get the impression that I must lay siege to encourage you to raise it. I did not think that I was the enemy.'

'You are not my enemy, my lord.'

All my senses told me that I must keep my wits keen. In this mood, the sardonic Duke was unpredictable. What's more, he was confident. I could see it in the flare of his nostrils, the glitter in his eyes. He expected to win this encounter. I raised my chin, prepared to resist. There would be no easy victory here for either of us.

'So why, madam, have you built your defences against me?' the Duke pursued, showing his teeth in a smile that was not a smile, for the sake of a passing servant.

'Because I am uncertain of my position, sir.'

'I thought I had made your position clear.' His brows rose, his tone was acerbic. He knew I was fencing with him, while I, knowing full well that I was crossing swords with an expert, would not cry defeat. Nor would the Duke: 'You have a place in my household. I am your lover. You share my bed to our mutual enjoyment.'

How cold, how flat the statement of our relationship, yet there was fire in his eye. Assuring myself that we had no audience:

'I am afraid,' I announced baldly.

'Afraid? Of what?'

'Rejection.'

'God's Blood, Katherine!'

'I see your affection for the Duchess growing stronger. I fear I am superfluous,' I said. 'I expect it is the penalty a mistress must pay if she is absent for the months of childbirth.'

'What penalty? There is none, except of your own making. You have closed your door against me!'

'And you defended the Duchess quite superbly,' I retaliated. 'I recall perfectly. She is your wife and mistress in the eye of God and Man.'

'Ah, so that's it! Constanza's childish game-playing!' His brows continued to express disbelief. 'What would you have me do? Open you both to scandal through some malicious game?'

'Of course not.'

'Constanza is my wife.'

'I know she is.'

'She deserves my respect.'

'I have always known that too,' I said, withdrawing behind my bulwarks in the face of such obvious statements.

'And I have always been honest about my marriage to Constanza. What do you want from me, Katherine?'

There was the direct attack I had expected. I thought about this. How difficult to explain, but I did so with all the self-possession I had held to in past days.

'I share your bed, my lord. I have carried your child. I think I need to know that you still need me in your life, that I am not here as some passing pleasure when the mood takes you.'

'Reassurance?' The attack was still dynamic, his jaw taut with annoyance at his inability to wear me down as he had hoped. 'Is that what you want? You have it, Katherine. I never promised you more than what I give you now.'

'You did not promise me anything.' Oh, I was calm, if perhaps not altogether fair.

'There is no more that I can promise you. What do you ask of me?'

'Nothing that is not of your own volition,' I replied bleakly, as I held out the book. 'Take it. I am in no mood for love poetry.'

'I never do anything not of my own volition.' His arrogance was truly impressive.

'I know. Nor do I question your authority.' I lifted my eyes to his and held his dark stare and spoke the words that had lived with me for so long. 'I also know, my lord, that not once in all the time we have been together have you ever said that you love me. You speak of need and desire. Of passion. But not of love.' I touched my tongue to dry lips, appalled at my courage, yet I repeated the fear at the centre of my heart. 'You lavish words of romance and yearning on me. You kiss me and cherish me, but never have you spoken of what is in your heart. I have never asked it of you, but never have you offered me love.'

The Duke looked as if I had doused him in icy water, the planes of his face flattening under the unexpected. He was certainly stuck dumb.

'I expect that is because, for you, it does not exist.'

Then, when he took the book, frowning, rather than have me drop it onto the beautifully patterned tiles at his feet, I walked away, more despairing than I had ever been since I stood in my courtyard with flood-water lapping round my ankles. Nothing was settled between us. The emotion that I took to bed with me that night was one of raw distress that I had compromised my principles for nothing in the end, because he would send me away.

He has given his son into your keeping. He trusts you to educate his daughters and the heir to the great Lancaster inheritance. His physical desire for you is as strong as it ever was. You cannot doubt him.

But I did. He did not love me. I waited for formal dismissal: it might suit the ducal pair very well. My deliberate challenge to the Duke's legendary sangfroid might just tip the balance.

Chapter Ten

W̲hat an occasion it was, here at Kenilworth, celebratory and formal, announced by a fanfare which caused a rich undulation of Castilian and Plantagenet banners along the walls with the movement of air through the great chamber. With its huge traceried windows and soaring hammer-beamed roof, it provided the perfect setting for this event. Sir Robert Swillington, our Chamberlain, grandly formal in his tabard with staff of office to the fore, paced along the length of the hall before the Duke who led his wife by the hand, both of them magnificent in fur and cloth of gold. This was Constanza's occasion as she took her place on the dais. Receiving the grace cup from Sir Robert, the Duke raised it and surveyed the assembled party, addressing us in a voice that carried with its superb modulation to every guest present.

'To my fair wife who had given me an equally beautiful daughter. Today we celebrate them both, particularly Katalina on this first commemoration of the day of her birth a year ago.' He smiled down at Constanza who had her eyes trained on her clasped hands. 'We hope for a restoration of

Castile for our daughter's future dowry when we look for a husband for her.' He smiled, as did the guests. 'A little young as yet but one day…'

He drank and passed the cup to Constanza, who at last looked up and, inclining her head graciously at the Duke, she drank too. There was a glow in her eye.

'And we hope for a son to become King of Castile in my name,' she added, her voice vibrating with emotion. 'Do we not, my lord?'

'So we hope.' He bowed gravely, raising her fingers to his lips, whilst I clenched mine against an all-too-recognisable bolt of pure envy. What a wearying emotion it was, but I could not shake myself free of it.

'It is my life's work to take back your kingdom, my lady.'

'And to provide me with an heir,' she reiterated.

'We would both welcome the birth of a son.'

I sat, conscious of my magnificence in my new rose-pink sleeves, extravagantly embroidered and edged in thick sable, conscious also of Lady Alice's warning to be wary, to keep my jealous inclinations under control. Consequently my nails dug painfully into my palms, until we were summoned to echo the toast, raising our cups to fill the room with an oscillating sheen of gold as the candles warmed the precious metals.

No sign of Lady Alice's doom and gloom for the marriage here. At the same time my position was still secure in our removal to Kenilworth. The Duchess was more than content. I was no longer even sure that she saw me as a rival to the Duke's affections. I began to relax with a cup of good Bordeaux at my elbow. As I sipped it, it seemed that she was not even aware, and that my suspicions of the night of the charade were misplaced.

The banquet was drawing to a close, the musicians and

entertainers, jugglers and dancers who had so fascinated the ducal children were praised and paid, and as a final flourish, Katalina was brought in by Alyne, her small form clad incongruously from head to toe in Castilian heraldic motifs. We drank a toast, admired the baby heir to Castile (until a brother was born), and the gathering began to disperse.

For a moment Constanza remained on the dais with her damsels, working the delicate material of her skirt loose from where it had caught in the high carving of her chair. She smiled at her ladies, her voice as it carried to me light and happy. It had been a good evening. The servants were beginning to clear the tables, folding the no-longer-white cloth from the dais table with a snap of fine linen.

I stepped into my place in the procession behind my sister with thoughts on the dancing in the room that had just seen extravagant completion in the Duke's building schemes.

'Katherine de Swynford.'

The Duchess's voice carried from the dais with as great a clarity as the Duke's.

I turned, curtsied with a polite smile, my senses lulled by good food and music and the potency of the Bordeaux. 'My lady?'

'I would speak with you.'

That same hard, clear timbre, infinitely polite, yet I knew, with a deep beat of a major bell in my chest, that this was the moment. This was where Constanza's revenge against me would be played out.

What a fool I had been to persuade myself that Constanza was unaware. All through that long evening of ritual and ceremony she must have pondered the content of the rumours, and yet with regal control, as formidable as a charge of English knights on the battlefield at Crecy under the hand of King Edward, she had chosen to play the role of contented wife. She had known when she instigated the courtly game. She had known, and chosen to bide her time. Until now. Until she could confront me at a time of her own choosing, after an evening when the Duke had shown her every consideration as his wife.

Despite my sinking heart, her tactics in dealing with a despised mistress had to be admired. Would I not have done the same? Now I must face her wrath that I had stolen the loyalty of her husband from her, and if not his love, certainly the duty of his body. If I were in her place, that is how I would react. And thus I must withstand whatever attack she saw fit to make against me.

I stood straight-backed, arms at my sides, and waited for the fall of the axe. I could already sense its edge against my nape.

With an imperious gesture from the Duchess, the damsels had left us except for her most intimate trio who stood at her back. Shutting out their expressions of bright delight that I would at last receive my just deserts, I retraced my steps until I stood at the foot of the dais, the Duchess above me, her skirts no longer encumbered. Clearly a clever ruse to remain behind and isolate me. For the first time I acknowledged in my mind just how powerful a force the Duchess was to be reckoned with. I was on trial, and I would be judged by an authority far greater than my own.

'How dare you.'

Her accusation was surprisingly dispassionate, her expression as well-governed as mine. She knew she had the upper hand for I was part of the ducal household. I was hers to play with, to dismiss. She did not even ask if the rumours were true.

'You stand there before me, so brazen, so seemingly innocent.'

I held my head raised, my eyes on her face. I could feel the tremble through every muscle as I kept my spine erect.

'Were you my husband's leman, were you sharing my husband's bed before he married me?'

'No, my lady.'

I answered without pause even though my heart thudded. Here was a moment for truth between us.

'Then when we were first wed? Even though I was carrying his child, were you his whore when I was travelling here, full of hope, for a new marriage and a new life?'

'No, my lady.'

'So it was after I took you as my damsel.'

'Yes, my lady.'

Still I trembled but I would not show it. I knew that she would never accuse the Duke to his face, but she would accuse me. Had I not always known that this time would come? How cruelly accurate were her assumptions. My conduct was about to be thrown into high relief, a disgraceful patchwork of immorality and sin.

'Do you know the humiliation for me, of having Lancaster's whore foisted on me as my damsel, accepting my daily patronage?'

Lancaster. She called him Lancaster. We were both in receipt of her bitterness, but I was the one to be singled out. As it must be. My courage showed a tendency to slither away under Constanza's assault, as I foresaw my dismissal, but I held firm. I would not be shamed for a decision I had made in cool certainty, and would make again and again. My life was entwined with that of the Duke. For however long he wanted me by his side I would be there. I would not be shamed.

'When the Duke wed you and welcomed you here, I was not his whore,' I replied.

'How bold you are, Lady de Swynford,' she sneered. 'Then when I gave birth to Katalina? Did he know you more intimately than he knew me?'

'Yes, my lady. We were together then.' I did not see that it mattered, but it did to her. And I supposed it would to me too.

'And now I hear that you have a son of Lancaster's begetting.' I heard a note of fury creep in. 'When I could only bear a daughter.' She picked up her gloves from where they had been cast aside on the table, her fingers tearing at the gilt edging. 'You were my damsel. I actually asked for your service because you had experience. And now you are *magistra* to Lancaster's children. And what is it that you teach them? When you are so lacking in morals, how can you be *magistra*?' She spat the word. 'How can that be, that you are allowed to have influence over such valuable young lives and minds? Do you think you have the moral compass to educate my husband's children?'

The accusations were as keen as a raptor's talons slicing through my flesh but still I replied with composure. 'I teach them to fear God and to value their education, my lady.'

'Do you fear God, Lady de Swynford? Does a whore fear God? Were you his whore when you took my daughter to King Edward's court? Did you enjoy the pleasures of the flesh at The Savoy, then carry my daughter into the royal presence, in those arms that had seduced my husband into committing adultery? How dare you prate to me about morals and God fearing!'

So I was the one to seduce. The blame was to be laid at my door, was it? I was seized with a need to leap to my own defence, rather than meekly bow my head. I had stepped into my relationship with the Duke with my eyes fully open, knowing that I would be universally condemned. Had I not undermined my faith and my respectability for love? But I had done it. There was no going back and although my heart was sore for the Duchess, I could not, would not, apologise for a step I had taken in full knowledge. That would indeed be the mark of hypocrisy. Nor would I take the blame. The dignity that I had embraced all my life would keep me from retreating in the face of Constanza's hatred.

'Yes, I fear God,' I replied, holding her gaze where anguish had suddenly doused the fury. 'And I know that I must answer to Him for my sins at the end of my days. But I am no whore,' I affirmed, aware of a wash of colour tinting my cheeks. 'I am not paid for my services in your husband's bed. Nor can I be accused of seduction. If you are to apportion blame, it must be in equal measure. Yes, I went to my lord of Lancaster's bed, but I was no wanton seductress.'

She had not expected such a vehement response, nor such an open confession. I heard the in-drawing of her breath, the sharp sound of the cloth of her gloves tearing under her busy fingers as, suddenly, I was not the only object of her loathing.

'What is Lancaster thinking, taking a mistress when I am his wife? Keeping her here, to my degradation?'

I could say nothing. I would not answer for the Duke. All I saw was Constanza's disgust and the eyes of the damsels, shining with malice.

Constanza's thoughts veered, her focus returning to me. She leaned towards me, gloves abandoned, her knuckles planted on the wooden boards of the high table. 'Does he mock me when you come together?' Her head whipped round when a servant appeared from behind the kitchen screens at the far end. 'Get out!' she shrieked. And then, when the maid scuttled to obey, to me in a fierce whisper. 'Can you tell me that? Does he compare me with you? Does he think you are more beautiful than I can ever be?'

The cry of every slighted woman, and in this mess of

conflicting emotions, my heart melted in pity for her, and sorrow that in her short marriage she had learned so little of the Duke's loyalty to her. It was the last thing he would do.

'Never,' I stated. 'My lord would never be so lacking in chivalry.'

'He lacks it enough to take you to his bed! Does he compare me with you?' She could not let it go. 'Does he compare my lack with your undoubted talents?'

'He has too much honour, my lady.'

'Is it honour to take another woman to the marital bed?' She paused, horror stretching the planes of her face. 'Has he had carnal knowledge of you in his own bed, when he has fulfilled his duty to me?'

And, snatching them up, she threw the mistreated gloves. One landed on the floor at my side, the other struck my much-admired sleeve. I bent and picked them both up, as Constanza's beautiful figured veils quaked with anger about her shoulders.

'Did you seek the position of Lancaster's mistress for the power it will bring you?'

'I did not seek it...'

'I advise you not to hope for what will never be yours. My lord will not give away his power, and I do not think you have the guile. You have to be a strong woman to take on the Plantagenets and use them for your own interests.' Her eyes flashed. 'I will and can. I, Constanza, Queen of Castile. My lord will take Castile for me. What are you but the wife of some minor knight, daughter of some insignificant family? You will not use his authority for your own ends. I will not allow it.'

'I do not seek power,' I repeated simply. It was an accusation easy to deny.

'I do not understand you. I do not believe you! Would you

not wish to promote your family? Enrich your children? Expand your lands in this bleak and distant Lincolnshire that you talk of?'

The question surprised me. 'No, I do not seek to promote and enrich.' For that was true enough. 'It is my desire to hand the estates in good heart to my husband's son, Thomas. That is all. My employment here enables me to do that. But I seek no power.'

'Then what do you want from him?'

What could I say? I could not, would not say: *I love him*. I could not say; *I am as jealous of you as you are of me*. Instead: 'I want nothing.'

'You lie.'

Constanza would never understand that a woman could be drawn to a man for other reasons than wealth and power. She would never understand that I had rejected every moral teaching of my youth simply because the Duke had wanted me and I had been unable to resist his allure.

'All whores seek advancement,' she stated, now cold as February snow, her eyes glittering like obsidian. 'I do not want you here under my roof.'

I placed the gloves carefully, palm to palm within my own hands, as I chose my words, hoping that they carried weight. 'But I am not your damsel, my lady.'

'You are living in my household and I do not want you in it.'

'I am in the Duke's employ, my lady.'

Had he known this when he changed the nature of my appointment? Had he deliberately taken that step to protect my position in the ducal home? Perhaps he had foreseen this—as I too had anticipated it—but nothing could spare me the Duchess's righteous anger.

'I do not want you here,' she repeated, her voice rising

to a shriek again as if I were the hapless servant. 'Get out of my sight!'

Robbed of her gloves Constanza lunged and picked up one of a pair of salt cellars that had still to be collected and returned to the buttery, and drew her hand back to hurl it. I flinched, automatically raising my hands to shield my face as she threw. The salt cellar missed its mark and thudded to the floor far to my right, leaving a spray of salt crystals over the hem of my skirt that glittered in the candlelight.

Fired with her fury, Constanza picked up a gold platter with both hands.

'Get out! I want you out of this place before the morning!' She raised the dish.

'No!' There was a limit to my pity. Anger flickered, even as I cowered, expecting the platter to find its mark. 'I will not go.'

'I say that you will!'

'That is enough, Constanza.'

The quiet voice stopped her as I could not have done.

I turned. Halfway down the length of the Great Hall stood the Duke. In the extremity of emotion run wild, we had not noticed his approach, but now he stood there, motionless, so still that the light barely shimmered over his cloth of gold. His hair was a perfection of ordered waves, his tunic fell in elegant folds to brush his thighs. All was in control and yet, even though his hands were relaxed at his sides, I saw the tautness in the carriage of his head, the set of his shoulders. This would be no easy negotiation, for any of us.

'Enough, my wife,' he repeated softly.

My wife. His choice of words made my heart hammer. How understanding of her predicament, as I knew he would be. But what of me? How painful it was for me who could never look for that honour. I turned back to face the Duchess, all emotion stripped from her face, the platter, forgotten now, but still clutched in her hand. The damsels were a frozen backdrop. All I could do was to wait, all senses stretched, uncertain of the outcome. I felt the Duke approach behind me, heard his measured footsteps grow louder on the painted tiles, then he was beside me, but stepping past until he stood before his wife, as if she were the only woman in the room. He lifted his hand for the platter. Constanza gripped it hard, raising it slightly as if she might still consider hurling it at my despised head. The Duke said nothing, simply waiting with infinite patience.

Then, when she did not respond: 'Constanza. It is not fitting…'

'She is your whore,' she hissed, the word slapping at me again.

'You will show Lady Katherine more respect.'

'Why should I? She is the source of your sin in our marriage. She should be driven out. Look at her! How unabashed she is in facing me. I demand that you rid yourself—'

'No, Constanza.'

I waited, caught between his implacable refusal and the Duchess's adamant insistence.

'No,' the Duke repeated into the little silence that had followed, 'Lady Katherine will not be sent away.'

'I demand it. I will not have her here.'

'It is not for you to decide. Will you throw that? Your aim is not good, and it will spoil a good piece of plate.'

With a sharp movement of distress she released into his hand the platter, which he placed on the table.

'You will dismiss your damsels.'

'I will not.'

'Will you discuss your private affairs before women who

have no thought of discretion? They are vulgar and indiscreet.' For the first time the air had become spiked with his anger although his voice remained smoothly even. 'It will be better that we have this conversation without them.'

'Better for her?' The Duchess acknowledged me with a toss of her chin.

'For all concerned. For the whole of my household. You are not the only member of it, my lady.' He did not wait for her response but swept a hand to encompass the little knot of women who now hovered uncertainly behind the Duchess. 'You will leave us,' he commanded. 'Nor will you discuss what has been aired here today.'

The Duke bowed as they stepped from the dais, courteous to the last, but his face had the rigidity of the carvings on the walls of Westminster Abbey.

And then we were alone in the vast hall. Three individuals overwhelmed by the space and height, cast into nothingness by the great hammer beams above our heads and by the oppressive air. I sensed the tension building and knew that these two people would soon fill the space with the clash of their will. They faced each other while I stood, an uneasy third point in the pattern. An unnecessary point. The outcome was as impossible to read as the expression on the Duke's face.

'Did we wed for love, Constanza?' he asked.

She lifted her chin. 'No.'

'Do I not honour you, before all women, as my wife?'

She looked away, lips pressed tight.

'Have I not vowed to restore Castile to you and your descendents? To our descendents?'

'Yes.'

'Do I not show you every respect, furnish you with everything you desire?'

'Yes.'

'Do you lack for anything?'

'No.'

'I spend the time I can with you…'

'As you should,' she snapped back now. 'But now I learn that you spend time with *her*!' She pointed a derisive finger at me. 'I am Queen of Castile. I am your *wife*.'

'But you do not always act as one, if that implies an intimacy in our lifestyle.'

I held my breath. So, I could see, did Constanza. The stillness echoed. Such a criticism in so few words

'My behaviour as a royal wife is beyond criticism.'

There was a frown between her brows.

'If by that you mean acting with propriety in public, then that is so, but when did you last express a desire to spend time with me? Travel with me when I visit my properties? Have you ever shown a desire to visit the King or my brother Edward?'

'I am not at ease away from my household…'

'Then take them with you. There is no need to shut yourself away at Hertford or Tutbury. I think you were even reluctant to come here to Kenilworth.'

'You should stay with me.'

'But that is not the manner in which we live. I have a duty to my father the King, and to England.'

'And I know which comes first!'

'As it must. You knew that, Constanza. You knew the way of life for such as us.'

I saw his regret, his compassion for this difficult woman. But I also saw the harsh ruthlessness that would always come into play when his authority was questioned. There was the inflexible, driving ambition that could make him appear merciless in the eyes of some, and I wished myself elsewhere. I felt as if I was spying on an impossible marriage. I should not be there. They did not need me as witness to such personal and passionate recriminations.

The Duchess shook her head. 'I did not expect you to take a mistress within the first year of our marriage!'

'I will not excuse what I did. It was a choice for me to make.' I heard him take a breath in a little pause, and then I heard the deepening of his regret. 'When did you last welcome me to your bed, Constanza? Much less invite me? We do not love each other.' Soft-voiced, infinitely gentle, but the questions were applied with dire precision. 'I will support you and honour you. But Katherine remains in my household.'

It was as if he had set a flame to a torch. Constanza's fury leaped into vibrant life.

'I will not allow this. How can I tolerate her presence here? She has usurped what should have been mine. I demand—'

'No,' responded the Duke and raised his hand to touch her wrist, to still her.

Allowing his hand to fall to his side, the Duke turned on his heel, a strangely brisk movement as if driven my some inner compulsion, to face me and look at me. And that is what he did. For what seemed to be endless moments of time his gaze encompassed me, moving steadily, slowly over me as if seeing me, Katherine de Swynford, for the first time, and finding something in me to claim his interest. There was no change in his expression at first. His face remained stern, his eyes alight with the wild mood of the moment, his lips firm pressed, while all I could do was stand there under his regard, entirely at a loss. I thought I knew his moods well, but I could not interpret this disconcertingly dispassionate appraisal.

As the emotion in that magnificent hall built and built, so

that I could scarce take a breath, I felt warm colour flooding my cheeks and I smoothed the palms of my hands over my skirts, which little gesture of unease on my part the Duke must have seen, for at last his face softened. Not into a smile but suddenly all the tension in him was gone.

He looked as if he had been lacerated by the point of a lance.

'Katherine.' He spoke my name softly, as if weighing it in his mind, on his tongue.

'My lord?'

'I have a debt to pay to you.'

'There is no debt,' I denied, caught up in the moment.

'But there is.' And then: 'No,' he addressed Constanza, but his attention was all for me. 'She will not be sent away. For here is the truth, Constanza. Katherine is the woman I love. She is the woman I wish to have beside me.'

Katherine is the woman I love.

Such a declaration, made to me as much as to Constanza, made with such apparent restraint, was too much to take in. My heart gave a single unruly bound, my throat tightened with disbelief at what he had done, and the manner of its doing, as the Duke turned back to his Duchess.

'I love Katherine, Constanza. You must accept that.'

And, as the Duke's words sank in, my heart shattered within me. He loved me. He had chosen me. Still holding her position on the dais, eyes glittering, Constanza flung back her head as if he had struck her. If she was wounded, so was I. Astounded, incredulous, I felt my nails dig deep into my palms. The air between us was rent with agony.

'No…' she whispered. 'Do not say that.'

'I love her, Constanza. I always will.'

And with those few words, even as exhilaration sparkled in my blood to my very toes, my heart was moved with a sharp pity for Constanza. How would she face this momentous declaration that brought me happiness and her nothing less than degradation? I had not truly envisaged the full scale of this difficult relationship, but now it was writ clear. How could I not have compassion for the Duchess when her marriage was one of pure ceremony? Perhaps she did not love the Duke, but her resentment of me and what I meant to him was fierce, and I understood that resentment, as one woman would understand another.

I moved a step backwards, so that the Duke turned his head to look at me. Still in command of voice and actions he might be, but his face was as pale as death.

'I need to go, my lord, my lady.' Curtsying, I forced myself to be formal, to bring them back to the reality of the three of us.

Coolly decorous, as if the matter were of no moment, the Duke took my hand and without another word led me to the door, where he kissed my fingers and bowed me out, but his hand had been rigid under mine and his lips icy cold, a wash of rare colour chasing along his cheekbones.

'Forgive me. You should not have been asked to be a part of this.'

And he pushed me gently through the door.

'I will not have her in my household—'

The final words I heard, the Duchess's voice rising dangerously as the Duke closed the door behind on me.

What would pass between them now? That was not for me to know. The only thought of any importance was that the Duke, in such a tense moment, had proclaimed his love for me. Had spoken it aloud, as if it was a discovery that needed to be made known.

Katherine is the woman I love. The woman I wish to have beside me.

With that declaration before the most crucial audience the Duke had ripped apart all my doubts and insecurities. How could I doubt his love now? It blazed indelibly in my mind but there was still this for me to face: would Constanza's need for the Duke's reassurance, for his loyalty, force his hand? What man of true compassion would be able to withstand the Duchess's tears, her pleas, as I could imagine them as soon as I had left the room? His duty to her was far greater than it was to me.

Would I be prepared to wager on my still being at Kenilworth by the morn, in the face of Constanza's hatred?

I would not.

'That,' the Duke announced, 'was worse than facing a charge of French cavalry.' There was no humour in this caustic statement, only an intense tiredness. 'My wife has lapsed into Castilian, and with nothing more to throw, has retired to her chamber to curse my name and yours.'

It had taken two hours before there had come the peremptory rap of knuckles on the door that I had not barred, and the Duke entered, still clad incongruously in festive magnificence. I gave no words of welcome but waited, my breathing shallow as he stood before me, the candlelight layering glints of red through his hair, deepening the lines between his brows. I could almost see the remnants of energy shimmering around him as I acknowledged the same in my blood. Much had been made clear in the ragged emotions of that formal chamber. Much had been laid bare, and now we must acknowledge the repercussions.

The Duke looked unutterably weary. I had no idea what he saw in me. The air around us crackled with tension, while incredulity held me, silent, in its power. I would not admit to impatience.

The Duke pre-empted any question I would ask.

'It is not in the Duchess's power to dismiss you,' he said, harsh in the aftermath of Constanza's turbulence. 'The power is mine, and mine alone. And I will not.'

For a long moment I allowed relief to sweep through me. Then, because my heart and mind were full of what he had said:

'You said that you love me.'

'I do. God help me, I do.'

'Not once,' I continued relentlessly, 'have you ever said that you love me, in all the months we have been together. Until tonight.' My mind was still trying to catch hold of the magnitude of his announcement.

'And it is to my regret,' he said. 'How long has it taken me to recognise my love for you for what it is?' He might speak of love now, but the Duke's voice remained rough-edged. 'Tonight, when I saw you standing there alone, defending yourself with such composure, such courage, I knew what you had come to mean to me. That you are as necessary to me as the air I breathe.'

I took a laboured breath of that air. 'Say it again,' I said. 'Let me hear it again. Unless your words are indeed only troubadour's fripperies and I need set no store by them.'

He was in the act of lifting the heavy livery chain over his head, but that stopped him. The Duke's shoulders braced.

'Am I facing another angry woman?'

'It depends.'

His answering smile was wry as he tossed the chain onto my bed. 'Should I be pilloried for a day, outside the walls of The Savoy?'

'Or even two days.'

The rings, stripped from his fingers, followed the chain. A vagrant smile touched his eyes, the weariness lifting.

'But would such penance absolve me of my sin? I think I need to kneel at your feet in reparation.' He had the grace to blush as he crossed the space between us and gathered my hands into his. 'I am deep in love with you, Katherine de Swynford. I love you in every way known to man. Before God, you are my soul, and I will love you and serve you as long as there is breath in my body to do so.'

The Duke might not kneel but the tension between us was beginning to dissipate and I could breathe again. The sheer intensity of that avowal made me shiver, which he felt through our joined hands, so that he raised them to his lips, softening his tone, but his words remained unsparing of himself.

'My insensitivity unmans me. Tonight it had to be laid out in plain sight, for Constanza to know. And for you too. This life of constant subterfuge and pretence that we were forced to lead was hurting you. I could not permit it.' He raised a hand to my cheek, the gentlest of caresses with the tips of his fingers. 'My beloved…I need Constanza as she needs me, to preserve a public face for my household and for England. You know that she must always have a place in my life—it is vital that you accept that.' His clasp on my hands tightened painfully. 'Because if you cannot it will continue to damage what is between us.'

His sigh was barely perceptible, as he sought for the words to state what he knew he must.

'All I know is that you, Katherine de Swynford, are a constant flame of light in my life. You are as necessary to me as the sun rising at the start of each new morn. You are the one I think about at the end of a day when we are apart. You are the one who is there in my mind on waking. You are ever-present when my mind slides from the demands of duty. Never think that I do not love you, or that you mean less to me than the woman joined to me by law. You mean more.' His kissed my lips, the most fleeting of caresses. 'So much more. I cannot help myself. Nor would I wish to.'

'Hold me,' I said, completely overwhelmed.

And he did, but lightly, as if still uncertain of the events he had set in motion.

'I know you doubt me. I understand now why you believe your feet to be on an unsafe path. I did not see the difficulties for you at the beginning when I took you simply because I wanted you. You intrigued me, you roused a need to protect you, I desired you with a passion that scorched like a strike of lightning fire. But, to my everlasting shame, I had no intention of laying my heart at your feet. You once accused me of lust, and so it was. Will you forgive me? But here my heart is: I give it to you.' He flattened our joined hands against the gilded emblems on his breast. 'My love for you will never die, that I swear. Let your heart rest, Katherine. You are mine, and I am yours.'

He tilted his head, as if to read my expression.

I doubted that he could. My own thoughts were still in turmoil.

'But if remaining here is too hard for you to bear,' he continued, 'then you must leave me. I will not ask you to withstand more than you are able. My love for you is great enough to let you go, if that is what you wish, my dearest love. And whatever your decision, you will have my regard and my loyalty until the day that death claims me. You will have my love for all time.'

There it was, the offer to soothe my heart, even though, in denial of his words, his fingers linked with mine as if they would never release me. Was it not the supreme extent of his love? To give the choice back to me, with all his magnanimity.

And what of me?

Freeing myself from the embrace I had desired, creating a necessary distance, I looked at the man who offered me all I could ever dream of, seeing first the unquestionable authority of a royal Plantagenet in the ceremonial tunic, the jewelled chain, the layering of fur on silk damask, the sword still clipped to his side. And then the handsome man who drew all eyes, fine features, dark hair highlighted with russet tones, compelling eyes. And at last the man I knew when passion claimed him, a man with clever hands and outrageous pride but an understanding that few would guess at. He was the man I loved.

I saw it all. I heard the Duke's avowal of love. All I had ever wanted was here in the palms of his hands, offered to me. The depth of love that the Duke had once given to Duchess Blanche, that I had believed could never be mine, had been expressed so plainly for me—for me!—that I could not mistake it. It was like unwrapping a Twelfth Night gift, to discover a treasure I had coveted but believed I could never own. And there it was, shining and impossibly precious. The Duke of Lancaster loved me.

Raw astonishment, and a strange incapacity to absorb what I had desired for so long, still rendered me mute.

By now the Duke of Lancaster's eyes were alight with singular impatience.

'Tell me, Katherine. Tell me what you wish to do. Can you live here with me, in the same household as my wife, with some degree of peace of mind?' The lines between his brows became even more clearly etched. 'Don't, in God's name, tell me you need to borrow a book of French poetry to help you decide. I won't lend it. You must know your own mind by now.'

Which made me inhale sharply in exasperation. Had I

not lived with the knowledge of my love for him for so long, afraid to speak of it aloud? I had controlled my words, my responses, masking any emotion as dangerous as love behind light dalliance, for fear that he did not desire something so oppressive as love from me, and here was the Duke, in this moment of his own blinding awareness of love's power, demanding an instant response from me.

'No, I don't want a book of French poetry,' I said with enough asperity to catch his attention. 'And yes, I do know my own mind. I have known it longer than you, it seems. There's no need for you to berate me for being astounded by your ducal decree.'

'What have I said? Can you not love me enough?' he demanded, unconsciously arrogant, brows flattening ominously. 'Or will you go back to that benighted spot in Lincolnshire that owns your allegiance? By the Rood, Katherine! I think I should never have offered you your freedom, because you might just take it. I think, in fact, that I will rescind it and command you stay with me.'

'Command me? What of this love you have just discovered, that is strong enough to let me go if that is my wish?' With laughter in my heart as I acknowledged that the Duke would never change, I stepped forward to grip his sleeves. 'I cannot leave you. You know that I cannot,' I cried, the words tumbling from my lips. 'For I love you, John. I have always loved you, and I always will, however hard it is to live with you.' And then, when I allowed the exasperation to return and hold sway: 'How could you not know it? It must have been written on my face, in every kiss, every caress. I carried a son for you. How could you be so very blind?'

'I have no excuse to offer,' he replied tersely. 'You never said that you did.'

'Because I couldn't compromise you with a burden that

you might not want. But I say it now, so that you are blind no longer and must, perforce, carry the burden as I do, for I declare that my love for you is not a negligible offering. I love you, John. I return your love in equal measure. And I will live with you. Is that what you wish to hear?'

For a long moment he stared at me as I had stared at him.

'Tell me, John,' I ordered, as he had demanded from me.

And at last there was a smile in his eyes. 'I deserve your censure, don't I? I have been so very wrong, Katherine. Do you have the generosity of spirit to forgive my blindness?'

'Do you have to ask?'

The distance between us was closed, his hands clasping my shoulders.

'There will be no turning back for either of us. There can be no more insecurities between us. Yes, we will continue to hold fast to discretion, but my people will know that you are the woman I have placed at the centre of my life, because, before God, I realised tonight that my love for you is more precious than even the crown of Castile.'

Sliding smoothly, so that my heart quivered with it, the Duke's hands stroked slowly down the length of my arms to take possession of my hands, and I clung to them as he said all the words I had yearned to hear, savouring every nuance of this breathtaking proclamation of his love for me.

The Duke bared his soul to me that night.

'What shall I say to you? What troubadour's fripperies would you like to hear?'

'"I love you, Katherine," would be a good place to begin.'

And at last his face was illumined with laughter. 'I love you, Katherine.'

The fewest words. The simplest, most beautiful words. What a magnificent assertion it was, to fill all the cavities of my mind and heart with inexpressible delight. This was the value of his love, the fortune in gold coin he was returning to me. Joy unfurled its wings within my breast and took flight.

When he held out his hand in invitation, when, without hesitation, I placed mine there, with a little bow he led my towards my bed where the covers had already been drawn back, as if to celebrate a bridal. Turning me again, he began to unbraid my hair, then to untie the laces of my court dress.

'Would you have refused to let me go?' I asked.

'Yes.'

It was unequivocal.

'I am not your legal wife.'

Still I felt the need to say it, to force him to acknowledge in cold reasoning rather than haughty pride what we were doing. Constanza had never intruded so forcefully into our lives as she had that night. Every servant, every official, every member of the household at Kenilworth would know by the morning in whose bed the Duke of Lancaster had spent the night hours.

'But I will make it as if you were. This night. This moment.'

Laying aside my precious sleeves, folding the weight of my skirts, he proceeded to lavish kisses on my shoulders, my throat, a prelude to the delights that were to follow. Legality was not in my mind, nor the whisperings within the walls of Kenilworth. I had chosen to be with the man I loved beyond all things when I made that decision in the library at The Savoy, with all its promise of present passion but ultimate heartbreak. Now I had made that choice again, with pride, with calm acceptance and clear-sightedness.

'I will never leave you. Nor will you leave me,' the Duke said as the light of morning touched the sky.

'I will not. I will never leave you,' I repeated.

'Do you suppose love outlives death?' he asked.

'We will prove that it does.'

How love illuminates, so that we shine like the angels in heaven. My love for the Duke was strong enough to carry me through that day and all that followed. His for me, superbly, had been flung down like a gauntlet, and I rejoiced.

We would be together in happiness for as long as fate allowed.

Chapter Eleven

My dreams were full of blood, of vicious wounds and death, so drenched in it that I awoke with my heart pounding. My days were full of the darkness of loss. The Duke was campaigning, the silence between us heavy with terrible portent in this, my first real experience of the separation of war. Why had terror not struck me to the same measure when I had lived apart from Hugh? This was a grinding, gnawing fear, day after day. My whole existence seemed to be centred on every new rumour that reached us.

'What is happening in France? Is Castile invaded yet?'

If the Duchess demanded an answer once, she demanded it a dozen times a week.

And we had no reply to give. Not even I. I could have asked it myself, but that was not my way and I hugged my worries close. If I had posed the question, I would have asked: 'How does the Duke of Lancaster fare? Does he live?'

Yet I knew he lived as I wore out the steps to the turret and wall-walk at Tutbury, as I had once done at Kettlethorpe when the storms kept him pinned in the Channel. The open skies made it seem as if I could reach him if I allowed my mind the freedom to span the distance, for now he was much further away from me. The embarkation had gone according to plan, that much we knew. The Duke, as Captain-General, was in France, marching south with an army of six thousand men. How hard it was to live with any degree of equanimity in those months of not knowing. I longed for news, yet when we were alerted to the approach of a courier, I found myself tempted to hide in the cellars or take refuge with the kitchen maids where they stirred and ladled under the eye of Stephen of the Saucery.

Which would be worse, I pondered, as the weather continued to bless us and the countryside donned summer dress, to know or not know? That was the only thought that lived with me. Hope was better than despair. What would I do, if I were to hear a courier pronounce in heartless exactitude that the Duke was dead, struck down by some stray arrow or caught up in a fatal charge of cavalry?

Commanders were not exempt from death.

'Don't leave me,' I had said at the last moment of his departure when my courage fled.

Stern, severe, wholly the King's son, seemingly without compassion, his response put me in my place. 'I must go. You must not ask that of me.' Even in his newfound love for me he could be harsh when any obstacle appeared in his path, even one presented by me. 'You must know that you cannot always command my presence.'

He softened the reprimand with a smile and a brief salute: nevertheless it was a lesson I learned quickly, as I had learned so many, that a royal mistress must have the strength to live her own life separate from her lover. I never asked again. It would demean both of us.

But now, with the rumours not good, I found the distance

hard to stomach. I did not see the blossoming trees or hear the love-struck birds.

And then the couriers began to arrive, outstripping the rumours. They must, of course, be heard, their news dissected and assessed with due formality and detailed accounting in Constanza's audience chamber. How far were they from Castile; how long would it take to reach that Holy Grail? Was her despicable uncle Enrique of Trastamara still alive, still claiming her crown?

Only then could I take the hard-travelled rider aside into any quiet space I could find, to badger him with question after question as he consumed bread and ale before his return.

I cared little for the progress of the war, for the destructive march of the *grande chevauchée*, with its plunder, looting and killing. It mattered not to me how far the Duke might be from Castile, or whether Enrique could be driven out of his ill-gotten gains. England's victory might touch momentarily on my conscience and my interest, but it was the Duke who consumed my thoughts for I received no personal communication from him. How could I? I could not be his primary interest. I did not expect it. All I wanted was to see his return.

Not so the Duchess.

'That is good,' stated Constanza to every description of the march south by the English army and its final arrival at Bordeaux. 'Nothing will stop him now. He will destroy Enrique before the end of the year.' A smile lit her face. The Duchess did not often smile. I noticed how pale and thin she grew.

I did not smile at all.

'Is the Duke in good health?' I asked as the courier gulped his ale and crammed bread into his mouth. 'And the army.

Does the winter affect them? Do they suffer?' Because if the army suffered, so would the Duke.

His face set as he finished chewing. Constanza had not even asked.

'Badly, mistress.' He wiped the crumbs from his chin with his sleeve. 'Half the army dead for one reason or another. Floods and cold and ambush. They're starving...The Duke tries to remain in good heart. He'll not be in Castile this side of the grave,' he growled. 'She'll not see it—but so it is if you want my opinion.'

'And the Duke?'

'As hard-ridden as the next man. He's not eating either. Looks as if his belly's clapped to his spine.'

Which only served to double my fears. I gave him coin for his trouble.

'She's not bothered, is she?' he grunted as he rescued his gloves and satchel.

'She has other concerns,' I tried to make the excuse.

Nine months of separation. I lived through those days without him, anxiety treading in my footsteps, while Constanza bloomed at the prospect of her beloved Castile being restored to her. She closed her mind to the rumours that were increasingly hard to bear.

I did not.

Until the day that the Duke returned to England.

'*Un desastre!* All he promised me. All lost in futility.'

Constanza stormed from one end of the audience chamber to the other, cheeks no longer pale but flushed with heat. 'Why did he not engage in battle? What of England's reputation now? Trampled in the mire of failure!' She glared at the carrier of bad news. 'I do not wish to see your face. Leave me!'

I stood silently. The courier—a different one, a young man but with features imprinted with a similar brand of near-exhaustion—bowed himself discreetly out. I sensed that an eruption was imminent. Constanza could no longer pretend that the rumours of English failure were anything but the truth. So preoccupied was she that she failed to notice me, but I supposed eventually that she would. I wished I could join the suffering courier in the kitchen.

'He promised me he would force Enrique to surrender and hand over Castile. He promised me!' She tore the document—was it a letter from the Duke?—into two pieces. 'And what has he achieved? Nothing. An English army on its knees, begging for its bread. And now he has abandoned them.'

'Not abandoned, my lady.' Lady Alice attempted to distract with wise words.

'He is not there to lead them on, is he? Should he not be planning a new campaign? The days are lengthening.' It was April into the new year. 'Soon it will be May when the days are long and the campaigning is good. That I know. And where is he now? Come home to England to lick his wounds while I mourn the loss of my true inheritance.'

Tears streaked Constanza's cheeks as she turned on me, eyes fierce.

'Where is he?' she demanded.

'I do not know, my lady.' I had not even known that he was back in England. The letter passed to me by the young courier lay flattened against my skirts, still unread.

'I suppose it matters not to you whether he wins Castile or not.'

Constanza, unconscious of all dignity in her frustrated grief, fell to her knees, arms clutched around her belly as if struck down with intense pain. Her howl of nothing less than agony echoed from the walls. Surely her slight figure could not support such excess of humours. We leaped to her, to lift her, to comfort her, but Lady Alice waved me aside.

'Go,' she ordered. 'You'll do no good here. She'll not listen to reason. She will never listen to reason when Castile is the issue, and you won't help matters.'

I retreated, my relief at the Duke's return heady, only to be replaced by another, different grief. In the quiet of the schoolroom, where Philippa and Elizabeth, having read their catechism now wallowed in the romance of Lancelot and Guinevere, murmuring to each other, I unfolded the letter from the Duke with care as if the contents might snap and bite.

I am at The Savoy and have no plans as yet to travel
further. Come here to me. I find I have need of you.
The knowledge of your love has sustained me through
some of the worst weeks of my life.

The words caught at my heart, brief as they were. Brief and—despairing? Was that it? Although I tried to fathom the quality of his mind, despair was the only word that came to me from that bleak request. I could not imagine his being so low in spirits, his pride so smeared by the defeat. I had never seen desolation lie so heavily on him, unless it was after Blanche's death when black mourning had stalked him.

I think England will not forgive me this setback. The
King will not. I have undone all that he had achieved
in his glorious lifetime. And yet what more was there
to be done?
I will talk to you when you come.

I sat and stared at it, with only one thought in my head. I must go. As I had known I must since the courier's news, if the Duke asked me to go to him, because he had a need of me, then I must obey, for his sake as well as mine. How scathing must the criticism be, to hack away at the Duke's self-worth in this manner?

I must go to The Savoy.

'Is the letter from my father?' Philippa of Lancaster asked, her eyes, abandoning the tragic romance of Lancelot, now fixed on me with a degree of speculation.

I returned her regard. At fourteen years she was almost a woman, grown and aware that her own days as an unmarried girl were numbered. I should have known, from my own experience, how fast girls grew up at court.

'What does he say?' Elizabeth immediately asked, pushing aside the book and standing. 'Does he ask about us?'

'No,' I said as calmly as I could. 'Your father is at The Savoy. His thoughts are involved with matters of war.'

'Then why does he write to you, Lady Katherine?' Elizabeth's fair brows creased.

'He wants you to go to him, doesn't he?' Philippa said.

A statement that took me aback, and I found myself seeking wildly for a suitable reply, a reply that would cast neither their *magistra* nor their father into a contentious light. But before I could, Philippa was standing, curtsying, for there was Duchess Constanza in the doorway. She walked regally across the room, ignoring me, to see what it was that they were reading.

I waited, hands folded. I knew right well that the Duchess was not here to interest herself in the education of her step-daughters.

'Read me that,' the Duchess commanded, as if needing proof that they were learning anything of value under my care.

After a few lines, when both girls read with their usual fluency, she stopped it with a sharp gesture of her hand.

'Have you said your prayers today?'

'Yes, my lady,' Philippa replied, raising her eyes from her book with confidence.

'And studied your catechism?'

'Yes, my lady.'

'And you too?'

The Duchess directed her question at Elizabeth, but without waiting for an answer, spun round to face me. The tears were dried, her earlier fury contained, her features composed as if she had come to a hard-won decision. She pointed at the open letter that I had carelessly left to lie for all to see on the desk.

'Is that from him?'

'Yes, my lady.' It came to me that to prevent further recrimination I should have disguised it, but I replied without dissimulation because all I could recall was that throughout her intense disappointment, Constanza had not once asked after the Duke's well-being. I could not forgive her that.

'Where is he?' she demanded.

'At The Savoy.'

'For how long?'

What did she wish me to say? Was she concerned for him despite her condemnation of his lack of achievement? And then beneath the anger I saw the torment in her face and could only pity her. In spite of everything between us, this woman retained the power to rouse my compassion. All she had ever dreamed of was lost to her, all her plans destroyed: my conscience was touched.

'If you go to him at The Savoy,' I found myself saying, 'my lord will be able to explain what he intends to do.'

'Go to him? I? And why should I do that?'

'So that when my lord explains that the campaign will be renewed, your mind could be put at rest.'

Any compassion she had stirred in me was violently rejected. 'Explain? How can he say more than the facts prove? I will not go.' Irritably she kicked her skirts aside. '*You* go to him,' she snapped with excruciating bitterness. 'Help him to lick his wounds. That's what he wants, isn't it? That's why he wrote to you.'

I hesitated.

'He wants you with him, doesn't he?'

'Yes, my lady.' It was an unequivocal response to an unequivocal question, and I expected an eruption of her fury against me.

'He wants you, not me!'

The Duchess halted an arm's length from me. When she stretched out her hand I almost flinched, recalling the affair of the salt cellar, but it was only to pick up the letter, which she allowed to fall before she had read more than one line of it. Her regard had the hardness of flint within it. I expected her refusal, and she knew it.

'If I refuse to give you permission,' her voice grated, 'would you defy me?'

Which cast the decision fairly into my lap. To defy the Duchess so openly would fling her lack of authority over me in her face, and yet I did not hesitate. If Constanza had planned to forbid me, to exhibit my lack of power as the Duke's mistress compared with her own as his wife, she had failed. I knew where my life lay and I had within me the strength to stand before her without the degradation she had envisaged.

'Yes, my lady. I would defy you.'

I held her gaze as the air drew taut with tension between us, the girls sitting motionless as if they too were aware of the critical balance of power here. Here was a new layer in our relationship, wife and mistress, and, now certain of the Duke's love, I would not retreat.

'Can I stop you?' Constanza demanded, eyes wide and fathomless, fingers slowly clenching into fists at her side.

'No, my lady,' I said softly, my defiance coming readily to my lips. 'Not unless you resort to chains and a dungeon.'

Her laughter was brief and hard, lacking any humour.

'So what do I say?' She swung away from me, then back again, the motion of her skirts wafting the letter from table to floor. She paused, her tongue skimming over her lips. 'Go to him.'

So this was the decision she had come to. I could barely believe it, my body still tensed against her expected rebuttal.

'Do you not hear me?' she repeated. 'Go to him.'

There was the outcome I had hoped for, and relief swept aside every other emotion, but here was no time for triumph. I knew what it must have cost the Duchess to give me the victory. She had my compassion, even thought she would have despised it, but the only thought in my mind was that I need never fear the extent of her authority again.

'I am grateful.' I curtsied. 'Do I take any message, my lady?'

'I care not. I will not see him. He has no thought for me.'

Which caused justice to take a hold. 'But he does, my lady.'

'How can you say that? When he has banished my damsels to some distant place of confinement? So I am punished!'

I could think of no reply. The Duke had ordered the gossiping damsels to Nuneaton Abbey to learn discretion, but any

attempt on my part to defend the Duke was superfluous—
the Duchess marched out, leaving a palpable lightness in the
air of the schoolroom. I inhaled sharply, pondering what I
had achieved in my troubled relationship with Constanza,
until I grew aware of Philippa standing quietly beside me.

'Are you going to see my father?' Without asking permission, she picked up my discarded letter, and I allowed it,
since her tone was not judgemental. I let her be.

'Yes. I am.'

'Will you come back to us?'

It was a question that startled me in its maturity. Philippa
was old enough to understand the implications of that recent exchange, and condemn me for the choice I had made.
She was no longer the little girl who had clung to my skirts
when I had left the household after her mother's death. I
must tread carefully here if my authority over her, and our
affection, meant anything to me. I did not want to read disdain in her youthful regard, and so I tweaked the soft folds
of her coif, raising the glimmer of a smile.

'Do you want me to?' I asked lightly.

Philippa did not answer. Instead: 'My father says here
that he has missed you.' She looked down at the letter that
was still in her hand as if she had every right to read it. 'It
does not say that he loves you. I thought he would have written that.'

I stiffened, unable for a heartbeat to dredge up a reply,
then decided that she deserved my honesty, and I her disapproval if she chose to give it. Philippa could not be cushioned from what the household knew and she had the right
to respond as her growing mind saw fit, even if her disdain
hurt me.

'How do you know that he does?' I asked.

'I've seen him look at you.'

'And he gave you a merlin,' Elizabeth, who had joined her sister, added.

I raised my brows at a logic I could not follow. 'So he did. The Duke gives many presents. He is a very generous man.'

'Yes.' Philippa picked up the point, tapping her sister on her neatly braided head with the letter. 'He gives costly gifts. When he does not care about the receiver, he gives a silver cup, jewelled and with a cover. But to you he gave a merlin, because he knows you enjoy hunting.' Then, after reading to the end: 'My father says he wants you to be with him. Is it a sin, when my father is wed?'

I regarded her steadily. 'It is not what I would advise for you.'

'I think I would want a husband of my own,' Philippa agreed, returning to her seat and the exploits of Lancelot and Guinevere, another adulterous couple. 'But it must make you very happy. To be so greatly loved.'

Astonished at her calm acceptance of a relationship that might justifiably have stirred her to rank disapproval, I could think of nothing to say other than 'Yes, it makes me very happy.'

And, oh, it did. Deliriously happy, as it did in that moment. It had the power to stir the flames of the most intense joy that could be imagined when we were together. That it could cast me into a pit of despair when we were parted was a consequence of that love that I must accept.

But I said none of that.

I was packed and gone within the day, stopping only when the other Philippa, my sister—and far less accommodating of my disgraceful lifestyle—made her way to my side in the courtyard.

'Will this happen often?'

'When he needs me.' I was trenchant.

'And you need him.' How blistering she could be, in so few words.

'Yes. When I need him. When will I ever not need him?' Short of time, risking a rebuff, I stepped forward and hugged her before she could retreat. And since she did not, we kissed, a sisterly reconciliation of sorts.

'Give him comfort,' she whispered.

'I will.'

Constanza's acquiescence had instilled in me a new power, an assurance that seemed to grow within me with every breath I took, with every mile I covered towards The Savoy.

The Savoy was uncomfortably quiet to my mind, without children's voices, the servants solemn and soft-footed. As if there was an illness in the house. Or a death. I did not like it.

'Where is my lord the Duke?'

'In the library, my lady.'

'I will announce myself.'

I did not knock, and he did not hear as I opened the door, absorbed as was often the case. He sat at a table where the light fell on his work, but, unusually, it did not seem to me that he saw the documents in front of him or the contents of the coffer to his right. Rather his thoughts were far away, taken up with some planning, some regret perhaps. Some ghastly scene from events in Aquitaine. Always lithe and rangy, I thought he had shed weight that he could ill-afford, but then starvation was no respecter of rank. I walked towards him until I stood at his side as once before. And as on that first time, I placed my hand on his shoulder.

For a long, wordless moment his gaze held mine, in its glitter a great distancing and a wealth of grief and disap-

pointment that wounded my heart. The failed campaign had
touched him heavily.

'John...' I said. There was nothing else to say.

Then his self-command was back in place, and he smiled
as if for me to be there with him was the most natural thing
in the world, the most looked-for blessing. As if there were
no restrictions on either our movements or our loyalties,
and in the face of such a welcome I felt tears gather in my
throat, and my heart seemed to be so swollen with love for
him that it filled my breast so that I could scarcely breathe.

'I wanted you to come.'

'Yes.' I took the liberty of touching his cheek with my
fingertips, the gentlest of caresses. 'If you recall, you ordered me to do so.'

How sure I felt in my decision. Constanza had given me
leave, not just by her dismissal but by her rejection of the
Duke's suffering in her cause. Her lack of compassion, her
vicious criticisms of all he had done, her lack of interest in
his present state, had presented to me the freedom I needed
to leave Tutbury and be openly with him here. None of which
I explained. The Duke would not see my need for permission, or even necessarily understand that guilt still had a
habit of perching like a hungry raptor on my wrist. Sometimes I was impatient with that wily bird. But Constanza's
condemnation of her husband had ensured that the raptor
took wing: I was free of conscience.

The Duke had captured my hand, and was engaged in
kissing his way across my knuckles in what could be con-
strued, my fluttering heart announced, as light-hearted seduction.

'I will listen, if you want to tell me how bad it was,' I offered, still uncertain of his mood.

'No.' How wrong I had been, for there was suddenly no

control at all in his face. Nothing at all of light-heartedness. Only rampant desire in the rawness of his voice. 'This is not the time for exchanging views on English policy.'

Standing abruptly, arms sliding around my waist, he clasped me close, his mouth hot and demanding on mine.

'You will stay.' A command.

'As long as you need me.'

'For ever.' He framed my face in his hands. 'Before God, I want you, Katherine. I want you now.'

I shivered at his expression, at the slide of his fingers against my throat before he all but dragged me to the chamber I used at The Savoy, delighting me with his concern for my comfort in familiar surroundings despite the hot emotion that drove him.

'When did you last sit at ease and laugh and talk of inconsequential matters?' I asked, striving to keep the moment free from high drama.

'Laughter? What's that?' He was already loosening his belt, sitting to unlace his boots with urgent fingers.

'Do you realise how long it is since we were last together?' I asked.

'I'm sure you will tell me,' he replied, actions governed by intense need.

'Almost a full year.'

'Then we will celebrate our reunion. We have spent enough time apart. We will spend no more. Stop talking, and come to me.'

Then high drama overtook us, and neither of us was in a mood to deny it as the Duke stripped me to my shift, and then took even that from me, trailing his fingers over the silvered lines of past child-bearing. They were not too disfiguring in the soft glow of costly candles whose flickering hid the worst ravages, and he knew them well anyway. I did not flinch from his appraisal.

It was a reunion of passion, tumbled and heated with no time for soft seduction. I had no need of it, and the Duke was stirred by an inner need to re-own me. It was a statement of love and longing and joy in being together again, a rejection of the failure and despair across the sea. Pain and loss were fast subsumed beneath the fire of lust that used no words, no endearments, nothing but the slide of flesh against flesh, hot kisses on even hotter skin. We feasted on each other, a glorious celebration in the end, to prove that love could conquer all and give relief from anguish.

What was there to say? We were together and our love could burn as brightly as the sun at noon, or as softly as the lapping of a kitten's tongue.

He made me laugh anyway, and I reciprocated, my lips and fingertips explored anew the ducal skin. He made me sigh too for notwithstanding the driving force, the Duke sought my pleasure as well as his own.

'Allow me to caress the arches of your delectable feet. I think I have neglected your feet.'

I was devastated by his success. My whole body was light with exultation.

'You cannot imagine how I have missed you,' he said, pinning me to the bed.

'Of course not,' I agreed. 'I have been far too occupied to give you a second thought.'

My eyes were wet with tears, which he kissed away with tenderness. He understood all that I would not tell him. He knew how hard it was for women to be left behind and imagine the worst.

'My love for you knows no end,' I informed him when we at last took time to draw breath.

'For which I thank God,' he replied, and he was smiling at last.

Yet although I slid into some species of exhausted sleep in his arms, I knew that, as unconsciousness claimed me, he lay awake.

I woke to find him gone from the bed, but he had not left me. In shirt and hose he was stretched out on the low window seat, back propped against the stonework, a little pottery bowl in his hand. I thought that he was at ease, until I realised that the scene beyond the window did not take his attention. So I had not dragged his mind from the loss of English life for long, or from whatever it was that had now placed its hand on him. Grief, I would have said, studying the stark lines. I lay and watched him for a little while, shocked to see such torment. He was eating steadily from the bowl, as if the delicacy would assuage his worry as well as his appetite.

Eventually when I could remain apart no longer and the dish was empty—how could I enjoy my own happiness when he was clearly bleeding from some inner wound?—I wrapped one of the linen sheets round me since no other garment came to hand and walked slowly to stand at his side. But there I was even more disturbed, for although he acknowledged me with an arm sliding comfortably around my waist, a mask instantly fell into place to hide the rank despair of minutes ago. The mask was good, the muscles of his face relaxed and I followed his lead, calmly relieving him of the dish, placing it on the floor beside us, because I dare not tap the ugly depths of that distress.

Kneeling beside him, resting my head against his shoulder and feeling the tension there that the mask could do nothing to hide, I changed my mind.

'Was it very bad?' I asked. I thought he needed to speak of it after all. He did not resist.

'It was bad. Our army suffered beyond belief.' Then: 'I hear no good of what I did.' Straight to the point, as ever.

'No.' I could not deny it. The loss of men and land had come in for scathing criticism, the Duke's reputation ravaged.

'My policy in France has been stripped bare. Once we ruled a mighty Empire stretching from Calais to Bordeaux. And now we hold the towns but no land to connect them. Our Empire is no more and I failed to bring England a victory...' He looked away towards the window, as if he could absorb the grumbling complaints from the London streets even at this distance. 'What do you think?'

'How can I judge?' I combed my fingers through his hair. Nothing I could say would make matters any better. He would have to face his demons, as the burden demanded by royal blood, but I would stay at his side as he faced them. He would not be alone.

'I am of a mind...' He hesitated. 'I think I was wrong...'

'And I never thought to hear you admit that.' I essayed a little humour.

And indeed the faint remnants of a frown were smoothed out by a wry twist of his lips. 'Do you accuse me of arrogance, Lady Katherine? Many would.' And then with a lift of a shoulder: 'What value is there for England in such a war, to hold fast to territories so far away and surrounded by those who would take them from us?'

Such an admission astonished me, and he saw it.

'Should I not admit to it, when I am coming to believe that it is true? What do we gain, except a drain on our wealth and the death of our soldiery? The Pope is calling for negotiations and a lasting peace. I think we should do it.'

'It will not be well-received,' I ventured.

'I care not. It's a storm I must weather. I am not popular now, and the losses at Bordeaux will bring more invective down on my head, but who can harm me?' The Duke's sardonic smile became even more pronounced. 'Consider the advantages. Peace will bring an increase in trade, lower taxes. We cannot continue as we are with this vast drain of money and taxation so high that it all but beggars our merchants. The stain on England's reputation is a wound on my soul.'

'Parliament will not support peace with France,' I suggested.

'God's Blood! I'll be damned if I let Parliament dictate my policy.'

Which promised no good for the future when foreign affairs and finance must collide. 'Will the King agree? To peace-making?' I asked, to divert into calmer channels.

'I must persuade him. Since my brother is too ill to hold the reins himself it's for me to take up the banner of England's future. I'll do it readily, with or without Parliament behind me. They'll follow me if they know what's good for them.'

And as I felt a single, solid beat of his heart beneath my hand, my presentiment that this was not the full cause of his wretchedness was enforced as the Duke turned his face against my hair and, beneath my hands, in his laboured breathing, I felt the earlier grief rush back in a torrent.

'John...' I whispered aghast.

He shook his head but I persisted. When he might have pulled away, I held onto his shoulders so that he must look at me. It was all I could give him. And by some strange female intuition, I realised what it must be to make such pain live in his eyes. The breath continued to shudder in his lungs.

'It's the Prince, isn't it?'

'He's dying.'

My heart throbbed with reflected pain. His much-loved older brother, his hero, the perfect prince.

'I doubt my brother will live to see our father die.' And then because the pain had spread its tendrils much further: 'What will England do with a child king? I doubt Richard will be more than ten years when the crown drops into his lap. What then?'

'I will tell you what then,' I replied with smooth urgency, fastening my hands tight around his wrists. 'You will stand at Richard's side. You will support and guide him until he is of an age to rule in his own right. You will do it for your father and your brother and because it is your duty to your name and to England. That is what will happen.'

I could not reassure him about the Prince's health, but I could paint a bright picture of the future in which his role would be so very important. I pressed my lips against his brow as I felt at last an infinitesimal softening in his shoulders.

'You see it very clearly,' he observed.

'I see the truth,' I replied. Here was no place for doubts, and so I lightened my tone. 'Would you argue the point with me? I don't advise it.'

And the Duke's eyes were now clearer, and his mouth curved in a vestige of a smile. 'My thanks, Lady de Swynford.'

'My pleasure, my lord,' I responded archly, still intent on distraction because I could do no other. 'And I have to say, you have eaten all my sweet pears.'

'I have?'

I nudged the empty bowl with my toe. 'What do I demand in reparation? I swear you have as great a sweet tooth as young Henry, and I've never seen any boy clear a dish of marchpane as fast as he can.'

He laughed, a little rough at the edges, but still a laugh. It was not from his heart, and I had perforce to accept the limitations on my powers. It was his brother who weighed heavily in his mind, and I had to allow it as I acknowledged that I could do nothing to lift the burden, and yet my heart was steadier, for the Duke had opened a new door for me, one that I had never been allowed to step through before, allowing me the right to trespass in his own emotions and fears. But only as far as he saw fit. All I could do, with gratitude that he gave me freedom to know the thoughts that troubled him, was distract and wrap him around with my love when he needed it. It was my pleasure and my heart's delight to do so. I knew that he laid that burden down before no one else.

Was it not a precious milestone in the journey that we were travelling together?

'You should sleep now, John,' I said.

And he did, deep and dreamless. For the first time, I thought, for many nights. I lay awake to watch over him. Was that not the essence of love? It was for me. Sometimes it was all I could do for him. And was that not another lesson for me to learn? I had had no recognition of the inner strength I would need to draw on as the truth of our relationship was exposed. Now as our love grew, I needed to be strong for him too. For who else was there for him to turn to in grief or despair?

He could turn to me, and I would answer all his needs.

It had its repercussions, our reconciliation at The Savoy. When the Duke left Tutbury, en route to London in August to commemorate the sixth anniversary of Duchess Blanche's death, he held me close in a final embrace, for I was not to accompany him. His arms were firm, his lips soft, then he raised his head and looked at me. And looked again, trailing the palm of his hand over the panels of my close-cut gown.

I drew in and held my breath, perhaps still a little nervous.

'Are you breeding?' he asked.

'Yes.'

'When?'

'At the start of the new year.'

'Does it please you?'

'Yes.'

'It pleases me too.'

He kissed me, lingeringly gentle but with the underlying passion that was now part of my life. I smiled. I would never again need to flee in fear that the Duke would reject me and this new child. Our love would stand firm against everything.

Chapter Twelve

July 1376: The Savoy Palace, London

I sat at Blanche's bedside. How had I not realised how small she was despite the passage of years? Philippa and Elizabeth, particularly Philippa, were now grown to be young women, but Blanche was still my little girl. She was twelve years old. The hangings of the bed dwarfed her, the pillows seemed far too large to support her frail neck.

She had the dreaded sweating sickness.

I remembered Henry with similar symptoms, here at The Savoy as we were now, how he had responded with all the vigour of youth to the powerful mix of leaves and potions I had administered. It should have soothed me to recall his fast recovery, but anxiety over my daughter's health built, stone upon stone, until it presented a rampart against any comfort. I had been here at her side for five days now but saw no improvement in her condition as she lurched from frenzied delirium to fractious mutterings, the bed linens soaked with the heat of her poor body.

Administering another dose, I settled a little as Blanche fell into a more restful sleep. Perhaps this time the fever would not return. Her forehead was cooler, her breathing less laboured. I thought it was evening, but I could not tell. Nor did it matter. Nothing mattered but Blanche's ability to recognise me again. To sit up and laugh and demand her singing finches to keep her company.

Brother William Appleton, the Duke's own physician, entered quietly, hands tucked in his sleeves, to stand at my shoulder.

'How is she?'

'Better, I think.'

'I'll watch her for you. You need to rest.'

'I cannot.'

'You can. You will, if you desire to bear this child safely, my lady.'

For I was breeding again. My ankles were swollen and my back ached. Very near my time, I was burdened with this third Beaufort child as I had been burdened with no other.

I went to my room but I could not rest, and was back at Blanche's side within the hour.

'I will sit,' I promised. 'I won't exert myself.'

'Only worry yourself to death.' Brother William pressed a hand lightly on my shoulder. 'You are exhausted. The Duke will not thank me if I do not take care of you too.'

I tried to smile. 'I'll take no harm. Pray for me. Pray for Blanche.'

'I will, of course.'

He brought me a cup of wine and left me, with dire warnings, to my night watch.

Where are you, John?

It was a silent cry from my heart.

I knew where he was, dealing with a recalcitrant Parliament and a failing King. Despite the much-vaunted peace policy between England and France, unsteady as it was, England had once more a need for an army, and Parliament, faced with a demand to consent to high taxes, was flexing its muscles under its ambitious new Speaker. This man, Peter de la Mare, had the Duke in his sights for all the ills of England. A scapegoat was needed and who better to target? The Duke was considered to be too high-handed, too powerful, too intolerant, usurping the royal power that should have been wielded by the King, even though King Edward, his mind afflicted, was incapable of wielding any such power.

So the Duke would be striving to keep his temper, or perhaps not even striving at all in the face of such outspoken opposition. A man renowned for his ability to negotiate between hostile parties, he would not always choose his words with discretion. All I knew for certain was that he was not here with me, when I most had need of him.

Never had I felt so alone, for Agnes was at Kettlethorpe and the Duke so terribly preoccupied. He had not returned to The Savoy since the day before Blanche had slid from her knees in the chapel into a miserable little heap of flushed face, aching limbs and raging fever.

'Hush now.'

The effect of the henbane, to cool a fever, was beginning to wear off, so that Blanche became restless again, struggling against the bed linen. My holding her hand and speaking to her, trying to calm her, had no effect. Although her eyes were open, they held no recognition for either my face or my voice.

'Hush now. Drink this. You will be well. Philippa and Elizabeth miss you and ask for you. They are waiting for you to be well.'

She drank the potion but her expression was wild, her face and chest mottled with heat as I bathed her tortured limbs, the cool, sharp scent of lavender pervading the room.

'Sleep now.'

It calmed her, but Blanche seemed to be fading away before my eyes, her skin translucent in the light of the single candle beside the bed. My fingers moved over the coral beads of my rosary as I petitioned the compassion of the Blessed Virgin who knew all the travails of motherhood.

In the end I fell asleep, my body awkward, my cheek turned on the coverlet beside her. My rosary fell to the floor.

Hours later I woke in a state of confusion, unsure of my surroundings, before it all swept back to squeeze my heart dry. I looked around, thinking that the physician had returned. And then at the bed.

Blanche lay still. Impossibly still.

I stood, abruptly, clumsily, my hands in the small of my back where my muscles were taut and stiff. Had the fever broken at last?

And then the absolute breathless silence pressed down on me, filling the room, filling me. Blanche lay unmoving, all the heated anguish of past days now gone, her face pale, eyelids closed, her lashes spiked and fragile on her cheeks. She might have been asleep, so perfect, so beautiful her features. I touched her cheek with the back of my fingers to prove my fears.

She was not asleep.

I had lost her. I had lost my daughter.

Holy Mother. What do I do now?

My mind cried out with the agony of any woman losing her first-born child. There was nothing I could do. I sat on the bed so that I could lift her gently into my arms, as if she might still wake and fling her arms around me, telling me what she had done that day that had given her joy. She did not stir. How light she was after the days of fever. What a beautiful young woman she would have been. Blanche Swynford, much-loved damsel to the ducal daughters. Incomparable daughter of Hugh and Katherine de Swynford.

'I am so very sorry, Hugh,' I murmured against her hair. 'I could do nothing for her. I could not save her.'

My Blanche, my lovely Blanche was dead.

I laid her back on her pillows, combing her hair, straightening the neck of her shift so that it lay in a seemly fashion on her chest. And then I sat, my hands clasped, my eyes fixed on Blanche's face. I could not weep. It was as if all my tears were frozen in an endless sea of ice. If I had stayed awake, could I have saved her? Could I have anchored her to this life, until the fever had worn itself out? But I had not, and she had been taken from me when I had been unaware.

The hours stretched emptily, wearily before me. I had lost my daughter and the man I needed could not be with me, and therefore I must bear my grief alone. Was I not capable of that? I dried my tears and went to arrange for my daughter's body to be carried to the chapel.

I was desolate. I was beyond desolation. I would carry my grief with fortitude.

It was two days before the Duke returned to The Savoy.

'Before God, I'll not have it! Do they think I'll bow the knee to their demands?' he blazed, exhibiting a royal temper in vituperative flow. 'Do they think they are kings of this realm, in their pride and arrogance?'

He flourished a document like a war banner.

He did not know about Blanche. No one had told him.

'Do they not know my lineage?' he continued, casting the offending missive into the fire. 'Would they dare to take it into their heads to curb royal power? The effrontery of it. I'll have de la Mare's balls stuffed with rosemary on a platter. Our Parliament complains when our army fails, yet will not grant the funds to make a campaign across the sea viable. You can't have one without the other, as they well know. It's merely a damned ruse to attack me and bolster their own authority.'

The Duke had entered one of his private chambers at The Savoy—where I was sitting in discomfort, in spite of cushions and a footstool—with the force of a winter storm. Now he prowled the length of the room, much like one of his hunting dogs, out for blood. This was not the man who had wooed and beguiled me. This was the Duke, hard-eyed and driven, plotting revenge against those who questioned his right to use the power invested in him with the decline of the King. I remained silent for he was in no mood to accept advice.

'Those mealy-mouthed members of Parliament have no authority other than that given to them. God rot the lot of them!'

I abandoned the embroidered panel on my cumbersome lap. What matter that the girdle was incomplete? I would not be wearing it for some weeks yet.

'They dare to accuse me of corruption! Parliament is dissolved. I'll have no more of it. And God save us from sanctimonious prating priests,' the Duke continued, with no apparent recognition of my silence.

And I knew all about this too. Thomas Walsingham, a priest with a gimlet eye and a vicious pen. A man seeing himself as an upholder of God's morality on earth, intent on bringing the Duke down. Were not England's losses in

France to be piled at the Duke's door? Walsingham did not mince his words either.

Setting aside my embroidery, I reached to the coffer at my side and poured a cup of ale and held it out.

'John…'

Without thanks the Duke took it as he strode past me and continued to prowl. 'Do you know what he's done?' The Duke's eyes were alight with fury. 'He's stirred up the old slander all over again.'

I had not the energy to ask which one, but listlessly picked up my stitchery again. He told me anyway.

'I only arranged the murder of Blanche's sister Matilda. I poisoned Matilda of Lancaster, by the Rood. So that the whole of the Lancaster lands fell to Blanche and so to me. Would I do that?' he growled, coming at last to a halt in front of me. 'Would Blanche have agreed to wed me if I had done away with her sister?' he demanded.

It was all too much.

I took a deep breath and, tossed the fine cloth to the floor at my side.

'John, I need to tell you—'

'They are saying that I already have my eye on the throne since my father is sinking fast by the day,' he stated, full of ire. 'When the King dies I'll snatch it from my nephew, they say. Did I not give my solemn oath to my dying brother that I would be loyal to his son as king? That I would serve Richard as his friend and counsellor?'

I was so weary. 'Richard is only nine years old,' I observed. 'No older than Henry. Is it surprising that they will suspect you of naked ambition if you stand beside him?'

'Richard is the heir. Would I oust him?' Heated emotion had him in its thrall again. 'Do you of all people believe such rumours too?'

And it was as if the emotion poured over me as well. 'No! I of all people do not. I of all people at this precise moment do not care overmuch!'

He stared at me. 'I would like to think that I had your support.'

I could not force Blanche's name past my teeth. 'You don't need my support,' I snapped back. 'You have enough confidence for both of us!'

Uncontrollable tears welled up again in my throat from what seemed a bottomless source. My mind was too sore to be compassionate. My bright, loving Blanche was dead, and all the Duke could think about was Parliamentary disobedience. My breath caught. Blanche, my darling Blanche, lost to me. All that sparkling promise wiped out by some nameless fever that would not respond to common henbane or doses of wood sorrel. There was no room in my mind for politics and power-brokering when my daughter lay cold and still in the chapel. I stood in the middle of the room, my mind in turmoil, any pleasure I might expect to feel that he had at last come to me refusing to settle, flitting round the edges of my thoughts so that I could not grasp it.

I knew that I must be strong enough to contain my grief, not allowing it to encroach on this moment, but I could not. It threatened to overwhelm me. Perhaps it was due punishment for my great sin. Had Blanche been taken in penance for my immorality? I shivered in the upheaval of my despair.

'And of course, our august members of Parliament claim to believe every word if it,' he continued. 'And that I wed Blanche only for her inheritance. Next they'll be arguing over that old dispute that I am not my father's son. A changeling, by God! Who would dare accuse my lady mother of infidelity! Do I not have more than a resemblance to the King? But it has its uses as an arrow to loose at me. As a royal bastard, was I not doubly disloyal to Blanche, not fit to wed her? So I duped Blanche into...'

Blanche...

I burst into tears.

'Katherine...?' For the first time I thought that he truly noticed me.

'Blanche is dead. My daughter is gone from me and nothing will bring her back.'

Pressing my fingers against my lips I ran as well as I was able from the room.

I took refuge on the wall-walk, even though the effort to climb the steps took my breath, where the wind from the Thames would cool my cheeks. Could such a loss ever be overcome? I knew that I must learn to be thankful for her life, and not weep whenever the name Blanche was mentioned. When I heard footsteps loping after me and recognised the ownership, I braced my shoulders but did not turn.

'Forgive me, Katherine. I did not know.'

His voice was even, with none of his earlier anger.

'There is nothing to forgive. You have your own loss to mourn,' I sniffed.

For Prince Edward had succumbed at last to his endless sufferings. We had all been in mourning robes in that year. Even worse, the Duke going to Bruges to attend peace negotiations had taken Constanza with him where she had given birth to their much-longed-for and prayed-over son, only to have him die within a few short weeks.

A unbearable time of death and loss, but for me Blanche outweighed all.

The Duke kept a discreet distance at my side in so public a place.

'I can't comfort you. Not with every eye on us.'

'I don't expect you to,' I replied, drying my tears. My mood was as fragile as my waist was thick.

'I am so very sorry, my dearest love.' And abandoning all decorum, he pulled me into the corner of the wall-walk where the steps led down, pushing me to sit on the top one. Disturbingly, he chose to sit below, his back against the wall, holding my hands. If any of his household saw us, he ignored it as his eyes searched my face.

'I feel your anguish, and I am so sorry. For the death of your daughter. For my own concerns that I cannot push aside,' he said with some difficulty, before lowering his forehead to rest against our clasped hands. His face might be hidden from me, but his compassion was as soft as a new snowfall, wrapping around me. 'I regret the comfort I can't give you. I regret my own anger that drives me, even when I know that your loss is even greater than mine in that it is new and raw. I knew my brother Edward was dying. Forgive me, Katherine.'

I rested my cheek against his hair. How complex was this man I was privileged to love. From hot temper to infinite tenderness; from stormy pride to deliberate abasement.

'Blanche was my godchild, and I mourn her with you.'

The Duke stood and lifted me, his lips warm against my forehead, his gaze full of all the grief that lay as hard as granite within me. When I began to weep again, he drew me into his arms and at last I rested there for they were a defence against the world. I luxuriated in them. He was mine again, for those few moments, and he gave me the comfort I needed. The rock inside me began to melt.

'I am afraid,' I said, 'of your enemies who use every means to attack you.' I had never admitted it before, even to myself. 'Of the wedge it drives between us, because you are taken up with Peter de la Mare and I am too irritable to accept that…' My breath hitched.

And so he finished the thought for me. 'That private grief must step back in the face of England's demands. We mourn the ones we love, but sometimes we cannot choose the time or place.'

'Yes. That's it.' It was a heavy burden. 'I am afraid I will forget my daughter. That I will not mourn her as I should.'

Which made him kiss away the tears. 'You will never forget Blanche. Nor need you be afraid for me. I will win the day against de la Mare.' He pressed my head gently against his shoulder. 'You are too tired for this, my dear love. What you need to do is to rest.'

'But what if…?'

'We will not talk of it. I will deal with Walsingham and de la Mare. I've a mind to show de la Mare the interior of one of my dungeons.' He smiled fiercely as if enjoying the prospect of a lengthy incarceration until, when I sighed, he fixed his mellowing eye on me once more. 'You will go to your chamber. You will order your maid to pack what you need.' And when I shook my head against his restraining hand: 'It will be better if I don't have to worry about you too. Sometimes, my love, we both know that it is better if we are apart. This is one of those times.'

Which I had to accept. We could not be together, but our love would never be dashed against the rocks of volatile politics.

'I'll go to Kettlethorpe.' I surrendered, reluctantly, to good sense. 'I need to take Blanche home.'

I did not wish to. I did not wish to be separate from him. My spirits had never been as low.

'No, this is what you will do.' The note of command was

unsparing beneath the gentleness. 'I need to know you are somewhere safe, away from the politics and the threats of riots in the city. I don't want you where you cannot defend yourself, and Kettlethorpe has no defences. You will go to The Countess of Hereford at Pleshey Castle.'

I had an acquaintance with the Countess of Hereford, but had no wish to take up residence with her. 'I don't wish to go to Pleshey. I'd rather go to Kettlethorpe.'

The Duke remained unswerving, even as he dried my tears with my oversleeve and kissed my sullen mouth.

'What you want has no bearing on the matter. You will go to Pleshey because I say it shall be, and you will give birth to this child in comfort and safety. Countess Joan will welcome you in my name, and you, my dear love, will be pleased to be there. I will arrange for Blanche's burial beside her father at Kettlethorpe. It is decided.'

I went to Pleshey Castle. The Duke kissed me and dispatched me with a substantial retinue, arranging highhandedly for Agnes in the company of John and Henry to join me there, as he arranged for Blanche to go home for the last time, where she would lie in peace beside the heart of her father. The Countess, as a close friend of long standing and blood relative of the Duke, opened her doors to me with a quizzical expression as she took stock of my figure.

'When are you planning to give birth to this child?'

'Two months ago, I think,' I replied, heaving myself from the litter.

Countess Joan smiled at me. 'Come and be at ease. I will look after you.'

It was there that I gave birth to a daughter, who emerged into the world with placid acceptance of her change of surroundings and predictably dark russet hair. I called her Joan in honour of the Countess who allowed me to mourn Blanche on her broad shoulder and kept me abreast of affairs beyond our walls when John could not, for King Edward had died, sinking the court into mourning and keeping the Duke fixed in London.

'When you return, all will be well,' Countess Joan announced with all her years of experience of court affairs. She set the cradle containing Joan rocking with one practised foot as we sat together in the nursery. She had two daughters of her own. 'It's a new reign and everyone's of a mind to rejoice and look for new beginnings with a handsome young king at the helm. John's being astute in his dealings with his enemies, and they're of a mood to come to terms with the man who stands at the side of the new King.'

It was a good omen. Had the Duke not knelt at the opening of the new Parliament at Westminster to swear his allegiance to King Richard, denying any charge of treason or cowardice on his part? Had not the peers of the realm and Parliament received the Duke with honour and begged him to be comforter and councillor to King Richard? Even the City of London asked pardon from the Duke for their past criticisms. The Duke was safe, restored to favour, no longer threatened by vicious Walsingham or self-seeking de la Mare.

My mind steadied into serenity with the birth of my new child, my world tilting back so that my thoughts steadied and I was comfortable again. Blanche would always remain a scar on my heart but I would learn to bear my grief with gratitude for the loving child she had been. I would never forget her. All my fears for the Duke were unfounded. How foolish I had been. Even knowing that he had imprisoned

Speaker de la Mare in Leicester Castle with no hope of a trial did not disturb me to any degree.

And when the Duke wrote: *Come to me at Kenilworth*, I went.

April 1378: Leicester

It was one of those soft spring days that only April can produce, as if by magic, after the bleakness of a cold March. Shower-clouds had just cleared and the pale sun turned all the drops on thatch and wood and budding leaf to crystal. Even the rubies sewn into the Duke's gauntlets and pinned to his cap were dulled in comparison.

We were in Leicester together, one of the precious moments we would snatch before the Duke must turn his mind once more to English policy abroad and the continuing education of the young King Richard, and I to the building chaos that was Kettlethorpe and my trio of Beaufort children once more ensconced there.

I had never been as content as I was that day in Leicester, for were we not together? My happiness was so intense that I could taste it, sweet as a new honeycomb on my tongue. Since my enforced sojourn at Pleshey I had learned to live from day to day, to savour every moment, and today it was enough to be with him. He would be away at war in France before the end of the summer, and there would be no more idylls for us to linger in. The English fleet had already sailed from England a week ago with the purpose of crushing the fleets of France and Castile, and the Duke must follow.

But for now, I could be with him, confident in my position at his side even as I acknowledged the undercurrent of desolation that was always present, and always would be. I knew I could never experience true happiness, simply because of the life I had chosen for myself. There would always be that piercing grief that I could never have a permanence in his life.

I found myself smiling, if a little sadly. How remarkably innocent I had been when I had thought that I could simply step into the role of mistress, enjoy the glory of being with him, and not have to pay any price of merit. How irresponsible. I had thought I could bask in our love without penalty. Now I was worldly-wise enough to see that there would always be a cost, and I accepted it, even the rank disapproval of the Duchess of Gloucester who turned a very obvious cold shoulder against me, making no effort to hide that she despised me. Did she not have royal blood in her aristocratic veins? I, of course, was nothing but a commoner in her eyes. I had become used to her superior condescension by now. I was no longer wounded.

'My Lady of Swynford?'

I blinked in the sunshine, recalled to my immediate surroundings. It was the Duke, regarding me across a motley of merchant hoods and felt caps and stalwart wool-clad shoulders.

'Forgive me, my lord,' I replied formally as I gathered up my reins, which I had allowed to slacken dangerously, and rearranged the voluminous folds of my skirt. We must be preparing to move off. I sighed a little at the prospect of more business.

Instead, he pushed his mount towards me until we sat side by side, and he lowered his voice, eyes appreciative on my face. 'Where were you?'

'Far away, I'm afraid.' In fact, with my daughter Margaret, who, to her own satisfaction, had taken the veil at Barking Abbey. It was an honour and I was proud for her.

'But not so far that I cannot reach you. Can we escape

from this endless discussion of town rules and regulations, do you suppose?' There was a jaunty air to the Duke's manner, and his less than discreet comment surprised me. Impeccable as his courtesy usually was in company, he had grown weary of the merchants' demands and the Mayor's persistence over the contentious issue of taxes. Indeed, he waved them aside with casual indifference, blind to their annoyance, careless of the official disfavour of his high-handed rejection of their pleas to pay less. 'I am finished here,' he said, and turning from them to me: 'Unless you, my lady, are of a mind to purchase a basket of oysters?'

As he gestured towards the woman who advertised her wares with a voice worthy of a royal herald, I saw the gleam in his eye.

'I might,' I replied lightly, not averse to a flirtatious exchange since he was obviously of a mind to respond, even as I was uncomfortable with his ability to make enemies when the mood was on him.

'Can I persuade you not to?' Now the gleam was accompanied by a grin.

My heart melted, my discomfort evaporated. The Duke was his own man and would order his affairs with the same nerveless assurance that he always did. As for me, what other woman in the length and breadth of the country could claim to own the total love and adoration of the one man who filled her own heart? Was there any woman as fortunate as I? I thought longingly of the island of peace, isolated behind the formidable walls of the castle. We would eat together—probably not oysters. Walk in the gardens. Talk of whatever came into our minds. The Duke would read to me, if I asked him, weaving the enchantments of the old legends in his beautiful voice, which he now used to my persuasion.

'I say we should make our apologies, before the Mayor

can find some other matter to claim my attention. Such as the state of the town midden.'

He turned his horse towards the castle, saluting a farewell to the Mayor and aldermen who still sat in a knot of frustrated corporate business, and I kicked my mare to follow him. Recalcitrant animal that she was, she promptly balked at a cur that snarled round her legs, and planted her feet. The ducal retinue came to a chaotic stop behind me.

'Will you move, you foolish animal!' I demanded, aware of my flushed cheeks as I used my heels to no effect.

Without a word, the Duke turned his horse about to come to my aid. He grasped my bridle near the bit and hauled the mare into a spritely gait to keep up with him.

'I'll give you an animal with more spirit,' he offered. 'This one goes to sleep on every possible occasion.'

He kept the bridle in his hand, forcing her to keep pace with her companion, as we wound through the streets, through the townsfolk busy about their own affairs, towards the castle; the Mayor, aldermen, cleric and our own retinue followed behind.

'Have you decided where you will go next week?' the Duke asked as we manoeuvred around a woman with her baskets of apples, small and wizened from the previous year's harvest.

'Yes, to Kettlethorpe. To see how the rebuilding is progressing. I may have a hall fit to receive visitors by the end of the summer. And to see the children, of course.'

The Beaufort children. For a moment I felt the weight of his regard full of compassion for me, the brief pressure of his fingers on my hand, acknowledging that my Swynford children were no longer all under my care. But John and Henry and Joan waited for me at Kettlethorpe with Thomas Swynford. I smiled, to reassure him that Blanche's death was not about to reduce me to a bout of tears as it could still sometimes do.

'You'll not see me in Kettlethorpe,' the Duke gave solemn warning. 'The fleet's sailed and I must follow without more delay.' He led me round a stall selling pans and cooking pots. One of the pans fell to the floor, dislodged by a climbing child, the clang and roll making my mare skitter again, and John laughed. 'I'll send you a gift.'

I caught his glance. 'An iron pan?'

'Do you want an iron pan? I cannot imagine why. But if that is what you want…Why give a woman something she will not make use of?'

'Like a chain of rubies.' I nodded at the chain around his neck. 'Your daughter Philippa once told me that you only give valuable gifts to people you don't particularly care for.'

'Did she?' His eyes registered bafflement.

'Like silver cups with lids.'

'Have I ever given you one?'

'Yes. But I think she's right.' I laughed. 'So I'll have the iron pan and the wagon-loads of wood or the prime venison or the tun of wine…'

'Well, it must prove something if I'm concerned for the roof over your head and your sustenance,' John admitted, still amused, still holding tight to my bridle, for the mare, scenting her stable now that we were in the environs of the castle, was keen to have her head and continue through the gateway. 'I was not aware that Philippa was so observant.'

What was it that made me look up, away from him? Something caught at my senses in that moment, like the threatening drone of a hornet before it stings. Except that it was no wasp. It was no sound that alerted me. I looked around at those who rode with us. The Mayor was occupied only with the list of complaints clutched in his fist, the merchants merely jostling for position. The priest might have drunk sour ale from the downturn of his mouth, but I had rarely seen him smile. I glanced at the Duke who had turned to cast an eye over an altercation between two men over the sale of a horse, and seemed entirely unaware.

There was nothing for my concern here. We continued on our way, until the street became uneven and I took control of my own creature again, falling behind at the parting of the ways when the conversation once more ranged over rents and tenancies, and then the ducal party was alone.

'What is it?' John murmured, once more riding beside me on the final stretch, quick to pick up my unease.

'I'm not sure. Perhaps nothing.'

There was nothing here to give me cause for worry, to spoil these last days. Once in the castle courtyard, as I slid from saddle to ground, Simon Pakenham, our Leicester steward, approached and bowed as he took the mare's reins from me.

'I trust you enjoyed your day, my lady.' His voice and face were sombre, but then when were they not? Few of the Duke's officials were quick to approve of me.

And there was the Duke walking beside me.

'Are you anxious over something?'

'No. Not a thing. Except that you will leave me.'

Our leave-taking was passionate and bittersweet in private.

Don't leave me.

Once I would have said it. Once I did. I no longer shamed myself or him by putting my longing into words. It was not the life we led, to be together, to be able to map out the pattern of our days for month after month. What purpose in my dreaming over an existence where our days together could be enjoyed without interruption? What I knew was that wherever duty called him, he would return to me.

In private we allowed emotion to rule. In public he handed me over to my escort, formally putting me under their protection with a bow and acceptable words of farewell.

My journey to Kettlethorpe was without incident, my reunion with Agnes and the children one of noisy delight. Not even a pair of squabbling storm-crows on the new roof of my manor gave me pause for thought.

I had seen the little cavalcade of three horses and single baggage wagon from my chamber and idly watched it draw nearer. After two weeks at Kettlethorpe I had decided that Master Burton, Master Ingoldsby's young and enthusiastic replacement, had my new hall well in hand. It had no need of my supervision, leaving me free to return to my position at Hertford. I would take Agnes and the children with me. The days of hiding my Beaufort children were long gone. They would join the nursery at Hertford.

If I was not waylaid by chance visitors.

I held Joan in my arms, pointing out the newcomers. Master Burton would offer them ale and bread and chivvy them on their way. The need to return to Hertford had begun to lay an urgent hand on me, even though the Duke would not be there.

The travellers pulled into the courtyard, but not before, Joan still clutched hard against me, I was down the stairs and standing beside the leading rider. They had barely drawn to a standstill.

'What is heaven's name are you doing here?'

Not the most unctuous of welcomes but, as I very well knew, this visitor had no taste for Lincolnshire seclusion. She slid down to stand before me and it was only then that I saw the expression on her face behind the weariness of travel.

'Philippa! What is it?'

I could not imagine what had brought my sister all this way from Hertford. And then when she simply looked at me without replying, terror rose in me, filling me to the brim like a winter storm drain.

'Is it Margaret?'

'No.' Briefly her expression softened. Blanche's death had touched us all. 'Margaret is well. And my children too.'

'Then the Duke—'

'It nothing to do with the children or the Duke. No one's dead,' she interrupted. There was no mistaking the emotion in her eye, and it seemed to me that she had ridden the whole distance with some gnawing worry as her constant companion, a burr beneath her saddle that gave her no peace.

'What has happened?'

'The sky has fallen on your head, Katherine.'

'What?'

Pale of face, jaw clenched, she was making no sense.

'And all things considered, on my head too. I thought it better if I was not part of Duchess Constanza's household just at this moment.'

'Why not?'

'It is not something that I will discuss out here.'

'There's no one out here to hear!'

Her servants had gone, Master Burton directing the horses to my smartly renovated stables. There was no one to eavesdrop apart from Joan who was more intent on watching the ducks marching across the grass behind me.

'I would still prefer to say what I have to say in the privacy of four walls. The words are not ones I normally find a use for.'

I thought for a moment through the complicated weaving of my sister's thoughts, still unable to imagine the cause of her distress. There was only one possibility.

'Is it Geoffrey?' I asked finally.

And she burst into tears.

Five minutes later we were in my chamber, my sister divested of her outer garments, seated on my bed with a cup of wine in one hand and a square of linen in the other. Her sobs had become mere hitches of breath although her eyes were still bright with tears and undoubtedly hostile. I sat beside her, Joan on the floor at my feet.

'What has he done?'

'Who?'

'Geoffrey!'

'It's not Geoffrey I've come about. It's you!' Philippa dragged a breath into her lungs and expelled it. 'How could you be so stupid?'

It was as if she had struck me, a sharp open-handed slap.

'What have I done?'

'Only destroyed you reputation!'

'No…' This must be some mistake.

'Do you want me to tell you what is said and written about you?'

Not waiting for a reply, she told me. The words used against me filled my room with such vile hatred that I could barely stay enclosed within it, but as I stood, my sister's hand shot out to drag me back and anchor me next to her on my bed.

'Listen to it, Katherine. See what you have done. This is what you have created. A monster. A whore.' Philippa did not spare me. 'An unspeakable concubine. A foreign woman who lured the Duke into shameless fornication and adultery. A prostitute who seduced the Duke from his lawful wedlock.'

At first I was disbelieving. Of course the Lancaster household knew of the duality of my position, but never had I heard such a string of vicious epithets and I knew it would not be from Constanza's lips. To remain silent and circumspect would shield us all from widespread disgrace. Of course there would be talk outside the Lancaster walls, but from where had this diatribe been born?

'Where has this come from?' I asked. 'Surely no one would believe such nonsense.'

'They would when it's from the mouth and pen of Walsingham!'

The name sent a shiver down my spine. Thomas Walsingham again, bitter priest and vile writer of letters. He had been silent since the mending of relations between the Duke and Parliament a year ago at the start of the new reign.

'Walsingham? But why would he turn his wrath on me?'

'You don't know?' Philippa's venom continued to pour out, her mouth ugly with her anger. 'As I understand it, it was your stupid, stupid ride through the streets of Leicester. And don't tell me you didn't do it. I'm quite certain you did.'

'Leicester?' What on earth had I done in Leicester to warrant such ignominy?

'Yes, Leicester. Where you rode with the Duke!'

'Of course I rode with him. But I don't see that it makes me a whore.' It was hard to make my tongue form the denunciation.

'How could you have been so careless, Kate?'

'Were we? We have always been careful not to draw attention—'

'And I suppose his taking your reins and leading you

back to the castle was the height of discretion. Is that what happened?'

And I saw it now in my mind's eye. My mannerless mare. The Duke's solution to an immediate problem. And I saw the intimacy of such an action between a man and a woman.

'Is it?' Philippa repeated.

'Yes. Oh, yes.'

'Katherine, you fool.'

'I did not think. The Duke did not think.'

'And look where that has got you. You knew it would happen one day if you could not keep your lust in check.'

'It was hardly lust to let the Duke curb a difficult horse.'

'It was the height of stupidity to show the world that there is a deplorable intimacy between you.'

'No! I don't accept that! Let me think.' I stood, pulling away from her now, to stand before my prie-dieu, but I could not kneel. This was no time for prayer. This was time for some cold hard facts and I allowed my mind to return to that day of such happiness in Leicester, when I had thought I had sensed an air of disapproval, and rejected it as my own imagination, looking for shadows where there were none. I had allowed the Duke to seduce me with the bittersweet emotions of parting. I had refused to *see*.

But there had been shadows after all. Oh, I had not been mistaken, for I had sensed the atmosphere in that little group with conspicuous accuracy, as well as the disfavour in the eyes of the steward. But how had it grown from that minor shimmer of disapproval in the streets of Leicester to a thundering diatribe under the pen of the Duke's greatest enemy? Becoming too complacent in our love, we had forgotten the need for discretion and thus we had fallen into his hands. Our ride through the streets had offered him the opportunity for a vicious onslaught. But here was the surprise that caught at my throat…

'But why would he cover my name with such filth?' I asked, looking over my shoulder to where Philippa still sat, folding and refolding the damp linen.

'Because he is a hater of women as daughters of Eve. And what a weapon you put into his hand, the pair of you. Besides, it does not matter why he does it. The damage is done.'

We had become reckless in our love. Bold even. Careless of how the world would see us. Intense dismay washed over me, to destroy all my assurance and complacency. I could never be complacent again. I had become notorious.

'Walsingham says you are a witch.' Philippa was not done with me yet.

My eyes snapped to hers.

Witchcraft? Here was a deluge of dangerous invective falling down on my head. What damage could Walsingham make in my life?

'I am no witch.'

'That's as may be. He says you are a promiscuous adulterer, not fit to be the governess of the Lancastrian princesses. Flaunting yourself, humiliating the beautiful and loyal Duchess who should be secure in her marriage…'

Anger began to burn, replacing fear.

'He says that you are blatantly unashamed. And what's worse, you are of low birth. Can he find anything worse to say than that? I'll tell you if you think not. He says that—'

'Be silent!'

Philippa subsided a little before my anger. 'I thought you would wish to know.'

'When you have finished lashing at me. Tell me what he says of the Duke.'

My guilt could not be measured. All my thoughts had

been centred on what Walsingham had said about me, but what calumnies had he levelled at the Duke? If he saw me to be a worthy target, what fuel did our behaviour provide for Walsingham to use against the Duke of Lancaster? I shivered as Philippa delivered them in the same flat tone that she had used against me.

'He has deserted his military duties in France for the sake of a sinful union. Any failure in England's campaigns will be placed at his door. And at yours.'

'That is not true.'

So I was to blame for that too.

'He had made himself abominable in the sight of God. He is a fornicator and adulterer. A pursuer of luxury and lechery. He is not fit to have authority in England. He is not fit to have the ear of the young king.'

It was worse, far worse than I could possibly have imagined.

'He says the Duchess was with you at Leicester. That she was riding with you when you publically slighted and humiliated her.'

'Which is not true. By the Virgin! Would the Duke have paid court to me with his wife riding at his side?'

'I don't know,' she muttered. 'I no longer know what is and is not beyond you.'

I ignored her taunt as well as I could. 'Is there anything else I should know?'

'Isn't that enough?'

'What is the Duchess saying?'

'Do you really want me to tell you? It is loud and in Castilian for the most part.'

'Has she seen the Duke?'

'Yes.'

'Then there is a lot you are not telling me.'

'I don't think I need to.' Philippa tilted her head. 'I thought to see more reaction from you.'

'What would you wish me to do?' I was cold, imagining the confrontation between the Duke and Duchess: Constanza's fury, John's pride when under attack. But there my imagination came up against the usual formidable barrier. Would he defend me? Or would he ask forgiveness for Constanza's mortification when the adultery of her husband was picked over by the vultures in the English Parliament? Would he allow me to carry the burden of guilt?

'What is it that you wish me to do, to vent my spleen?' I repeated, as I picked up a precious glass vessel, one of the many gifts from the Duke, from the coffer beside my bed. 'Destroy something of value?' I held it as if I might allow it to drop and destroy itself. Then replaced it as carefully as I had held it. I would not allow Walsingham or my sister to drive me to wanton destruction or despair. I would put my trust in the Duke's love for me. And thus I harnessed every ounce of willpower to answer calmly.

'Do I weep and moan my sins? Cast myself on my knees before the priest? I will do none of that, Philippa. I think I have been waiting for this moment since the day that the Duke told me that he desired me above all things. One day, if I became his mistress, I must be discovered and held up for shame. I just did not think it would be quite yet. How easy it is to turn a blind eye to how the world will view our union, when happiness beckons. I just did not think that it would be quite so vicious. But no—I will not weep.'

I could not weep as fury flooded through me that the cruellest accusations were directed at me. The woman. The daughter of Eve, guilty of seduction as she had been since the beginning of time. The one guilty of enticing the powerful man to her bed so that he would abandon the invading army, leaving it without leadership to fend for itself against hostile forces. It was my fault.

And now the price of that supposed seduction might be demanded from me. How high could that price be? Would the Duke be able to keep Parliament's teeth from my throat?

Not if he is fighting for his own political life.

Fear gripped hard. But I would not bow weakly before it.

'Well, you have delivered your good news,' I announced with brittle humour. 'Do you wish to remain here for the night, or is sharing the bed and board with a sinner such as I am become too much for your conscience to withstand?' And then I remembered. 'But you have come to stay, haven't you?'

My sister had arrived with her servants and a wagon full of her belongings.

'Yes.' There were tears on her face again.

'Why? Is it just the Duchess who has cast you out? Or is it…?'

And then she was weeping again. 'Geoffrey and I have decided to live apart.'

I went to her and, with a sigh, took her in my arms, two stricken women.

'We barely lived together through the whole of our marriage. I don't suppose I will notice…'

But she was hurt. I rocked her in my arms, murmuring words of comfort, while all the time in my heart was no comfort at all, and to my shame, my concerns were not with my sister's predicament. The true span of the price Walsingham demanded might colossal. What might he ask from the Duke as reparation for our sin? Or, in the face of this unexpected attack, how much might the Duke be prepared to pay to silence the vicious priest?

For here was the thought that preyed on my mind as I held Philippa close. Would I be the price demanded for the

Duke's reinstatement in the eyes of England? Would I, the vile daughter of Eve, be the one singled out as the sacrificial lamb? I had of late been so secure in our love, so mindless of dangers from without. Nor did I question the strength of the Duke's commitment to me even now, but in truth Walsingham was a powerful enemy, with a voice loud enough to swing opinion in England.

What of my own turbulent conscience, since Walsingham had called me harlot the length and breadth of the country? That night, with Philippa fallen into fitful sleep, I lifted my mirror, recalling how, under the attack of Constanza's damsels, I had scrutinised the face of the newly branded whore, questioning what I saw there, despairing that I would see the marks of shame on my soul. Dismay had been a heavy cloak, that I had failed to see my ruin as the Duke's beloved.

I had not seen the half of it then, cushioned as I was by the Duke's care. But who in England would not now regard me with utter contempt?

I placed my mirror face down. On the ivory cover a lady crowned her lover with a chaplet in stiff perpetuity. I could not contemplate my reflection, to see this object of sin, as fear returned, more lively than ever with cruel claws. I had always known that, one day, I would be separated from my lover. Had I not known it from the very beginning when I had given him a faded rose and my respectability? The cloud was always there, hanging over us like an ever-present sword of Damocles to divide and destroy.

Was this to be the moment, when the Duke must choose between me and England's glory? My mind was filled with trepidation, knowing that the choice was his to make; I would be unable to sway him. With his duty to England, as the puissant counsellor of the new untried King Richard at the forefront of his mind, I must not even try.

'I have come.'

It was all he said. It was enough.

'I knew you would,' I replied.

He stood in the refurbished splendour of my Great Hall, clad in wool and leather for travel but, as I would always expect, still with the gleam of jewels beneath the film of dust on hat and tunic. The flamboyance of his acknowledgement was as gracious as if Philippa and I were two high-born foreign dignitaries, rather than two unhappy women garbed plainly for domestic work.

'You are right welcome, John,' I said, as I had on so many previous occasions. My voice felt compromised to my ear, a little rough with all the underlying anxieties that had cavorted incessantly through my days.

With one glance at the Duke's expression, a brisk curtsy and a warning glance in my direction—as if to say: 'and don't do anything to worsen to what is already an appalling situation'—Philippa made herself scarce.

And there we stood, contemplating the destruction of the life we had made together. How many times had we stood like this, some chasm of guilt or duty or conscience separating us? How often had we stepped over that chasm to be together? But perhaps this one was too deep for our courage; too critical with the swarming mass of Walsingham's diabolical accusations.

I waited for the Duke to speak.

And while I did, I refused to relive the sleepless night-hours when I had been all but wrenched apart by the fear that he might, for the sake of his reputation and his marriage, for the sake of his authority in England, even for the sake of

England's success in the foreign field, renounce me, putting me quietly aside as a thing of danger. Once I had lived in dread that Constanza would be the one to call on his honour. Walsingham, I acknowledged, was a far more dangerous foe.

And if the Duke asked me to free him, so that he might restore his good name and his place at the young king's side, what would I say? Could I step back and let him go? Would I have the strength to do that?

I trembled at it.

As I stepped towards him, the Duke raised his hands a little, palms turned out, his gesture as disciplined as his face. His cheekbones were sharp, the skin pulled taut, as if he had ridden far and fast. The familiar lines that I knew so well, that I had frequently traced in the aftermath of passion, were engraved more deeply than usual.

The words, yet unsaid, hung in the air between us with the smoke from the fire.

'Are you going to invite me somewhere more comfortable than this hall? Have you a room where, just at this moment, I don't have to face your scowling sister?' He spoke with something that might once have passed for a brush of humour, but not today.

What was he thinking? No matter how carefully I searched his face, his eyes that were dark agates, I could not tell. I never could unless he wished me to know. He would not talk about the effect Walsingham's attack had had on him. That was not why he was here. But what then did he have to say to me, which had brought him this great distance to Kettlethorpe when his whole concentration had been engaged by the invasion? I was full of fear as I opened the door into the inner chamber.

One inside, I faced him and said, 'My sister says the sky has fallen on our heads.'

'So it would seem,' he replied with a lift of a shoulder.

Here was tension. I asked: 'What did we do that was so very bad?'

'We drew attention to ourselves.'

'I am so sorry.'

'It was my fault, not yours.'

'That's not what Walsingham says.' How the words had hurt, and did so again as I repeated them. 'He says I am a seductive whore.'

The Duke's mouth tightened. 'I should have been aware. I took your bridle and led you through the streets of Leicester, under the eye of every merchant, tradesman and gutter urchin.' His hands had clenched into fists, but his voice was without inflexion. 'For those who would make trouble for me—and for you—it was translated as a symbol of our disgrace, that I have control over you. That I have possession of your body. It was no better than shouting it from the rooftops. It might be one thing for me to take you to bed privately at The Savoy or Kenilworth or Leicester Castle, but to show ownership of you in public could not be tolerated.' He took a deep breath, as if he had not breathed deep for some time. 'We forgot to be discreet, Katherine. We forgot.'

I could see all the damage we had done, so heedlessly, on that bright morning when I had daydreamed and he had prompted a flirtation over a barrel of oysters and an iron pan.

'I had been warned,' the Duke said. 'I should have taken heed.'

'Warned?' I was startled, and not a little angry. 'So I had already been singled out as a blight on your life.'

He did not reply. It did not need saying. His priest, his advisers, even Sir Thomas Hungerford in his role of steward of all the southern Lancaster estates would have warned him against me. How many jibes and slights could there be to wound me?

'Why did you not tell me?'

'It was not important.'

Taking cognisance of his shuttered expression I knew he would say no more.

'Can Walsingham harm you?' I asked.

'There is nothing new in his firing arrows at me,' he replied, again avoiding my question.

'It seems to me that he has more and heavier ammunition now.'

'Perhaps. I will look to my defences.' All the pride of a Plantagenet prince rested on his brow like a glittering coronet. 'But I am not here to talk about Walsingham.'

It was my turn to take a breath. 'Why are you here?'

'Why do you think, Katherine?'

And I read the sudden blaze of fire in his eye, the physical desire in his face. No, he was not here to talk about calumnies and reputations. He was here to see me, to show me that Walsingham could not sunder what existed between us. Whatever the future held, whether we lived together or apart, our love would remain inviolate.

In my bedchamber, where Philippa was not scowling, there was no place for a complex exchange of words, for soul-searching, for regrets. Here was no place for what the future would hold for us. I would not think that our parting on the following day might be our last, if the Duke decided to repair the damage to his own standing.

I would not consider that this was the tender precursor to his leaving me.

Of course he will sever your relationship, if he has any sense, Philippa opined in my ear.

I banished her.

You have degraded me. And still do, spat Constanza, lurking in the shadows beside the clothespress.

I banished her too.

You are an evil seductress, intoned Walsingham from the bed tester.

I turned my back on him.

I warned you, did I not? Even Agnes had a face of stone. My breath caught that she too would condemn.

'What are you thinking?' The Duke had quietly closed the door and was watching me as I walked a circuit of the room.

'That this room has suddenly become entirely too crowded.'

'It looks empty enough to me.'

He approached me for the first time.

'Of course it does.' I forced myself to rest, although it was not difficult with his arms enclosed around me, and I laughed a little as I leaned my forehead against his shoulder. 'Even the mice have been cleared out in my rebuilding.' My breathing was already shortened. 'John, my life, my love. I have had such a need of you these past days.'

His heart leaped beneath my hands. 'I love you. I adore you,' he replied.

I held his hand in mine, as I took him under my dominion in a chamber where there were no shadows, only ours.

'I think I should not be with you,' I whispered, but despite all Walsingham could do to destroy us, desire thrummed through my blood, as if I were a new bride, united for the first time to the man she worshipped. I allowed him to lead me to the bed with no coy resistance.

'What is it?' he asked, detecting some nuance as he busied himself divesting himself of his own clothing and mine, impatient as ever over the buttons on my sleeves.

I would have denied what was in my mind. Instead: 'I

could not look at myself in my mirror,' I confessed, the words tumbling out, even as my breath caught at the slide of his hand on my skin. 'I was afraid of what I would see. I have committed a great sin, you see. I have always known it was, but I did not fully understand...'

Eyes fathomlessly dark, the planes of his face severe, the Duke looked at me as if discerning for the first time the essence of the sacrifice I had made. With one finger he traced the outline of my lips, before running his knuckles under the line of my jaw. Then finally framed my face with his fine hands and kissed my lips, soft as a promise.

'I owe you every apology, Katherine de Swynford, from the depths of my soul. I took you for my own pleasure, without thought, as I have taken everything in life. Who has ever thwarted me? Who would gainsay me? We are both guilty of sin, but I did not consider how vastly a woman of such integrity would suffer. I regret that. I wonder that you can ever forgive me for my placing your feet on this particular path that many would say leads to the fires of hell. I did not consider how the world's condemnation would wound you. I should have. You should have been my first concern.'

The contrition in his eyes, bleak and cold, took my breath, and in the face of so brutal a confession I could do no other than raise my hands to his cheeks, to return the kiss.

'I'll tell you what you would see in your mirror,' he said when our kiss was ended, 'because I have the true image here before me. You would see a woman with the courage to accept what is between us, whatever the world says. A woman with the fortitude to love me. A woman with the spirit to allow me to love her. I can only honour you for the choice you made to link your life with mine. Nothing I can do or say can ever express the love that is in my heart for you.'

'My love. My dear love…' Never had I thought to hear the Duke place himself at my feet. Emotion threatened, but I would not weep, for an inner joy was unfolding. 'I thought Walsingham had destroyed our happiness,' I said, kissing him again. 'I thought that when we came together, his words would taint what we have.'

'No. He cannot. You are lodged in my heart. Are we not complete in each other?'

As so often before, we shut out the world, even Walsingham. I even succeeded in banishing the fearful anguish, although our lovemaking had a strange quality of despair about it, as if we should snatch all the fulfilment we could before storm clouds threatened. And yet there was such an exultation, such a sense of triumph that we were untouchable, that there was no possible room for regret.

I was awake when he rose at dawn. I had been awake for some time, taking note of each beautiful feature as the daylight strengthened, committing all to memory. Then I kissed him and allowed him to dress without comment. What was there to say about our love that had not been said throughout the dark hours? That had not been proved by the drift of his hands, the power of his body as he took ownership of mine in earnest.

As for what still had to be said between us, I would not pre-empt it.

Hosed and shod with fine, elegant lines, his tunic laced and belted, he came to sit on the bed beside me, to wind his fingers into the turmoil of my hair.

'I always forget the magnificence of your hair. Its richness takes my breath.' He barely paused. 'I cannot stay. Not even for a day.' He released my hair, as if it seared his flesh.

'I know. I would not ask it of you.'

'Thank you,' he murmured, his lips against mine.

'For what?' My heart thundered against my ribs. Surely he would hear it, or feel the vibration of it as he cupped my face and placed a succession of soft kisses on my lips.

'For not asking. I can see the question circling in your head.'

'There is only one for which I need an answer. And which I will not ask.'

'You do not need to ask it. You know the answer. The answer is no. It is too late for that. Far too late. Do we not both know it?'

No, I did not have to ask it after all. I held tightly to his hand, raising his palm to press a reciprocal salute there.

'Will you stay here?' he asked.

'Where else would I go?'

I doubted I would be welcome with Constanza. How could she turn a politic blind eye, now that the whole country knew of the depth of sin between her husband and his daughters' governess? What had been a brave tolerance could no longer be preserved under the condemning eye of every man and woman in England. My role in the Lancaster household was at an end.

'And you?' I asked, thinking that he would tell me which port he would make for.

Instead: 'Constanza and I are estranged.'

That was all he would say. Such a momentous step explained in so few words. I imagined the blow to his pride, and to hers, but I made no comment. He never would discuss her with me and I honoured him for it.

'I will pray for you,' I promised.

He kissed me. 'God keep you.'

He walked to the door, then returned, surprising me by

lifting my rosary from my prie-dieu before coming to kneel beside the bed.

'Did I not promise that I would protect you? I swear that I will. I will never again allow you to suffer from the choice you made to join your life with mine.' He sighed, an infinitesimal exhalation that I noted because I knew him so well as he pressed the crucifix to his lips, then folded the coral and jet and silver into my hand. 'Remember me. And God keep you.'

And I carried it to my own lips in acknowledgement of his vow.

Bundled into a chamber gown, my hair roughly braided and lightly veiled, I was watching the Duke ride out when Philippa came to join me, in no better mood than on previous days.

'Where is he going?'

'To The Savoy and then Southampton.'

'So he has left you,' she observed with a cruel complacency.

I was fretful. Whatever the Duke might say to reassure me, I knew that Walsingham's attack could do nothing but harm to John's already unstable reputation. Parliament would take every opportunity to sharpen its claws since Walsingham had accused me of being the cause of the Duke's failure to accompany his fleet. The Duke of Lancaster had been so weak as to allow me to seduce him from his duty. I knew it was all lies. He did not sail with them because he was commandeering extra ships, but there were many who would give credence to Walsingham.

'He has left me because he must,' I replied, swallowing my anxieties in front of Philippa. 'I do not hold him back from going to war.'

'I did not mean that.'

'I know you didn't. But I felt that it needed saying. It was an unfair assertion, on both of us.' My eye remained fixed on the distant Lancaster colours until the last possible moment when distance enclosed him. Walsingham had had the temerity to accuse the Duke of cowardice in not sailing with his men.

'I meant,' Philippa persisted, 'that he has cast you off. Has he given you an annuity for past services and wished you well for the future?'

Since the Duke was out of sight, I turned to look at her.

'Sometimes I wish there was more charity in your soul, Philippa.'

'What have I said that is not the truth? He did not even kiss you when he left.'

I would say no more. I did not have to. All our kisses had been exchanged in private. And the question that I had not asked, and had not, in the end, needed to:

'Do we part for ever, to put you and England right with God?'

And his answer: 'No. It is too late for that.'

The Duke had not left me. He had not cast me off. How could we be parted, when our love was indestructible, resilient enough to withstand the brutality of Walsingham's particular brand of warfare. Our love could never be denied.

Eyes narrowed as if I might still catch a final glimpse of Lancaster banners, I recalled comparing my long-ago existence to a line of plainchant, predictably moving along familiar paths, without highs or lows. How different was this love with which we had been blessed. This love, breathtaking, unsettling, held the complex interweaving of the glorious polyphony from St Stephen's Chapel at Westminster. Unpredictable, extreme in its ability to move to joy or tears, superbly glorious, the power of this music of our hearts overwhelmed us both.

Whenever the Duke came home, from war, from Parliamentary debate, from negotiation, he would come to me because I was at the very centre of the intricate harmony of his life, as he was of mine. I would stand at the last before God's throne and proclaim my love for him. As I knew he would for me.

Chapter Thirteen

June 1381: The Manor of Kettlethorpe, Lincolnshire

'It's bloody insurrection, m'lady,' Jonas, my blacksmith, informed me with lugubrious self-importance before going about his business.

'No it's not,' I replied firmly to his back.

Jonas regarded me over his shoulder, scratching his nose with a black-nailed finger.

'You mark my words, m'lady. Bloody insurrection!'

'Well, don't tell the diary maids,' I called after him. 'They've enough to gossip about without this. Cheese is the last thing on their minds as it is.'

The foundations of the world I knew had begun to shake.

My sister Philippa had ultimately left me to return to Duchess Constanza's service, with some relief on both sides. Constanza had decided that she approved Philippa's companionship more than she detested her as the sister of the ducal whore. I wished Philippa well. She would be far happier at Tutbury or Hertford—or anywhere the Duchess chose to live apart from the Duke—than at Kettlethorpe. Their estrangement continued, meeting only for ceremonial and family purposes.

Yet I was not lonely for female companionship, for I had the other Philippa, the Duke's lovely daughter now grown to adulthood, for company. Usually a confident young woman, self-possessed behind the facade of her striking features, she had decided to put distance between herself and her sister Elizabeth, who although the younger daughter, had recently engaged in a dynastic marriage with the youthful Earl of Pembroke. It had made Philippa restless for her own future.

And then the rumours began to reach us. At least they took our collective mind off Elizabeth's crowing, Philippa's disappointment and the loud demands of my new son, Thomas, born in the depths of a wintry January with a voice fit to raise the dead.

At first we listened in disbelief, strengthening into sheer denial.

Surely the stories were mere fabrications, magnifying out of all proportion a spark of disgruntled opposition over a tax demand that would be quickly stamped on by local magistrates. I would not give the rumours credence.

Yet the news continued to be carried by every group of travellers passing our door, of trouble-making peasants massing in Kent and Essex. I listened and worried but in a mild way. Kent was far from us in Lincolnshire, where the days passed in unrelenting monotony with no unrest other than a squabble over the slaughter of chickens by an unleashed hound. What had this uprising to do with me? What damage could they do to us? We were safe, isolated and unnoticed, as we always were. No need for us to jump at every shadow.

Besides which, I informed my household, the defences of London were strong enough to stop a parcel of peasants even if their complaints sounded horribly familiar. Had they not been voiced at any time over the past dozen years? Hatred of the poll tax, failure to win battles in France, restrictions on wages when labour was in demand after the Pestilence. What was so different now?

My reassurances had their effect, leaving my mind free to follow the Duke. It was a month since I had parted from him at Leicester. He was going to Scotland. With the Scottish truce about to expire, Richard had sent the Duke to open negotiations. He would probably now be at Knaresborough or Pontefract or even at Berwick, so he would be in no danger.

The distant clatter of hooves on the road took my attention.

I sighed, handing sleeping Thomas over to Agnes, taking Joan by the hand. 'Another party to spread fears of death and destruction, if Jonas has not done enough…'

I walked slowly, through the door into the courtyard, shielding my eyes from the sun, keeping Joan firmly anchored, to her annoyance, and any complacency vanished. A small escort of soldiers had muscled their animals, dusty and well-lathered from hard riding, into the confined space before me. I stiffened, pushing Joan behind my skirts, for there was no identifying mark on them. Had I been careless in believing us to be safe in the depths of Lincolnshire? Then as the leader, obvious by the quality of his half-armour and weaponry, dismounted and strode up to me, I recognised the face beneath the shadow of his helmet.

One of the Duke's captains.

I exhaled my relief, retrieving Joan to lift her up into my arms, but my relief was short lived when the man gave the briefest of bows and barely paused for breath.

'An order from my lord of Lancaster, my lady.'

An order? I smiled and extended my hand. 'Come within.

There will be ale for you and your men. You look as if you need it—'

'No!' He shook his head as if to deny his abruptness, and I realised that he had kept his troop mounted. 'No, my lady. You are to pack up what you need—only enough to be carried on horseback—and come with me.' He cast an eye on Joan who, unexpectedly shy, hid her face against my neck. 'All of you. You need to take refuge. The country's in the hands of rebels and your safety cannot be ensured here.'

'Tell me—' I gripped his sleeve as the warnings of the past days rushed back in full vigour, yet still I would not believe that I stood in any real danger. I needed proof if I was to agree to a full-scale upheaval.

'No time,' he replied, and as if he had read my mind: 'My orders are to be gone from here within the hour. You are in danger.'

It did not make sense. The countryside lay about us, basking at peace in the June heat. All I could hear was the usual clamour of a household at work and Thomas's lusty yells.

'But why? Why am I in danger?'

'It's the Duke who's in danger,' the captain responded with an impatient exhalation at women who would not obey a simple order. Then even more brusquely: 'And all who belong to him. My lord says he cannot risk your staying here if the rebels' accusations turn into actions.'

So the rebels were flinging their accusations at the Duke. I frowned at the captain. Had the Duke not weathered all the past storms with Parliament, despite the nagging problems of taxation and failure to win any notable victory in France? Would he not mend the toppling fences once again? I saw no need for my own household, including all the children, to be uprooted.

'But why can I not stay here? We are isolated enough. Or if you consider us too vulnerable, we could go to Lincoln.'

Now the captain grunted in frustration. 'Have you had no word of the uprising, my lady? You're a marked woman. You are known here for your...your closeness to my lord.' His skin flushed but his gaze remained direct. 'And in Lincoln too I warrant. You are to come with me to Pontefract.' Then he added, as if this made all beyond argument: 'By my lord's orders. You must lie low at Pontefract, until things change.'

I looked round at those who, alerted by the voices and crush of soldiery, had followed me out into the courtyard. Philippa standing anxiously at my shoulder, holding tightly to Henry. Agnes carrying the baby Thomas whose cries had subsided. John who had emerged from the stable, smudged with charcoal. Were we truly in danger?

And then there was my other family. Thomas would be well protected in the Duke's own retinue. Margaret would be safe enough surely, within the convent at Barking.

Still I was reluctant to accept that my life was in any real danger. Was not the Duke the most powerful man in the country? No one would dare to lay his hands on me. The rabble, stirred up by Walsingham, might deplore my lack of morality as a royal mistress, but I could never accept that they would attack me or my family. I said as much.

'Do you say?' responded the captain with laconic patience fast running out. 'They are at this moment murdering Flemings in London—and elsewhere. You are labelled foreigner. Will your fate be any better, lady?'

'I am not a Fleming. I am from Hainault. It is no secret.'

'They'll not stop to ask the difference, as I see it. Fleming or Hainaulter, you will be a target for their hatred.' He shook his head. 'All I'll say—look to yourself and your own family, lady.'

I stared at him. 'You are not wearing Lancaster livery,' I accused.

His reply was immediate, his hand clenching on his sword hilt. 'No. Nor will I. And if you want to waste even more time knowing why, I'll tell you—you'll not be seeing the young squire Henry Warde again. It's death to those marked as Lancaster's men who fall into rebel hands.'

'What?' It came out as a whisper. I knew Henry well, a stolid lad with dark hair and a quick turn of foot.

'Picked out by the mob in Essex, he was, as one of Lancaster's men, and done to death, for my lord's mark on him.' He must have seen my shock, for his voice gentled. 'But I will serve my lord well, with or without livery, to the day of my death. Which might be sooner rather than later if you don't make haste, my lady! And my lord sends you this as a sign of his regard.' He cleared his throat roughly. 'In case you should consider ignoring his advice.'

He gestured to one of his men at arms who, with a sly grin, unstrapped from his own saddle a wool-lined pannier. A perfect size for carrying a six-month-old child on a long journey over difficult terrain. And I smiled too despite the rumble of fear in my belly. The Duke might shower his dependents with silver hanaps but he gave me what he knew I needed.

'Well, my lady?'

'We will come.'

The Duke knew me very well, the pannier tipping the balance, and I was persuaded, acknowledging in that moment of shining clarity that I must protect his children. The Duke had enough to contend with, without my intransigence.

Within the hour we were packed with the little that we would need, and incongruously, foolishly, a little silver chafing dish, a new gift from the Duke, elegant with its three legs and handle, chased with a pattern of ivy, that I could not bear to leave behind. And then we were gone, a flight through the night. An unnerving ride when dangers seemed to lurk behind every bush. Agnes and the children and Philippa, Thomas packed snugly into the pannier, the other children passed between us. We stopped briefly to take a cup of wine, a snatched mouth of bread, but the captain urged us on. And through it all my thoughts were with Duchess Constanza and Elizabeth and my sister. Safe, I prayed, in Hertford. As I and my companions would soon be in Pontefract, the Duke's headquarters in the north, strong enough to repel any attack with its towers and walls and great barbican.

Yet still my mind would not accept. This was not real. This rioting was merely a stirring-up by this man Wat Tyler. King Richard's advisers would take the right steps. Tyler and his cohorts would be pacified with promises and sent back to their villages. All would be well.

Would it not?

Of course it would, I reassured myself, as we flew through the night, and were refused entry by the Duke's cautious Constable at Pontefract until our credentials were vouch-safed. We were safe until better times.

Yet ensconced in Pontefract, I could allow my anxieties about the Duke to escape my control. Thank God he was safe behind the stout walls at Berwick.

Oh, how I raged when the news first reached me. And then, in private, I wept. A sign of a shallow mind, some would say, to waste such emotion on the works of man, the dross of earthly wealth. Why would I weep over the destruction of gold and silver, of fine jewels and even finer tapestries, when men and women ran in fear of their lives? And some lost them.

The guards at The Savoy had lost theirs.

I wept because these elements of wealth and power, the beauty and grandeur of The Savoy, were an integral part of my memories of the Duke and the bonds that pinioned us. And with their destruction, my memories, of such inestimable value, had become tainted with horror. With terror of what was to come.

'How is it possible? Could no one stop it?' Philippa asked, eyes dark with dismay.

The Savoy Palace, John's glorious, magnificent, luxurious home on the banks of the Thames, that superb masterpiece of craftsmen's art where we had first expressed our love, was no more. Laid waste; utterly ruined. All destroyed, stamped on, brutally razed to the ground by Wat Tyler and his rebels, the contents flung in the river or burned in vast glowing pyres as the great swathe of rioters breached the gateways and walls, invading the public audience chambers, the chapel, the Great Hall, the private parlours. The intimate bedchambers.

All I could do was sit and stare in shocked disbelief, to the unease of the itinerant friar, allowed through the gates after close questioning, who had revelled with what seemed to me an unholy enthusiasm in its telling. At first I had refused to believe it, that the King's own uncle, a royal duke, should be so despised, that his property should be the subject of such vitriol, but now, as the details flowed on and on, I must. As I must accept the scarcely credible events in London where the Archbishop of Canterbury and the Lord Treasurer had been hauled out for execution on Tower Hill.

Even Brother William Appleton who had given me his strength when Blanche died had paid for his allegiance with his head. I could not comprehend it.

Oh, John. My love, my dear one. How will you deal with this?

My flesh crept at the image that I could not erase from my mind. Men I had known, men I had conversed with, sat at supper with. Men whom the Duke had known and respected.

The friar's voice trailed off, his tale told, and I dispatched him for food and ale, accompanying him briefly to the kitchens, handing him over to Hugh, the cook, who was avid for news. Here was no place for ungoverned emotions. There was far more of horror and destruction for me to face than the looting of The Savoy. Slowly I returned to my chamber.

'It is vile.' Waiting for me there, at my side throughout the telling of desperate events and destruction, Philippa sniffed and wiped her eyes.

'Yes.'

'Will our household at The Savoy be safe?'

'I expect they will have taken refuge in the city.' I would not tell her what I knew of the fate of the guards.

Philippa wept again, but I was in control, as cold and restrained as I had ever been. I would not tell her. Or not yet. Perhaps when affairs became clearer and her own emotions were less overthrown. The destruction of stone and timber, gold and jewels was not the worst of it. Yes, they could be replaced by any man of great wealth such as her father. The Duke could rebuild and refashion as magnificently as before. But why had such a vengeful attack been launched against him, even in his absence? Why were even his servants reviled? I knew the answer to that.

On our journey to the kitchens, I had pulled the friar to a halt in the buttery where we would not be overheard. 'Why was it done?' I held his eyes when they threatened to slide away. 'What do the rebels say when they set fire to tapestries? When they fling precious vessels into the Thames?

Why of all the buildings in London do they disfigure The Savoy?'

The friar's eyes still managed to evade mine.

'Tell me!' I tightened my grip. 'I can't believe you don't know.' Finally I sought in the purse at my belt and extracted a coin. 'This might jog your memory.' I tried not to sneer.

'Because they fear him. They despise him.' The accusations made my blood run cold. 'They say he would usurp the King's throne. "We will have no king named John," they bellowed as they…'

So simple. And what I had feared. There could be no other reason, could there? The home I had known and loved was destroyed as the ultimate symbol of the Duke himself. Lancaster's home, Lancaster's base in London, from which all his power as royal duke and uncle to the King emanated. And thus it had become the target for all their hatred, as if it were the Duke himself, bruised and battered and destroyed beyond recognition.

'But why single him out?' Although I knew the answer.

'They won't blame a fourteen-year-old youth who has barely hair on his cheeks, mistress.'

Of course. They needed a scapegoat, as they had always done. Who better than the man at the young King's right hand? How could they hate him so much?

'They blame him for their ills,' the monk repeated, as if able to pick up my thoughts. 'The poll tax is a heavy burden. The lords refuse to pay more for the labour on their estates.' He shrugged, the worn cloth releasing a sour smell. 'Who to blame but the man whose hand is on the reins of government?'

And the thought crept into my mind. What would they have done to the Duke, if he had been at The Savoy? Would they have treated him with the same lack of respect as they did the contents of his private chapel?

'What are they saying about the Duke?' My final question before I released the monk to his bread and ale. He did not hesitate. Perhaps he felt the determination in my grip.

'They demand his head as the worst of all traitors. They've sent a petition to the young King. They want revenge for their sufferings. The Duke's head will do it.'

Still the questions hammered at my thoughts. Could they not see the Duke's sense of justice, his dedication to England's greatness? Perhaps when the air cooled they would be satisfied with their revenge on property and possessions. What would the Duke do? Would he gather his forces and ride south to put down the rebels in the King's name?

In all the years that I had loved him, I had learned to accept his absences, to govern my own desires to be with him every moment of every day, but in those days at Pontefract I wished I could have been there in Berwick with him. I would have gone to him if I could. Instead, I lived on the edge of an anxiety so sharp that it drove me to my knees in the chapel.

'Holy Virgin, turn your face towards John of Lancaster. Preserve him from his enemies. Keep him safe from harm. I will offer up a novena if you have mercy on him.'

I lit a candle at the foot of the statue.

If John was spared, I would make recompense. If John was spared I would have candlesticks made in gold for the altar at Kettlethorpe. I smiled as I realised I had called him John in my mind, which I never did. A token of my anxiety.

'Holy Virgin, have mercy on us both.'

I was reassured by the calm stillness around me. The Blessed Mother would not allow my prayers to go unanswered. The Duke would be safe.

Every day I stood on the battlements at Pontefract and

allowed my mind to seek him out. I knew he was alive. I knew he was in health and spirits. Soon we would be together and the ravages of these days would be put right. He would stand at Richard's side and deal with the rebels with justice and clemency. He would rebuild The Savoy. He would return to me and kiss away my fear. Perhaps I would bear him another Beaufort son. I spread my fingers over the folds of my gown and I smiled.

The sense of him settled on my shoulders, around my heart, as a goose-down quilt on a winter's morn.

There was something wrong. I could not fathom it. All I knew was that there was something out of kilter, something I could not quite see in my mind's eye, or hear; merely the whisper of it in my head when I caught it unawares. The whole castle seemed to be redolent of a sense of unease.

It was not the dire news we had received from the south where events leaped from bad to worse, attacks unbelievably launched against the Duke's castles in Hertford and Leicester. We had thought the Duchess and her household to be safe. Pray God that they had fled, forewarned, perhaps to Kenilworth whose massive walls would hold an entire army at bay.

No, it was not that, although prayer filled our days and fear our nights.

Nor was it the desperate tale from Leicester where the furnishings and ducal possessions, five cart loads of them, were hidden in the churchyard in Newark by a terrified Keeper of the Wardrobe who could find no other refuge, in spite of the Mayor of Leicester calling out the militia to keep order. Even the Abbot had turned him away.

No, it was not that.

We doubled the guards on the walls at Pontefract and

watched the road, to north and south. We did not expect the Duke who was still, as far as we knew, tied up in Scottish negotiations. We would have to stand in our own defence if the rebellion spread its net to encompass us so far north.

But it was not that either. Pontefract was strong and well provisioned. We too could withstand a siege of a major army.

Yet there was something that stirred the atmosphere.

Philippa had become sprightly, displaying an artificial high spirits unlike her usual solemnity, as if she were attempting to obliterate some image too noxious to contemplate. It was as if, in my presence at least, she had set herself to charm and entertain. It had an air of a jester's role about it.

'Is something troubling you?' I asked, finding her cheerfulness unnerving.

'Not a thing,' she pronounced. 'Why?'

'I just thought…' I did not know what I thought.

Her eye did not quite meet mine. 'I am in excellent health,' she announced.

'It's not the prospects for your future marriage?'

'Certainly not!'

I let the exchange die a natural death, unconvinced.

As for the Duke's officials, Sir William Fincheden, the steward, obeyed my every order with efficiency and a face of stone, while the Constable was encouraging with brisk goodwill and frequent exhortations that all would turn out well, just wait and see.

Agnes had developed a habit of watching me, eyes fluid.

'What's wrong?' I demanded.

Denials showered me from all sides.

It was as if there has been a death in the family, a death of which I was not aware, and they were keeping the bad news from me. At least the children were the same boisterous quartet that they ever were, Joan shadowing me with her poppet, the two older boys pestering the soldiers with demands for tales of gore, and Thomas beginning to crawl with lightning speed.

I tried to pin it down, when had it exactly begun? Since a party of benighted travellers, heading south from Richmond, had asked for hospitality and been given food and overnight lodging. I had not seen them, leaving the good offices to the steward since Thomas was letting his sufferings be loudly known as a tooth began to appear, but perhaps their visit had lit the smouldering embers of unease. Some hideous violence discovered on their route, perhaps.

At the hour for Compline the household joined with me to kneel in the chapel to hear the priest say prayers for our comfort in troubled times. To ask for succour and peace of mind. For holy protection. He addressed the Almighty with assurance.

Then his voice wavered.

'We pray for Lord John, Duke of Lancaster. That he might have strength to uphold what is right under the pressure of this day. Grant him acceptance of his sins, O God, and Your blessing on his desire to do what is right and good.'

'Amen,' we intoned.

I frowned behind my closed eyes. *Acceptance of his sins?*

'Grant him, Almighty God, your succour in his courageous battle against the evil that has pervaded his life.'

'Amen.'

To my left, Agnes sighed heavily.

'We pray, Almighty God, that You will grant him comfort for his soul in these dark days.'

Evil? Comfort for his soul?

'Amen.'

'We pray that he will make recompense for all the offences he has committed, whether privately or publicaly, against King Richard and the realm of England. We pray that Lord John might mend his reputation.' I heard the priest draw in a breath, and swallow heavily. 'We pray that he will no longer be blinded by earthly desire.'

'Amen.'

What was this? My eyes snapped open but could not look at the priest. I dared not. I felt Philippa's glance slide across to me, alighting on me with heavy concern. Over by the wall, Steward Fincheden, spine rigid, stared ahead as if carved of wood.

Was the Duke dead! Was that it? For that single moment I could not breathe, but then I immediately thrust it aside, taking myself to task for such foolish imaginings. If he was dead, brutally done to death in Edinburgh, or on the road south, we would be holding a requiem Mass, not the evening service of Compline. This was merely the product of too many long days of no news and too many fears.

If he was dead, would I not know? I could not imagine his passing from this world without my awareness.

But the priest's words had the cutting edge of a newly honed dagger. Sin. Evil. Succour during dark days. The priest continued, voice stronger into the final blessing, but when I turned my head at last to look at her, Philippa was flushed, her expression anguished before she schooled her features.

I stood abruptly.

'Come with me,' I said without preamble and strode out.

She did not demur, although I thought that she might have liked to. Agnes took it upon herself to accompany us to my chamber.

'Close the door,' I ordered Agnes who was hovering. I faced them, keeping my voice light and steady despite the lively fear.

'What is it? What is troubling you that you are not tell-ing me? And why are you not telling me? Why did we have a need to pray for the Duke's strength in destroying the evil in his life? I am not aware of there being any evil in his life.' I felt a worm of hysteria curling in my belly. 'Tell me what you know, Philippa.'

And as if she were still a child in the school room facing her governess, with head bowed, she replied: 'Nothing, my lady.' She could not look at me.

I changed the object of my attack. 'What prompted the priest to call for God's strength against evil and sin?' I de-manded of Agnes.

'Ah…'

Fear grew inordinately, and leaped in my throat. 'Tell me!' My voice was no longer light or steady. 'Am I too weak to carry the weight of it?'

Agnes and Philippa exchanged glances.

'It is obviously about the Duke. And he's not dead. Is he in danger?'

Agnes lifted her hands in what could only have been de-spair. 'Tell her.'

So Philippa, in her honesty, her clear-sighted affection for me, her inability to lie, did exactly that. Her words were plain and brutally frank.

'My father has made a public declaration. It was when he heard of the rebellion and the destruction of The Savoy. He has repented of…' She paused, then rushed on. 'He has repented of the misdeeds of his evil life. The sin that has forced God to turn his face from him and from England. And he made his repentance in public so there could be no doubt, and no false rumour.'

'In public? A confession in public? He would not!'

I heard the disbelief shrill in my voice. It was impossible.

Risible. The Plantagenet pride would never prompt the Duke to make confession of his sins before an audience. Before a priest, of course. But in some public declaration? Yet here was Philippa, ignoring my dissent.

'It is said that he wept…That his face was awash with tears as he admitted the…the sins he had committed.'

'He would not!' I repeated. 'Where does this calumny arise?'

'From the mouth of a traveller who has passed our gates. And those from Richmond,' Agnes stated, the dismay that I was rejecting lively in her eyes.

'I have not heard.'

'You have not spoken to them.'

No, I had not, yet still…and I knew that I had not heard the worst of it.

'Very well.' I tried for calm. 'So the Duke has repented. Do we not all repent?'

They shared glances again.

'My father has admitted that he is to blame,' Philippa continued. 'That God has chastised him, and because of his wickedness, God has chastised England too, by causing bloodshed and rebellion.' I watched as she bit her lip. 'He has…' She looked to Agnes, a look of such anguish that my belly clenched.

'I think you should sit down, Katherine,' Agnes said, abandoning all formality, as if she were my nurse once more.

'I will not.' By now terror had its cruel hand around my heart.

'Then hear this. My lord of Lancaster has confessed openly to the sin of lechery,' Agnes said.

Lechery. Sins of the flesh. Cold hit me, spreading from my belly as realisation hit hard. If he had confessed to such a sin, it could only be with me.

'Is this true?' It was no longer a denial, but a plea. 'The Duke wept that he had a relationship with me?'

'So it is said.'

I dragged off the padded roll that secured my hair and veil. Suddenly it seemed too heavy to tolerate. Casting the abused material aside, I released my hair from its pins. My head throbbed with pain.

'I don't think that I can bear this after all.'

I must have looked shattered. They pulled me to sit down on the bed, one sitting on either side of me. I refused to let them hold my hands, clasping them hard together in my lap instead.

'Tell me the rest.'

So they did because they must. All the cruel, hurtful details of the Duke's public repudiation of me, which reduced me to wordless despair.

'Do I believe this?' I asked at last, when between them they had destroyed all that made my life worth living. All the joy that had welcomed me on waking to each new day, all the contentment that accompanied me to my bed. The delight in my knowledge of his love for me that had kept me company through the hours of work and family duties. All was laid waste at my feet.

'It must be true,' Philippa urged. 'For your own good you must believe, Katherine. Walsingham has praised my father for turning away the wrath of God so it must be true.'

I was stunned, hardly able to breathe for the solid rock that seemed to have lodged in my chest. 'Where did all this happen?'

'In Berwick. But now we think my father has taken refuge in Edinburgh. We are told…' Philippa paused.

It was Agnes who continued, smoothing a large hand over my disordered hair, as if I were five-year-old Joan. 'They say that my lord the Duke has summoned the Duchess to travel north to meet him. He wishes to be reconciled with her.'

I think I sobbed.

I covered my face with my hands.

'He has renounced you, Katherine,' Agnes said softly. 'The blame is his for taking you in sin, and he must make amends. He has renounced you.'

Once I had thought we would never part. Even an hour ago, I was so secure in the passion that kept us strong against any divisive attack. Was our love not as unbreakable as the interlocking links in a gold chain? We would never part until death claimed one of us.

Yet now…How could I ever envisage that the Duke, my beloved John, would be the brutal instrument of that parting? Suddenly I did not want Agnes's soothing. I pushed her compassionate hand aside and stood, putting distance between us, then whirling to face them. I would make recompense if he were safe, I had vowed. And all the time I was pledging gold candlesticks for Kettlethorpe, he was engaged in casting me aside. When I was offering up prayers and reparation, promises of an endowment in return for his safety, he was throwing me to the wolves. *I will protect you*, he had once sworn on my crucifix.

He had destroyed me.

I stared at the pair of them. 'And when were you going to tell me?'

There was the glance of collusion between young and old.

'When we thought you would be strong enough to accept it,' Philippa said softly.

'I will never be strong enough. Give me a woman strong enough to accept that the man she loves has damned her as the cause of his adultery.'

John, I called out in my mind, in an anguish of pain. *What have you done to me?*

There was no answer. Only my dire knowledge that he, my life, my love, had rejected me as the cause of his lechery.

In the days that followed, I read every nuance in the expressions of those with whom I lived in the garrison at Pontefract: censure, pity, sometimes malicious enjoyment. Expressions that I would have to learn to confront for the rest of my life.

I had been pilloried.

I had been held up as the cause of the Duke of Lancaster's great sin.

It would not go away. It would never go away.

At first, as with any foolishly self-indulgent woman faced with unpalatable truth, I refused to believe it, remaining fervently, dogmatically, adamant. The travellers were misguided, devious mischief-making trouble-stirrers. I could not believe that the Duke would be guilty of a step so outrageously cruel. It was just not possible that the man who had owned my heart, had shared my bed, had fathered my children, had been the creator of all my joy, would lock me out of his life and his household. And what's more, if the Duke had fallen out of love with me, he was the last man to reject me by public proclamation so that the whole world would know it before I did. As for weeping in repentance, on his knees before any gawping onlooker...

I laughed at the enormity of it, but he had become the Duke again in my mind.

I could accept that the Duke might make reparation if he thought some guilt was attached to his arrogance, as many saw it, in wielding power in England in young Richard's name, but not that he would reject me in this manner. Never that.

As for his reconciliation with Constanza. Had his words of love for me been no more than the rattling of a pebble in an empty pot? Never. I would never accept it.

Frustrated, eventually irritated with me, Philippa and Agnes left me to my furious denials.

But now the rumours flew thick and fast, like wasps around the sticky sweetness of wild plums, demanding that I listen, accept. Bloody tales of fire and looting and destruction along the wharves and streets of London, that made me fear for the country I knew, the life I had taken for granted. Flemish merchants in London, dragged out of the church where they had taken refuge, to be beheaded in the street. As a Hainaulter I had indeed been in danger. They would not stop to test the difference.

And then there was the praise for Duchess Constanza. Her goodness, her tolerance, her love for her lord. The perfection of her beauty. Her courage in bearing the humiliation heaped on her by Lancaster and his whore. The whole country had take Constanza to their hearts.

I looked for word in writing or by Lancastrian courier from the north, from the Duke himself, an explanation setting all to rights, and one that I could believe. There was nothing. Had he returned from Edinburgh to England? Perhaps he was even now moving south from Berwick and he would come to me. Of course he would. And when he did he would enfold me in his arms, chastising me for my lack of faith and all would be well. He would take me to his bed and show me that his love was greater than my fears. His adoration would be no rattling pebble but a velvet assertion.

I watched the road. I was not proud. Philippa stood at

my side, stern with disapproval, shivering with fears that matched my own despite the heat of the days.

'Will he come?' she asked as another day drew to its close.

'When he can.'

Don't leave me here in ignorance, John. The pain of not knowing is too great. My heart is torn in two.

The days were endless.

As one June evening sank into late dusk: 'There's an approaching force, my lady. More than travellers.'

The Constable, severe and gruff, stood at my shoulder. In the past week scouts had been sent out for the first time that I could ever recall, as if we might come under attack. In the face of such unrest, coupled with the uncertainty over the Duke's state of mind, our garrison was taking no chances.

'Who? Do we know?' Automatically I strained my eyes to the north for a glimpse of Lancaster banners.

'No, my lady. But they're from the south.'

My hopes, so quickly stirred into life, were quashed.

'And riding fast with outriders,' he advised. 'If they have livery, then it's hidden.'

I forced my thoughts into practical channels of hospitality. 'Do we open the gates?' It would be hard to leave someone benighted in these troubled times.

'We wait and see, my lady. I'll do nothing to put your life in danger. My lord would have my skin if I did.'

'Even if he has spurned me?' I heard myself ask bitterly, the words escaping before I could stop them. Too late: besides, the Constable would know everything there was to know by now.

'Even then, my lady. You were sent here for your protection. And the lady.' He nodded his chin towards Philippa who had emerged from the shadows to join us. She rarely left me alone for long, as if she feared for my sanity. There was nothing wrong with my mind. It was my emotions that were raw and ragged. 'I will do my duty now, and answer questions later.'

We waited, looking south, but not for long before a small force, well mounted, well armed and in close formation, drew rein outside the gate. And no, there was no badge of livery to identify friend from foe.

'Who are you?' bellowed the Constable. 'Make yourself known.'

Immediately at a gesture from the leader of the cavalcade, a pennon was unfurled. Even in the deepening shadows the lions of Lancaster, worked in gold, glimmered as the breeze shook out the folds. Lancaster. But this was not the Duke. A second pennon told its tale. The gilded castles of Castile. My heart leaped with a jolt, then settled to a heavy thudding against my ribs as I leaned against the parapet to peer down.

'Open the gates!' The voice of authority from below was clear enough.

'Who demands it?'

'I speak for my lady the Duchess of Lancaster, Queen Constanza of Castile.'

And the full Lancastrian standard was unfurled, gold-fringed, to hang and lift with languid power. Constanza was here. Constanza was travelling north to meet with the Duke.

Shock. It was shock rather than misery that swarmed through me from head to foot, my fingers clinging onto the hard stone coping. All my attempts at self-delusion had been destroyed in this one hideous, unforeseen arrival, which could only confirm what I had denied, as the lions and the castles on the banner entwined themselves sinuously together. The Duke had sent for her. And as my brain finally accepted that here was Constanza at my door, surrounded by symbols of Lancastrian power, I saw a figure, swathed in a heavy cloak despite the heat, ride forward from the centre of her escort. She pushed the hood back so that, face pale, she looked up to where the voices reached her from our vantage point above the barbican. Beside her I now recognised the captain of her force from the garrison at Hertford. It was his voice that was pitched to us now.

'My lord the Duke of Lancaster has requested that the Duchess come to join him, as he travels south from Edinburgh. It is her wish to stay here at Pontefract until my lord comes to greet her.'

So it was all true. This simply added an even heavier layer of confirmation. The Duke had summoned Constanza to meet with him. I sought her features, expressionless in the distant shadows, but I imagined her lips tight-closed in determination, her eyes bright with the courage it would have taken for her to make this journey. The Duke had asked her to come north, and in her eagerness to be with him she had agreed, riding the length of England, on horseback, risking any dangers. When the Duke had requested her company to travel to the Low Countries it had taken nothing less than a ducal command to dislodge her from the comforts of the palaces and castles she knew. Now her husband had held out his hand to offer her reconciliation, and she had leaped to accept it.

Desolation dragged down on me, mingling with the misery, and out of its coupling, an even deeper emotion leaped into life, and one of which I was not proud. Dry-eyed and furiously cold, I continued to watch, aware of the Constable standing at my side, Philippa silent and watchful at my shoulder. There was a decision to be made here. A lamentable conversation, spiked with fury, played out in my head.

Do I order the gate to be opened for her? Can I bear to spend hours, let alone days, in Constanza's company?

She was constrained to spend days in yours, when you were the favoured one!

But I cannot. I don't have her fortitude. Not when the foundation of my life has been ripped from beneath my feet.

She has the right to demand admittance.

Do I not have the right to refuse her?

No, you don't.

But I have the right not to be present at her reunion with the Duke.

Then go back to Kettlethorpe so you won't have to bear witness...

And then the thought, the despicable thought, slid into my mind that I would indeed refuse her. I would turn her away. Too far distant as we were from each other for our eyes to meet, yet the air between us was stretched, tense and haunted. Was she aware that I was there, on the gate-house parapet, deciding on her future? Motionless, she sat upright in her saddle, without doubt weary to the bone but determined not to show it.

Philippa stirred beside me, a hand to my arm. 'We have to let her in.'

'Yes. I suppose we do,' I said tightly.

The Constable looked at me. He knew that too. But as our eyes met, I sensed a curious level of understanding pass between us, as if he absorbed the depths of all my selfish concerns in denying the Duke's wife the right to come under the same roof as I. Constanza had won. The Duke had chosen her over me, his wife over his mistress. I did not think I could tolerate it, watching her take precedence over me in all the trivial matters of day-to-day living. I had withstood it well enough in past years, because I had been sure in the

Duke's love. But no longer. No longer. He might not love Constanza but he had surely proved in these desperate days that he did not love me either.

How could I possibly be present at their reunion, knowing that she was his choice?

Oh, John! What have you done to me?

For a long moment the Constable waited for my response. Then, receiving no instruction, he leaned over the parapet and informed those who waited below: 'Lady de Swynford is in residence here.'

My breath leached out between my clenched teeth. What had he indeed read in my face? I felt Philippa clutch at my arm. Below me it was possible that Constanza stiffened on her mount, for it sidled restlessly as if her hands had clenched on the reins.

'I don't care if the Devil himself's in residence,' the caustic reply came back from Constanza's captain. 'There's room for any number of households here. What's stopping you opening the gates, man? We need admittance.'

I felt the Constable's glance again before he replied. 'It might be better if you take the Duchess on to Knaresborough.'

'Do you dare to refuse entry to the Duchess?'

The Constable answered without hesitation. Perhaps only I noticed his knuckles, clenched as white as mine against the stone coping.

'I do refuse you. My lord placed Lady de Swynford here for her safety. The castle is in my charge. The Lady Philippa is also here. In the circumstances it is not fitting that the Duchess reside under the same roof. It is better if you go on.'

The refusal swirled in my head. A specious argument, there was no logic to it, only perhaps a desire to protect me from humiliation. From Constanza's biting tongue. The Constable's support was a strange comfort when all around me was black with despair.

Below a laconic conversation occurred between Constanza and her Captain, resulting in: 'The Duchess is afraid to ride on. Notwithstanding the circumstances, she begs that you will give us accommodations for the night.'

Philippa's fingers tightened even more.

'I will not,' our Constable rejoined with astonishing calm. 'Make haste to Knaresborough before the light fails totally.'

'Lady Swynford.' It was Constanza, her voice thin but perfectly audible. 'Lady de Swynford. I beg of you.'

So she had known I was there all the time. I stepped back, as if to hide from her would make my refusal more acceptable, even as I knew that nothing could. It was a deplorable act, lacking in Christian charity, yet although guilt might aim a punch at my heart, I could not do it. It was the Constable who settled it for me.

'The decision has to be mine, my lady. Go on to Knaresborough. You will be safe enough. We have had no disturbances hereabouts.'

Without another word Constanza and her retinue, banners and pennons refurled, turned and rode off towards Knaresborough.

And I?

Could I really allow this? I found that I had taken that step forward again to the parapet. If I raised my hand now, speaking out before one more moment passed, I could halt this debacle. I could call to Constanza, claiming a misunderstanding. I could send a scout riding fast after them to bring them back. If I gave the order the gates would open and she would ride in, the Duchess of Lancaster, in authority in her husband's name. I would curtsy before her and stand aside. My conscience would be clear.

I lifted my hand.

I let it fall. I said nothing, made no attempt to recall them to safety.

'Katherine…!' Philippa's whisper was harsh, her hand on my arm a grip of steel. She had long ago abandoned calling me formally. At twenty-one she had acquired the maturity of years, and of judgement which at this moment was unsparing. 'This is wrong. You can't let it happen. If harm comes to her the blame will be yours to shoulder.'

I shook her off, already riven as I was with that guilt, walking the length of the battlements to watch the vanishing cavalcade, identification once more hidden. Today I had rejected compassion, good manners, duty. Obedience to those who employed me. Had I not in effect, disobeyed the Duke also? Would he not have expected me to offer shelter and safety to his wife?

I was horrified at what I had done. But I could not admit her. I could not.

'We should not have done that.' Philippa, relentless, had followed me. It did not help at all that she had acknowledged the joint decision.

'It is better so, in the circumstances,' I replied flatly. 'It is not far to Knaresborough.'

'But if any harm comes to her—'

The echo of my own words. How devastating they were, stitching in bright colours what I had done.

'Then I will take the blame,' I said. 'You had no part in it. I will answer to the Duke.'

And to God.

Refusing her company I went to the chapel where I prayed to the Virgin, for her intercession, for forgiveness, my thoughts all the time flitting away from my prayers to scenes invisible to me. My self-justification was like the constant and ineffectual pecking of a bird.

Constanza would be safe. She would be reunited with the Duke. The country held her in its heart, in the highest of esteem. Constanza would not be seized and done to death as a detested foreigner. No one would wish harm to her. I was the evil one. If anyone dared attack her she had only to reveal her name, and she would be revered, whereas I was the one who would be torn to pieces. She would place her hand once more in that of the Duke and, his reputation salvaged, all would be put right. For her. For him, in the eyes of England.

I was the one who would be punished.

What a formidable, vengeful mistress England was.

I tore my thoughts away, back to the chapel with its candles and the reminiscence of incense. Even the kindly face of the Virgin was closed against me, stern and unsmiling, as I undoubtedly deserved. It seemed that her downcast eyes deliberately turned away from me. I pressed my clasped hands against my lips, begging for her compassion. Shame was a heavy cloak.

I felt a movement at my side where Philippa was sinking to her knees.

'I will pray with you,' she said. 'The Virgin will listen.'

'I think she will not,' I replied.

'But she will. She will not condemn you for a broken heart. For loving too much.'

Oh, Philippa! Tears welled in my eyes but this was no time for tears. 'I was wrong.'

'You had your reasons.'

'Not such that God would forgive. I was vindictive beyond measure.'

Philippa did not reply but bent her head to her task, her fingers moving over the beads of her rosary. I made to follow her example, then realised as I saw the beads of coral and gold that it was the rosary that the Duke had given me. I closed my fist over the beads. I could not use it. It would make me more of a hypocrite than I already was.

Philippa eventually raised her head, making the sign of the cross.

'It must be true, then,' she said, addressing the altar. 'What my father has done.'

'Yes, it must.'

I saw a long dark road stretching ahead of me, leading me to I knew not what. For the first time in my life I felt frightened and vulnerable. I felt beyond hope.

From the chapel I refused Philippa's companionship and climbed to the battlements once more, despite the darkness, to look north. How often had I done this? Once I would have sensed him. The direction of his thoughts. Sometimes a brush of his emotions. His love.

Tonight there was nothing.

It was as if I faced a stone revetment or a wall of shields. A fortified bastion, I decided fancifully, although I was in no mood to be fanciful.

The Duke had shut me out.

I lifted my hands in silent plea, in despair, then allowed them to fall as a patter of approaching footsteps grew louder. I knew who they belonged to before he raced up the steps.

'John.' I took his hand in mine, letting my hand rest on his head. 'You should be in bed.'

'I escaped from Agnes.'

'I expect you did.'

And then, predictably, Henry. I lifted him into my arms so that he could see over the wall.

'Where is my father?' asked John.

'I wish I knew.'

'Will he come soon?'

'I don't know.'

'Does he know we are here?'

'Yes he does.' I lowered Henry to his feet. 'And now we will go down, or you two will face Agnes's wrath.'

They ran in front of me, surprisingly agile on the turn of the stair. I could imagine them both excelling at military skills as they grew older.

Life would have to go on, for my sake and theirs. I did not know how I could.

What should I do now? Frightened and vulnerable, I never expected to experience such draining emotions, but the sturdy confidence that had built within me over the years now drained away, no matter how often I told myself that I was not without resources. I had Kettlethorpe and Coleby in my son Thomas's name, my annuities, my connections in Lincoln. Margaret and Thomas were provided for. My Beaufort children would never lack. I knew the Duke well enough that whatever might stand between the two of us, his sense of honour was far too strong for him to neglect these children of his blood.

Had I no strength of character to withstand this terrible blow?

Go back to Kettlethorpe.

But I couldn't. I could not yet cut the cord. Caught up in a maelstrom, I remained at Pontefract, wrought with indecision. Until the decision was made for me.

I was in pointed communication with the cook who was overseeing the messy task of dismemberment of a carcass with an eye to making brawn with the brain and offal. I would have retreated long before this, except that his complaints about the quality of the meat and the lack of it were legion, and so it was there that I received a letter. The courier had been directed to the kitchens.

'I was instructed to deliver this to your hand, my lady.'

I took it, and the opportunity to turn my back on the chitterlings, except that they no longer seemed to matter. The letter took all my attention for the inscription was in the Duke's own even script. I opened the cover to find a single page. It was strikingly brief, as if written under duress with haste a necessity. It lacked even a superscription, such as my name.

Do not leave Pontefract. I command it. You must not leave until I can come to you.

And, below, a scrawled signature.

The Duke was coming. He was coming to me.

Rereading it took no time at all. Nor did my decision-making on the strength of this imperious command. I had no intention of leaving. There were things that I needed to say.

A movement at my side made me look up to see the cook, cleaver gripped firmly, watching me. So was the courier, if less overtly. It would be far easier to slink away, back to Kettlethorpe, where I might lick my wounds in private without too many prurient eyes watching my every move. Eyes that, as now, were keen to strip the flesh from my bones.

'Will you sit, my lady?'

What emotions had the cook read chasing across my features? I shook my head but I took the cup of ale he proffered and sipped, feeling the blood flow back beneath my skin at cheek and temple. No, I would not run away to Kettlethorpe. I had been Lancaster's lover for nine years, I had borne him four children. I would wait and hear what he had to say. I would not weep at his feet as, the rumours said, Constanza had done when they met on the road. The emotionally vivid account of their passionate reconciliation had reduced me to unutterable fury.

It swept through me again now, and I cast the letter into the fire in a fit of pique, noting with satisfaction that the wax image of John of Lancaster, King of Castile, surrounded by all the accoutrements of his authority, melted away to nothing in the flames.

What could he say to me that would reinstate him in my good graces? Could I ever forgive him for what he had done?

'Was it important, my lady?' The cook, abandoning his cleaver, nudged me to sit. I must appear to be more fragile than I thought.

'No. Not important at all,' I said with an attempt at a smile. And I did sit, for my legs seemed to have no strength.

But I would wait. I would be here when he arrived. And I might listen.

Chapter Fourteen

The Duke of Lancaster rode with his retinue into the courtyard at Pontefract.

'You waited until I came.'

'As you see.'

It was not an opening that boded well for what was to follow. The courtyard was grey and glistening with the earlier heavy rain that still pattered on my head and shoulders as if in a final lingering defiance. Much like my own frame of mind. I would not take shelter until he had dismounted, even though it was to my discomfort. I would wait as he had instructed. I would be calm, obedient, open to his persuasion. I forced myself to stand and observe with commendable dispassion as he swung down from the saddle and gave his reins to his squire. Throughout all his movements his eyes had not left my face.

It had crossed my mind that I should stay in my chamber. That I should keep him waiting. But that, I decided, would be a sign of immaturity. I would acknowledge his arrival, as I had so many times before. I would listen to what he had to say.

The Duke signalled for his retinue to dismount and take shelter.

'I note the castle is well garrisoned.'

As well he might. It was bristling with military.

'Yes,' I replied. 'We received your orders.'

Apart from my one line of instruction, it had been the only direct communication between the Duke and Pontefract throughout all those difficult weeks. His gaze continued to hold mine as I allowed the silence between us to lengthen. Even in the courtyard with all the noise and bustle of the Duke's dispersing entourage, I felt the power of his regard. It made me shiver. Not from pleasure, as once it might. I kept the contact, every muscle in my body braced against what was to come.

I had expected him to look weary, from travel, from the shock of such vehement hatred flung at him by the rebels. From the loss of his most beloved possession, The Savoy. Even from the acknowledgement that his life had actually been in danger at the hands of Englishmen. In the blackest corner of my damaged heart I hoped that he would look at least careworn. If I felt older than my thirty-two years, why should not he, at a decade older? I resented the little lines that had become ingrained between my brows, the smudge of shadows beneath my eyes from lack of sleep. My mirror was no longer my friend. As I stood there in that inhospitable courtyard, growing wetter by the minute, I studied his face, a very female resentment building as my gown clung in sodden folds.

Why did I not have the sense to go inside?

Because I had anticipated this meeting for so long. I had

longed for it as much as I had feared it. I knew that what
had been between me and the Duke of Lancaster, the overwhelming emotion that had encompassed us in the face of
all tenets of morality and good judgement, would never be
the same again. I could not retreat from it.

And so I took in every inch of him as he stood a good
arm's length from me, remarking that there was no inordinate sign of strain in his visage, and his movements were as
elegantly controlled as I had ever seen them. If the lines between nose and mouth were well marked, I had seen such an
effect when he was faced with a problem of moving troops or
supplying a garrison. A cup of warm ale would soon smooth
away the tension. No, there was no hint here of the man who
had begged God's forgiveness on his knees in public, with
tears staining his cheeks.

The man who had in so cursory and public a manner rejected his lover of nine years, before informing her of his
decision.

I bit down on the little surge of wrath.

'I see you are in health and good spirits, Lady Katherine,' he remarked.

Good spirits!

The flapping of my veil, wetly against my neck, was the
final straw. I raised my chin. Without courtesy or any acknowledgement that he had addressed me, I turned on my
heel. He would follow if he needed to speak with me. Was
I in health? It was the least of my concerns. As for my spirits…I strode on, up the staircase, aware of his footsteps behind me, relieved that he followed me, and yet anger burned
through any relief. I flung back the door into one of the
chambers used by the family for celebrations, empty now
except for a chest and a pair of backless stools, an empty
dais at one end. The walls, usually hung with magnificent

tapestries, as were the rooms of all the Duke's accommodations, were bare and grim. In a corner there was a stash of boxes and trestles, on one resting the folded tapestries.

A bleak place for a bleak reconciliation.

There would be no reconciliation here.

I walked to the centre of the chamber, where I turned.

'We will speak in here. Where there is no one to eavesdrop and pass comment on my shame—or yours.'

The Duke inclined his head, before closing the door quietly at his back, then casting gloves onto the chest, dislodging a swirl of dust as he did so. Something I must take in hand, I thought inconsequentially. The room had not been used of late, nor would be, for we were in no mood for celebrations. What emotion would it witness now? The Duke made no further move to approach me, but stood, hands clasped lightly around his sword belt, the dim light glinting on the breastplate of his half-armour.

'Well?' When my voice sounded annoyingly shrill to my own ears, I tempered it. 'I have remained here as ordered. What would you say to me, my lord?'

The pause was infinitesimal, but I noted it. 'You will have heard by now.'

'Yes. I think I have been the recipient of every piece of rumour about the pair of us that has run the length and breadth of the country.'

I would not make this easy for him.

'They have destroyed The Savoy,' he said.

I raised my brows. Did not all the world know of that? I would not respond.

A muscle in his jaw leaped beneath the fine skin, but so it often did when he might struggle with a document from a difficult petitioner. I folded my hands, one on the other, over the clasp of my girdle. I had had many days to consider all that I knew, almost as many days in which the developments had festered like an ill-tended wound. It would astonish him how much I had gleaned from the gossip of passing travellers. I tilted my chin, as if I might be mildly interested in what he had to say.

I stopped my fingers before they could clench into fists. I would hold fast to composure. I would be reasonable. Understanding. I would, by the Virgin!

'Why have you come?' I asked.

'I had to know for myself that you were safe.'

'Safe,' I repeated unhelpfully.

'But I knew you were. God sheltered you from all harm. I asked Him to.'

My brows remained beautifully arched. 'I am flattered. Or I suppose I am.'

'And I had to come and tell you myself.'

He took a step forward as if testing the water, as if there might be an unseen pit below the surface, into which he would haplessly fall and drown.

My lips thinned and curled minutely. 'So you said.'

His spine was as straight as an ash sapling, his voice raw, but that might be thirst after a long journey. I offered him no refreshment. It was his castle. He could summon his own steward if he so wished.

'It would be discourteous,' he continued in the same limpid but impassive tone, 'for you to be the subject of gossip and not know why I did…why I did what I did. I have come to try to explain…So that you would not remain ignorant…'

Not once had he moved, his breathing as level as if he were purchasing a horse.

'Explain?' I would be understanding, would I? My fingers clenched anyway, nails digging deep into my palms. I kept my voice low, yet even though, raised as I was to impeccable good manners, I knew it was unforgivably venomous, I chose every word with precise care.

'Explain? And I should thank you for that? I have, of course, to be thankful that you have considered my situation to any degree. In the circumstance of my being—what was it you said?—an agent of Satan? But then, you have always considered the welfare of all your servants, have you not, my lord? How charitable of you to dismiss them from your service in Scotland, so that they need not suffer with you in your painful exile there, far away from friends and family. If I had been with you in Edinburgh, doubtless you would have done the same for me. Would you have wept over me, as I am told you did over them? For it seems I am no better than a servant to you.'

My tongue hissed on the word servant. I had not realised the true depths of my bitterness.

'That is not so.' His lips barely moved.

'Ah…Were the rumours then false? I did not think so, but I am willing to be persuaded. Answer me one question, my gracious, chivalrous lord. Are you sending me away?'

The silence in the room was as taut as a bowstring before the release of the deadly arrow.

'Yes.' He took a breath as if he would have said more. Then repeated: 'Yes. I am sending you away.'

My anger bubbled dangerously, too dangerously, near the surface.

'I don't think I can ever forgive you,' I said between clenched teeth, 'for the manner in which you did it.'

'What have you heard?'

'You would not believe what I have heard. I did not, at first. Until each repetition came as a slap in the face.'

'And now you believe what is said? You hold it to be the truth without hearing me? To know why I took the decisions that I did?' His hands remained clenched at his belt. 'Do I not at least deserve a hearing from you, of all people? If you love me, you will hear me out.'

For a moment I closed my eyes against the pain of that thrust. But only for a moment.

'Oh, I will give you a hearing, my lord. I will listen,' I said. 'But it is difficult to give you the benefit of the doubt, is it not? When Constanza rode past my door, intent on an emotional and intimate reunion with you.'

He had not expected that from me. His eyes widened a little.

'Is that what happened?' I asked.

'Yes.'

A flat affirmation, all I needed, all I dreaded. It was what I had feared more than any other. I turned my back on him because I could not look at him without weeping, and marched to the window, the thick glass grown opaque with rain and gloom, where I smacked my knuckles hard against the stone surround.

'Oh, they relished telling me the detail of that little event,' I announced to the view I could not see. 'What pleasure to give all the details to the whore, of the triumphant victory of the ill-used wife.' I looked back over my shoulder as I fought to control my voice. 'They told me how you met on the road at Northallerton. How the distraught Duchess fell on her knees in the dust at your feet and begged your forgiveness for her lack of affection towards you. Three times she prostrated herself, so they told me. Three times, with tears and wailing, until you lifted her up and reassured her that all would be well between you. Is that how it went?'

I saw my lips curl again with wry appreciation, a grey reflection in the glass, but there was no humour in it. Poor Constanza. Had she accepted at last that she had had a part in causing the rift between them? Did the attack on her precious Hertford stir enough terror in her heart that she saw the need to humble herself and beg her husband's protection? In my own loss I had no sympathy for her. I turned my face away, so that he would not note the gleam of moisture on my cheeks, to watch him in the reflection.

'Did you? Did you lift her into your arms?'

'Yes.'

I nodded as if in agreement. 'Of course you did. That is exactly what you would do. And then you escorted her to the safe luxury of the Bishop of Durham's house where you marked the occasion of your joyful reunion. Until daylight, I understand, with great merriment and celebrations. You asked pardon for your misdeeds and she willingly forgave you.' I looked up, stretching my neck, noting the carving of a cat stalking some misbegotten creature in the stonework above my head. I had never spoken to him in this manner before, but I did not care. I did not care if it roused the fire of his temper. 'Before God, John, *I* was not invited to the safety of the Bishop's lodging, was I! No place for me. No place for the whore.'

'No.'

Again that cold affirmation of my accusations, that flat acceptance, when my soul longed for his denial.

'No,' I repeated. 'There could be no place for me, could there?'

In my mind I saw our two disparate reunions with the Duke, Constanza and I placed side by side, one dramatic and emotional, a true reconciliation for the Duchess, with intimate kisses and promises for the future. The other, as we stood here now, the width of the room between us, bitter and redolent of raw grief, a portcullis of iron lowered between us.

And as that vision filled my mind, without warning all

control vanished. I swung round, pressing my back against the stone. 'You rejected me. You denounced me. An evil life, you said, that you had led with me. A life of *lechery*.' I all but spat the word. 'Was our love lechery? You stated it, for all to hear. I'm amazed that you did not get your herald to announce it with a blast of a trumpet. You will drive me from your household, you said. Banish me. That's what you said, isn't it?'

'Is that what you believe?'

'It is what I am told.'

Every muscle in his face was still. The jewels gleamed flatly, without movement. It was as if all his Plantagenet pride was under restraint. I had never seen it so. I could only attribute it to guilt.

'And is it true that you labelled me a she-devil?' My voice broke on the word. 'An enchantress, who lured you into breaking your marital vows? Am I a snare of the Devil, to entice men into sin?'

I saw him take a breath.

'They were not my words.'

'No? Well, thank God for that!'

'But you believe it of me.'

And there I heard a note of self-loathing, which I ignored. 'I expect you implied them since they were well reported. Or you did not make too much haste to deny them. It would not be in your interest to do so, would it? What pleasure Walsingham must have had in putting such venom into your mouth. I expect he fell to his oh-so-pious knees before God and gave thanks for such a confession from the mighty Duke of Lancaster, the would-be King of Castile.'

His title shimmered into the silence as I drew breath at last. I was beyond remorse. He might have accepted for himself the vile charge of adultery, but he had coated me with the filth of witchcraft. What manner of attack would this lay me open to? I could not comprehend the horrors of my being brought to book for witchcraft.

'Have you nothing to say?' I demanded. 'I accuse you, but you do not defend yourself. Is there no defence? Are you guilty as charged?'

For the briefest moment he studied his hands, then he looked at me, and I saw what I had not seen before. His eyes were tired. Hard and grim. The eyes of John, my love, they were not. They were those of the Duke of Lancaster, putative King of Castile. Here was a different creature, not the man I had thought I knew.

How easy had it been for him to stop loving me?

'I did not put the blame on you, Katherine,' he stated.

'Ha!'

'But yes, I said that we must part.'

'Oh, I know you did. For the good of your immortal soul. Was I nothing more than a court concubine? Is that all I was to you, through nigh on ten years of sharing your bed and the travail of four children?' My hands were clenched hard in my skirts. 'I have given up everything for you. I was a respectable widow when you issued your invitation. Did I lure you into that? I don't think so, my lord. As I recall the impetus was all yours. And yet you call me an enchantress, using witchcraft to undermine your strength of moral will.'

'I have said…' How quiet his voice, how undemonstrative, but now the engraved lines that bracketed his mouth were deep. 'The words were not mine.'

'Yet you have repulsed me. You have destroyed all we meant to each other, stripping it of all that was good, stamping it into the earth as the grossest of sins.'

As his nose narrowed on an intake of breath, I thought he

would react but he did not, except to say: 'It was a sin, our being together. We both knew it.'

'Yes, we did. Both of us. And we were prepared to live with it. And yet you reject me now. I gave you my good name. I gave you my unconditional love, my body, my conscience. I put them into your safe-keeping.'

'Perhaps you should not have done that.'

Which took my breath. I could not answer so monstrous an assertion, that I had been wrong to trust him with my life, my happiness. My soul.

'And our children?' I whispered against the grinding agony in my chest. 'Are they also a sin?'

'No, they are not.' His hands now unclasped, he flung them out at his sides. 'Katherine, the sin is mine.'

'Forgive me. But a greater part of it seems to be mine.' The edge that crept back into my reply could have sliced through a haunch of venison like Hugh the cook's cleaver. 'I am despised by all, but Constanza has emerged in glory, in blinding-white robes. Oh, I know I cannot defend myself in helping you to commit adultery, in undermining Constanza's position in your life and household. I am not proud of my flaunting our love before her, or of stepping into the place she should have had at your side and in your bed. But she did not want you. I will not take all the blame.'

A pale fleeting emotion that I could not read touched his face.

'There is no reasoning with you, is there?'

'No. None.'

'What more can I say?'

'Did you weep, as they say you did, when you bared your soul in public?' I could not imagine his weeping in public penance. I could not. It was the most ludicrous of all the rumours.

The Duke did not reply. The austerity was hammered flat with intense weariness under my relentless assault. Instead, starkly, brusquely: 'You must understand the new threat. There are French plans to invade England. The most effective way for us to prevent it is to make an alliance with Portugal. Between us we can invade and crush Castile, France's ally.' I could see that his mind was already taken up with the planning. 'If I am to invade Castile I need to be reunited with Constanza. Enrique is dead, but his son Juan reigns in his stead. I need Constanza's authority behind me if I am to oust King Juan and reclaim Castile. As it has always been…'

Another dart in my flesh, upon which I pounced with cruel delight, ignoring the high demands of English foreign policy. 'And you put your authority in Castile before me? Of course you do. I would expect no other. Have you not always done so?'

He inclined his head in due acceptance, yet still, to my mind, twisted the blade.

'I am a man of ambition. You knew that. You have always known that.'

There was no denying it. Unable to face him any longer, my limbs trembling with damp and too-fervent emotion, I stalked to the side of the room, and, spreading my skirts, I sat on one of the stools. It was not seemly for me to berate him like a fishwife. I would return to reason.

'So you have done with me at last, my lord. I suppose that ten years is a fair record for a mistress.' I was proud of my light pronouncement. 'I am banished to Kettlethorpe, with my children. I have no further place in your life.' I stared down at my interwoven fingers. I was suddenly so weary of it all and beyond anger.

'There is more fault to tell, Katherine…'

'Over and above the rest? What more can you possibly have done to hurt me?'

I heard his heavy inhalation. 'I have not kept faith with you. When I repented...I renounced all the other women I had taken to my bed.'

'All?' I exhaled slowly.

'You were not the only one with whom I sinned.'

'There were others?' And without allowing him to reply: 'Before God, John! And are you going to argue weakness of the flesh? Opportunity? Availability?'

He stiffened, with a flare of temper burning through the control like fire through a field of dry grass. 'I am a man with a man's appetites. But I have no excuses.'

I could not comprehend. I felt lost, everything I had believed in laid waste as if by the fire and sword of an avenging force. There had been other women in the ducal bed. When I had thought his love was mine alone, his body had betrayed me with other women. I could not contemplate how many, how often...

'How many? One? Two?' I stood abruptly. I could not sit, but swept to the door. I could stay here with all the hurt and humiliation no longer. 'Am I the last to know? Does Constanza know?' I could not bear the degradation of my lover handling my heart with such contempt.

'Not as many as the rumours say,' he said, as if that would make a difference. It lit my wrath again.

'Does that make it any better?'

'No. My penitence can never make it better for you. My heart was yours, but sometimes—'

'Sometimes you needed to indulge your physical needs,' I broke in. 'And any woman would do.'

'I cannot defend myself, Katherine. I have known times

when the demands of my body overcome the loyalty of my soul.'

'On campaign?'

'Yes.'

'Here in England?'

'Yes.'

I simply stared. If I had been hurt before, I was now devastated. Fleetingly I recalled standing on the wall-walk here at Pontefract, with at least some hope still alive, even as I acknowledged my hurt. I had not known the half of it. There was no hope, none at all.

'In the bed I have shared with you?' I asked trenchantly.

'No. Never that. Katherine.'

He took a step towards me. I took one back until the door stopped me, as a sudden unadorned thought struck me.

'Not my sister! Please God, not that.'

'No!' The planes of his face were set with anguish. But so, I thought were mine. 'Not your sister. I would not do that to you. Would you believe that of me?'

I could not think, not knowing what to believe, what to say, except, in infinite desolation:

'You have wounded me unto death, John.'

Without answering, he walked to look out from the same window that had taken my attention. I saw his face reflected, shimmering, pale as a ghost. Then he swung round to face me and for the first time in all that exchange, he retaliated against me, the jewels leaping into life.

'I must turn away God's wrath, Katherine. I must live by His dictates. How can we deny God's anger when we are faced with such rebellion and destruction in England as we have seen these past months? If I am the cause, if my manner of living has drawn down God's punishment on this nation, then I must of necessity repent and make reparation.'

All spoken with an awful, calm, precise, relentless certainty.

But I in my dismay refused to listen.

'Then I hope you sit in heaven at God's right hand on the strength of it.' And then, a cry from the heart that I could not prevent. 'Have you grown tired of me? If that is so, then I wish you had told me—'

'I could never grow tired of you. You know that.'

'But I don't know it. I am struggling to understand any of this.'

I saw no reason for his denial of me. I had been swept behind the tapestry as if our love had been a sin. A crime. Was that all I had ever been to him, a convenient whore? My mind came back to that one point again and again until it sickened me. I could never forgive him for that.

'I am well-served, am I not? I remember the day when you proclaimed your love for me before your wife and your damsels. You cannot imagine the depth of happiness you gave me. Now you have disclaimed your love before every man and woman in England. You have broken my heart.'

I put my hand on the door-latch, hoping against all possibility that he might say something profound and ameliorating, to sweep away the anguish of the last minutes. I looked back, over my shoulder, at the fine-drawn handsome features, the braced shoulders, the motionless control that was back in place.

'You have wounded me, John. You have destroyed all my happiness,' I informed him.

His reply was severe. Deliberate and unhurried.

'I cannot heal the wounds for you, Katherine. Nor my own. Perhaps we don't deserve happiness. Perhaps, by seizing our own desires, we have caused too much damage, to too many people. And now we are called on to pay the price of our wilful carelessness.'

It was as harsh a blow as any man could possibly deliver, to chastise the senses. A slap of a hand. A deluge of freezing rain. The fear engendered by a bolt of lightning striking a tree in the forest. Our happiness, recklessly, selfishly pursued, had undoubtedly hurt others, forcing on them difficult choices. Who knew what compromises Philippa and Elizabeth had been called on to make, out of their love for their father? Constanza had had to make the greatest.

It was not an argument that I could ignore, as he well knew.

And I resented it, resented his forcing me to see the obliteration of my moral bearings. I had not expected my lover to stab me in the back quite so effectively.

I opened the door, looking back for the final time. An empty room, stripped of all past glory, except for its owner with the spangle of rain still in his hair and marking his velvet and armour. What a fitting place to end a love that I had thought would last for all time. What a fitting place to utter the words I never thought I would, and immediately wished I had not.

'Do you not love me anymore?'

In horror and shame, for such a question could only bring down humiliation on both of us, I pressed my fingers against my lips, dismayed that they had so betrayed me. The Duke, eyes stark, skin lacking all colour, simply looked as if I had driven home a knife into his flesh.

He made no reply. I walked from the room. He did not try to stop me.

We had not touched, not once.

And the thought came to me as I walked rapidly to my chamber, how little he had said, to explain or to justify.

Merely that he must turn God's wrath away from England. But then, there was nothing to explain, was there? It was the first time that we had met since the earliest days when there was not even a smile exchanged between us. But then, there was nothing to smile about either.

If our love had been hacked and laid low by Walsingham's cruel blows, even more had it been dealt its death wound by the Duke's despicable sense of duty.

I gave no thought to the dust in the chamber, as any good housekeeper should. I did not care if I could inscribe my name in it, on the top of the coffer. By choice, I would never enter that room again.

I was done with Pontefract Castle. I was done with the Duke of Lancaster, with the world he inhabited, his newly awakened sanctity. I was done with it all and for ever. The decisions made through one sleepless night, dry-eyed and wrathful, were not difficult. I could not stay here.

I hugged my beloved Philippa as I oversaw the preparations for my departure, but was fit to say little to her beyond farewell.

'Write to me,' she whispered against my hood.

'I will. And you to me.' I dredged up some suitable thoughts from the well of my own self-pity, managing a grimace that might pass for a smile. 'Tell me when you have a husband. Tell me of Elizabeth.' I did not think Elizabeth would write to me.

Her eyes glistened with anxiety. I gave up on the smile.

'Where is he?' I could not call him by name. The castle buzzed with gossip, mostly accurate, except that I had not drawn a blade against him. I had behaved with perfect propriety, principally because there had not been a dagger to hand in my chamber of choice. The sharp blades had only been those stitched in the folded tapestries.

Now I would leave with the same cold composure that had governed my every public action since I had heard what he had done.

I did not wish to meet him. Not again, while my heart was so sore. And after what had passed between us, it would be best if it were never again. I slammed the door closed on all my unsettled emotions, turning my thoughts to the practicalities of packing my belongings into the wagons, settling the children into the vast horse-drawn litter. All the necessities for my return to Kettlethorpe. How had we managed to acquire so much since our flight to Pontefract, reassured that the Duke held my safety close in his heart? No matter. I belonged to the house of Lancaster no longer.

'I don't know where my father is.' Philippa cast a glance at the windows of his apartments above our heads. There was no sign of movement there.

I took a breath to swallow what might have been a twinge of regret if I had allowed it. We had slept apart in cold, lonely beds. He had not come to break his fast with me. He had not come to bid me adieu.

He does not know you are leaving, honesty murmured in my ear.

Well, he should know. He should have known that I would not stay. And unless he is deaf he will have heard the racket of departure...

The lively voices of John and Henry, the chatter of Joan and the cries of Thomas, could hardly be ignored.

I mounted and rode out through the gateway. I would never return to one of Lancaster's castles.

The moisture on my cheeks was, of course, caused by the brisk wind.

* * *

I rode in silence for the first half-hour beside the sergeant-at-arms, aware of nothing around me, not even the clamour of children's voices and Agnes's occasional sharp rejoinder, as my emotions swung wilfully into a well-worn track. I would live alone. I would take a vow of chastity and, although not shunning society, I would order my days with piety and seemliness, wrapping myself in the ordered emotions of a nun, as many grieving widows were drawn to do. I would beg God's forgiveness for my life of unspeakable sin. All the fire in me that the Duke had once admired would be quenched. Cold ash, grey and insubstantial, would replace bright flame. I would devote myself to being Lady of Kettlethorpe, supremely gracious. Completely unresponsive to excess of feeling.

John of Lancaster would hold no part in my life, in my thoughts. Not even in my dreams. Now that all his perfidy was laid bare, beyond question, it would be a simple matter to close and lock the lid on this coffer of memories. What's more, I would drop the key into the well at Kettlethorpe.

Surreptitiously I blotted the persistent tears.

And meanwhile I would draw on my reserves and converse with the sergeant as any sensible well-mannered woman would do.

I asked about the villages through which we were passing.

'Quiet enough,' he said, showing the direction of his thoughts. 'They're my lord's own lands, of course. It's only the bloody Percys who've turned traitor.'

'What of the Percys?' I asked, momentarily distracted. I knew the Percy family, the powerful Earls of Northumberland who ruled their territory in the north as autocratically as any prince.

'They only snubbed him, didn't they? A bloody insult. And all my lord could say was that he understood their divided loyalties. I'd have ordered a sharp punitive attack against one of their bloody castles, but of course, my lord would have none of it.'

'Tell me,' I said.

'When we were coming south from Berwick. My lord would have stopped off at Bamborough. The big fortress on the coast, you know? So what did Harry Percy do? Only send a message that my lord would receive no welcome there. He closed the gates. And Harry Percy supposed to be an ally. Lancaster was not welcome to stay in any of his castles, he said, until King Richard informed him—personally, mind—that the Duke could be trusted. A bloody insult, I say.'

He had not told me of that. That the Duke of Lancaster, the most powerful and experienced of all English nobles, had been treated as if he were an outcast.

The fire was not quenched, not quenched at all, nor were the memories locked away in their box. The flames danced and flickered as the lid on my memories flew open, and tears for the humiliation he must have faced slipped silently down my cheeks. I wiped them away with the back of my glove and raised my chin. I would not be swayed by tales of his suffering.

If I was to live alone for the rest of my life I would need fortitude, and best start now.

'Halt!'

At the sudden command from the sergeant, startling me into tightening my hands on the reins, my mount tossed her head as our little entourage came to a ragged halt, the litter swaying on its supports.

'What is it?'

I could see no problem. Was one of the horses lame? We

had travelled no distance, since we made slow progress with the cumbersome litter.

'Horses approaching…Behind us.'

As the sergeant gestured to his three men to draw arms and move to the rear, so shielding us from any direct assault, I picked up the faint beat of hooves. It did not do to be complacent even in the Duke's lands, not as matters stood, despite the sergeant's confidence. We were approaching the crossroads where I would turn east for Lincoln, a spot with a bad reputation for ambush and bloodshed. Fear mounting with every second, I drew my mare to the side of the litter where John and Henry had pulled back the leather curtain to investigate, unaware of any danger. I said nothing as I loosed the dagger I kept in my sleeve when I travelled.

The sergeant rode to my side.

'Is it robbers?' I asked.

'No. Too many. Too well organised.'

The beat of hooves grew louder to echo the thud of my heart. They were travelling fast, a sizeable body.

'Perhaps some knight and his retinue, my lady,' the sergeant said, yet I saw the apprehension in his grip on his sword, which he had drawn from its scabbard. Then his face cleared and he grunted. 'Nothing to concern you, lady.' He nodded to the body of horsemen that had emerged through the trees on the bend in the road. 'It's my lord.'

I momentarily closed my eyes, for in that moment of foolish embarrassment I thought I might truly have preferred a rabble of cutpurses and footpads. On top of all my ungovernable feelings, beyond all reason, fury filled me to the brim, that he had given me cause for such fear.

How close I was to anger in those days.

Decidedly unfriendly, I sat and watched as they approached at a smart canter, the splash of colour on tabard and banner so vivid that I absorbed every detail of it, as if I were not involved. Here was no effort to hide incriminating livery. The Duke was travelling in full glory of red and gold and blue, royal colours, splashed with emblems of Lancaster and Castile, sun glinting on the half-armour, his gauntlets, on the blood-red jewels in his cap. Beside him his herald rode with tabard, staff and horn. Behind him an escort of a dozen men emblazoned with the quarters of Lancaster and Plantagenet, two of them leading pack horses.

Oh, it was a magnificent impression, deliberately made by a man who knew how to squeeze every drop of splendour from personal appearance, as I well knew. The sun blazed on the profusion of gold thread and costly jewels. This was not the Duke of Lancaster, penitent and downcast at the enormity of his sin. This was a royal Plantagenet in full fettle.

But why? Was it pure coincidence that the demands on his time would bring him on this road, at this exact moment? It might, of course. Even their slackening of speed proved nothing. He could hardly ride on past me as if he had no knowledge of me when everyone in his company and mine knew that we had shared a bed, frequently and scandalously.

I watched as he drew his horse into a sedate walk towards where my mount still stood. What if he had come to reclaim me, to take me home? Was it possible that he had, after all our vicissitudes, made the choice, of me as his mistress, his love, over the demands of a vengeful God and a neglected wife? Had he come to put all right?

No. That could never be.

They drew rein in a jingle of horse-harness and a stamp of hooves on the road. The Duke swept off his splendidly glittering hat and bowed low.

I sat and stared.

What are you doing? Why have you followed me? To heighten the pain of my grief?

'I am here to mark your departure, Lady de Swynford, since you left Pontefract betimes.'

'There is no need, my lord,' I replied quickly, hoping to bring this to a fast end, my throat as arid as a summer riverbed. I did not want this mark of consideration. I hoped that my tears had dried without incriminating marks. I was in no mood to retract any of the things I had said the previous night. 'We said all that needed to be said yesterday.'

'Do you say?' he responded. 'I think not. There are things that need to be done before any man or woman leaves my service.'

Face stern, voice laconic, words clipped, he was enjoying this as little as I, as I could tell by his gloved hands planted one on top of the other on the pommel and the manner in which he addressed me, as if I were a troublesome petitioner for his charity. He saw this as a duty, unpleasant, tedious even, but one that could not, in his cold and chivalrous heart, be ignored.

'What are you going to do, my lord? Offer me another pretty silver chafing dish? Or should I return the one I already have to you. Constanza would value it. I have it here with me.'

His lack of reaction was commendable under such a jibe, but I knew I had hurt him when he inclined his head, acknowledging the hit. His manners were better than mine.

'I can do better than that, my lady.'

'I need nothing from you, my lord.' My features felt stiff, frozen in my desire to rebuff. I found it difficult to choose the words I wanted, but I did so and they were not kind. 'You owe me nothing and I have no claim on you.'

Ignoring my lack of grace, the Duke gestured to the herald who urged his mount to my side to present me with a folded document, which I took it with my gloved finger tips, but did not open it.

'This is my recognition of your service, principally to my two daughters, but also my son, my lady.' How formal he was, unperturbed by my lack of decorum. 'I could not have chosen better. My daughters will for ever be in your debt. It is a pension of two hundred marks a year for the term of your life for your exemplary attention to their education and happiness.'

'No!' The ignominy of being paid for my services. I let the folded sheet with its seal fall to the floor.

'Have you not earned it?' he continued. 'Would you decry the benefit of your care for my daughters? Shame on you, Lady de Swynford, to deny me the opportunity to reward your service in my household.'

I felt my face heat with embarrassment. How clever he was at making me see the unworthiness of my response. When the herald patiently dismounted and retrieved the smeared document, I took it, as if it had been dropped by a moment's carelessness.

'I am unable to express my thanks, my lord. I ask pardon for my unwarrantable demeanour.' There were still no fair words in my acceptance, but I had been shown the error of my ways. Pray God that that was the end of it, that I would be free to continue my journey. Pray God that this arrogant man would make no more claim on me. I gathered up my reins, but was stilled by the herald, still standing at my horse's withers. He took hold of my bridle, even when I frowned down at him.

Touching his horse with his heel, the Duke rode closer.

'It is not to be permitted that you leave my employ and my household without my marking the occasion. It is not fitting that you flee like a thief in the night.' He raised his hand to summon the little group of servants from the rear of his escort. They rode forward, leading two horses laden with luggage and a richly caparisoned riding horse. 'If you will honour me by dismounting, Lady de Swynford...'

I balked.

He dismounted, to stand looking up into my face. His might have been engraved in stone.

'If it please you, my lady.'

He took my bridle from his herald's hand, his fingers clamped around the leather, and I read in his eyes that if it did not please me he would drag me from my mare. Clutching the document—I would not drop it again—I dismounted in cold dignity.

A snap of his fingers and his squire approached. Without any word being needed from the Duke, the young man took the document from my nerveless fingers, unfastened the brooch that pinned my cloak—a fine cloak, I had thought— and with a flamboyant swing of costly material, replaced it around my shoulders with one of fine woven wool lined with sable. The riding horse was led up and the squire tucked the document into one of the panniers, my old cloak folded away into the other.

Throughout the whole procedure, the Duke stood in silence. Within the travelling litter, Agnes looked on with a mix of astonishment and baffled amusement. I was furiously compliant.

'I do not need a new cloak,' I informed the squire who was neatly fastening the pin that gleamed with gold and the splash of blood-red. So I was to be bought off with sables and jewels, was I?

'It is my lord's wish,' the squire said with a bow.

'I have a horse.'

'And now you have a better one, my lady,' the Duke re-marked, with more than a hint of warning. He would not be gainsaid. 'The packhorses carry meat and wine. The escort will accompany you to Kettlethorpe. For your peace of mind.' His eyes were direct. 'And mine.'

So I was to travel in full ducal splendour as well. What level of recognition was this from the Duke of Lancaster, for all to see and comment on?

'Why are you doing this?'

Without replying, the Duke walked to the litter where, leaning an arm on the support, he stooped to peer in. For the first time since he had drawn rein, his features softened a little. He ruffled John's hair, restored a little armed knight to Henry after lifting him back onto the cushions, spoke softly to Joan and straightened her bonnet, and touched the cheek of Thomas.

I could not look. I could not watch without my heart being torn in two. They were as much his as mine. Did he not care? He was abandoning them too. I would not look.

But I did. The children said not a word, in awe of him in this gleaming splendour. And then John grabbed his sleeve.

'Do you come with us, sir?'

'No. Not today.' His smile was forced, his reply ragged. 'But my men will keep you safe. You will ride with an escort, as a young prince should. What do you think?'

'I think I will be a knight one day,' John replied.

'So do I think it. You will be a great knight.'

He turned and again nodded an unspoken instruction to the squire who, with a polite request, took my arm and helped me into my new saddle. The Duke remounted too, and bowed, hat in hand.

'I commend you and your children to God's care, Lady de Swynford. To his forgiveness for what has been between us. I will make restitution for the wrong I have done to you. You will want for nothing.' His authority, in the centre of a road in the depths of the country, was formidable, his diction pitched for all to hear. 'I accept your reluctance to receive anything from my hand, but I hope that time will heal, and that you will not refuse my gifts. My sons and daughter should not be allowed to suffer.'

While through it all I sat angry and silent and hard-eyed. Did he think I would let pride stand in the way of his support for the children? Did he truly think I would let my humiliation guide my future decisions for their well-being? I would not!

'I will know that you have reached Kettlethorpe safely.'

'My thanks, my lord.' It was all I could say.

'If you are ever in need, my lady, in any danger, you will send word.'

It was not a request. I did not respond.

'I will keep you in my thoughts, Katherine.'

I turned away. I made no reply. I rode away from him, cloaked, caparisoned, as superbly mounted as if I were of royal blood. Dry-eyed and stern faced, I vowed to fulfil my promise to the Virgin to clothe the altar at Kettlethorpe in gold. The Duke was safe, alive. It behoved me to do what I had vowed before the altar, even though he had broken my heart.

Well, everyone in our joint retinues now knew the truth about us. And the need to gossip being what it was, it would spread like an unpleasant rash.

I did not know what to make of it. It stunned me, such overt recognition of me and what I had been to him, for all to hear. Another public confession, in effect. An admission of guilt and responsibility, risking the wrath of God one more time, risking the wrath of the Church in the nasty guise of Walsingham if he got to hear of it. As he would.

And yet this had been a very intimate recognition of my place in his life, and of his children.

Why had he done it? Was it to win my forgiveness? Was it to assuage his own guilt that had made him follow and award me such astonishing recognition?

Well, if that's so, he's failed.

I would not forgive him. He had pilloried me just as harshly as Walsingham had, so plainly that I was known to every man and woman in England as Lancaster's whore who had dragged him into a life of sin.

I rode away from him, with no inclination to look back. I would not. I rode on a new horse with a new cloak and all the ducal panoply around me, and a gift of great value in my pannier, the confirmation of my pension almost burning a hole through the leather. Two hundred marks a year: a vast sum, which, for the sake of our four children, I could not refuse.

But in my chest was a hole large enough to encompass the heavens.

It would be better when I had returned to Kettlethorpe, I assured myself. There I could forget and set my feet firmly on a different path.

The magnificent cloak proved to be far too heavy for the clement weather but in sheer defiance I wore it all the way home.

It was not better. It was not better at all. Why would this love not let me go? Why did it continue to yearn, hopelessly, helplessly for reconciliation?

There was no hope, yet it would not let me be.

I wished my love for him dead, but it would not die.

Kettlethorpe became a place of sorrow to me. Since I was no longer part of his life and his household, what right did the Duke have to prowl through my thoughts and dreams, reminding me at every turn of what I had lost? I could not accept, I could not sufficiently grasp all that had happened, all we had been to each other, now destroyed. My heart shivered in its desolation, its absolute aloneness.

In its total bafflement.

Were we still not held captive in that grand passion that allowed us no freedom to exist apart from each other, like silver carp from my fishpond trapped in a net? Even when I hated him I longed to see him ride through the arch of my newly constructed gateway into the courtyard as he had done so many times. How could we deny all that we had said and done together? All those words of love and honour, torn up and scattered.

The silver carp might wish to escape the net; in my heart of hearts, I had no such desire.

The empty space in my chest continued to grow until it all but swallowed me.

Nor were my thoughts stirred into liveliness when my sister Philippa appeared in my hall, informing me with infuriating lack of feeling that she considered me in need of her advice. The Duchess Constanza, in her reinvigorated marriage, could manage without her for a week or two.

'Look at you, malingering and wasting away,' she announced.

'I am neither malingering nor wasting,' I replied briskly, drawing her into my parlour, another new addition to my home. Even if I was, I would not exhibit such weakness to Philippa.

My sister, with narrowed eyes, taking in the evidence of my unfortunate pallor and the loose neckline of my gown, was not to be deflected.

'If he means so much to you, are you going to accept this estrangement? If your love is as strong as you say it is, go to Kenilworth. Tell him that you will not accept your banishment from his life. Tell him that—'

'How can I? How can I fight against England and God?'

'I did not think that would stop you!'

It made me laugh. But without much humour.

'He has hurt me. He has hurt me too much.'

'You should remarry,' my sister remarked when we sat together at the end of the day, her eye to my flushed cheeks as we stitched.

'And why do you say that?' I asked, smiling brightly to hide my dismay. Was this to be the pattern of my days, those who knew me encouraging me to bury my disillusionment under some new relationship?

'It will take your mind off Lancaster.'

Philippa, never less than forthright; Agnes, sitting comfortably at her side, nodding her agreement.

'And who of status would be interested in taking on a woman with my notoriety?' I asked. I resented their matrimonial dabbling.

'I can think of any number who would take on a woman with a guarantee of income from Lancaster.'

'And four bastard Beaufort children?'

'Why not? They will be well provided for.' Philippa shrugged as she stabbed with her needle. 'Lancaster will not leave you bereft, even with a new husband.'

I bent my head over my sewing, noting that the stitches were awkwardly uneven but was not of a mind to unpick them. Marry again? Could I see myself, ensconced in a different manor house, or enjoying a town house in Lincoln? With another unknown man to share bed and board. To share thoughts and ideas at the end of a long day. To carry another child for.

'I will not,' I said.

'So it's to be a vow of chastity, is it? To live as a nun, without the cloister.' Philippa slapped her hand down on her lap. 'In God's name, Kate, you are still young enough to have your own life. Will you flounder in misery because one man had turned his back on you?'

'I am not floundering.'

'I say you are. There is no reason why you should not visit friends. Even go to Court. The King has always had a high regard for you, and with the prospect of a new young wife, he would welcome you. And yet you shut yourself away here as if you have nothing to look forward to but death.'

I stared at the pair of them, rejecting their advice out of hand. The young King might welcome me to his new court with his beautiful young wife, Anne of Bohemia, but the Duke of Lancaster would also be there. And so would Constanza.

'No, I will not go to Court. And it is not true—I have not shut myself away. I have merely taken up my duties to Kettlethorpe and Coleby for my son. I am content. I will not visit friends. I will not go to Court, even if King Richard invites me. I will not remarry. We will just have to survive here together, three abandoned females, without a man to add disruption to our lives.'

My smile had long since vanished.

Philippa, equally with no hope of a reconciliation with her much-travelled husband, cast her stitching onto the floor. 'I can think of a better way of life.'

So could I, but I would not admit it. 'Then if that is so

you must return to the Duchess,' was all I would say. In my present mood, I wished that she would, whilst I lived like the nun the Duke had made me.

Chapter Fifteen

I heard of the Duke's movements, his achievements, even when I would rather not. What a magnificent sacrifice he had made, how superb the outcome for him. I should have rejoiced that his rejection of me had brought about his glorious reinstatement. The Royal Council, once so hostile, received him with honour, praising him when he refused to be avenged against those who destroyed The Savoy. Walsingham smiled on him, praising his determination to undo a past life of debauchery. So did King Richard, who gave the Duke the office of welcoming the new Queen, escorting her through the streets of London.

I was right not to go. I could not have smiled on him.

Duchess Constanza was seen frequently at his side, enjoying their restored relationship. Arrangements were being made for a new campaign to conquer Castile.

The Duke and Duchess of Lancaster had been truly blessed, but in the harvest it was I who was stripped bare of all my bloom.

I took all the jewellery the Duke had given me over the

years, every single piece of it, and dropped it into the bottom of a coffer in which I kept garments I no longer wore. I turned two little brooches over in my hand, remembering when he had pinned them to my bodice, less than a year before. A little gold heart set with a diamond. A clasp with two hands interlocked around a ruby. I added them to the hoard in my coffer and turned the key, but not before placing the coral and gold rosary there.

I would never wear them again.

In a week at the beginning of February, when it was possible to travel the roads again because of a hard frost that froze the mire into something passable, a courier beat his way to my door, bright with Lancastrian livery.

'Now what? Does he plan to win my good graces with ale and venison this week? I swear he will not do it.'

I had no patience with anyone in those dark days after the new year. I took the package with bad grace.

We had been apart a matter of weeks, but to my mind I was living in the depths of a black well. Every day was a struggle to remain calmly courteous to those amongst whom I lived. I accomplished it, because it behoved me to be courteous, by encasing my emotions in cold apathy, like a suit of armour that would let nothing come close and hurt me. I repelled all friendly overtures. I refused to ride the new mare despite her confiding manner and satin hide. The sable-lined cloak I consigned to the coffer along with the jewels. I was a *femme sole* and would espouse my title as Lady of Kettlethorpe as I had never done in the past.

I carried the packet into the nursery, picking up the baby from the floor as I sat. Thomas was a year old now and sturdy of limb. I hugged his solid little body, my eye on the document. It was very official, surprisingly so. I thought it might be some form of financial security for the children. Yes, that would be it. Setting Thomas squarely on my lap, I ran my hands over the bulk of it. I could feel a seal.

'Are you going to open it?' Agnes was hovering, sensing my reluctance, but overcome with curiosity. 'It won't improve for being ignored. It can't harm you, can it? I'll take the child.'

'No.' For some reason I felt the need to keep Thomas close, and smiled at Joan as she came to stand at my knee, dropping a kiss on her forehead where her russet hair had escaped from her little cap.

'Shall we see what your father has to say to us? Yesterday two barrels of fine Gascon wine. What will it be today?'

Breaking the seal I took off the protective cover, letting Joan take it from me, as I unfolded the two enclosed sheets, one more legal than the other, which took my attention first.

Yes it was formal, a legal document, written in a clerkly hand. I let my eye travel to the bottom, to the impress in the seal. And yes, this was from the Duke. My heart began to trip a little faster. I held Thomas firmly around his middle as he began to squirm. Why would the Duke need to send me so legal a document? It had nothing, on first scan, to do with my annuity or the children.

I started to read, crooning to Thomas.

My crooning stopped abruptly.

Let it be known that we have remised, released and, entirely from ourselves and our heirs, quitclaimed the lady Katherine de Swynford, recently governess of our daughters...

My eye swerved back, to fix on that one word. *Quitclaimed.*

I could not prevent a little cry of distress.

I read on again, line after line.

...neither ourselves, our heirs or anyone else through us or in our name, may in future demand or be able to vindicate any claim or right concerning the afore-mentioned Lady Katherine, but from all actions let us be totally excluded...

What was this?

In testimony of which we affix our private seal to this with the sign of our ring on the reverse.

This was a quitclaim. I knew what a quitclaim was.

I rubbed my cheek softly against Thomas's hair, as if for the comfort of his warmth, for my heart was as brittle as a shard of ice as I read between the legalistic lines.

This was the Duke of Lancaster, relinquishing all his rights and interests in me, and, what was worse to my mind, mine in him. We were severed, by law. He had no future claim on me, nor I on him. Our relationship was irrevocably at an end, signed and sealed.

If I had ever clutched at a forlorn hope that one day our estrangement might be healed, that one day in some distant point in the future we might once more stand together, this quitclaim had crushed it into dust.

At the end, when the words ran out, I simply sat and stared, unseeing, as humiliation trickled through my body, as honey would drip from a honeycomb.

Did he actually think I would pester him for money? For support for his children? Did he think I would arrive at the door of Hertford or Kenilworth, my children and household packed into travelling wagons, demanding his recognition? His hospitality and his charity?

Pride stoked my temper. I would not, even without this cold legality. But now he had made sure that I could not, as if I were an importunate beggar who needed to be manacled by the law. Neither I nor my children would have any claim on him ever again. He had severed the connection between us as assuredly with this red wax imprint as with a sword.

...from all actions let us be totally excluded...

I sat and looked at it, horror growing strongly through my shame as I acknowledged what it was that the Duke had done. I was legally banished from his life. Was he not satisfied with simply sending me away and denouncing me as an enchantress, with its overtones of witchcraft, so that all the world could point and pry? I would never take advantage of our past, and yet he suspected that I might take an action against him in law to demand my rights. What rights? I had never claimed any rights, except those of love.

Did he know so little of me, after all I had been to him?

Dismay churned in my belly. This legal separation was unnecessary, as was the cruelty in sending it with a courier. The crevasse he had excavated by this deliberate action lay dark and deep between us. How could my love for him survive this?

I let the quitclaim drop to the floor. I could not vindicate him from this despicable act towards me and his children. Nor could I weep over this cruel blow. My desolation was too intense to allow the luxury of tears. Instead, anger burned as I recalled our meeting on the road from Pontefract.

You owe me nothing and I have no claim on you, I had said.

How right I was. We were parted for ever with the weight of the law between us. Perhaps in my most wretched moments I had been hoping for a reprieve. Perhaps I had thought he would not be able to live without me. I had been so wrong.

'How could you turn the blade in my heart like this?' I cried out. 'I despise you for it.' I bent my head over Thomas, struggling against tears that finally threatened to fall as the emotion grew too great to contain.

'My lady.' I felt Agnes's hand on my shoulder, her voice soft and steady, everything that mine was not. 'He would not hurt you in this manner.'

'I know what he has written,' I cried out in sudden agony. 'I know what he has had written for him by John Crowe, his clerk. Why would he write it himself when he has a minion to do it for him?'

All I could see was the damning words of the quitclaim, as if they were written in blood.

... from all actions let us be totally excluded...

I was unaware of my sister coming in, until she removed Thomas who had begun to fuss, and leaned to look over Agnes's shoulder at the quitclaim. She took it from me, out of Thomas's reach.

'Ha! Well, there's a man's hand in that, for certain. Why do you weep, Kate? What did you expect from him now that he is back in Constanza's grateful bosom? She probably put him up to it, and since his eye's on Castile again, with full Papal blessing for all who accompany him, he'll have no compunction in obeying her. What man puts the woman who has warmed his sheets for a dozen years before his ambitions? None that I know.'

'He is not Geoffrey,' I remonstrated, still torn asunder by disbelief. 'I never doubted his love. I never had cause to. After that day when he faced Constanza and stood as a shield for me, how could I have ever doubted him?'

'More fool you, then. I learned my lesson, didn't I? Men have no loyalty where their loins are concerned or their ambitions. You should know better than to cast your honour and your reputation under Lancaster's heel. But you did it against all my advice because you thought that love would prove stronger than ambition or public disgrace. He had no loyalty to Constanza, and he has none to you. He deserves every criticism. Any reputation for chivalry has been torn to shreds. Men have no chivalry when their own interests are in the balance.'

Her vehemence, against the Duke and men in general, shocked me, although perhaps it should not have. Philippa shrugged, tight-lipped with disapproval as she ran her eye once more over the document. Then gave a harsh bark of a laugh.

'I see nothing to laugh at.' I snatched the letter back.

'That's because you don't see what is in front of your nose. That's because you are still besotted with him.'

It was too much. Gripping the two letters, one still unread, I strode from her, from the nursery, her accusations against me and the Duke still ringing in my ears. He was untrustworthy. Lacking in honour. Not worthy of the epithet chivalrous. Whereas I was blind and wilful and deserved my present heartbreak.

Forget him. Banish him from your thoughts.

Was this the final ending of our love? Destroyed by the Duke himself, not by Walsingham? When Walsingham had called me whore, the Duke had raised me up from the depths of my anguish. Now I was alone to weather the storm.

Had I not known that our love would one day meet some impossible obstacle?

But not like this. Never like this.

* * *

I spent the rest of the day supervising the cleaning of the few tapestries of which Kettlethorpe could boast. Then when I was exhausted, cobwebbed and coated with dust, but my thoughts settled to some semblance of steadiness, I retired to my parlour and, with a sigh to see that it was unoccupied for the fire was unlit and the room cold—I unfolded the second sheet that I had not yet read, from where I had kept it in my sleeve. It could hardly be of any great importance compared with the rest and I was weary of official documents. Fortunately it was brief enough to be taken in at a glance, sealed with the Duke's own seal but in the recognisable script of Sir Thomas Hungerford.

An invitation is issued to Lady Katherine de Swynford and her daughter Joan Beaufort to attend the household of the Countess of Hereford at Rochford Hall in the county of Essex in April of this coming year. It is hoped that Lady de Swynford will apply her skills in attendance on Lady Mary de Bohun, Countess of Derby.

I stared at it for some time, able to feel, despite my own woes, some sympathy for the child bride, Mary de Bohun, barely out of her first decade. Married to Henry of Lancaster, now Earl of Derby, the young couple were both considered too young for the physical demands of matrimony. It had been agreed that they should not live together until Mary was of an age to welcome childbirth.

Who can pronounce on such matters with confidence? The attraction between the two ran deep, Mary was smitten and Henry lacked the willpower to hold back. A sweet girl, here she was at thirteen years and carrying the ducal heir. Such a young child to give birth, younger than I had been when I had carried Blanche. It was no surprise to me that the Countess of Hereford, Mary's concerned mother, had solicited my aid in this immature pregnancy.

Except that it did surprise me. Barred from the Lancaster household, why would the Countess open her august doors at Rochford Hall to me as she had once accepted me at Pleshey Castle?

Considering, I folded the invitation, sharpening the creases with my thumbnail.

This invitation did not come from the Countess's lips. Was this not simply another attempt, on the Duke's part, to cushion his rejection of me? Another attempt to salve his conscience, together with the pension, and the frequent delivery of wine and the venison that would surely arrive any day soon on my doorstep? Why would he burden himself with these futile overtures? Since the quitclaim had made his future path as clear as day, I would have no compunction in refusing an invitation to attend the household of the heir to the dukedom and his child bride. I would not!

I crumpled the sheet in my hand, then in a fit of petulance, I ripped it into little pieces and scattered the whole in the cold hearth. I would not go. I would not go to Rochford Hall in April or at any other time. All connections between me and the Duke of Lancaster were at an end.

As for the quitclaim, I pushed it into my coffer, my fingers brushing against soft fur as I did so. I reacted with a hiss of breath, as if my flesh had been singed, and I dropped the lid closed. I had had quite enough of the Lancaster household for today without the lure of those magnificent sables.

I went to Rochford Hall.

Despite all my proud pronouncements, all my much-vaunted self-sufficiency, life at Kettlethorpe after another month of rain had palled enough to make me see sense.

'You are right welcome.'

A formal acknowledgement of my arrival. After an initial hesitation—I had become conspicuously sensitive to both real and imagined slights—the Countess of Hereford drew me from entrance hall to private chamber, anxiety stamped on her broad features, her fingers clenched in the furred edge of my sleeve. The heavy damask of my skirts brushed against the painted tiles. How satisfying it was to have the opportunity to wear court finery again, but anxiety at the quality of my reception made me stiff and formal in reply.

'I am honoured by your invitation, my lady.'

The words sounded cold when addressed to a woman who had stretched out her hand in friendship to the extent of allowing me to give birth under her roof, but that was before I was branded a witch. That was before the Duke had condemned me as the cause of his grievous sin.

Come to a halt in the tapestry-hung luxury of the Countess's chamber, I waited for the predictably chilly response. It crossed my mind that the well-connected Joan FitzAlan, Countess of Hereford, might have agreed to this invitation under duress. Perhaps I should have stayed with the miseries at Kettlethorpe, with the rain and flooding after all.

Countess Joan released my sleeve, with a little shake of her head as if embarrassed to be discovered clutching it.

'I was planning to send a courier direct to you if I did not see you this week,' she announced. 'We may very well have need of all your knowledge—and more besides—of foolish pregnant wives and babies who arrive before their time.'

My daughter Joan, self-important at being invited to accompany me at the age of five, stood with quaint gravity, but pushed close against my skirts. I had against all my good intentions taken up the shredded invitation because it was a situation that gave me some concern, involving women as close to me now as my own family. I could not turn my back on the Countess in her troubles, or on her daughter, however abrasive our new relationship might turn out to be.

But that did not mean that I would be won over by Lancaster's apparent wish to keep me connected to his family. I would give my knowledge freely. I would bring my skills to bear for the Countess and for Lady Mary, with the happiest of outcomes if that was possible. And then I would take Joan and return to Kettlethorpe.

And in a spirit of rebellion I had ridden the Duke's last gift to me. Why waste such generosity and neglect such a pretty mare? Had the labourer not been worthy of her hire? But I would not wear the cloak with its valuable sable. I would never wear it. Somehow to feel it warm against my skin was too personal.

Sometimes the depth of my cynicism startled me.

Standing in the Countess's parlour, testing the atmosphere, I regarded the Countess who might see me as the vile temptress of John of Lancaster. Once she would have thrown her arms around me and hugged me with a spontaneity that always surprised me, and I would have returned it. I found it impossible to be spontaneous. On my first appearance in exalted company since the Duke's denunciation, I simply resorted to formal courtly manners.

I curtsied, eyes respectfully lowered.

'I will do what I can, my lady,' I said.

The Countess sighed pointedly.

My eyes flew to hers.

There she faced me, fists planted on substantial hips as if she were no better than a fishwife in the marketplace when faced with a beggar who filched from her stall, rather than a lady whose marriage had been attended by her kinsman, King Edward the Third.

She was staring at me, not best pleased.

'My lady?' I queried. This could be worse than I thought.

'Well, the first thing that you can do, Katherine de Swynford, is take that sour expression off your face and call me Joan, as you have done any time over the past decade! Did I not sit at your side when you howled curses down on John's head for inflicting this little moppet on you?' She swooped, quick and friendly, to pat her namesake Joan's head and plant kisses on her cheeks. 'And you called her Joan for me! I thought we were friends. I've enough to worry about without a slighted mistress on my hands.

'And if you're thinking the Duke will be here to harass you, well he won't. Or not that I've had any indication of. He's too busy courting Constanza at Tutbury, trying to put right a decade of neglect on his part and disinterest on hers. Castile is on their joint horizon again and he's hoping to persuade Parliament to vote the funds. If you have any thoughts of revenge against him for his pinning you in the pillory for all to gawk at, I think you'll have it in the frosty atmosphere in their bedchamber, where they're doubtless trying to achieve a male heir for Castile.' She laughed immoderately, eyes gleaming with the prospect of gossip. 'If I were you, I wouldn't give it a minute's thought that I had stirred Walsingham's pen to vitriol once again. And whether John meant what he said and did—'

I braced myself against the warmth. If I did not, I would weep at the unexpectedness of it. Instead: 'Of course he meant it. He told me so,' I responded, all my ills rejuvenated, with enough ice to smother the heat in a cup of mulled wine.

'Never believe what a man says when his power is under threat.' The Countess now patted me as if I were no older than Joan. 'Enough about the man. Cheer up, Kate, and let's see what we can do between us for my errant daughter.'

Pointing to a stool, where Joan dutifully sat, the Countess pushed a cup of wine into my hand, nudged me to a cushioned settle where she joined me, drinking deeply as if her cup held the elixir of life.

I was startled. And then I laughed. What a relief it was to hear it all put so bluntly. At least it seemed that I might have one true friend in the world. To believe that I had none had begun to undermine all my self-confidence.

'Forgive me, Joan.' I sighed and sat, shocked by the emotion that packed all the spaces in my breast. 'I'm as miserable as a cat with a cold.'

'Then drink. It's the best wine we have. Better than anything you have at Kettlethorpe. Or perhaps not.' Her eyes, wide and ingenuous, glowed. 'I wager John still supplies you?'

And I laughed again, enjoying the closeness I had lacked. And drank. 'Tell me about Mary,' I invited.

'Come and see for yourself.' She was a little brusque, more than a little worried, but not given to condemnation of either of the pair. Just as she had not condemned me. 'Foolish children,' she observed. 'I'd say they should have known better—at least Henry should—but youth will have its day. Perhaps I should have kept a closer eye on Mary, but how would I have guessed? And what's done now is done so no sense in weeping over a spoilt pail of milk. I am everlastingly grateful to have you here.'

For the first time in months I forgot my anger, my despair, my desolation. I continued to forget my purely self-centred concerns in the demands of the coming weeks.

* * *

The child was born in April, to full term, not an easy birth, leaving both young mother and infant weak with the effort. I wrapped the squalling mite in a linen cloth and carried him out to where Henry, covered with mud and sweat from having ridden hard and fast from the jousting in Hereford to be with his wife at the birth, waited in the antechamber.

'You have a son, my lord.'

I thought he was due some formality on this most auspicious of days, and enjoyed the quick grin in response. A son. I held him out. Small but hopefully with a grip on life.

Henry touched his son's tiny hand tentatively, with a look of shocked awe that he and Mary had managed between them to create this child.

'He won't break,' I said.

'I know.' Whereas I had expected him to be clumsy, more at ease with a sword or bow than a day-old infant, Henry took the child from my arms with surprising competence. 'Edward. He will be Edward, after my grandfather, the old king.'

'A good name.'

The years swept back, as they must, showing me a different scene, but not so different in the audience chamber at Hertford. There I was, as now, carrying a newborn infant, but receiving me with desire in his eyes was the Duke. All those years ago, when all was still so bright and new between us. My heart clenched with grief for what I had lost as I watched Henry, unaware of my turbulent feelings, bend his head to kiss his son between the brows. Then laughed a little when the baby wailed and Henry clenched his grip as if he might drop his son.

'Is Mary well?' he asked.

'Yes, my lord. She is tired. But you will see her soon.'

'And you are very formal, my lady. I recall you stripping me and dropping me in a bath of water when I had managed to fall into the midden at Kenilworth. You had no sympathy and scrubbed me unmercifully. You always used to call me Henry. What has changed?' He paused, then added solemnly, 'What is between you and my father does not alter my regard for you, Lady Katherine.'

How easy it was for control to slip away from me at the least show of affection, for the emotion to well up again, but I took the baby from him, moved beyond measure when he leaned to kiss my cheek in formal greeting, with the same elegant grace that his father might once have used towards me.

There was a shadow in the doorway that made Henry lift his head and turn. Henry must have heard the footsteps but, forsooth, I did not. I had no premonition of it, no sense that the Duke had accompanied Henry to Rochford Hall.

How could that be? Once I could touch his mind, at some immeasurable distance, when we were bound in love. It had proved on so many occasions to be a comfort, a strength. Now I could not sense his presence even when on the threshold of the same room. I had lost the ability to call him into my thoughts.

Had I closed my mind to him so effectively? Or had he closed his mind to me? A rank chill ran over my skin. How powerful, his betrayal of me. It was as if an impenetrable thicket of oaks stood between us, and I must accept that it no longer mattered. I no longer had any call on him.

But my loins clenched when the door to the antechamber was pushed wider, and there he was, striding across the room to his son's side with loose-limbed elegance. The same imposing presence, the same statement of regal authority, and my wits, without time to marshal them, were scattered, my responses adrift. This was the first time we had stood together, sharing the same space, the same air, since his deliberate farewell on the road outside Pontefract. And between then and now rested the horror of the quit-claim. I could not decide what to do, what to say. For want of anything else, I held the baby tighter.

His eyes were on my face, light and calmly assessing, superbly confident in his powers, as if he had gone through some great passage of torment, and emerged on the other side, more certain, more driven, than ever. As I knew he must be. The Duke of Lancaster was once again accepted as a man to be reckoned with, at the right hand of King Richard. His rejection of a life of sin, together with the penance wrung from him, had been a resounding success.

Impressive as he was in that small room, even the youth and energy of his son, rejoicing in the birth of his own first-born, could not compete. It was as if, for the Duke, our parting was complete, the unpleasant reverberations in his life long gone. He had taken his decision to step away from me and was now at ease at its completion. The advantages for him had been momentous after all.

Whereas my heart thudded in my throat and the chill along my spine persisted, he was magnificently composed, but then, he had known I would be here. He had had time to order his initial response to me into strict line. I continued to stand motionless, a figure in a tableau, waiting to see what he would say, all the time wondering if I still had the power to move him. I could see no evidence of it in his clear gaze, his proud stance. There was no suffering here. I must accept that the alienation between us was for him a matter of no further importance.

In equally proud response I schooled my features into polite acknowledgement as I performed a brisk curtsy, the briefest bend of the knee.

'Monseigneur.' I was capable of wielding exquisite politeness like a weapon: like a battle axe to the head.

So, of course, was he. The Duke bowed, hand on heart. 'My lady.'

And that was the sum of our exchange. The Duke turned from me, placed his hand on Henry's shoulder.

'A son.'

'Yes.'

I saw the Duke's grip tighten. 'You must wait now, Henry. It is not fair on her.'

Henry understood very well. 'I know. We will. Lady Katherine says I can see her soon. I need to tell her…'

He shrugged with a sudden blush from chin to hairline. He was a young boy again.

'Soon,' I reiterated, my smile for him, not the Duke. I spun on my heel to carry the baby away, managing a few steps before:

'Madame de Swynford.'

I halted, but did not turn.

'My thanks. For coming here.'

'I was invited,' I replied, addressing the space before me. 'The Countess of Derby had need of me. I could do no other, my lord.'

'Is the Countess of Hereford with her daughter?'

'Yes. I will tell her that you are here.'

It was an agony as I took myself and the baby away from that cold impassivity. I reminded myself that he would be gone within the week. We had no relationship. What need had I to know what he was thinking?

And there was the Countess of Hereford, standing just beyond the doorway, where she had been all along. She nodded as I passed. Did she consider that we had been in need of a chaperone? That we might have fallen into each other's arms and renewed our illicit affair?

How wrong she was. Henry and the baby had been chaperone enough. If the Duke of Lancaster and I had been alone on a deserted moor, he would not have touched me, nor I him. Neither of us was of a mind to do so. The Duke saw his path to the future at the side of Duchess Constanza, whilst I, unable to either forgive or forget, would walk mine alone.

And yet...

And yet there was one thought that accompanied me to my solitary chamber. I loved him. I loved him still. In spite of everything, I would always love him. I might rant and fume, but when the Duke had walked into that room, it had been impossible to deny that, for me at least, the distance between us had fallen away. The passion that had bound us was not dead.

It should have been a time for rejoicing. A new heir for Lancaster. The beginning of a new generation of Plantagenet princes to become, one day, owner of Kenilworth and all the power that was attached to it. A banquet was planned. A mass was held. Toasts were drunk.

The celebrating was short-lived. The child died after four days of life, succumbing to a virulent fever that refused to respond to any remedy that we knew. All was despair.

Mary wept. Henry was desolate.

And between the Duke and I there existed a yawning distance.

It was his obvious wish to avoid me.

Sometimes, when he behaved with the cold propriety worthy of the Archbishop of Canterbury rather than an erstwhile lover, I felt as if I carried a leper bell.

But then my own response in his company was that of a nun who had foresworn the company of all men.

If anything could have made it clearer to me that our

estrangement was absolute, it was printed and illuminated on vellum in those brief days at Rochford Hall. The Countess's constant and not always subtle presence was an irrelevance. There was nothing to say between us. We did not try.

Sometimes, almost drowning in my loss, regardless of my furious denial of him, I wept at my inability to reach him, or his desire to respond to me. I wished I was not there. I wished the Duke had not accompanied Henry. My only joy was that Thomas Swynford was there, in the retinue of his new liege lord. How proud Hugh would have been of his son.

The Duke gave no acknowledgement of me. It was an icy distancing on both our parts.

Except for that one shocking, inexplicable explosion of temper.

Our paths crossed, as it was impossible for them not to cross, in the rabbit-warren of Rochford Hall's chambers and antechambers. My thoughts with the grieving Mary, my feet on a return from the stillroom with a bowl of dried herbs guaranteed to impart serenity and ease of heart, I stopped abruptly at the sight of the familiar figure just stepping through the opposite doorway, and immediately made to retreat. I was weary and drained by the excess emotion at Rochford, and was beyond verbal fencing.

The Duke too stopped, mid stride, face blandly indifferent. I might have been a servant, caught out where I should not have been.

'If you will excuse me, my lord,' I retreated another step. It would be simple to escape. One more step and I would be free of the room and him. I was becoming adept at it.

'There is no need to run away,' he remarked, his voice carrying clearly across the room.

I flushed. It was exactly what I had planned to do.

'I had no thought of flight, my lord,' I replied. Then could not resist. How illogical is the female mind? 'Since you do not seek my company—nor have you for a se'enight—I am merely relieving you of it.'

I took another step in retreat. The door to my escape was close at my side.

'I would say that you, for your part, have been remarkably invisible, Lady de Swynford.'

His tone was as dry as dust. I ignored it. And, with a surprising spurt of temper, I also ignored the threatening rumble of thunder beneath it.

'I am surprised that you have noticed, my lord.'

It was like casting a torch onto a stack of timber at the end of a summer drought. His face blazed. So did his words, a blast from the fires of hell. How had I ever thought him to be unmoved by our close confinement? They were delivered with the precise exactitude of an arrow loosed from a bow. The arrow was aimed at me.

'Do you think I have found it easy to preserve a distance between us, when you are in my line of sight day after day?' He was approaching me slowly, inexorably, with the graceful step of a hunting cat, and his words cut me to the quick. 'Do you think it was a matter of no moment for me, to make so public a confession of my sins? Do you think it gave me any satisfaction, having grovelled in the dust of Berwick, to have Walsingham pawing through the grubby corners of my life to extract what he would consider a mortal sin? And then to have him smile on me, on *me*, a royal prince, and grant me absolution so that England might once again rest in God's good grace? Do you think these last months have had no impact on my soul? By God, they have, Lady de Swynford! There has been no self-satisfaction in any of this for me.'

I blinked at the sheer glitter of fury in his face. I had seen the Duke in the grip of such passion before but never aimed at me, only at a recalcitrant Parliament, or overambitious courtiers who questioned his right to exert power. Never had I been the object of such rage, and because my patience was a finite thing, I retaliated in kind, deliberately to hurt. As he had hurt me.

'Oh, no, I'll never accuse you of self-satisfaction, John,' deliberately using his name when I had vowed that I never would. 'How could a man as proud of his Plantagenet blood as you appreciate having to bare your suffering soul before the masses of England? I know that your arrogance has no rival anywhere in England.'

'Arrogance?' His nostrils narrowed on a fast intake of breath.

'I remember your one and only communication to me at Pontefract,' I reminded him. '*You must not leave until I can come to you*, you said. Not forgive me. Not I have done you a great wrong. *Katherine de Swynford is a vile temptress*, you said—'

'I did not say that.'

'They say you did. A vile temptress, amongst other epithets that I choose not to recall.' I recalled every one of them, as if engraved on my heart. 'What I do recall is that I was no enchantress. It was you who demanded that I share your bed.'

'I did not demand.'

'You hunted me remorselessly.'

His temper flared again, bright as the sun on a dagger blade at dawn. I think I had hoped that it would. Experiencing far too much of his cold dignity, it would please me to stir him into wrath. A blast of emotion would be no bad thing.

'Before God, woman!'

'As I see it, you should be eminently satisfied, John. Restored to the bosom of God's grace, and Walsingham's, of course. Reunited in marital happiness with your Duchess. How could you have tolerated me for so long, when all the advantages for you were to deny me and return to the moral fold of legal matrimony? I hear that Castile is once more on your horizon, with Constanza's blessing. How magnanimous she is in her victory. Was it worth her kneeling in the dust to beg your forgiveness?'

Oh, how my rancour leached out, to coat us both.

His shoulders became rigid, his whole body poised to repel my attack. 'Cynicism does not become you, Katherine.'

'I have learned that it becomes me very well.'

'And you misjudge me.'

'I think not. I judge what I see and hear. I have heard no regrets from you. Two tuns of wine delivered to my door do not buy you a dispensation. And then, of course, the quit-claim.' I had to take a breath. Even the thought of it stirred me to immoderate speech. 'Did you really have to do that? You had already beaten me to my knees. There was no need to batter me about the head with a legal denunciation and formal separation.'

That brought him to a halt.

'That was never my intention.'

'No? To issue me with a legal binding that I have no further claim on you or your heirs, nor you on me. Did you expect me to come begging?' I saw him raise his hand, and spoke to stop him. 'No, I am not in a forgiving mood. Perhaps God is more forgiving than I. How could you do it? How could you?'

Which failed to quench his anger but instead goaded him once more into action. With three strides he was in front of me, his hands gripping my wrists without mercy. The bowl of *potpourri* that I had been carrying, that I had been gripping through all this brutal exchange, fell to the floor, shattering, the cloud of dried herbs scattering over my skirts and the floor. Over him too.

'What would you have me do?' he demanded. 'Do I allow England to suffer God's anger for the sake of my personal happiness? Or yours? Do I? You know as well as I the problems the King faces. Failure to hold onto England's possessions abroad. Rebellion and unrest at home with peasants raising their hands against Church and State. A young king who has neither the age at fifteen years nor the experience to take it in hand? Richard needs me. England needs me.' Colour had risen to mantle his cheekbones. 'Richard needs me, without blame, to be strong for him to offset the influence of men such as Robert de Vere who would seduce him from his duty. He will not listen to me if my soul is black with sin, or if the country turns against me. I had to repent. Would you blame me for that? Would you have Richard fall even further under de Vere's control, or some other unworthy favourite who will snatch power from his stupidly generous hands?'

Even though my wrists ached with the strength of his fingers banded around them, I considered his impassioned plea. Honesty, reluctant but necessary, coloured my reply, but there was no warmth in it.

'You have every justification in doing what you did. My own happiness, as you say, is nothing compared with the glory of England. How could I have thought that it might be? I consider it unfortunate that I should be cast in the role of the sacrificial lamb.'

For a moment he looked away from me, towards the far door, where footsteps sounded. Then when they faded, his eyes bored into mine again.

'Do you think that I do not rail against God? Against the

unfairness of it? Do you believe that my love for you was a mere charade? Do you not know that it still burns within me, every minute, every hour? Would you have me do nothing to protect you from those who attack me? Am I really so selfish as to place my own desires before your safety?'

As one question followed another, each driven home with the strength of a sword thrust, I held his gaze, all thought suspended, this new idea intruding like the point of a needle into fine linen, to add another, more complex stitch to overlay the first. Yet still I replied bleakly, holding onto my sense of ill-usage because it was the only familiar emotion in the whole of this morass that threatened to drag me down and suffocate me. 'I have no idea. I no longer know what you think or do. It is no longer any concern of mine, of course. You are quit of me.'

He looked as if would like to shake me, only to be rejected.

'No. I regret that you no longer see it as your concern.' The fires of temper were banked, the chill of frost reappearing. 'I have constructed a magnificent fortification between us, have I not?'

'Yes. It is a formidable structure. You should be proud of it.'

'It serves its purpose. It achieves what it was intended to achieve.'

I did not understand his meaning.

'You are bruising my wrists, my lord.'

Immediately his hands fell away. 'Forgive me. I have hurt you too much already.' His expression was stony, his restraint palpable, and with the briefest of inclinations of his head, the Duke left me to stand alone, but not before I had glimpsed what could only be raw emotion in his eyes.

I watched him go, thoroughly unhappy, thoroughly unsettled, all my resolution to withstand the power of the man I had loved—still loved—undermined. If nothing else was clear to me, this one fact was. The Duke was as unhappy as I.

In pure reflex, to offer comfort, in spite of everything, I stretched out my hand to him, but his back was turned. He did not see me.

'John!'

Nor did he hear me.

Thus ended our only conversation at Rochford Hall. Angry, accusatory, trenchant in its tone, before retreating into frigid withdrawal. Perhaps I deserved no better. Perhaps it was time I stepped back, away from him, allowing both of us to continue our lives in calmer waters.

Beyond weariness, I knelt to collect the pieces of the dish, which seemed a meaningless task when the floor was strewn with the dried herbs, so I simply sat back on my heels and surveyed the results of our discussion. Why had he been so very angry? He so rarely in my experience allowed emotion to rule to this degree, and yet his temper had bubbled like an untended cauldron, blistering me with its power. Grief at the child's death? It would have touched him deeply, but not for him to blast me with such venom, and hold me as if he had no sense of the fragility of my flesh within his grip. The marks were faint, but I could see them. I could still feel his power as he had heaped his anger on my head.

How easy it was for him still to hurt me.

For a long time I simply sat, unmoving in that empty room, all our bitter words descending on me to swirl through my mind, to land finally on some that gave me pause.

Would you have me do nothing to protect you from those who attack me? Am I really so selfish as to place my own desires before your safety?

Had I been wrong? Had I misjudged him? Had he in truth been protecting me?

Suddenly my erstwhile certainties that the Duke had betrayed me were as scattered as the *potpourri*.

I left the pottery shards and the herbs where they were. The sleeves of my gown were long enough that there was no evidence on view to rouse comment.

The Duke left, taking Henry with him. Back to more exhibitions of jousting skills, I surmised in uncharitable spirit, for both of them. It took little to drag a man's mind from grief. A thorough burst of male energy with sword or lance and all was put to rights, while Mary still wept for her loss, and I raged inwardly at my inability to overcome my grievances as I renewed the bowl of herbs that proved particularly ineffective in restoring either serenity or ease to anyone.

As they departed I stood in the Great Hall with the rest of the household to make our farewells. When the Duke spoke at length with Countess Joan, I turned to go, but at the end looked back over my shoulder. He was standing at the door, head turned. He might be engaged in pulling on his gloves, but he was watching me. Our eyes held, his arrested, but by an expression that I could not interpret. Unless it was a longing that could never be answered, by either of us. I was the first to turn away, thoroughly discomfited, thoroughly unsure.

'Well, he has gone,' Countess Joan observed as she caught up with me later in the morning. It was becoming time for me to leave also. 'Was it very painful?'

'No,' I lied. I managed to smile. 'Your chaperonage was wasted, I fear. Our desire to leap into each other's arms is a thing of the past. There is no impropriety.' I touched her hand in thanks. 'The Duke's infatuation is dead.'

She tilted her head.

'Do you say? I saw a man on the edge of control. If you had stayed, you would have seen him spurring his horse away towards London as if the Devil was breathing fire on his heels. Did nothing pass between you?'

'Nothing. What had I to say to him, or he to me?' I forced my brows to rise in a magnificent imitation of disbelief at what she might imply. 'I think the death of the child would light such a fire,' I responded gravely. 'He cares very much for Henry—and for Mary. I see no connection with me.'

Countess Joan eyed me for a long moment.

'It's not what I see—but perhaps you are right. Who's to say? And what of your long infatuation, Kate? Is that too dead?'

But that was a question too far. I would not answer.

I could not.

I was no longer certain of anything.

Chapter Sixteen

'Have you heard, Lady de Swynford?'

'Heard what?'

My servant barely had time to open the door of my rented property in answer to the thud of an urgent fist. The Dean of Lincoln Cathedral stood on my doorstep, black-clad like a bird of ill-omen, a look of horror dragging at his thin features.

'Come in, sir.' Such was the hammering that I was at my servant's shoulder. 'Are you ill?'

'No, my lady. I mean, yes—I will come in.' He stumbled on the paving. 'It's bad news.'

'Then you must tell me.' I took the Dean's arm and led him through to the comfortable setting of one of the Chancery's spacious parlours. 'Sit there and tell me what troubles you.'

The Dean enjoyed being the purveyor of bad news, mostly no more than some wild behaviour in the town that had encroached on the Cathedral Close. Today I was aware of no such disturbance yet still was pleased to extend my hospitality.

Unable to settle at Kettlethorpe after my sojourn at Rochford Hall, I had taken Agnes and the children to Lincoln, renewing my renting of the Chancery from the Dean and Chapter of the Cathedral.

Lincoln. My life in the very centre of that busy town over the years was as much of a pleasure as I could hope for.

The Chancery offered me a comfortable property well suited to my standing, providing me with a great chamber, perfect for entertaining visitors, my own private chapel and a solar on the first floor, a well-proportioned room where I slept and lived out my private life. With its carved doorways, immaculate stabling, courtyard and gardens full of fruit trees, its sophistication suited my state of mind. I had made a new life for myself in Lincoln. I was not without resources.

Three years had passed since the Duke's blistering temper at Rochford Hall and my stiff-necked intransigence. Three years in which I was free to reconsider the Duke's motives. If he had wished, by the quitclaim, to deflect Walsingham and his ilk, he had succeeded, for I was left alone, but of course, I would never know. There was no longer communication between us.

Perhaps for me the pain of living alone had grown numb. I liked to think so and gave a fair imitation of tolerance of our parting. My love for the Duke, my memories of our life together, had faded as all things fade with the passage of time.

'Tell me, sir,' I encouraged now. The Dean gulped the wine I poured and handed to him. 'You said it was bad news,' I prompted.

'Yes, my lady. The worst.' He leaned forward, his voice tinged with awe. 'The assassination of the Duke of Lancaster.'

My lips parted.

My fingers gripped my own cup.

My mind was frozen.

Misinterpreting my silence: 'Perhaps you already knew, my lady?'

I shook my head, utterly speechless.

He was dead. The Duke was dead.

My face felt clammy and pale.

Oblivious, the Dean launched into the facts of the plot to rid the King of his overbearing uncle, while I struggled not to be submerged in absolute despair. What would the Dean think if I fell to my knees before him and buried my face in my hands? Instead, I sat upright. It was a surprise to no one, the Dean observed, relations between the Duke and King Richard being as they were at a perilously low ebb—they had been for many months, since Richard fell under the influence of Robert de Vere. The royal favourite desired control of royal power, did he not? Nor was the King averse to escaping permanently the severity of the lectures on good government from his royal uncle. De Vere's plot was to have the Duke killed at a tournament.

I could no longer still the trembling in my body, my thoughts cavorted without pattern. Holy Virgin sustain me! Killed at a tournament. He was dead, his dear body was cold clay. He no longer lived and breathed and laughed and raged. My mind could not encompass it.

'Fortunately, it went awry—' I heard.

'Wait.' I gripped the Dean's arm, coming to my senses at last.

'Yes, my lady?'

I swallowed the rock in my throat. 'Is he dead?'

'No, no, my lady. Did I not say?'

'No. No, you did not.' I exhaled but the shock of relief gripped me with cold nausea.

'The plot failed,' the Dean continued busily, unaware of my distress. 'But it was a near-run thing. The Duke's living on borrowed time, I'd say. When the King and the favourite are against him. But for now the Duke has made his peace with the King...'

I thanked the Dean, barely listening to his tale of reconciliation between Richard and the Duke, and finally made my excuses, leaving my servant to usher him and his unwanted observations out.

In my chamber, all I could do was to wrap my arms around myself, to still the shaking. *Borrowed time*, the Dean had said. And had Richard concurred with this despicable plot? It could only be presumed that he had.

I found myself overcome with an urgent need to speak with the Duke, to simply see him in the flesh, yet at the same time I knew that it could not be. What would we say to each other now? Nothing. Nothing.

Did ever a woman miss a man like this? There was no tolerance here. I was bereft, hopelessly alone. I adored him. I always had. I always would because it was not a choice for me. He had drawn me into his heart and I was entrapped there for ever, manacled with steel.

I brought him into my thoughts so that he stood before me, as he had at Rochford Hall three years before, full of anger, yet as gloriously Plantagenet as I had ever seen him, full of vital life. And he was alive now. I must hold onto that one vital thought.

But I could not. Fear gave me no respite. How long could such a reconciliation between King and Duke last? It was one thing for me to step away from the Duke, learning to live without him as I had for three long years, but what if he were dead and I did not know? Could I remain in ignorance if his life was snuffed out by an assassin's dagger? Or by some malpractice at a tournament?

How could I continue to exist if he was done to death?

'You will continue to live as you do now, because you are woman of good sense,' I upbraided myself. 'You have acquired the skills to show a calm face to the world. You will continue to avail yourself of them.'

I bared my teeth at the sheer conceit of my advice, then turning my head as I heard the rattle of the latch, quickly smoothing my skirts and the flared fall of my sleeves of my new houppelande.

'Have you been weeping?' came the abrupt query.

'Certainly not.'

I turned away again so that my face was not lit by the cruel light.

'Well, that's a lie! I thought you had banished Lancaster from your thoughts.'

Philippa, who had come to keep me brief company, had hunted me down before I could put my much-vaunted skills into practice. Clearly she had heard the news.

Sometimes I wished Philippa had not come to Lincoln, but then rebuked myself for my ingratitude. Despite her sharp tongue, she was my sister and so dear to me. I pitied her matrimonial state, a wife yet not a wife, her children dispersed, Thomas taking up arms and Elizabeth the veil like my own daughter. Just as I thought that she viewed me with pity, in my isolation from court circles. I would give her no further cause to pity me.

'I no longer think of him,' I remarked with stately and superior calm worthy of the Duke himself. 'Our lives follow different paths. That is as it should be. I am done with men.'

I expected her to agree with me. She always did where

the perfidy of men was concerned. Her estrangement from Geoffrey, as far as she had confided in me, had never been mended. Now as she moved restlessly from bed to a seat in the window embrasure to look out over the well-cultivated grass of the Cathedral Close, lifting my lute into her lap, her glance was suitably sly.

'So you don't know what happened?' She drew her fingers over the strings in indolent fashion, her head bent over her fingering so that she could not see my scowl. 'It was of no interest to you to discover all you could of Lancaster's meeting with the King after learning he was to be done to death on the tournament field?'

'No.'

'You don't know what they said to each other at the Tower, where Richard apologised profusely for the attempt on Lancaster's life.'

'It wasn't the Tower. It was at Sheen. And Richard was as intractable as ever.'

I stopped with a hiss of exasperation.

'There now!' Philippa cast aside the lute, which she had never learned to play well, with a dull twang of strings, her eyes sharp on mine. 'You know every last detail, I swear. You still care. You are still besotted with the man.'

So I had fallen into her little trap, yet I clung hard to my pretence. 'No, I am not besotted. But that doesn't mean I wish him dead.'

Philippa folded her arms with a good show of belligerence. 'Well, he isn't dead, so you can stop worrying. That's the second plot to relieve the Duke of his life that's come to nothing. De Vere's double-dealing is a thing of wonder, but Lancaster has a charmed life.'

I knew all about it. Had we not all been aware of the growing influence of Robert de Vere, Earl of Oxford, young, well born, attractive and ambitious, just the man to catch Richard's admiring eye. And Robert de Vere was keen to extend his influence, encouraging Richard to ignore both Parliament and ministers. Of course he would make a target of the Duke who might be the one man in the land to stand in his path to dominating Richard.

Dangerous times indeed, with the Duke at the centre of them, dependent on his nephew's good sense and loyalty, when he appeared to have neither.

Did Philippa think this meant nothing to me? I took a breath, to stop myself from allowing my anxieties to flood out, managing to inform her with commendable gravitas: 'I have washed my hands of all this. If he is wounded he will have Constanza to minister to him and soothe his fevered brow. He doesn't need me.'

'I hear what you say, Kate, but there are still tear stains on your face.'

And, as if one of the Lincolnshire dykes had been broached, all my previous, well-guarded despair flooded out.

'He had to wear a breastplate to approach the King with any safety at Sheen. Can you believe that?' I wiped ineffectually at three years' worth of tears that I could not stop. 'And he had to have an armed escort to guard his back. What sort of life is that to live? What sort of King will Richard become when he reaches his majority?'

I knew the Duke would see it as his own failure. Richard, lacking strength and good judgement, was not the King the Duke would have hoped for.

'I cannot bear it for him,' I added. 'Nor can I live with the fear that the next piece of news I hear of the Duke will be that he is dead with a dagger in his back.'

'He does not need you to bear it for him,' Philippa objected.

'I know! That's what makes it so much worse. Why are my emotions so strongly engaged after three empty years? Why will this longing not die and give me some peace?'

How had I ever persuaded myself that my love for him had lapsed into some form of mild affection? It had not. It never would.

'Dear Katherine.' Philippa leaned to take my hands, pushing the lute aside to make space for me on the settle, surprising me as I read an unexpected compassion in her face, and in her softened voice. 'It can't go on, your mourning what is over and done with. There are things you must come to terms with.'

'There's nothing to come to terms with,' I denied, furious with my inability to command my responses in any matter where the Duke was concerned. 'When we last met at Rochford Hall he hadn't a word to say to me.'

'Nor you to him, as I understand.'

I had told no one of our single bitter exchange.

'I don't think of him. Not very often,' I tried.

'Katherine! You have a man who loves you, who had stood protector to you, even when you see no good in him.'

I stared at her, absorbing her impassioned words, startled at this unlooked-for turnabout. Now I snatched my hands away.

'Stood protector? How can you say that? And are you actually standing as his advocate? Is it the gift of yet another hanap that's swayed your judgement? Or being reinstated with the Duchess?'

'None of that. I am realistic, where you are not. The Duke cares. He cared for you, even when you shunned him just as adamantly as he spurned you. If you had not been so tied up in resentment, you would have seen it for yourself. Why do you think he sent you away?'

'To put himself right with God, to remove the stains on his soul,' I replied, still perplexed. 'To rescue England from God's displeasure. He told me that at Rochford.'

'I thought you had no conversation at Rochford.' She shook her head. 'But never mind that. Why do you think he issued the quitclaim?'

'To sever all ties. So that I can have no claim on him.'

'And did you take note of the date he had it written?'

The date? How should I? It was three years ago now…

'No.'

'Well, you should have. It was the fourteenth day of the month of February.'

'Of what importance is that?'

'The feast of St Valentine, my foolish sister. St Valentine's Day, when all the birds of the air rejoice and find their true mate. Or so Geoffrey says in one of his more flowery of-ferings.'

Diverted, I struggled to recall, since Geoffrey's poetry had been the staple diet in the Lancaster household. In Geoffrey's flamboyantly written *Parliament of Fowls* he had linked St Valentine's Day playfully to romantic love when celebrat-ing the betrothal of King Richard to the young and comely Anne of Bohemia.

'For this was on St Valentine's Day, When every fowl cometh there to choose his mate.

'Or some such,' Philippa recited, flushing as she saw me register her detailed knowledge. 'Not that Geoffrey would know much about romance outside the pages of a book of courtly romance. Or not with me. Not on any occasion that

I remember.' To my astonishment, her words dried as tears began to well in Philippa's eyes. 'Sorry,' she gulped, wiping her face on her sleeve. 'It's Geoffrey…'

'Well, I thought it would be! But since you are no longer living together I don't understand why…'

For a long moment she simply looked at me, then, expression tortured, told me everything in short bursts, her voice hoarse with the tears she refused to shed.

'Geoffrey had an affair. He has a son. He was accused of rape and she's called Cecily.'

I simply stared at her, unable to respond. Rape? My image of Geoffrey did not tally with this.

'Or at least it was a seduction.' Philippa was undeniably honest in the end. 'She released him from any legal charge against him. The boy's called Lewis. I could never forgive him for that, even though we had agreed to live apart. And now he has another son by that woman.'

Which was rather muddled but I got the drift and understood the turmoil of her emotions.

'Oh, Philippa. And you didn't tell me?'

'It hurt too much. And you were swamped in self-pity,' she added bitterly.

'But I would have understood. Infidelity is not unknown to me, is it? Oh, my dear silly Philippa.'

'I know you would have understood but I could not bear it. I had lost everything, whereas the Duke cared enough for you to do all he could to save you. To protect you. And you should have had enough faith in him.' She stood, drawing me with her, so that we stood as we rarely did in a sisterly embrace. 'Think about it. Think about what you know of him. You don't have to be torn apart by anger for the rest of your life. And there! You were always supposed to be the clever one. I swear he still loves you.'

'I know,' I admitted at last, to myself as much as to my sister. 'But I was so angry...'

He had tried to save me. To protect me. Had I not begun to doubt at Pleshey, when the Duke had intimated as much? *Am I really so selfish as to place my own desires before your safety?* he had asked, but I had been too furious to listen.

He had sent the quitclaim on the very day that love was in the air.

Three years I had had now, to weigh and balance, to admit to what my heart had always known.

How could the man you loved, whose children you bore, have been so heartless as to issue the quitclaim simply to be rid of you? This is the man you knew intimately, for whom you turned your life on its head. This is the man who still calls to your soul. How can you believe him capable of such cruelty? You have known for so long that this was not how it was.

It was time, it was long past time, for me to abjure self-pity and listen to my heart.

I went back to Kettlethorpe, Philippa accompanying me as she planned to journey on to Tutbury. There were letters waiting for my attention in my private chamber: more litigation over the clearing of my stretch of the Fossdyke, a royal licence giving me the power to enclose three hundred acres of land and woods to form a deer park around Kettlethorpe, the notification of a substantial annuity to my son Thomas Swynford from the Duke. I turned them over, discarding them to be addressed later with a cup of wine.

My breath caught, my fingers resting on a final document.

This was no litigation or complaint from neighbours.

I picked it up with my fingertips, balancing it between them as if it would scorch my skin, before sinking onto the edge of my bed where I folded back the creases. This could not wait. Perspiration prickled on my brow, down my spine, as I held this ghost from the past in John's own hand. I recognised it immediately as if was my own. I began to read. Slowly, carefully, absorbing every word.

To my dearest Katherine.

As a young man, I never thought I would have need to write an apology for my actions. But I find that I must. I could not live with my conscience otherwise. On two occasions in the last twelvemonth I have been forced to consider my death at an assassin's hand. If I died without seeing you again, without attempting to put things right between us, how despicable would that be?

I know that my actions were abhorrent to you. Nor do I seek to justify what I have done. I could not answer your accusations at Pontefract when you were so full of fury, and I of despair that I had been the cause of your anguish. Rochford Hall was no better. I recall my anger towards you with more disgust than you could ever heap on me.

Now, with time and reflection for both of us, I must try to make amends.

You must understand that it was important that I turn the wrath of the Church, and hostile parties in England, away from you. You must never allow the quitclaim to harm you. When you consider it with calm in your mind, you will see that I tried to draw the sting for you.

I was not calm. I was not calm at all. But I read on.

Forgive me, forgive me, my dearest love. I mourn your isolation and my inability to come to you. The legal distancing in the form of a quitclaim will ensure your future comfort and your safety. You and our children will never come to harm through me. You and our children must never be allowed to suffer.

For my comfort and safety. My eye returned to the words. My brain began to work again through the emotion as I read of what had afflicted England three years ago.

As you will know, my physician, together with one of my squires, and others of my people were murdered for their loyalty to me. If the rebels would draw the blood of my physician, what horrors would they inflict on the woman with whom I chose to share my life? I could not allow you to come under attack because of your continued association with me. For that reason I legally ended our union. No charge can be laid against you that we have any claim on each other. You will be secure from any future retribution.
   I could not have you punished for my sin.

He had feared for my life and that of his children. I had been vilified as foreign. As a foreign mistress I would be an easy target. The urge to read on was compelling.

I had to reinstate you in the eyes of England. I had to wipe your name clean and restore you to respectability. Thus it was necessary that we live apart.

So that was it. He had done all he could to remove the slur from my name, even at the expense of blackening his own, when I had seen only what I had considered to be his self-interest in turning away from me. Had he not promised to protect me? Oh, he had, yet I had been quick to condemn him when I thought that he had held me up for public denunciation to save himself. *God sheltered you from all harm,* he had said, *I asked Him to,* and I in my blindness had been scathing in my reply. Had the Duke taken God's punishment for our sin on his own shoulders, so that I might be free of it?

I knew that he had. Now my mind understood what my heart had always known.

Guilt that I had raged against him was a two-edged blade.

The date of issue of the quitclaim should have given you a thought to consider. It was not accidental, but to express all that I was no longer free to proclaim. I think, from our meeting at Rochford, that you had not acknowledged it. My dear, foolish Katherine.

And I, foolish again, sought and found the quitclaim in my coffer to look again, to reassure myself, smiling at the unexpected indentations of Thomas's teeth along one edge. There it was, the fourteenth day of February of the year 1382.

What a gift he had made me. One of protection, generous and loving protection, restoring to me my independence and freedom from attack and abuse. My property and the gifts were my own and safe from confiscation. No future accusations against me would hold any weight. At last, three years too late, it was as if I could feel the love flowing through the parchment.

Why do you think he sent you away? Philippa had prompted me.

To put himself right with God, I had replied curtly.

And so he had, but so much more. I made myself sit and think over all I now knew, all I had gleaned in the last five minutes. And I forced myself to review the Duke's actions with far more honesty. Less prejudice, Philippa would have said.

I could not have you punished for my sin.

I grimaced silently, but here it was. The Duke's rejection of me, reassessed in the light of my new knowledge, was to make amends for his sins, to prevent God's retribution in punishing England with defeat abroad and bloody unrest at home. How could I expect a man of chivalry to do any less? The overt hatred of him that drove the rebels to obliterate The Savoy must have inflicted agonising wounds on a man imbued by pride and self-worth from his cradle. I had to accept the demands on the Duke's freedom of choice as he stood in his self-imposed role of counsellor to his nephew, the child-king. England's glory must be pre-eminent. I must acknowledge that he could not put me first.

As for his reconciliation with Constanza, to make a strong stand with her since hers was the blood-claim, it was a necessity to further his dream of winning Castile. It was harder for me to accept this, but he was an ambitious man. This was the man with whom I had fallen in love. There was no future, as there had never been, for his authority in England—he had to look elsewhere.

My thoughts flitted on.

His acknowledged guilt of fornication. My mind flinched from it, but I forced myself to consider. All the months we had been apart during the years of our love. So many of them. What man, what vibrant man, could live with chastity for so long? Weakness of the flesh indeed, but I could not change what had been done. Was my love for him strong enough to resist such knowledge, to set it aside as a disturbing element of the past but one that need no longer trouble me?

There was more to read.

If you ask me: Do I love you? My answer must be: Too much. My heart is yours. My soul is an echo of yours. I have never questioned your love for me, nor must you ever question mine, despite my sins of the flesh. All I can ask is the gift of your forgiveness.

So I could no longer thrust this decision aside: could I accept his infidelity? I must. What choice had I? This was the man I loved unto death. This was the vigorous, powerful prince who had called to my heart all those years ago, with all his faults and iniquities. Was I without sin? My life was as blemished as his, tainted with temper and intolerance and that greatest of sins that I could not renounce.

Yes, I decided, in my new balanced maturity, I could and must accept in my lover such sins of the flesh. My love was strong enough to forgive.

I have granted land and money for the foundation of a chapel dedicated to St Katherine and the Blessed Virgin Mary at Roecliffe in Yorkshire. Prayers will be offered up to the saint of your heart to guard and watch over you, since I cannot.

My heart warmed in my chest, and tears were not far behind.

We must be apart but my heart lies with you, my thoughts too.

My tears flowed like a cataract in spate.

*I did not use the vicious words that have been ac-
credited to me. I never would make you the subject of
such ignominy. If I wept, it was not in self-indulgent
penance for my own sins but in grief for the anguish
I knew my actions would inflict on you. Walsingham
and his minions saw it of value to put the phrases into
my mouth. If you were an enchantress, as perhaps you
are, I would only see it as good. The intricate web of
your love remains woven around me, and will remain
inviolable until I am laid in my grave.*

    *I am your servant. And will remain so for this day
and for ever.*

And there was his signature. His name, not his title.
John

So there it was. The necessity for the quitclaim. Loving,
not vindictive. Caring, not callous. A release, not a rejection.
And what had I done at Rochford? I had believed the worst
because I had not thought beyond my own pain.

Now my hurt was sharper than ever, and the guilt too,
jostling with renewed anguish. He loved me, as he had always loved me, and yet we must of necessity remain apart.
Any suspicion that we were not living distantly, and Walsingham would descend on us with sword and fire, like St
Michael on the evil power of the dragon.

My isolation was even greater than it had been.

And yet perhaps not, I decided as I dried my tears, for
now I knew beyond doubt that the Duke's love for me was
a precious thing, far more valuable than gold or silver
hanaps, and I brought to mind that moment when he had left
Rochford Hall. When he had looked across the room at me.

I had thought him ruthless and unfeeling. He was not. I denied that he had felt any wretchedness comparable to mine. How wrong I had been. His sorrow had been equal to mine, if not greater.

I had thought he had grown weary of me, that he no longer wished to touch me even in a formal farewell. That I was nothing to him. Now I knew. To draw attention to us would be far too dangerous. He had been aware of every potentially prurient eye upon us at Rochford Hall, despite Countess Joan's careful presence. He had had to do it for me, and for himself.

His final lines, each one scrawled, one after another, written with such a sense of loss, near broke my heart anew.

It is an agony that I must accept that I will never touch you again when all I need is to hold you in my arms and know your lips against mine. To do so would be too dangerous. Even to acknowledge you in the public eye would draw unfavourable comment. Rochford was a torment for me, as it must have been for you. For the sake of England I made this painful bed. Now I must sleep for ever on it.

I have condemned you to sleep alone too. Forgive me, my very dear and most loved companion.

England must thrive. I must make amends to Constanza if I can.

And I must reassure you of my love, for now and all time.

I cannot hope that you will have the generosity to forgive me.

He loved me. He still loved me. And now I knew why he had been so very angry. I had been cold, shunning him, with no understanding of what it was he had done for me. I had been intolerant, unbending, because I had not, in my hurt and my anger, seen the true value of what he had accomplished. Now, older, and I hoped wiser, with my sister's trenchant advice hammering in my head, I knew I had to let go of my perceived wrongs so that I might once more live in peace with myself. And with the man I would always love, even though I could never live with him again. I must acknowledge the unbreakable ties of heart and soul and mind that bound us still, and simply forgive.

I had wronged him. Now I too must make amends.

I knew what I must do. I thought about it, ruining the nib of one pen, frowning at Philippa when she intruded so that she withdrew. She was still with me at Kettlethorpe on her journey back to the Duchess. She would take the letter for me.

Whatever level of contact there was between myself and the Duke, it must be as discreet and quiet as a mouse raiding an apple-barrel in my cellar. I might express my grief at the past wrongs I had heaped on him, but our relationship must be that of the spirit, not of the flesh. The Duke had made his choice and I must respect it. Most specifically I could not undermine what he had done, so cruelly for both of us, however much my heart raged against it. All I could do was reassure him of my understanding, reassure him that his sacrifice had not been in vain. The fortifications he had built between us, for all of England to see, would not be demolished by any careless word from me. His reputation had been restored, and I was glad of it. There was no going back for either of us.

So now—how to write it?

I would write under cover of estate business, one land-

owner in gratitude to another despite our disparate rank.
Why would I not write my thanks, in an entirely impersonal
manner? Philippa would ensure that it reached his hands,
not those of Sir Thomas Hungerford. But just in case it fell
into other hands...

> *To Monseigneur of Lancaster.*
> *In thanks for the recent delivery of trimmed oaks for*
> *use at Kettlethorpe. I am grateful for the timber as I*
> *plan an addition of rooms to the manor house.*

I wrote fast and fluently, yet another paragraph of inconsequential detail on my rebuilding. And then I began, the
first, the only personal letter I had ever written to him. How
difficult it was. Another quill went the way of its predeces-
sor. Now, knowing what I knew, I must say what was in
my heart, yet hiding the joy that danced in my soul that
he still loved me and I was free to love him, albeit from a
distance.

> *As for the quitclaim...*

That looked suitably legalistic, I decided.

> *You must have thought me unresponsive to the real-*
> *ity of that legal document at our last meeting at Roch-*
> *ford Hall. I confess to not understanding the essence*
> *of the quitclaim as I ought. Now I understand, and I*
> *have come to my senses at last.*
> *Due to the explanation I have received, I am able to*
> *take this essential step in informing you of it.*

There! Dry as dust! Would he understand? I thought that
he would. I swallowed against the emotion that I dare not

write, but that threatened to scatter the page with tears. There would be no cause for me to weep over a discussion of pasture enclosures. I continued with rigorous attention to my choice of words, written in the coldest of terms.

> *I understand what you did and why you did it. It has been a long and very painful road for me to get to this place. I know that I must accept what drove you to do what you did.*

I ruined the quill with my fingernails. And then, against all good sense, I wrote:

> *You must know that my sentiments towards you remain as they have always been, unconditional and all-encompassing. I pray for your safekeeping and for God's grace to protect and uphold you. I will listen for news of you.*
> *I only ask that you will keep me, ever a loyal servant to the house of Lancaster, close in your mind.*

Not one word of the love from which I would never be free. Leaving a space, in bold script I cushioned my confession with an account of one of my local projects, to deflect any prying eye.

> *I am involved in much time and effort to enclose local pastures into the park at Kettlethorpe. It is troublesome and there is local opposition but I have the King's permission and I will prevail...*

I laughed softly through my sorrow as I completed the final lines. He would think that I had lost my senses, until he realised what I was doing. But how to finish? I knew what I wanted to write.

> *I love you now, today, as I struggle to write this, as much if not more than I ever did. I will love you tomorrow and tomorrow. What strength comes to us under adversity. My heart remains yours even as the years pass. My soul rejoices in the knowledge that you love me. Keep safe, my dear love.*

But it would be far too indiscreet. Instead, I wrote simply,

> *With thanks again for your generosity and concern for the management of my estate. I remain, and always will remain, your grateful servant,*
> *Katherine de Swynford*

I reread it with something of desolation. A poor attempt at contrition, a poor contrivance. It was the best I could do, and I handed it to Philippa with instructions. I hoped that he would understand all I had dared not put into words.

'Well, I'll deliver it, Kate. But don't expect him to come to you,' Philippa advised, perhaps seeing the hope in my face. But indeed she was wrong. I had no hope of that. There would be no physical reconciliation.

'You have to learn to live without him,' she continued. 'He and Constanza are hand in glove. Or at least sharing the bed-linen. She is hopeful of carrying his child.'

'Then I must wish her well.'

It was the only response that I could make against another dart that lodged in my heart.

I have handed the letter to the Duke.

Philippa wrote to me at length.

It hurts me to tell you, but the Duchess is much re-stored in spirits, praying fervently that she will carry another child at last. The Duke is very attentive. He is planning another assault on Castile, to be preached as a Crusade. There is much optimism and happiness here. The Duke and Duchess are in accord. If a new child were to be born in Castile, it would be a marvel-lous coup for them. My thoughts are with you, Kate, if, whatever your denials, you hoped for any reconcilia-tion from your letter.

I understood. Of course I did. I expected no reply. It was enough that he should know of the direction of my thoughts. The days of bitter heartbreak were long gone.

But there were nights when I mourned my lost love who must continue to bolster the fortifications between us in the interests of reputation and England's glory.

'Agnes! Agnes! You'll never believe what he has done!'

All dignity as Lady of Kettlethorpe was forgotten. I hitched my skirts and ran into my beautifully refurbished hall with no thought at all for the improvements or the bright display of newly purchased tapestries.

Agnes emerged through a door on the floor above me, drawn to the top of the staircase by my strident tones.

'What is it? What who has done?'

'I can't believe it!' I was already taking the stairs two at a time.

'What?' Agnes demanded, now scowling fiercely.

But I couldn't say. Not yet. I hadn't the breath for it. I had been in the courtyard, in desultory conversation with one of Lancaster's waggoners. I was surprised by this wagon-load of timber and wine that had struggled through the slush and mire of January in the New Year. Not the usual time of year for such inessential journeying. The waggoner handed me the bill of lading as he climbed stiffly down and, taking it, I let my eye travel down it. There was also a basket of rabbits somewhere in there and a bolt of fine cloth.

But there was a postscript added to the short list of items.

And then a list. A list of five names at the very bottom. I knew every name on the list intimately.

It had the power to drain all colour from my face.

'I say you should go inside, mistress,' the waggoner advised. 'A cup of ale will do you good. Me too…'

But I was already running up the stair, the waggoner, wood and rabbits forgotten.

'Agnes!'

I could not believe what I had read.

I pushed past Agnes and Joan, who followed me to my chamber in some bafflement. Where I cast myself on my knees beside my coffer.

'What are you looking for?'

'This!'

I lifted out my sable cloak, letting Joan take it from me, smiling when she began to stroke its folds, picking out twigs of mugwort and lavender. The heavy perfume filled the room. It was easy to smile that day.

'And there! I was thinking that we were being invaded,' Agnes muttered. 'All this fuss about nothing but a fur cloak you've never worn.'

'You said you would never wear it again,' Joan observed, female enough to hope that I would give it to her.

'I've changed my mind.'

'God be praised. It's too good to be kept locked in a box.' Agnes's eyes narrowed on my ingenuous expression. 'Why?'

'I'm going to Lincoln.'

'I don't see that a visit to Lincoln would make you willing to flaunt this evidence of past sin.'

'Did I call it that?' I looked up with a laugh, as if I were a girl again. I could not recall when I last felt so foolishly happy. 'I am going to see the Duke.'

Agnes grunted, taking the weight first of the fur and wool from Joan, and then from her own feet as she sank onto a stool. 'And not before time, some would say!'

It was a shock to hear her concurrence. 'I didn't think you would approve.'

'Well, I do—and I don't. Which makes no sense, mistress. But when a woman's blessed with a love such as you have been given, it's a sin to waste it. That's what I say.' Her face was as flushed as mine. 'I'd best make preparations. How fortunate that I kept the moth from my lord's precious gift.'

Chapter Seventeen

The slender columns in the circular space of the Chapter House of Lincoln Cathedral rose powerfully around me as my sable-lined cloak fell in sumptuous folds to the floor, and I thought that my pride must have shone around me like the gilded haloes painted on the saints on the wall. My gratitude, my immeasurable gratitude, could not be expressed in mere words. Maternal tears trickled into my smile, no matter how hard I tried to present a dignified composure on this most auspicious of days.

But perhaps no one would blame me for it. I took the square of linen silently handed to me by Agnes, acknowledging the brush of her fingers against mine. She felt it too.

Once I had thought that there was nothing more of joy for me to look forward to, nothing that could ever again fill the corners of my heart with an expression of pure happiness. I had been so very wrong. On this day, beneath the stone ribs and austere beauty of such grace and power, my blood sparkled with it. What's more, I had every right to be here. It would be expected of me. This was a matter of family loyalty, and would bring down criticism on neither my head nor the Duke's. I raised my head and let the pride of the moment fill me from head to foot.

'Look.' Joan, at nine years, had acquired the self-control to whisper. 'There's Robert.'

Still her voice rose a little in excitement.

'Hush!' Agnes admonished, yet stroked the sumptuously embroidered shoulder of Joan's best gown.

'Doesn't he look grand?'

'He is very smart,' I whispered back.

Sir Robert Ferrers was fourteen years old, very serious and now the betrothed of my little daughter Joan. Sir Robert was in direct line to the considerable Boteler inheritance in the west, an excellent alliance, arranged by the Duke, and since the young man's spirit of mischief and quick smile had taken Joan's eye, I could be no other than grateful.

'He's a good lad,' Agnes murmured, her eye on Henry and Thomas who stood with us, warned of the necessity of good behaviour.

And I smiled again. I could have listed any number of proud noble families who made no provision for their illegitimate offspring. The Duke could never be accused of that.

I folded my hand over my girdle, where that innocuous bill of lading was tucked, as precious as a talisman. I knew the words by heart. I did not need the evidence and yet still I kept it.

Come to Lincoln on the 19th day of February in this year of 1386 for the admittance of various persons of some interest to you into the Confraternity of the Cathedral. It is not possible for you to make excuses on this occasion.

When the Duke had last visited Lincoln, in the year after our clash of opinion at Rochford Hall, I had fled back to Kettlethorpe in distress, refusing to be there in the same town as the ducal party, afraid of meeting him. Now he had made it so that I had no choice but to present myself, for there was a list of five names, of those who would be received into the Confraternity of Lincoln, the prestigious order of the brotherhood. The Duke himself had been received when he was a mere three years old. I too had been given that honour. But now he had arranged so much more.

It is right that you should be there, he had added. *If you do not, I will send an escort.*

Although I had bristled at his presumption to order my movements, as would any woman of independence, yet here I was, for below his command he had inscribed the names. Tantalisingly personal. Impossible to refuse.

Henry, Earl of Derby
Sir John Beaufort
Sir Thomas Swynford
Mistress Philippa Chaucer
Sir Robert Ferrers

There they were now, standing in the magnificence of the Chapter House that I knew so well, members of my family who meant more to me than I could express, all awarded this signal honour, the whole ceremony encompassed without any suggestion of scandal between us. This was no deliberate ruse on the Duke's part to put the once-ducal mistress in England's eye. It was a solemn affair of family and God and life after death.

'And there's John,' Joan spoke out, refusing to be quelled.

I had not the heart to stop her. She was as proud of her eldest brother as I was.

And there he was, tall and lean like his father, a year younger than Sir Robert, newly knighted at the Duke's bequest. The Duke had been very busy on behalf of the Beauforts.

My two sons. My daughter's betrothed. Even my own irascible sister who for once appeared astonished at the honour bestowed upon her for her service to Constanza, as they were received into the prestigious Confraternity of the Cathedral.

I knew that he had done it to honour me as much as to honour them, awarding them God's blessing, a daily offering of prayers in their name at the Cathedral. A signal honour indeed.

Yet as I rejoiced, still there was that slide of fear that would spoil the day if I allowed it, for it was known to everyone that the Duke was putting his affairs in order before embarking on the new campaign to Castile.

I refused to allow it to trouble me. That was for the future.

I watched and marvelled at the maturity of my sons. I enjoyed Philippa's ceremonial admittance to the Confraternity as if it were my own, recalling my own initiation. And I allowed my gaze to rest occasionally on the Duke who stood in his place some distance in front of me. Tall, lean, upright. He looked little different from the man who had lived in my mind's eye throughout all the years of our parting, even when I told myself daily that I despised him.

My letter had not been in vain.

My heart began to sing a little, like a bird catching the first light of dawn. Even if we did not speak, it was enough for us to be here under the same roof.

'When will you go?' I asked my sister Philippa, in the little interval between the wine and comfits served to guests and new members of the Confraternity alike, and the general movement to the castle where a ceremonial feast would be held.

I had already offered congratulations to my offspring and Sir Robert, restraining my maternal affection, resisting the urge to hug them. Earl Henry had kissed my cheek. I had not spoken with the Duke whose attention was commandeered by the bishop. Perhaps it was better so, I acknowledged, hiding my irrational disappointment beneath the dramatic fall of sable as I questioned Philippa. She had decided to accompany the Duchess when Constanza travelled with the Duke to Castile.

'In summer, I expect,' she replied.

'Are you sure you wish to?'

'What's to keep me here in England? My daughter is settled in a convent. My son is now part of the Duke's retinue. Geoffrey is nothing to me—nor I to him.' Her smile was not regretful. I thought she was looking forward to it.

'I will miss you.'

'I'm sure you will.' Her smile became a little wry.

'Where's Constanza?'

'On pilgrimage to visit her favourite shrines to solicit an heir. Did you expect her to be here?'

'No. We are both sufficiently women of the world to keep our distance.'

'You may not have to, if the Duke can claim Castile at last for her. She'll live there. The question is…'

'I know what the question is. What will the Duke do?'

There was, of course, every chance that he would live in Castile for the rest of his life.

Don't think about that. Not now. Not yet.

* * *

I spoke with Thomas—Sir Thomas Swynford now, of course, and in service to Henry of Derby—who glowed with as much pride as I, although he was better at hiding it under an air of insouciance. After more restrained maternal admiration, I discussed a little matter with him that was on my mind. It was something I needed to do, and yet the ultimate decision would be his. I gripped his hands at his response and allowed myself to kiss his cheek. He blushed furiously but did not object. Hugh would have been full of admiration for his splendid son.

'Thank you,' I said.

'When will you tell him?'

'I have no idea.'

Nor had I.

'I will deal with it for you,' he suggested.

'You may have to,' I agreed sadly.

There could be no disappointments, could there? But there were, because the demand on the Duke's time was a heavy one in his role of host. As an occasion of official leave-taking, there were many guests of importance, and self-importance, who requested speech with him so that he was quickly swallowed up again into the crowd. At the castle it would be even worse, and as the noise rose and those who wished to commandeer a portion of the ducal attention seemed to double in number, I knew what I would do.

I would not stay. I would go back to the Chancery.

I allowed Joan to remain, because of Robert, under Agnes's strict eye as an amused chaperone, while I shepherded Henry and Thomas, too young for such festivities, back to the Chancery with me. And once there I would hold fast to my delight, to my pride in my sons and in what I had demonstrated to myself in that brief interlude. Being able to step away without distress was of such great importance, showing me that life without the Duke was not impossible. It had been a ceremony of supreme achievement for me, but now it was over and a woman of sense would see the need to make herself scarce. It would be good practice for the time when he and Constanza were crowned King and Queen of Castile.

I used Agnes's square of linen again. How easily tears came.

The evening was quiet here in the Cathedral Close, being too far from the castle to hear music and singing from the celebrations. I sat at ease, confident in the rightness of what I had done. I smiled at the thought of Joan, enjoying the importance of her young betrothed.

My attention was caught, my smile vanished, for there was a stirring in the garden beyond the parlour window. I listened.

Nothing untoward. A prowling cat mayhap.

Henry and Thomas were put to bed with a maid to keep an eye on them. I sat with a candle and a Book of Hours but the book did not keep my attention, not even the glorious colour and gilding of the illustrations. It had been a gift from the Duke, many years ago.

How strange that I should still refer to him in my mind as the Duke. It was how I had known him from the very beginning when I was a young wife. He was still the Duke, and I suspected always would be. Except when we came together, and then he was John. Or when I was angry with him.

I smiled.

The candle burned low as I found a quill and parchment and wrote the note I had discussed with Thomas.

My pen hovered at the end as I signed my name. My ears pricked.

There *was* someone outside. I rose quickly, to summon a servant to investigate, then sighed as youthful voices reached me. Here was no attacker, unless it was on the ear. My heart steadied as I walked from parlour to hall, to open the door to Agnes and Joan and my son John. Swaggering Sir Thomas was there at the rear, still laughing at some joke between him and Sir Robert. And there was Philippa, sleekly glorious in her damask and gold-thread houppelande.

I hugged Joan because she was the only one of them who would not mind.

'Go in,' I said. 'There is a fire in the parlour. I will send in ale. You've probably eaten enough for a se'enight.'

Their voices were shrill with lingering excitement. Philippa appeared radiant, some of the years of unhappiness fallen away, looking as I recalled her in our youth when she would laugh and dance.

I made to close the door and follow, then, abruptly, stopped, my hand on the latch. Of course they had been sent with an armed escort from the castle. I stretched out a hand to invite the man in for ale.

I allowed my hand to drop.

'Would you like to let me in?' he said. 'Or do I wait out here to take Thomas and Robert back to the Castle?' There was the slightest pause, as if he fought against laughter. 'It's freezing out here.'

'You shouldn't even be here.'

He could have sent a servant. An armed body of his retinue. He could have called out Oliver Barton, the Constable of Lincoln, with the local militia. Instead, had come himself with the young ones. This was not discretion. This was not good sense. This was Plantagenet self-assurance in action.

In spite of my desire to take him to task, a surge of protectiveness almost choked me. I could imagine Walsingham's eyes gleaming.

'You should not have come here,' I remonstrated, as if addressing young Henry.

'As I am aware, if I had any sense,' the Duke replied. 'And I might wish I hadn't. If you don't let me in I'll have to take refuge in the stable.'

I opened the door wide. Still he stood unmoving in the fitful light that shone out from the windows of the cathedral where some priest was going about his final observances. Beneath the dark folds of his cloak I saw the shimmer of blue and silver, the garments he had worn for the ceremony. More than that in the soft light I could not see, but I knew every line in his face, knew that his hair was still unmarked by grey. Knew that he was a hand-span taller than I and his shoulders were unbowed. The years of battles, both abroad and at home against pen and Parliament, had dealt with him with kindness.

How I loved him. I could never not love him.

I sighed softly, silently.

'Then come in and I can close this door,' I remarked.

He hesitated.

'On second thoughts, it might be better if you came out,' he said.

'Why?'

'I imagine your stable will at least offer us privacy.'

'You said it was cold,' I objected in contrary mood.

He swung the cloak from his shoulders, a magnificent sweep, and offered it.

'Unless you will reject this—as I thought you had rejected my sables. But did I not see you wearing them today? Perhaps it was simply because of the cold in the Chapter House that made you change your mind.' His speech was uncomplicated, his tone amused. He was making this easy for me. 'Is there somewhere private for us to talk?'

'You could join us in the parlour where there is ale and a fire.'

How hard it was to breathe. The cloak rested in my hands. He had seen me, noted what I wore. My mind hopped and flitted.

'Your parlour is full of Agnes and Mistress Philippa and the young ones, and will be so for the next hour. Do they never stop talking?'

'No. The Beauforts are very vocal.'

My mind had steadied again. I let him wrap the cloak around me, as impersonal as a servant, and because I could do no other, and because I wished to, I led him out, across the Close to the stable block. It should have been awkward between us at first, after so long with such a physical distance between us, but we were both possessed of enough grace to overcome it, and that little exchange on my doorstep had broken the threat of ice.

I was aware of his soft footsteps on the grass as he followed me, as we made tracks in the early layer of frost. And then we faced each other in the stable with the shuffling of hooves for company, enclosed by the familiar scents of horse and grain and hay. Before God, it was cold, but the thick folds were warm from his body, and the fur was close at my throat.

'You have honoured my family today,' I said hurriedly, because it was uppermost in my mind. 'An honour beyond anything I could envisage.'

'I had a debt to pay,' he replied. 'Your letter meant more to me than you will ever know.'

His voice was on a level and I was relieved. I could rely on him to keep all emotions at bay. Was that not what I needed, to part from him in calm acceptance of our new situation?

'I was trying to be discreet,' I said. 'You understood what I was trying to say?'

'Yes. Amongst the rabbits and land drainage.'

I shook my head, silence stretching between us, until broken by a stable cat slinking along the wall, probably with rodents in mind.

'Forgive me,' he said softly in the darkness. 'Forgive me.'

And all the past emotions surged within me. 'Yes. Yes, I forgive you.'

'Katherine…' It was a sigh from the heart.

'Once I did not think it possible to forgive,' I explained. 'But that was long ago. Now I know full well that it is.'

The muscles in his jaw relaxed. You would have to know him well to note it, but of course I did. The tension had been there all along, superbly hidden by a master of dissimulation.

'Katherine. Will you look at me?'

I realised I had been watching the gleam of light on his jewels as his breathing leaped with the old anguish in his words, but I looked up readily. And then my eyes dropped before the expression in his, as if I were a young girl again, afraid to acknowledge the fervour in a man's appraisal, rather than a mature woman who had known this man as her lover.

'No—let me look at you,' he murmured. 'Let me read your thoughts. Before God, Katherine, you are as beautiful as the day I first loved you. You still fill my vision.'

No, no. This was a mistake. I must talk about normal things. I could not withstand the emotion. Nor, I thought, could he. So for both our sakes…

I lifted my hands in despair. 'I cannot speak of this.'

'Then speak of what matters to you. Whatever words you say, I know what is in your heart.'

The compassion in his face almost destroyed me.

'Are things well with you?' I managed to ask.

And, as a ghostly barn owl flew in through a high window with a sweep of silent wings, he followed my lead into less contentious paths, responding to what I did not say, as he had always been able to do. How great was his love for me, how strong it still was in spite of all the strains we had placed on it. I thought there was relief in his face as he picked up the new simple strand, as I might in a particularly difficult piece of embroidery.

'We are prepared, a fleet gathered at Plymouth,' he told me. 'The King is pleased to see me go. He's praying for my success so that I'll stay in Castile. He resents guidance unless it's from the lips of Robert de Vere.'

'I heard about the attempts on your life.'

'They came to nothing,' he replied lightly.

'God keep you safe in Castile, John. Will I see you again before you go?'

'No. I'll not return to the north. I'm for London first, to persuade Richard to give me more ships. And then I go in June.'

We might have been two distant acquaintances, choosing subjects that were of political importance yet did not engage our senses. And that was good. There was no emotion here. I continued to step carefully, my voice politely interested.

'How long will you be abroad?'

'Impossible to say. It will not be a short campaign.'

'I hear that Constanza goes with you. Philippa told me.'

'Yes, she does. My daughters will also travel with us.' And then I saw a moment of indecision on his face. 'I have to tell you about my wife.'

I took a step forward, hands raised to stop the words before they could destroy the tentative, fragile bridge we had created between us. 'There is no need. I know. Or at least I can guess.'

'Then you see my way forward.'

I let my arm fall to my side. 'Yes. Are we not adult? Have we not always seen this possibility?'

'It is what she wants. I could not deny her.'

All my calm good sense fled.

'Oh, my love…' I whispered against all my better judgement.

'My most dear Katherine…'

I would swear my tears gleamed as brightly as his jewels. There was one thing I needed to do, before I wept on his breast, which would destroy his control as well as mine. It would give both of us a breathing space.

'Wait here.'

I left him to run to the house. To the parlour to collect the note I had written that very evening, then up the staircase to my own chamber. And then I was back in the garden, in the stables, my breathing harsh with more than the effort.

There he was, exactly where I had left him.

'I thought you had left me,' he said gently.

'No. I would not do that.' I held the folded sheet out to him. 'It is all I can do to show my love for you. It is too dangerous to speak of it, for both our sakes, but this will show you.'

He opened it. A promise of five hundred marks. A loan to help to fund the expedition to Castile.

'It is given with Thomas Swynford's agreement.'

He studied the gift for so long that I thought he would refuse. When he refolded the page his voice was raw: 'I will repay you. It is more than generous.'

'I know you will.'

And I knew that he understood the depth of my gift.

The silence stretched out between us.

'I must collect Robert and Thomas and go,' he said at last.

For the first time a frisson of fear crept into the spaces in my breast and, longing submerging good sense, I said what I had promised myself that I would never ask because it would compromise us both.

'Will you kiss me in farewell?'

The jewels gleamed flatly. 'No.'

I took a breath at the starkness of his reply for I had not expected such a denial. And perhaps I flinched for he spoke again, quickly.

'No,' he repeated. 'I will not kiss you. For if I did I fear I would never let you go.' His lips curved. 'I recall saying something similar once long ago. I was right then, I am right now. It would be wrong of me to turn a flame into a conflagration beyond control. Neither of us would enjoy that, I think.'

His eyes rested on mine. I returned his gaze, in despair and in gratitude. I might never see him again, but I had been thoughtlessly weak, and he had rescued me.

'I knew you would understand,' he said.

'Yes.'

'Farewell, my love. I think God will forgive me seeking you out this final time.'

'I think He will. I will think of you.'

'And I of you.' Someone had lit a lantern outside in the Close. In its wayward light he looked stricken. 'Remember this: where I am, there you will be also.' I saw his sigh rather than heard it, as I felt the weight of his gaze. 'You will never know how very hard it was for me to send you away. I don't think I ever did anything so difficult in the whole of my life.'

With a sudden rush of tears in my throat I could not reply to so tormented an admission, understanding that he would not wish it. Some memories of the past were far too painful. Stepping quickly, before he could make a retreat, I reached out to pin the pinchbeck Virgin to his tunic. The little pilgrim's badge given to me so long ago by Mistress Saxby with all her worldly wisdom on the road to Kettlethorpe. Worth so little but now it carried all my hopes.

'The Virgin will keep you safe.' Although my hands trembled, I was careful not to touch him, only the cloth. 'I seem to have spent all my life in saying farewell to you.' I buffed it with my sleeve but the pewter would never shine.

'I have always returned.'

But would he this time?

He bowed low, as if we were at court rather than in a stable with straw and oats underfoot, and then left me as I sank into a deep curtsy.

Yet he didn't leave. Before I had regained my balance I was caught up in his arms, and at the familiarity of his touch, every emotion I remembered swept back to engulf me. An expression of despair at our parting it might be, but his mouth against mine was enough to set a light to all the old passions, and I gloried in it. It was as if the past years had never been.

'Katherine,' he murmured against my lips, against my hair as he held me, so briefly. 'I'll risk the conflagration…'

'My beloved John,' I responded, fingers tight in his sleeves as if I would hold him here in that stable in Lincoln for ever.

'How can I leave you?'

Then I was released, the Duke's retreating footsteps clipped and rapid as if he wished to put a distance between us, as perhaps he did in the reawakened desire that threatened to break his control. Whereas I waited, listening, my heart thundering in my ears, my blood hot beneath my skin until the final sound had died away, leaving me to hold onto the essence of his body hard against mine, his lips a brand on mine.

War was a chancy thing, and so was peace. It might be that if the Duke was victorious he would be King of Castile in more than name and a golden diadem. It might be that we would never see each other again. As King of Castile, accepted and crowned, he would never return to England, and with my gift I was helping him to achieve this. Or his own death on some foreign battlefield. Love demanded a huge sacrifice.

Yet I felt renewed, at one with him. I was alone, but not alone. I could not be with him, but our estrangement was healed, and I would hold him in my heart against all the horrors of foreign campaigns.

And as I returned to the darkened buildings of the Chancery, my heart leaped for joy that he had not had the power to leave without embracing me after all. I pressed my palm against my lips as if I could still feel the imprint of his. I too would willingly withstand the conflagration.

What had he not told me? What had I guessed?

That Constanza was carrying his child. For a moment I pressed my hand against my flat belly, remembering. I must be thankful for her, and I was. The days of my jealousy were long gone, for which I thanked God.

I did not want to do this.

I mixed the ink and mended my pen with a sharp knife, but because my hand shook it was not the best I could manage. Nevertheless, lacking another quill to hand, I forced myself to open the cover of my missal to the first page that had once been blank. Now it recorded moments in my life over the past year since the Duke had sailed from England.

I did not want to record this moment.

I dipped the pen and prepared to write, but the ink fell in an unseemly blot on the page, like a single dark tear. This was impossible. I could not write it.

I mopped up the ink, abandoned the pen, and let my eye travel down the milestones I had chosen to make note of. Moments of joy. Personal moments of delight. A record of the celebrations of those I knew and loved.

But I had written nothing like this present knowledge, which wrenched my heart from my breast and caused my blood to run like a sluggish stream under winter ice.

I forced myself to read, trying to recapture the joy.

I had written of the Duke's departure to Corunna, but briefly, for it was not a time of rejoicing, even though I kept his words in my mind.

Remember this: where I am, there you will be also.

They comforted me when nothing else could.

Then began the list of marriages and of births, of the achievements of my own children as they grew and made their mark on the world. Of my dear Philippa of Lancaster's marriage to King Joao of Portugal in the magnificence of Oporto Cathedral, to cement an alliance. I had rejoiced over the birth of a healthy son at last, Henry of Monmouth, to Henry of Derby and his beloved Mary. And then of my own recognition by King Richard as one of the prestigious Ladies of the Garter.

All to be savoured and enjoyed.

But I could not smile as I picked up the pen again.

Some things I had not written because they were too painful. Of Constanza's loss of her longed-for child; another daughter born dead in Corunna. Nor had I recorded those days of intense dread when an attempt had been made to poison both the Duke and Constanza. Philippa's tragic miscarriage of an heir for Portugal too was absent. I did not need to write them. I would never forget.

Nor had I written of the failure in the war. The Duke would never win Castile by force of arms. His own ambitions and those of Constanza were at an end. All that could be salvaged, through wise negotiations with Castile, was a marriage alliance for Katalina, now fifteen years old, with King Juan of Castile's son Enrique. Constanza would never rule in Castile, but her daughter would share the throne, which seemed to me to be the best outcome possible.

But this—*this*—I must record this, despite the heartbreak, because without it there would be no evidence of a well-lived life.

So I wrote, grief heavy on my hand.

In this month of August in the year 1387 the death of Philippa Chaucer, born Philippa de Roet. Died of dysentery in the service of Constanza, Duchess of Lancaster, Queen of Castile. The place of her burial is not known.

Having done it in my best hand, I laid the pen down with quiet precision.

Thus the end of my sharp-tongued, difficult, restless, loving sister.

I knew so little of her final days, and tried hard to remember her as I had known her, not as I imagined her, racked by pain. There was no body to return, no heart to inter in England, as I had marked the death of Hugh. Her earthly remains were gone from me. But she would live in my heart. And in her children.

I bowed my head.

It was not real.

I drew a line beneath my recording. I would write no more in this missal. What could compare with this loss for me?

Chapter Eighteen

It was three years since the Duke had kissed me farewell in Lincoln.

Could a heart remain the same, unaltered?

Mine shivered with anticipation.

There was no need for anxiety, I told myself. We were friends. Once lovers but now friends with a host of memories between us. I had been invited here to Hertford as a friend, summoned indeed, as he used to do in another life.

Lady Katherine de Swynford is requested to attend on Monseigneur de Guienne at Hertford for the celebration of the Birth of the Christ Child and the New Year. The Earl and Countess of Derby will be pleased to welcome her in my name.

I smiled thinly at the new title. A sign of Richard's good graces, if they could be relied on, John was now Duke of Aquitaine, addressed as Monseigneur de Guienne. He would always be the Duke of Lancaster to me.

Duly received by Henry and Mary, during all the days

before the celebrations began in earnest I waited for him, my senses alert at the arrival of every new guest, searching every new face that appeared at dinner in the Great Hall, chiding myself for foolishness. As if he would slip in quietly and without undue fuss to take his place on the dais. Unless he had changed greatly in three years, Monseigneur de Guienne would arrive with as much ceremony and fanfare as he had always done.

And then he was there in our midst, and I hung back until Mary, chivvying the rest of the family whether they liked it or not, found entirely spurious things to do elsewhere, as clumsy a ruse as ever I had experienced, but it left the Duke alone with me in the Great Hall. It also left me nervous. It did not suit me to be uncomfortable in my own actions and thoughts after years of ordering my life to my own liking.

I looked at him. He looked at me.

I was right about the ostentatious impression. The Duke's herald had announced his arrival and his tunic was a thigh-length creation in silk damask, furred and gold-stitched, enhanced by an embroidered sash that crossed his breast from left to right. It was a pure expression of wealth and power and authority, for prominent in the embroidery was the sleek white hart, emblem of King Richard himself.

But that was not important.

He was here, he was alive.

'I am come home, Katherine,' he said.

So simple a statement. So lightly announced, so uncomplicated after all those years when we had said nothing to each other. How portentous it was, but I was too wary these days to grasp it without due care.

'And I am come to welcome you, my lord,' I remarked dutifully. My hands were lightly clasped too. I tilted my head a little, recalling us using similar greetings in the heat of denial at Pontefract, when all was black and full of pain. But now winter sun shone through the windows and gilded us, although the warmth that flushed my face with colour had nothing to do with the elements.

The Duke was exhibiting nothing but unimpaired urbanity. He bowed with infinite grace.

'Well, Lady de Swynford? What do you see?'

I flushed even more brightly. I had been very obvious. 'Forgive me…'

'Look your fill.' He raised his hands, palms upwards, in invitation.

So I did as invited.

The Duke had aged. At first my heart tripped a little in its normal beat, for the three years had taken their toll. Pared down, I decided. That was it. Pared down to the fine essentials by grief and strain and a good dose of poison. Lines I did not recall marked his face, between his brows, scoring the flesh between nose and mouth. They had never been so deeply engraved as they were now, and having lost flesh, his nose was blade thin. And for a moment the austere expression, coupled with all the old glamour and the magnificence of his clothing, particularly the glossy fur and those resplendent sleeves, distanced him from me. He was as superb as the peacock in full plumage, scarred with age and battle, but still triumphantly majestic. I could imagine him no other way.

Yet still I looked.

He was not wearing a pinchbeck pilgrim's badge. Of course he would not.

'Do I horrify you?'

He had lapsed into a familiar stance with hands clasped around his belt, chin raised, and it came to me that his energy was as great as ever. There was a hint of grey in his dark hair but it still sprang from his brow with all its old virility. His hands still had all their old grace and beauty. He was as confident as I had ever known him.

He was, I acknowledged, still the most handsome man I had ever seen. I was not too old to admire a beautiful man whom I had once known better than I had known myself. But that was many years ago. Eight years we had been adrift, unknowing of each other in any intimate manner. Such passion that we had enjoyed must surely have died. It could not be resurrected, nor would it be good for either of us if it were.

I frowned at the thought.

Which he took note of. 'I see that I make a grievous impression,' he remarked. 'I must apologise.'

He bowed again with impeccable gravity and a tightening of his lips. He had changed very little in one respect at least: his arrogance was as vital as ever. I shook my head, delighted that I had given him cause to reflect. But I did not smile: all was too uncertain here.

'You misread my expression, my lord.' And I added with some mischief. 'And do you look at me too?'

'I do, my lady.'

What would he see in me? Childbearing had, I feared, taken its toll on my hips, but I could wear the soft folds and high neck of the houppelande with fashionable elegance. My hair was not untouched by the passage of time, but I was vain enough to take pride in it when well covered with a crispinette and jewelled fillet. I was no longer young, but I did not yet abjure my looking glass. Nor was I a dowdy peahen. The rich cloth of green and blue, sumptuous with stitched flowers at neck and sleeve, would defy anyone to label me widow. Yet who knew how many young Castilian women, dark haired and dark eyed with flawless skin, had taken the eye of the Duke?

'You are still beautiful,' he said. 'Even when you frown.'

I had been frowning again.

'If I pour you a cup of wine,' he offered, 'and lead you to sit beside me on that cushioned seat by the fire, will that perhaps enable you to smile at me at last? You have been staring at me since I first entered this room as if I had committed even more misdeeds than those that separate us. I would make amends.'

'I don't need wine,' I said. 'Nor do I need to sit. But I will judge your misdeeds, if that is what you wish. Have you accepted the loss of Castile?' I found myself asking, as I might in the past.

And wished I hadn't, for his expression acquired the blandness of controlled disinterest, and his reply was bleak.

'I had no choice. It was the best solution, to disengage from an impossible situation.' He hesitated as if he might say more and then he deftly turned the conversation. Or not deftly at all. It was brusque and deliberate. 'You look well. As dignified as I ever recall.'

Here in his brusqueness but still clear to my eye at least was a draining sense of disappointment. All those wasted years, wasted lives, ending in failure. Yet I followed his lead, since he would not speak of it.

'My thanks, my lord. I am in good health.' I could adopt dignity very well after all these years of maintaining it in the face of public denigration.

'Are the children well?'

'Yes. When it comes to rude health, the Beauforts are touched with magic.'

'Constanza and I mourned the death of Mistress Chaucer. As you must have done.'

'Yes.' I did not know what else to say about this loss that still gnawed on my heart.

'I thought I would lose my daughter Philippa.'

'It was tragic,' I agreed. 'And the loss of the child.'

'She is recovered now.'

Was this why he had asked me to Hertford, to exchange family histories? Our conversation had become formally courteous, as flavourless as a junket, as we steered around intimate matters. Would he talk to me of Constanza, who had, on her return to England, shut herself away in her own household, as chaste as a nun?

He did not. So, with a similar bland smile, I would continue in the same vein.

'I hear you brought home great wealth.'

'Yes.'

'And that the King smiles on you.' I indicated the chain around his neck. Although the familiar Lancastrian livery collar I had known all my life, it had the addition of King Richard's white hart to match the embroidered figures. 'A lord of the Council, in fact.'

'Indeed.' He looked taken aback at my diversion into the political, but did not demur. 'Your interest in politics is as keen as ever I see. Today the King smiles on me. He rode out two miles from Reading to show the warmth of his welcome home, and took my collar of Lancaster to wear around his own neck.' The Duke's expression was wry as his hand rested on the royal symbol. 'Richard proclaims his love for me. Thus I was duty bound to follow suit and wear the white hart.'

This was better. Not personal, but with a cutting edge that I recognised.

'So what does Richard want from you?'

'He needs me to mend the bridges between himself and his other uncles, of course.'

'Can it be done?'

'It remains to be seen. We will work on it, to try to bring reconciliation.'

And that was as much as he would say. I sought for another less contentious path to go down. Unfortunately my mind was a blank.

'Now what shall we discuss, Lady de Swynford?' There was a glint in his eye.

Snatching at an innocuous subject: 'Henry and Mary are content,' I said.

'They are as smitten as two ring doves. She is carrying another child.'

'I know.'

There! What was left? Nothing, except appertaining to the two of us, which was apparently forbidden since we had commented on each other's ageing grandeur. Had he not kissed me on our last meeting, as if passion was not dead between us? Entirely frustrated, I raised my brows in polite but stricken query.

The Duke gestured towards a pair of stools set in a window embrasure and, because it would give me breathing space, I sat. Once he would have taken my hand and escorted me there but now he led the way, gesturing to a distant servant for refreshment. Receiving it, I took a sip of wine that I did not want.

I turned a level glance on him. I would dance to this staid tune no longer.

'You invited me here, John. Was there a purpose in it?'

'Yes. I never do anything without purpose.'

Which was true enough. Was he laughing at me? But there was no laughter in his face. Frustration at last got the better of my good intentions.

'Have we anything else to talk about? Your horses? The

health of your hawks and hounds? I could fill in half an hour on the new building at Kettlethorpe if it pleases you.'

I half rose, but his hand on my arm stilled me. A fleeting moment only, but it touched my heart, and I wanted more, except that every vestige of common sense told me that I could not have it.

'I have lost the knack of reading your mind, Katherine.'

'I have been unable to read yours for years.' My reply was sharper than I intended. 'Perhaps it is more comfortable for you without knowing what I think.'

There was no change in his expression. 'I expect it is. When your thoughts are ill-disposed towards me.'

'But I am not ill-disposed.'

'Then what are you, Katherine?'

His eyes held mine. All my possible answers raced through my mind like clouds scudding before a storm-wind.

I am afraid. All you have to do is touch my arm and I am tumbled back into the past when my whole life was governed by my love for you. You are not my friend. You are embedded in my mind, my heart, my soul. You never will be my friend, and I am afraid of new rejections. I am afraid of renewed pain. I don't know what is expected of me. To be close to you is sometimes too much to bear. I cannot see my future in your orbit, even though I am flooded with desire.

I love you so very much...

I said nothing of this, of course.

'What are you to me, Katherine, if not ill-disposed?' he repeated gently.

I wished I had not come. I wished I had not embarked on this conversation. And I stood deliberately, to escape his gaze that saw too much of the turmoil within me, and this time he allowed it, standing with me, taking the barely tasted wine and placing the cups side by side on the stone window ledge. From the breast of his tunic he produced a slim document, and handed it to me.

'What is it?'

'A part repayment of the loan you gave me for my campaign in Castile.'

My fingers closed round it. 'So now all your debts to me are paid.'

'No. Not all my debts. Only one hundred marks, so you cannot close the door against me. Besides, some debts can never be repaid.'

I would not be seduced by soft words. I hardened my heart and my reply. 'So this is why you invited me here. You could have sent it by courier.'

'No, that is not why I invited you. I invited you to ask you…'

My gaze lifted from the repaid debt to his face.

'I invited you here to request, in all humility, knowing how you have suffered at my hands, that you return to my side as my loving companion.'

'Humility?' I queried, barely able to breathe.

The Duke smiled but if he considered rising to the bait, he rejected it. Instead:

'I want you to return to me, Katherine. I want you to live with me again as mistress of my heart.'

I simply stood and stared.

'I love you. I want you.' And then in the interests of the humility he had claimed: 'Will you consider my request, Katherine?'

I marched off in the direction of the private accommodations, my thoughts as unstable as the current in a whirlpool. Desire had exploded through me with his simple invitation, but cold reason held me with a grip of iron.

He did not follow me.

The Duke was never humble.

Did he know what he was asking of me?

New Year at Hertford came and went, with all the plea-sure of the annual gift giving. Soon, after Twelfth Night, I would be free to make my farewells. I sat in the nursery for a little while with Countess Joan. I thought she had delib-erately sought me out there, perhaps for a final exchange of opinion before our parting. Lady Mary was busy organising the final festivities for her demanding guests. I sat with the newest baby, another Thomas, on my lap as he slept.

'Will you go to Kettlethorpe?' Countess Joan asked.

'No, to Lincoln for a few weeks.'

'You are welcome to remain here with Mary,' she replied comfortably. Then added after a pause. 'But perhaps you do not wish to. I think you have not been happy.'

Had I not hidden the growing turbulence in my mind? I thought I had, and now I did not know what to say. I would not wish to appear ungrateful. I valued her friendship far too much.

'Perhaps it is that you miss your sister,' she suggested helpfully.

'Yes.'

For I did. Sometimes her absence had the sting of a new-grown nettle, making me catch my breath.

'The children enjoyed themselves,' she observed. 'I see Joan preening in the gown the Duke gave her.'

'Yes. She is quite the great lady.'

'And the sword for Thomas.'

'An excellent gift,' I observed drily. 'I shall confiscate it when we go home.' Thomas Beaufort was nine years old and lacked discretion.

The Countess folded her arms across her silk-clad bosom,

much as Agnes did when about to take me to task, and stared at me. I would have escaped if I had not had a sleeping infant on my knee.

'What is it?' she demanded.

'Not a thing.'

'Katherine!'

I shook my head.

She leaned a little towards me. 'Anything you tell me will be in utmost confidence. We have known each other a long time. We've lived through difficult times and supported each other. If it's about John, tell me. You know I'll be sympathetic and you can weep on my shoulder if you have to.' She stared at me as I remained obdurately silent. 'Do you not love him any more?'

'I don't think my feelings towards him have any importance.'

'Then is it that you think that he does not love you?'

Which effectively breached the dam that kept my thoughts under control. For that was the crux of the matter, was it not? He had invited me to return to his bed, and since that request—nothing.

Had I expect a wooing? Yes I had, and was thoroughly ruffled when I did not get one.

Perhaps he had changed his mind after all. Perhaps my sour lack of response had made him reconsider. Perhaps the dark clouds looming over royal government had given him more important things to think about, or warned him that to dally in my company might bring the return of Walsingham's disfavour in another terrible dissection of his character and ambitions. Yes, that was it. The Duke was a man of political acumen who would not act foolishly. If he wanted a mistress there were younger, fairer girls to invite to his bed. A girl without past scandal attached to her name.

And yet my foolish heart yearned, such is the nature of a woman spurned.

Not once did he dance with me. No troubadours sang my praises. He did not choose my company when we went out hawking but rode beside Mary or the self-satisfied Duchess of Gloucester.

I had given myself more than one hearty lecture. I had been summoned to give my expertise to the fast expanding nursery. That is why I was at Hertford, and that is what I would do. Had I not desired to remain alone, acknowledging the comfort of keeping my distance from all emotional shackles? What right did I have to complain? Nothing must occur to rouse the old spectre of the Duke and his mistress. I must not on any account tell Countess Joan why my thoughts were tangled in a morass of sensible acceptance and heartfelt dismay.

But: 'Tell me,' Countess Joan urged.

'He gave me nothing,' I replied against all my good intentions.

'Ah!'

I stood, to place the baby in his cradle with the little carved birds, ever watchful, on their wooden supports.

'He gave every guest a New Year gift. But not me.' I felt my face flush with shame, and knelt beside the cradle to hide it, but it had hurt. I had been surprised how much it had hurt. 'There now! Was there ever such a show of selfish ingratitude?' Briefly, I managed to smile at her across the sleeping child. 'And I think you tricked me into a confession of which I am sorely ashamed.'

'Then tell me this.' The Countess's face was a masterpiece of gravity. 'What did *Henry* give you?'

I looked up again in some surprise. 'A gold ring with a

diamond set in it. It is beautiful.' I was wearing it and lifted my hand for the light to set a flame in its depths.

'And?'

'A length of white damask for a robe.'

'And did you not think that such gifts were unusually generous?'

'Yes.' More than generous, certainly, but then Henry has always been very kind.

'Did it not surprise you?' Countess Joan continued.

'I thought it was in recognition of my care for Mary and this little one.' I put a hand to the cradle to set it rocking.

'I'm sure it was. He has a great affection for you. But a ring with a diamond? Consider it, Kate.'

I stilled the cradle and stared at her.

'Young men are not noted for their thoughtfulness, unless they have been kicked on the shin to engage their mind away from tournaments and such like.' Her eyes gleamed. 'I'd say that Henry was persuaded. I'd suggest that John is a master of discretion these days. I don't know what he hopes for—that is between the pair of you—but without doubt he is being very careful.'

My thoughts were instantly engaged. Careful. We had not been careful in the past.

'Is this a wooing in disguise?' I asked plainly, disconcerted that I had not recognised it for what it was. 'If it is, it's too discreet for my appreciation.'

'Who am I to judge?' she replied.

'And if it is,' I continued, still to be convinced, 'I am being very unhelpful.'

'It is possible.' She paused. 'What do you want, Kate? What do you want from him?'

'I don't know.'

A question that I had been closing my mind to for so

long was now being asked of me. Would I put my trust in him again? Would I be willing to give my happiness into his keeping again?

'Do you not trust him? Do you love him still?' Countess Joan urged me to consider.

'Yes.'

'Would you be with him if he asked you?'

The difficult question, the impossible question, that I was avoiding.

'How can that be? We know the public scandal it would cause. John is still wed. We cannot step back into adultery and think we can do it without recrimination.'

'I don't suggest you announce it from the battlements. All I ask is: do you love him enough to give thought to it?'

'Yes.' I covered my face. 'I have never stopped loving him. Not even when I thought he was my enemy. I'm just not sure…'

'Of course you are sure.' She could be formidably bracing. 'And you must tell him. Before he crowds out the stables with even more horses for your use.'

I lowered my hands, much taken with the surprising comment.

'Have you ever thought about it?' the Countess asked with a crow of laughter. 'Why is it that you ride a different horse almost every time you ride out? And all of them animals of superior breeding?'

I had not considered it to any degree. 'I thought it was whatever animal was left after everyone else was mounted.'

'Go and look in the stables, Kate. And I'll come with you, just to see your face.'

I went immediately. So did the Countess. The stables were quiet apart from the satisfying chomp of horses in their stalls and the occasional clatter of shod feet, the work here having been done for the day, the animals fed and watered. As we entered, stepping carefully, Hertford's master of horse approached with a smile.

'I think my lord has a horse kept here for my use,' I said, ignoring the Countess's bark of laughter behind me.

There was a guffaw from the groom lounging on a stool in one of the empty stalls.

'Come with me, my lady.' The master led me down one line of stalls, stopping beside a little grey that I had ridden the previous day. 'There's this one.'

'I've ridden her.'

With a hand beneath my elbow to help me over the straw-strewn cobbles, he led me on. 'Then there's this one. And this one...'

I counted a half-dozen altogether.

'There's another six or so, my lady. At Kenilworth. You'll not be short if you've a mind to ride out, anywhere in England.'

The master remained remarkably straight-faced as I turned to look at the Countess and joined her in laughter. It seemed to be the first time I had laughed with such carefree amusement for days, and my heart was light.

'See what I mean?' Countess Joan asked.

'Yes. Yes, I do.'

And I did. He had wooed me after all in his own inimitable way. And, to my shame, I had not realised it.

It coloured the final days of the festivities and the joyous rompings of the younger people over Twelfth Night, yet even though the Duke's demeanour towards me in public was no different from before, now I saw it as a discreet lovemaking.

No, he did not ride out hawking at my side, still choosing to entertain the Duchess of Gloucester with lively wit, but the tercel I was given was new to the mews and very beautiful. My mount was a lively bay gelding I had not seen before. The gauntlets handed to me by the master of horse for my particular use were stitched in gold, entirely inappropriate to my mind for the stress of a hawk's talons, but a consider-ate gift that would attract no real attention.

A master of discretion indeed.

But time was running out before my departure. Was Countess Joan misguided? Had she misread the gift-giving after all? All I could do was keep myself busy, all the time failing to force my thoughts from their familiar distress-ing path.

'When do you leave?'

My nerves jumped. I dropped the spoon I was using to measure out the tiniest amount of ambergris into a bowl. I was in Hertford's well-stocked stillroom with Joan who had expressed a wish to be shown how to make a perfume for her own use. Intent as I was on persuading my determined daughter to lean towards the lighter scents of rose and cin-namon, he had crept up on me.

'Tomorrow, my lord.'

'What are you doing, Mistress Beaufort?' he asked Joan, who laughed at being so formally addressed and held up the phial.

'Making this,' she announced enigmatically.

'This looks very interesting,' the Duke replied with com-mendable gravity. 'Would you allow me five minutes of conversation with your mother? I would be very grateful. Grateful enough to exchange those five minutes for this.'

He extracted a silver penny from the purse at his belt,

which Joan took without a second thought. It disappeared with alacrity into her own purse.

And we were alone, the door closed on the small space, with the heady scents of ambergris and musk and rose petals with the heat of summer on them. And as if the perfume worked its magic, there was no dissimulation between us, no words that were not direct and lethally potent.

'That was bribery,' I accused.

'It certainly was. Don't go, Katherine. Stay with me.'

Command or request? The Duke took my hands in his and I did not draw back.

'Do you know what you are asking?'

'I know very well. I have paid my debt to England and to Constanza.'

'But Walsingham would not see it in such a light. If we are seen to be together, he will raise the old storm and condemn you. Are you willing to risk your immortal soul?'

'My soul is in God's keeping, not Walsingham's.'

It was an unexpected flippancy that troubled me.

'John…'

But he was not flippant at all. He touched his lips to my fingers, first one hand and then the other.

'Before God, Katherine, I have lived apart from you too long. I have done my duty by my country and by my family. Since I have failed Constanza over Castile she no longer has need of me. We have agreed to live apart except for the occasions when we must stand together for public show. We will separate our households.'

'I am so sorry,' I said. And I was.

'Now I must make my peace with you. Will you forgive me for the wrong I have done you? Will you accept what I can give you now? I am no longer young. I do not have the strength I once had. But the fervour of my love remains the same. Will you, dearest Katherine, be again my very dear companion?'

I never replied in words, but took one step. My lips pressed against his expressed all my love, whilst his returned the unspoken promise with a fervour I had forgotten. Glittering strands of disbelief and delight interwove to dance through my blood.

And then the stillroom did not give us what we needed. Taking my hand in his, he led me from the heady scents and sharp aromas. Led me to his own chamber.

'How long have we been apart?' he asked as he closed the door.

'Altogether?'

'Altogether.'

'Eight years, at the last count since Rochford Hall.'

'A lifetime. I have wooed you for two weeks. Is it enough?'

I did not question the wooing, since now I knew it for what it was. 'Enough for what?'

He released my hand to allow me to stand alone in that opulent room with its tapestries and polished coffers. With its vast bed, hung with gold and blue.

'Enough to keep us together for the rest of our lives. We have wasted such a very long time. We'll waste no more.'

I took a breath, moved by his determination, and equally by his desire to allow me to set the pace, when he looked hungry enough to devour me. His eyes were alight with all their old passion.

'Will you let me love you again?' He held out his hand. 'I have never stopped loving you, but will you allow me the right to show you?'

I did not reply straight away. 'You asked me what I saw when I looked at you,' I said instead.

'So I did. And you did not respond.' There was latent

humour in his eye behind the heat. 'Perhaps to shield me from the truth.'

But I remained solemn. 'Now I will tell you, in truth. I see a man of honour. A man of integrity and a wise knowledge of how to use the power that he has. I see a man whose heart and mind speak to mine.' How strongly I needed to say these words. 'We have both made mistakes. We have both hurt each other, but my love for you has never changed. It is yours now as it has always been.'

The jewelled chain that lay on the Duke's chest rose, gleaming, on a deep breath, and his lips firmed as if anticipating rejection. 'So what do you say?'

What indeed? The days of my youth and foolish dreams of courtly love as hailed by the troubadours were long gone. Since then I had travelled far, both with the Duke and alone, along roads that had been joyous and full of heartache. I feared that the evidence of age that put its mark on the Duke's still-handsome features was regretfully replicated on my own. Marks of experience and tolerance and acceptance. I was a different woman from the one who read the poetry of the troubadours and thought the world well lost for love. Not a better woman perhaps, but one more seasoned in life's battles, and more honest in my judgements. I knew full well that love was no easy burden, with all its depths and intricate twists and turns for those who are caught up in its toils. But who, being loved as I had been, was able to turn away from it?

I smiled at the thought.

'By the Rood!' He gathered up my hands in his. 'Are you going to keep me waiting again, Madame de Swynford?' And I laughed a little. Not much tolerance here. 'I seem to have been waiting on your decisions all my life.'

'No, John,' I spoke at last. 'No more waiting. If I had

intended to say no to you, I would not have come to your
chamber and made myself the gossip of choice of the whole
household here at Hertford. Take me to bed, John. Take me
to bed, my dear love, and heal all my wounds.'

No, we were not as young as we were, but neither were
we old. Less supple perhaps, less beautiful to the eye, so
many new wounds and abrasions for John, whereas my hips
and waist bore witness to the passing years. But here were
so many caresses and responses to revisit, so much to recall and renew to bring us back to the pleasure we had once
known in each other's arms. I had never forgotten how the
Duke could make my blood run hot, and I was not disap-
pointed, for there was no reticence between us. How could
there be? We were confident and demanding in our passion,
devouring each other with infinite and exquisite slowness,
before naked desire destroyed all self-control. My lack of
breath had nothing to do with age. Nor for him. Until finally lack of stamina dictated that we rest, my head cushioned on his breast.

'Would you not look for a younger woman in your bed?'
I sighed with happiness, daring him to agree.

'You are my younger woman.'

Still that last little seed of fear remained. He was not his
own man. Would England claim him again and snatch him
from me?

'John—if you regret this, if you turn away from me again,
I don't think I can live with it.'

'I have no regrets. I will never let you go.'

His kisses made me weep.

'Must we confess?' I remembered the heart-wrenching

confessions. How could I confess a sin when I would repeat it again within the day?

'If you wish it.' He smoothed the tears away. 'But you are my true love. I cannot believe that God will punish us for this. We harm no one. We love in true spirit.'

I sniffed, and smiled, still disbelieving that we shared the same small space, breathed the same air and would never be parted again.

The Duke leaned forward, and sniffed my hair. 'It smells of...?'

'Of ambergris. Joan's perfume.' I laughed as I realised. 'It is an aphrodisiac, so it is said.'

'Shall we prove it?'

And, oh, it was. It worked its magic on all our senses. Or perhaps we did not really need it. I would have loved him on a bed of straw in my stable at Kettlethorpe.

'You will be my love. But circumspectly,' he said when he could. 'We will not be reckless again. We will not ride through the streets together.'

There was nothing circumspect in our behaviour for the next hour.

We were renewed. Reborn. We gave permission for our minds to touch, to slide, to enmesh one into the other when we were parted, as we gave sanction for our bodies to become one again when time and duty smiled on us. It was a strange moment of transition from estrangement to reconciliation, marked by tentative steps at first.

We had hurt each other. How cruel the wounds we had inflicted on each other. Now we had to learn to step together again, in trust, in renewed loyalty. In harmony, picking out the same notes from the troubadours' songs of requited love.

'I regret our time apart with every drop of blood in my body,' the Duke said.

'It was a living death,' I replied. 'Without hope. Without happiness.'

But now, grasping our permission to bloom, our love would not be gainsaid. Soft as a blessing, fervent as a nun's prayer, it healed our wounds.

'You are the music that stirs my heart to weep at the beauty of it,' he said.

'And you are the succulent coney that enlivens my winter frumenty.' I would not allow him to be solemn for long.

'And there was I thinking that you preferred venison,' he growled, lips against my throat.

'Only when I have a rich patron to provide it.'

'Patron?' His brows lifted splendidly.

'Or lover.'

'So I should hope. Now why is it that you remind me of a plump roast partridge?' And there was the gleam that I had once thought never to see again.

As his brows winged at my culinary flight of fancy, and his hand slid over my hip, my blood warmed and my heart beat hard. I relented, and gave him kind for kind. 'You, my dear man, are the sweet verse that awakens my mind to love's glory.'

Our souls were replete in each other, as smoothly close-knit as the feathers on the breast of a collared dove.

Chapter Nineteen

Why is it not in the human condition to be satisfied with what we have?

Fear creeps in to spoil and destroy, like the first ravages of the moth in a fine wool tapestry, impossible to distinguish by the naked eye until the damage is done and the glorious hunting scene is punctured by as many holes as a sieve. So fear crept into my consciousness.

What if my lover, my dearest friend, my only heart's desire, the glorious apple of my very critical eye, were to wed again? What if the Duke of Lancaster should take another Duchess to his marital bed?

It was a thought that I despised, but one that kept me brooding company. I could see no reason at all why he should not. It would be good political strategy on the part of King Richard to arrange it. To insist on it, if he were of a mind to exert his authority over his family.

Duchess Constanza was dead. Constanza who had, in her eyes, failed to achieve her life's wish, had died. We had not foreseen it. How would we? There had been no rumour of ill-health, only of the end when it came, when in March at Leicester Castle, surrounded by her Castilian ladies, Constanza breathed her last of English air.

In Lincoln, I had known of her death before the Duke, for he was in France concluding a long-awaited, four-year truce with the French. What a blow it had been for him to return to this loss, full of the success of his diplomacy, and be plunged into funerary rights. Even though they had lived apart since the abandoning of the Castilian campaign, yet his respect for her, his Duchess for more than twenty years, was great. He was not a man to be left unmoved, and in moments of honesty his conscience troubled him. He had not always made life easy for her.

He had not talked to me of it and I was too careful to step mindlessly where I might not be wanted. My discretion these days was a thing of wonder.

But now the Duke was free, had been free for four months. In excellent health in mind and body, he would be an asset to any plans Richard had for a European alliance. Would the King put pressure on the Duke to wed again at his dictates? I imagined that Richard already had such a plan in his mind, so that before too many more months, the Duke would be participating in a third nuptial celebration.

I could not think of that. Not yet.

Such a prospect would bring me too much pain in a year that had seemed to bring nothing but pain. What a year of deaths it had been. Of tears and graves and mourning. A year of portents, when I had set my mind to luxuriate in my restored happiness, even during John's absence in France, but happiness is not in the gift of Man when God takes his due. For a year in which contentment should have enfolded me, blessed me, I spent an unconscionable length of time on my knees. And so did the Duke. Death had blown in without warning, as disturbing as a summer storm.

Now I knelt in Westminster Abbey with the royal court, for Queen Anne was dead from the plague, which took no account of her rank or her mere twenty-eight years. Richard, unhinged almost to madness, had ordered the rooms of the palace at Sheen where she had breathed her last to be razed to the ground.

I allowed my eyes to rest on the rigid shoulder-blades of the Duke. Straight backed, the Duke was suffering from grief too, and not only for the passing of Duchess Constanza. The wound of desperate loss was made so much worse for him for Mary, dear, sweet Mary, Henry's child bride, was dead at Hertford with her seventh child—a daughter, Philippa—in her arms. I was there with her, and heartbroken. Henry was inconsolable. Had he not sent her a basket of delicate fish which she loved to help her through the pregnancy? And now she was dead.

What a crippling homecoming for the Duke, to bury Constanza and Mary at Leicester, within a day of each other.

The ceremony was drawing to a close. Ahead, Richard stood, looking distracted. Was he already drawing up new marriage contracts for himself and for the Duke? All I knew of high policy was that Richard had confirmed my lord as Duke of Aquitaine and that the Duke was already preparing to sail to enforce his authority there. What if he came back with a wife, some Aquitainian beauty, as he had once returned with Constanza?

There were rumours. There were always rumours.

Be sensible, I abjured myself. *Rumours can be false as often as they are true.*

* * *

My abjuration had no noticeable effect.

'Do you intend to remarry? Will you return with a new bride?'

My demands were made as soon as I stepped across the threshold of the Duke's record chamber at Leicester on this eve of departure. I had barely taken time to greet my son John whom I had passed between stable and Great Hall.

The Duke looked up but did not stir from where he sat. Demands—other than mine—lay heavily on him, as I could see. He was harassed.

'And a good day to you, Lady de Swynford,' he growled.

I strode up to stand before the long trestle table that habitually occupied the centre of the room. It was covered with documents from one end to the other.

'I hear that Richard has a new marriage arranged for you. Has he?'

'And who would be the fortunate lady?' The pen was thrown aside. Elbows planted on the table, the Duke rested his chin on his hands and looked me in the eye.

'I have no idea. Would you not know before me?'

'I expect I would. Why would I want a wife when I have you to hound me?'

'I am allowed to hound you. I am your love.' I smiled with deceptive sweetness. 'I am told that you intend to wed again. For an alliance.'

'I *intend* to go to Aquitaine. If I can ever manage to get the fleet together and the forces to accompany me. And Richard has his mind set on his own new wife rather than on mine.'

I was almost intrigued enough to ask who she might be, but would not be distracted. He was short on temper, but then so was I. Short on patience too. I saw documents, lists and tallies under his hand. In the circumstances he might wish I wasn't there. I hunched a shoulder as I moved to occupy one of the stools set along the wall, as if I were a clerk waiting instructions.

'When will you return?' I asked.

'I don't know. I have to get there first.'

'When do you go?'

'Next week. From Plymouth if I'm allowed to get on with it.'

I breathed out, no better at bearing the looming absence than I had twenty years before, for that was at the heart of my ill-humour. I would be alone, without knowledge of him, for as many months as it would take. There were plenty who would try their hand again, to rid the world of the new Duke of Aquitaine, with a cup of poison. Or a hidden dagger.

The Duke stacked the documents into a pile, then the endless lists with brisk irritability, before tunnelling his fingers through his hair. The sun highlighted more silver than I had recalled. And I sighed.

'I'm sorry,' I said, quite as irritable as he. It did not sound like an apology.

For what?'

'For disturbing you when you might wish to be left alone. But I had to come.'

He stared at me. I knew he would wait until I had confessed all.

'And for thinking that you would marry again without telling me.' I scowled a little. 'I still think you might.'

The Duke thrust aside the papers, stood and stepped round the table and in one fluid movement, lifting me to my feet, took me in his arms. He could still move fast enough to take me by surprise. Especially when I did not try very hard to escape.

'If I take a wife, you will be the first to know.' He kissed me gently. Then more fiercely, after which I smoothed the line between his eyes with my finger. 'Does that settle your ill-temper?'

'A little.' I was almost won over.

'Where will you go?' he asked.

'To Lincoln. It suits me very well. Send word to me when you can.'

'You know that I will.' He kissed me again. Then, 'Pray for me,' he said suddenly.

'When do I ever not?' His urgency had surprised me.

'Pray that Richard isn't swayed into seeing me as his enemy who has an eye to royal power. Pray for me and for Richard, Katherine. He's not to be trusted in where he takes his advice. Who will advise him to have that good sense when I am away?'

There was no answer to the question. 'I will pray.'

'And pray that Henry can keep his head and not provoke Richard to something outrageous, from which there is no way back.'

'I will.'

For a long moment he rested his cheek against mine so that we stood, breathing slowly together, his arms holding me firmly against him, and I allowed myself to hold fast to what would be a precious memory in the coming months.

'I feel set about with worries for this kingdom,' he said at last.

'Then I will pray all the harder.' I smiled in an attempt to lift the burden by whatever small amount I could manage. 'If you kiss me. And at least pretend for the next few hours that you have time for me.'

He did. He did both.

Yet next morning when I left him to his arrangements, his embrace was perfunctory and abstracted. I would also pray that he did not return with a new bride of European importance. I could withstand it. But I would not like it.

It was January with snow on the ground yet the Duke, new returned from Aquitaine, had braved the roads to come to Lincoln with an impressive retinue. This no longer stirred any surprise in me, although his choice of travelling weather did. So what was afoot? I surveyed his arrival most deliberately from the vantage point of my parlour in the Chancery. There was the Duke, of course, swathed in heavily furred cloak and hat. A tight knot of soldiers and a sergeant-at-arms. A clerk, his confessor, a master of horse and sundry others of squires and pages.

My heart was thundering beneath the heavy volume of my houppelande.

And then my heart steadied. There was no female figure. He did not have a new wife with him. He was alone and here with me at last, filling my vision completely, and I was smiling when I drew him into my parlour, all the niggling worries of my days smoothed out like a new wool cloth. Once alone, he duly kissed my cheeks and lips in formal acknowledgement, and sank into the chair I pushed him towards. I did not bother him with personal questions or demands. It always took a little time for us to step across the divide that the months apart had created. The moments of intimacy would present themselves eventually, and would be sweeter for the delay

'Katherine.'

That was all he said. It was all he needed to say to restore the bond that held us after a full year of separation. His eyes, full of light, full of love, rested on my face.

'John,' I replied in kind, pressing my palm against his shoulder, then moving quietly to pour ale. He drank deeply from the cup, before placing it on the hearth, stretching out his legs to cross his ankles before the fire. His boots steamed, so did his travelling clothes, filling the room with the pungency of horse and leather and wet wool.

'It's good to be still for more than two minutes together.'

I sank to a cushion on the settle opposite, prepared to wait.

Briefly his eyes closed, his face such a mask of weariness that my hands clenched hard around my own cup. It was easy to forget how the years passed and added to our tally of age, but that was all forgotten when he opened his eyes and smiled at me. They were keen and bright, not weary at all. The austere lines of his face softened into the handsome man I knew so well.

'Well?' I asked in response to his smile, returning it. I had missed him so very much. Everything in my world tilted back to normality.

John leaned forward, arms braced on his thighs, looking across to me. 'Do you know what I most admire in you?'

'My intelligence?' I responded promptly. My hands relaxed in my lap. This was certainly the man I knew.

'Your intelligence is unsurpassed—but no, not that.'

'My hair.'

'Not that either. Nor can I see it since it's covered with that little padded creation that I understand has become the rage. I like the beads. You look like a Twelfth Night gift.' Those eyes gleamed as they had done in the past, dispelling for ever the image of age and death. 'I'll take pleasure in winding your hair round my wrist later and show you how much I admire it.'

I remained suitably stern. 'Then it must be that you admire my way with land drainage and poor crops and tenant squabbles.'

He laughed. 'Never! You'll never solve the drainage problems.'

'Then you'll have to tell me.'

'It is your ineffable patience. And your generosity of spirit.'

I tilted my head against the high back of the settle. If only he knew. How often had I run to my window, drawn by the sound of hooves? How often had I buried myself in a frenzy of paperwork to drive him from my mind when he could not be with me?

'I've been back a month and could not come to you. You never complain.'

'Agnes would not agree with you,' I remarked drily.

'Which makes your even temper even more marvellous. I was summoned to present myself at court by our illustrious King.'

'What now?'

'Ruffled feathers all round. Richard wanted my support.' The taut line of his jaw suggested that there was something else, apart from Richard's obtuse refusal to see the dangers that surrounded him. 'He wants a French alliance,' he continued. 'A French bride perhaps.'

'And what do you think?'

'I think that what I think no longer matters. My brother Gloucester abhors any such suggestion. Richard hopes I can persuade him, or at least hold the balance between the pair of them. They were at each other's throats like rabid alaunts when I got there.'

'Will he listen to you?'

'Richard or Gloucester? Who's to say? We all parted amicably enough, but I think my days of holding any influence over Richard are well and truly numbered. And then I went to Canterbury. A prayer before St Thomas never goes amiss.'

I watched his expression carefully, trying to read what he was not saying. 'A prayer for what, exactly?'

Which he ignored. 'Come here, my beloved.'

I knelt at his feet, as I had done so often before, expecting him to take my hands in his as a prelude to our seeking some privacy for the rest of the day, but instead he reached within the breast of his tunic and withdrew a document. I opened the single sheet without a cover as he dropped it into my hand. A letter. Or rather a copy of a letter, since it had no seals, but the signature was John's own although the script was that of his clerk. Then I saw the superscription…I saw the crucial, particular word. Carefully I folded the sheet closed again, looked up into his face and governed my voice.

'I knew it would happen, of course. I hoped it would not be so soon. I should be pleased for you.' My smile felt all wrong on my mouth but I fought to keep it in place. 'You know I will not make a fuss.' My whole body felt full of unshed tears. It was a request for a papal dispensation to allow a marriage. 'Richard holds you in a higher regard than you think,' I continued. 'Who is she?'

It would be some puissant lady from Burgundy or Aragon. Perhaps a connection of the powerful Valois family. A princess was not beyond his sights. Even an English lady whose family Richard wished to shackle to the Crown. Who was important enough for John of Lancaster, King's son, Duke of Aquitaine?

I considered. No, it was not unexpected, but that did not mean that it did not tear at me with sharp incisors. I held out the request, to return it to him. I should be gratified that he had ridden so far to tell me of it, for of course he could not refuse if Richard insisted.

Instead of taking it, The Duke leaned forward, surprising me by closing my hand over it, holding my fingers tight closed.

'Katherine, my dearest love.'

'It's all right, you know. You are too powerful to remain unwed. I have lived as your mistress for more years than I can count. You must know that a new wife will make no difference to my love for you. Has the Pope allowed it?' If he needed a dispensation, she must be close to him in blood line. I could not think who. I sighed. I had hoped for a little respite from marital upheavals. Jealousy was no respecter of age or experience. 'Do I know her?'

'Katherine, my dearest love,' he repeated. 'My dearest and most obtuse love. It is for you.'

I searched his face for enlightenment. I did not understand.

'It's a request for a papal dispensation...' he explained slowly and solemnly as if I were a want-wit. 'For us, Katherine. To allow us to marry.'

'For me?' My voice squeaked. My eyes blurred with tears so that I could barely see the tenderness of his smile. I swallowed and tried again. 'Why would you wed me?'

It was all I could think to say since, before God, it made no sense to me.

'I would wed you,' the Duke stated, choosing the words with care, 'because I can think of nothing in life I would rather do. I need please no one but myself. Surely I am of an age to follow my own heart.'

I simply stared at him.

'But why would we need a dispensation? I am no blood of yours.'

'Because we have been more than close for too many years, even before you came to my bed. I'll give no man the opportunity to claim that our marriage is without legality. Read it if you will.'

I read what had concerned him: the stages in our lives together that had given him pause for thought in his search for legality, primarily when he had stood godfather to my daughter Blanche, even before he had been in an adulterous union with me when he was still wed to Constanza. There were some who would question the closeness of such a long relationship. The Duke had asked that all such past impediments should be removed and papal permission granted.

Yet I could barely comprehend it. Permission to marry *me*, a woman no longer in the full flush of youth? A woman with no status, no standing of any importance? I looked up from the request, beyond words. He held my heart in his hands, as he knew. Why would he see the need to wed me? Princes did not marry their mistresses. Princes did not marry women of such social inequality as ours. Already I could hear the mass of voices at the royal court raised in condemnation of such an outrageously unacceptable step.

The Duke of Lancaster did not marry his daughters' governess.

'But you must not,' I heard myself say.

'Why not? I want to wed you.'

'Are you sure?' It was all I could manage.

The Duke huffed a breath as he cupped my face in his hands and planted a kiss on my lips. 'Now that has to be the most foolish question I have ever heard you ask, Lady de Swynford. Of course I'm not sure. I might change my mind any minute. You'd better hurry up and take me before I renege on any promise.'

I could not laugh. 'What did His Holiness say?'

'Yes. He said yes.'

'Show me,' I said, still sifting through his astonishing

statement. A papal dispensation for me to wed the Duke of Lancaster.

'I cannot, faithless one. It was not written, but sent by word of mouth, delivered by papal courier in full regalia and jewels.'

'Is it legal?'

'Oh, yes.'

'Does the King know?'

'Yes. He sanctioned it.'

'He did?'

'He did. A little cool perhaps but I did not have to harangue him.' With a soft laugh the Duke dropped his hands to mine again and raised my imprisoned fingers to his lips. 'There is no legal reason for you not to agree. Only your own inclination can dictate your choice. Of course, if you decide that you cannot tolerate me after all these years. Or if you have given your wayward heart to one of my squires...'

I sat there with the letter on my lap, tears on my cheeks, even as I smiled at last.

'I thought you would wed a lady of foreign consequence.'

'I know you did.'

'If you wed me, there are those who will rail against us. They'll detest it, as degrading to your lineage.'

'I know that too. Are we not equal to them? Will we let such judgemental minds dictate what we will do with the rest of our lives?' He lifted me so that we stood together, the damp of his garments spreading to mine. 'Katherine, my love. Will you wed me? I am no longer a young man—'

'You are not old—' I interrupted but he silenced me with a brush of his lips against mine.

'I think you could do better for yourself if you want a husband who can spend time with you. And I committed a great wrong against you. My sins are many.' His smile was sharply self-deprecating. 'I would put right what has been wrong all these years. Except that it was not wrong at all, was it? It was right. It was always right. It was ordained in some strange corner of the heavens that our lives should be indivisibly entwined. Katherine, my dear and constant companion, will you wed me?'

So long. So many years. What would it be like to be finally, legitimately, united with him? I could not comprehend the enormity of what the Duke was offering me. Tears welled and fell.

The Duke's brows arched predictably. 'What in heaven's name have I said to make you weep?'

'That you could love me enough to wed me.'

'Do you love me enough to accept?' the Duke asked.

'I don't know what to say to you.' My mind was still taken up with the shock of being wed to the Duke of Lancaster. How long would it take for me to give him the answer he desired?

'Say yes, Katherine. Say yes. How long are you going to make me wait?' he demanded, but I read no doubts in his gaze. He knew that I could not refuse.

'Yes, John.' Tears tracked down my cheeks but I was smiling. 'Yes I will.'

This was the day.

I knelt in the familiar surroundings of Lincoln Cathedral, and I was trembling. I still could not believe that it would actually happen, but the Duke had swept all before him. Now that we had got to this point, he announced, nothing and no one would be allowed to stand in the way of our marriage. And thus we were united in the eyes of God under the kindly auspices of the Bishop of Buckingham in Lincoln Cathedral in the rain-swept month of February.

It was the quietest of ceremonies, with no outward splendour other than the robes of the Bishop who cast us all in the shade. We were astonishingly circumspect still, although this would—as the Duke had also announced, as if challenging the Almighty himself—put all to rights. The bishop inclined his mitred head in agreement.

Kneeling together before the altar, my hands were joined with his. I made my vows to him, and he to me. The blessings were given. The Duke kissed my cheeks and then my lips.

There. It was done.

The Duke raised me, Katherine, Duchess of Lancaster, to my feet.

'Do you realise,' he murmured as we walked from the church, back to the Chancery with no panoply of trumpets or ringing of church bells, 'that until Richard remarries, you are the most important woman in England?'

My heart shivered a little. 'And that is intended to make me feel more confident?'

I felt no different. Except—I stopped abruptly at the end of the nave, where one of the Duke's pages stood ready to open the door for us.

'What is it?'

'Do you realise,' I asked, 'for the first time ever in our lives, I can take your hand and walk from this place for all to see? And even if there is gossip—and there will be—no one can denounce me for immorality.' I looked at him, splendid in soft browns and russet and sable fur at neck and hem. Perhaps the bishop had outshone me, but he could never outshine this man who was now my husband. 'Or yours, for that matter.'

'You mean that we have thwarted Walsingham.'

Lightly, I punched his shoulder so that the links of his jewelled collar shivered. Not even the shadow of our nemesis could spoil my delight. 'We will not mention his name on this happiest of days.'

'No, we will not. And since we are able to proclaim our legal state, then we will do it with aplomb.'

He raised my hand to his lips, linked his fingers with mine and led me out into the world beyond the walls of the cathedral, where I laughed with the joy of it, the sheer foolishness of it, for there was no one to see us except for a priest much taken up with the office of the day in his psalter and a pair of chickens scratching in the garth.

Was this reality?

But of course it was, for my hand was clasped in the Duke's and his smile was for me, as was the glow of sheer pride in his eye, whereas I was awash with emotion. How could I have ever believed that the Duke of Lancaster would be proud to make me his Duchess? I had reached my safe-harbour at last. And yet, the strangest of thoughts came to me. Once, in my youth when I had worried and yearned and doubted, this marriage would have been the embodiment of a beautiful dream, as proof of our love. A dream that could never be fulfilled. Now, older, wiser, infinitely more secure, I no longer needed marriage to act as a seal on our love. I knew it to the very marrow in my bones. Through all the partings, through all the fickle reverses and cataclysms, we had emerged with a binding as strong as death. As strong as life. Our vows before a priest could not make it any less steadfast.

Not that I would refuse my new status, of course.

I laughed again, causing the Duke to raise his brows.

'I am so very happy to be wed to you,' I explained.

'Which is fortunate in the circumstances,' he responded.

How much I had learned on this journey, which had provided no goose-feather bed of happiness but had allowed me to grow from the blinkered woman who had put love before family, before reputation, before harsh morality on that day when I had given the Duke a winter rose. Had I even realised what love would demand of me in those early, heady days? Now, holding hard to my husband's hand, I acknowledged how much I had had to learn, of jealousy and compassion for Constanza, of fortitude to withstand bitter taunts, of trust and inner conviction when all around was black and our love would seem to be blighted. Of forgiveness, that I needed to ask from my children, and from John for ever doubting him. I had thought that love was my right. Now I knew that love could not easily be won. It had to be earned, by forging a chain as tensile as the Duke's glittering collar. A chain that could not be shattered.

Had we not done it? We had created a love, held fast by our children and by my fingers linked now with the Duke's on our wedding morning. The Duke and I had earned the right to love each other.

My mind returned to the present, to the busy priest and the chickens. Now I was a wife again. I was Duchess of Lancaster.

'What do we do now?' I asked. 'What does a Duchess do after her wedding when there is no feast or celebration for her to attend?'

The Duke did not reply, but led me silently through my equally silent house to my own chamber. Only when the door was closed against the world that seemed in no way interested in us:

'We will celebrate alone. This is the first time in all the years that we have legitimately shared the sheets.'

Holy and sanctified we enjoyed the legal luxury of unclothing each other.

'I have to be grateful to the setter of fashion.'

'Why is that?' I asked on a breath as his fingers smoothed over my ribs from breast to thigh.

'A sleeve without buttons is a miraculous gift.' He groaned as I traced a similar path to his own with the nails of my right hand. 'But perhaps I would have just torn them off. A husband's rights after all.'

'Because you would then, as my husband, have to purchase a new gown for me.'

'I'll buy you a dozen.'

His gift to me that day was beyond price, a glorious affirmation. The physical expression of our love was as powerful now as when we were young.

'What will we do?' I asked again, when I rose the following morning, a married woman, and broke my fast with my household, still agog with the events of the previous day. 'Beard the court?'

I thought he might ask my wishes, but he did not. He never had. I doubted he would start now.

'Eventually. First we go to my own lands. I wish to introduce my new Duchess to my people at Pontefract.'

'I have no good memories of Pontefract.'

All I recalled of Pontefract were the days of fear and then increasing isolation. Of divided loyalties. My conscience still reminded me that I had refused admittance to Constanza when she was in dire need. The accusations that I had thrown at the Duke's head in that dusty chamber still haunted me.

'I'll make your memories there better for you,' he promised as he summoned one of the squires, to issue a stream of succinct orders that would take us to Pontefract where I would begin my life as Duchess of Lancaster.

Chapter Twenty

How astonishing the difference a marriage vow, to impose respectability, could make for me. The towering bulk of Pontefract Castle became a different world from the one I recalled when I was under duress.

'You know the lady well,' the Duke had advised his steward and Constable when we had first dismounted.

'Yes, my lord.' Sir William Fincheden, the steward—my steward now—bowed, the Captain likewise. They knew me very well.

'Lady Katherine is now my Duchess.' I had to admire the Duke's not beating about the bush.

There was the briefest of hesitations.

'Allow me to offer my good wishes, my lady.' Sir William's face had been impressively wooden. Why was it that stewards, in their officialdom, had difficulty in accepting my status, whether scandalous or superbly legal?

The Constable had bowed without hesitation. 'You are right welcome, my lady.'

The Duke took my arm to lead me into the hall and nodded. 'You will serve her, as you would serve me.'

It was in manner of a warning, of course, lightly given. It was all that was needed.

'If my lady would accept the grace cup?' The steward presented it to me, in my superior position on the dais, before the dishes were served at dinner.

'Perhaps my lady would try the venison?' The Duke's carver was keen to show his skill.

'Would my lady wish to cleanse her fingers?' The newest of John's squires knelt at my side with a finger bowl and pristine napkin.

I acquired a page, Guyon, to scurry at my heels and pick up anything I might drop. Doors opened for me as I approached.

'If it is your will, my lady…'

'And your head will be as big as a cabbage!' Agnes opined as the poulterer visited me to offer a choice pair of geese for supper. I seemed to have acquired my own personal poulterer as well as a master of game and Stephen of the Saucery who was intent on proving his prowess with a wooden spoon.

I sat at the Duke's side on the dais. I knelt beside him in the chapel. His chaplain beamed on us indiscriminately. I was able to make confession with a glad heart.

'Would my lady wish to take the merlin or the tercel this morning?'

I had a falconer too. And a groom to hold my stirrup when I mounted. I never had to shiver in the cold until my horse was readied for me.

I was the Duchess of Lancaster, in the home of the Duke. My wishes were of supreme importance. The Duke saw nothing noteworthy in any of this, but I did, after a lifetime of monumental discretion and subtle insolence.

I did not need it for my happiness, but it proved that my new status was no dream.

The Duke was John now in my mind as well as in my speech. I could think of him as John when he was my husband, in spite of the habits of a lifetime that still clung to me, as a cobweb clings to the hem of a gown. John grew stronger away from court and its network of cunning intrigues. His languor vanished with good food and no pettish demands from Richard. The hunting was good. Yet in all those days of comfort, when my mind should have been put at ease, I was restlessly anxious.

'Are you worried about going to court?' John asked with an insouciance to which I should have grown accustomed but still had the power to disconcert me.

'Yes.'

No point in dissembling. I had thought about it often, even if John had not. But it seemed that he had.

'I will smooth your path. It will not be so very bad. Richard has never been hostile to you.'

I knew he meant it, but how would it be possible? It did not take more than a woman's instinct to know that there were many who would resent my startling promotion. It was not Richard I feared.

'They will be astonished. It will be no more than a seven-day wonder,' John announced, turning his mind to the greater importance of ruffling the ears of one of his hounds.

Thus John brushed my megrims aside as a matter of inconsequence compared with a good run after a deer. How typical of a man not to see it. The inhabitants of the aristocratic hencoop would have much to say about my marriage, if I knew anything about them. They would be quick to put me in, as they saw it, my inferior place.

My daughter knew the same.

Arriving at Pontefract, Joan curtsied to me as if to the Queen of England herself before falling into my arms. The twinkle in her eye belied her stern expression as she stepped back and took stock. Married and newly widowed with two little daughters, she had lost none of her calm outlook on life.

'So you are Duchess now,' she observed, tucking her hand in my arm as we turned to walk indoors, out of a brisk wind that promised snow.

'So it seems.'

'And are you growing into your new dignities?'

'You know your mother.' John had arrived to kiss his daughter. 'She still feels an urge to supervise.'

I could not deny it when he saluted my cheek, despite the audience of grooms and soldiery and a smirking huntsman, and assured me that he would return before dusk. He always had a thought for my peace of mind.

'Go and gossip with your daughter,' he added.

'He looks happier than I have ever seen him, I think,' Joan said as we watched him ride out.

'Yes.' My eye followed him until the cavalcade disappeared into the grey of the winter's day. He did. The lines that had seemed ingrained on his return from Aquitaine had smoothed out. He was restored to all his old spirit. It pleased me that it might in some small measure rest on our happiness together.

'You look happy too,' Joan added, as if she saw the direction of my thoughts.

'Happy? The word does not express half of what I am.' There was nothing more to say.

Joan slid me a glance. 'You have thought about what they will say at court, haven't you?'

I had thought about nothing else.

'What's wrong, Katherine?'

Joan had returned to her own household with a new mar-

riage on her horizon, and I had ridden out with the Duke,
hawks on our fists, the hounds milling round our horses'
hooves. It was an exhilarating spring day and the rabbits
were good prey. John's face was bright with the whip of the
wind, and I rode beside him, trying to match his enthusiasm, until he handed over his hawk and mine to the falcon-
ers, and pulled my mount into a little space.

I raised my brows with superlative skill. 'Nothing. What
should be wrong?'

Without replying he removed my gloves, tucked them into
the breast of his tunic and proceeded to rub my cold hands
between his. 'How long have we been together?' he asked
with apparent inconsequence.

'Twenty-four years, I think.'

'There! And I thought you would know, to the exact date
and time.' I heard the smile in his voice as he rescued my
gloves and drew them back on. Then, having completed the
task, the Duke instructed firmly: 'Then let us try that again.
What troubles you, my love?'

For a moment I turned my face away so that he would
be unable to see how much I had been distressed, for I now
knew considerably more about the reception waiting for me
in London. *You are being ridiculous*, I told myself. *You have
faced far worse than this. Are you not capable of conduct-
ing yourself with perfect propriety and seemliness at court?*

But despite all good sense, my belly would not tolerate
food and sleep was a fitful thing with difficult dreams. I
tried to hide it beneath a facade of smooth conversation and
a loving spirit. I thought I was successful. The royal court
could hold no terrors for me. If I could play the mummer
through John's public rejection of me and the ignominy as
a whore at Walsingham's hands, I could preserve a smiling

equanimity as the wedded and bedded Duchess of Lancaster. Well, I thought I could.

But now my reply to my husband was stark enough because the truth was unpalatable.

'I have it on official authority that I am a mean, low-born woman, not fit to fill the shoes of the sainted Blanche or the courageous Constanza. Sorry,' as he frowned, 'I did not mean it to sound quite like that.'

'I know you didn't. And who says that of you?'

'The royal and courtly hen-roost.'

He grunted, his hand closing warmly around mine again, undoubtedly in comfort. 'And who specifically?'

'The Duchess of Gloucester, the Countess of Arundel. Others—anyone with an ounce of royal or aristocratic blood from as far back as...' My teeth snapped shut. I was having difficulty in keeping my temper. 'They are women I did not see as enemies. Once the Countess of Arundel and I exchanged experiences on how to dose a sickly child. She was pleased enough to accept my help then, with a dose of boiled tansy roots to dispel worms.'

'Worms?'

The Duke had a tendency to laugh at inappropriate moments. I grimaced at the banality of my attack. 'But now the Countess of Arundel and her like are sharpening their tongues and their talons. Perhaps they are not hens at all but hawks.' I looked over to where my new merlin hunched on her perch with her fellow raptors. They were all prettier than the Duchess of Gloucester. 'Or bitches!' I added. 'Even the Countess of Hereford has joined their ranks, so I am informed.'

And that wounded me more than all the rest. I had thought her to be my friend, my daughter named for her. How could we share the suffering at Mary's deathbed, as well as the joy at the birth of Mary's sons, and then she disown me?

John laughed. 'It's the marriage then. As we thought.'

'No need for you to laugh. You are denounced too.' Oh, the gossip, carefully expurgated by Joan, I had no doubt, had been detailed enough and Agnes had been bullied into repeating it for me. '*You* are guilty of defying convention, putting me above every woman in the realm, when I am not fit...'

I took a breath, entirely ruffled, angry with their ability to make me feel unworthy. Of course they would hate me. John had made me pre-eminent over every last one of them. But I ought to have the presence to withstand their hostility. That was the problem, of course. I had not expected quite such a degree of virulence from women I knew well and who knew me.

'It does not matter.' His fingers were smooth as they stroked the soft leather over my wrist where my blood thundered.

'It might.' I worried at it, like a loose thread on a sleeve. 'Men of power and title do not marry their mistresses. Oh, John—we should have foreseen this. Now I am condemned as an upstart while you are castigated as a fool...'

'I am?' I could just make out the little lines of a frown, not masked by the shadow of the velvet folds of his fringed and elegant chaperon. He never took kindly to criticism, but I might as well warn him.

'You are a fool, they say, because you could have made a grand marriage for profit or alliance.' I would not tell him that the epithet fool had come from the lips of his own brother of York. 'But don't despair. They'll forgive *you*, with your high blood and noble rank. Whereas I will always be a woman of questionable morals and tainted blood, from a family of low degree. My reputation is tarnished beyond repair. You are a fool, but I am and always will be little better than a whore who has been raised beyond her station.'

I watched as John's brows registered astonishment at my bitterness and at the vicious detail of my informant.

'Where did you get all of this?'

'From those who write and gossip. It's too good a scandal not to spread, isn't it? I seem to have been causing a scandal for most of my life.' My voice, caught on an excess of emotion, was whipped away by the stiff wind. 'I'm sorry. I know you'll say it's not worth such a fuss—and yet it hurts me.'

'I presume it's Walsingham?'

'Who else? He gossips worse than a woman. And to more effect, unfortunately.'

'His words cannot hurt you now. You are my wife.'

I was not soothed at all. 'And because I am your wife, the Countess of Gloucester and her coterie will take their revenge, to prove to me that I am not superior. Do you know what angers them most? Well, you did warn me of it, didn't you? That until the King weds again, you have made me the most pre-eminent woman in the land. The court women of my acquaintance are preparing to take a stand against me, to show me how inferior I am.'

'Which is not so. Your family is entirely respectable.'

'But not sufficiently noble for you!'

'You can withstand that. What can they do to undermine your confidence? You know to an inch how to go on at court. What Queen Philippa did not know about court etiquette could be written on one of your very pretty fingernails. You cannot be tricked or undermined. You cannot be humiliated, or your behaviour made to appear inappropriate.'

Which only repeated what I had told myself. And yet:

'Do you know what they are saying?' His compassion for

my situation I thought to be waning, as would any man's after such a deluge of hopeless misery from a woman who claimed to have superior intelligence. So I would shock him into seeing the fear that lived with me.

'The Duchess of Gloucester,' I announced, 'says that for them to acknowledge me as Duchess of Lancaster would dishonour them.'

My nails dug into John's hand. I was only aware of it when he flinched and changed his grip. The thought of the revenge they were planning, and such a particular one, had me in its maw.

'They say they'll never enter a room or attend a ceremony where I am present. They will turn their bejewelled shoulders against me. Can I tolerate that? They will refuse to sully their feet by walking on the same paving, refusing to consort with me, of so base a birth. And'—I took another breath—'they say that our marriage is not even sanctioned, that the word from the papal mouth does not grant a full dispensation. He has to actually write it down in sanctified ink to achieve that. And until it happens we are still living in a sinful union!'

There were tears on my cheeks, from anger more than grief that they had discovered the power to undermine my contentment. With legitimacy and respectability I had hoped for acceptance. The papal dispensation, which now apparently did not even exist, had been the bedrock of my position. But my marriage was not papally blessed. I was still a whore. I would be *persona non grata* for ever.

I scrubbed at the persistent tears with my sleeve.

Throughout which performance, John remained irritatingly undisturbed, as if this final dart aimed at our happiness was not news to him.

'This is what will happen, my dear love. We will approach His Holiness again, with a dozen purses of gold if we have to, and he will use his sanctified ink to our pleasure.' He leaned across the divide between our mounts to kiss my cheek. 'Richard will welcome you to court, where he will present you with garter robes. Which of the hencoop will dare raise a voice against you when the King sees fit to acknowledge you?'

I would not be soothed. I did not want to be the centre of everyone's hatred. I recalled having to stand against Constanza, living in her household when she despised every breath I took. I did not want to go through all that again, under the eye of every meddlesome, gossiping, blue-blooded court cat at Windsor or Westminster.

'I think I am too old to face this,' I said, not liking the despair I heard in my voice.

John wisely, but infuriatingly, decided to tread on safer ground by adopting an authoritative tone. He snapped his fingers to alert the falconer.

'You are my wife and my Duchess, Katherine, with all the authority that is mine now invested in you. No one will humiliate you. Your position in my household and at court is beyond question or debate. That's the end of the matter as far as I am concerned. There is nothing to stir up the surface of the placid waters of your life.' He stretched out his wrist on which sat a juvenile merlin, looking as ruffled as I had been instructed not to be. 'Now take this raptor and let's see how well she flies. Imagine every coney to be the Duchess of Gloucester, if you will.'

No, I did not doubt him, and because I loved him and regretted laying my troubles at his feet, I managed a smile to please him and put his heart at rest, as lovers will, even those of long standing. Particularly those of long standing. The merlin settled her feathers and flew well. Perhaps the coneys did have a look of the Duchess of Gloucester with her furred collars.

But when I slept that night I dreamed that I was standing alone in my striking garter robes, all blue and gold with the heraldic motif pre-eminent on my shoulder, in the centre of a vast room. Around the perimeter, little groups smiled and nodded. There was not one face I knew. And then as the edge of my vision faded, there were no faces at all.

'John!' I called out in my dreaming.

But he did not hear me. He was not there either.

'I am nobody,' I informed him, my desolation keen, as we broke our fast.

'You are everything to me,' he replied.

We had been staying briefly at John's lodge at Rothwell to the west of Pontefract, a more intimate establishment where the hunting was good, but now I was late for our departure. They were waiting for me, to begin the journey to Windsor. I hurried through the hall, down the steps where I knew that one of my pages would be holding the mare John had selected for me to ride on this first of many long stages—and I stopped, so abruptly that another page, closely shadowing me, trod on my hem.

'Forgive me, my lady.' He bent to pick up the cloak he had dropped, hastily brushing dust from its folds.

I barely noticed. My attention was completely snared, and I blinked.

John was there in the courtyard, clapping his squire on the shoulder, walking slowly towards me as I stood statue-like on the step, coming to a halt at the foot of the stair. He turned to take in the scene that had made my eyes widen in astonishment.

'By God, it's eye-catching,' he observed with a grin. 'I wager this won't leave you cold...'

I was speechless. I stood and looked. And looked.

'I've rarely known you with nothing to say.'

'Have you done this?'

'Of course. Who else? For your pleasure, my lady.' He took my unresponsive hand and led me forward. 'You are not no one, Katherine. How would I choose a woman who had no merit? You never were. You never will be. Here is your own heraldic achievement to proclaim to the world that Katherine, Duchess of Lancaster, is a woman in her own right.'

The whole courtyard was a blaze of red and gold, from the curtains of my litter, if I chose to use it for some portion of the journey, to the bridle and saddle cloth of my riding horse. The pennons carried by my escort displayed the same emblem, the ostlers who rode the heavy horses that pulled my litter were encased in red and gold tabards. John's blue and white was totally eclipsed.

'I don't know what to say.'

Continuing to grip my hand as if I needed to be steadied in the face of such startling opulence, John led me to my horse. The ostlers were grinning too.

'Do you approve?'

'You have done this? For me?' It was all I could seem to say.

'Well, you were not satisfied with my poor heraldic achievements of Lancaster and Aquitaine, now you have your own.'

And a warmth, as if emanating from the sumptuous red and gold, closed round my heart, dispelling in that moment so many of my fears.

'You wanted your own identity,' John went on to explain.

'I thought you would find St Katherine more than appropriate…?'

That was the gold that filled my vision. The three golden wheels of St Katherine, glittering on a red background, to create my own coat of arms. My very own, not quartered with John's or Hugh's. My own, Katherine de Roet, Katherine de Swynford, proclaiming my own identity even if I was also Duchess of Lancaster. And he had chosen my own saint whom I honoured more than any other, the virgin martyr St Katherine of Alexandria, who refused to allow her Christian faith to be broken on the cruelty of the spiked wheel.

And I laughed as I realised.

'What is it?'

'It is like the Roet wheels,' I said. My own father's emblem.

'As it should be,' John agreed. 'Transmuted into gold for a daughter of Roet and a bride of Lancaster named Katherine.'

I thought about John's choice of St Katherine for me: virtuous, erudite, devout, nobly born. I could not have chosen better for my own emblem. Bold and courageous too when her principles were challenged. And now her emblem was mine. This was truly a moment for rejoicing.

'I am honoured,' I managed when I had marshalled my thoughts again.

How could he have read my mind so well? And I knew the answer: he loved me. John loved me and would go to the ends of the earth to ensure my happiness.

Before helping me to mount: 'One moment.'

Opening the purse at his belt he extracted two livery badges. One he pinned to my collar, a gleaming golden Katherine wheel enamelled with red, while the other he attached to the grey fur that formed the upturned brim of his hat.

So he too would proclaim my livery.

His fingers were gentle against my jaw as he adjusted my collar, his countenance lit with his smile that was beautifully forbearing. 'So let us be gone and startle the populace from here to Windsor with our glory. They'll think it a papal visitation and ring the church bells.'

What reassurance that blaze of colour and gilded wheels gave me. Foolish? Undoubtedly. But I rode to Windsor with confidence and St Katherine's courage high in my heart and her wheels bright in my armorial for all to see.

John had done this for me.

I vowed that whatever was waiting for me, I would prove an entirely suitable Duchess for him.

We were expected, of course, so the chamber was thronged, and there were the women of the court who had vowed not to sully their feet on the same ground that I occupied. Well, here I was, for better or worse.

Let us see what they would do. Let us see who would win this bout. I was ripe for battle.

John took my hand and led me forward. And as the Duke smiled at me, I returned it with no need for pretence, for Queen Philippa's training from all those years ago was surging strongly beneath my embroidered girdle with its golden wheels as I walked slowly, smoothly forward, the skirts of my houppelande brushing against the floor with a soft elegance, my hair caught up in a sapphire-jewelled caul. I would not be hurried. I allowed my lips to curve into a faint smile as if certain of my worth as Duchess of Lancaster. Whatever happened here today would not hang on my incompetence or clumsiness in a formal situation. Court procedure ran in my blood, and where I might be unsure I could mimic insouciance to perfection.

Did I not have the master of such court ceremonial at my side?

I was sufficiently at ease to take in my surroundings. The Rose Chamber was as extravagant as I recalled, and much to the King's taste, where the decorations in blue, green and vermilion paint together with a quantity of gold leaf, defied any attempt to choose a gown that did not clash horribly. Notwithstanding I wore figured damask, glorious in blue with rioting leaves and flowers.

Ahead, seated on the dais, King Richard awaited us.

'There, you see. They have not cast you out,' John murmured, lips barely moving as we made our way between the ranks of courtiers.

I allowed my smile to widen. John might be pre-eminent but I knew which of us claimed every eye today. I had felt the weight of them, from the moment we were announced by Richard's emblazoned official. The high blood of England might be here, breathing the same air, but that did not mean they had any intention of enfolding me to their collective bosom.

'But they hate me, you know. Look at them,' I murmured back. 'They are sharpening their daggers already.'

John shook his head, with no time to answer for he was turning to bow to his brother Edmund of Langley, Duke of York, who bowed briefly in reply, even more briefly to me. At least he had not cut me dead. My expression schooled immaculately to one of cool pleasure at being returned to court, I surveyed the throng as we approached the King, registering all, giving no acknowledgement to any.

'You are magnificent.' John's final encouragement before we reached the dais.

'I know.'

But my heart quaked a little.

I knew who was there at the King's side. John's brother, Thomas of Woodstock, Duke of Gloucester, together with his Duchess who had vowed to have nothing to do with me. And there was the Countess of Arundel on my left, a Mortimer descendent of King Edward the Third, the royal blood in her veins heartily dosed with venom. The Countess of Hereford, once my friend, whose presence here smacked of bitter treachery. Others too.

I encompassed them all in a gaze of serene affability.

Then I was curtsying to Richard, gracefully sweeping the skirts of my court finery. All would hang on this reception. If he proved cold towards me, if he mocked me or showed any disdain for my antecedents, he would point the way for every one of his court to follow suit. I rose to my full height and lifted my chin a little.

But Richard was looking at John. 'You have returned at last, my lord uncle.' At twenty-nine years of age, he had all the Plantagenet arrogance, and was smiling, smoothly welcoming. The gleam in his eye reminded me of a cat perusing a tasty mouse. 'I have been in great need of your advice of late.' Suddenly he was frowning. 'And you were not here to give it.'

'I am here to give it now, Sire.' John's expression was a study in benign regret, ignoring the royal frown as he had probably done for the last decade. 'I know you will understand my absence, and excuse it, when I present my wife to you.'

'Your *wife*! And who is this fortunate lady?'

Which Richard knew very well. His bright gaze moved slowly and fastened on my face with spritely mockery. They were too bright, too full of mischief, as was the brilliance of surprise in his voice.

'My lady of Lancaster. We welcome you.'

'My thanks, Sire.'

His hair as darkly gold as the gilding around him, Richard was now of an age to make an impressive figure. The houppelande he wore, so they said, was worth all of thirty thousand marks. Swamping his slight figure in its heavy folds, the encrusted gems blinded in their quantity and brilliance. Fair and smiling, he was the epitome of a young king intent on making his mark on his realm and on European events. But what was his intent? How soon before the unmistakable air of mischief would turn to malice? Richard sparkled with it, wearing a false smile as easily as he wore his robes.

'We are pleased that you have joined our august circle, at last. After so many years of flirting on the periphery.'

'Yes, Sire.' The little barb did not quite glance off my skin, and I felt a flush creep past my embroidered collar, but I smiled as if it were wholly a compliment. 'I too am honoured to be received here at court as Duchess of Lancaster.'

His eyes flashed for a moment. Then gleamed. Had I earned myself a royal reprimand? But no.

'I think you know everyone here present? You ought to do.'

'Yes, Sire.'

'Good, good.' He rubbed his hands together with a flash of jewels. 'You arrival is most timely. I have ordered garter robes to be made for you for the ceremony next week.'

I had forgotten. Or not given it a thought. Now I felt my face flush, knowing exactly why Richard had mentioned it. The royal kitten, full grown into a stately cat, was flexing its claws. He allowed his glance to pass over those who stood as audience around us, inviting them to respond to his magnanimity towards me. Then, when faced with a tense silence that spoke volumes, he raised his hand in a wide gesture.

'I have need to speak with my lord uncle of Lancaster

about the French truce. And my proposed marriage to the Valois lady.' His glance at Gloucester and York, neither of whom supported the proposal, was supremely innocent. 'And you too my uncles of Gloucester and York. Perhaps Lancaster can persuade you of the value of this union.' Then to me: 'I will leave you, my lady, to renew your acquaintance with the ladies of my court.' Richard stood and bowed to me, before snatching up my hand to bring it to his lips, murmuring wickedly: 'They have all come here to meet you with you, you know.'

As I knew only too well. As John walked away in Richard's wake, I faced the little cluster of court women, Richard's playful malice a hard knot in my belly. And waited. Etiquette demanded that they curtsy to me. What a strange turning of the world on its head, where I could command their respect. But would they honour my new status? I looked directly at the Duchess of Gloucester, every one of her fine-boned fingers heavy with precious rings, knowing that her response would be watched by all. Boldly I kept my gaze— level and cool—on her face.

Eleanor de Bohun returned it, all expression governed, her lips a slash of anger.

I raised my chin infinitesimally. But it was enough.

Her curtsy was made, as an essay in brevity, but she bent the knee.

I shifted my regard to the Countess of Arundel, who copied the welcome to an inch but had the grace to say in the tightest of tones: 'My lady.'

Well, that was a step forward.

And then the Countess of Hereford, whose disaffection had given me sorrow. It took much on my part to anticipate the rejection in her taut stance. After all we had lived through together, at Mary's bedside in childbirth, at her tragic death.

'You are right welcome, my lady,' she said softly.

And after the briefest of obeisances, she stepped neatly across the floor and folded me into her arms.

For a moment I stood rigid in incomprehension, and then I knew what she had done, and allowed her to pull me a little distance away from the rest, where I gripped her hands, relief sweeping through me.

'We have been looking for you for the last month, Katherine. I have missed you. And such a shock when we heard.' I saw the loss of her daughter in her face, but nothing would silence her obvious delight. 'You look happy. I don't need to ask…although how you can be so, surrounded by this sour flock of vultures. As for the King's mischief, who knows what he's at these days?' And then, as emotion robbed me of speech: 'Have you nothing to say? Or has your marriage robbed you of your tongue—and your sense of the ridiculous?'

And at last I laughed. 'Are you sure you should do this?'

'What?'

'Welcome the black sheep into the pure white of the royal fold?'

'Why ever would I not?'

'I was under the strongest impression that I would be taught a sharp lesson.' I looked back over my shoulder, at the expressions of those who intended to do exactly that. 'I was told that you were one of them…' I admitted.

'And you believed it? Nonsense, Katherine! My name was attached where it should not have been.'

'And I am grateful. I have missed you too.'

'Good. We will talk later.'

For Richard, his discussion apparently at an end, was at my side, beaming indiscriminately on all.

'It is my intention to travel to France, to complete the negotiations for my new wife, the French Princess Isabella.' He continued to smile. 'I would invite you, my lady of Lancaster, and your daughter Joan, to accompany me. I can think of no one more fitting.'

My surprise masked, my courtly graces back in play, I curtsied my thanks. 'I am honoured, Sire.'

'My intended bride is very young—no more than six years. She will value your knowledge of life at the English court, and your friendship. I will wed her in Calais,' he was continuing, despite knowing that most of his audience were listening to his plans with strong disapproval. 'I know that as her primary lady in waiting for the ceremony—with my lady of Gloucester, of course,'—he bowed to the stiff-backed Duchess—'my wife will be made most welcome.'

'Thank you, Sire,' I murmured. 'I will do all in my power.'

'I know you will. I rely on you.'

And then with a bow he had walked on, while I took advantage of this situation deliberately created by Richard.

'So we work together to welcome our new queen,' I observed to the Duchess.

She managed a bleak curve of the lips. 'So it seems, my lady.'

'We will meet after supper,' I said, matching John's effortless supremacy.

'Of course, my lady.'

The Duchess of Gloucester would never call me sister. I saw no softening in her face, but it had been made as clear as day that it would be unwise for her to shut me out of the hen-roost. As I turned away I caught John's stare from where he conversed with his brother of Gloucester. It was full of pride for me, and of satisfaction which matched my own, yet there was no smile on his face, which conveyed a stark warning. Richard's games were obvious, even risible, but infinitely dangerous. I must never allow myself to be seduced.

Richard, watchful, brimful of devilry, beckoned to me. 'I would be honoured if you would accompany me, Lady Katherine—to give me your opinion of the apartments that I will have refurbished for my little bride. I know your taste in such matters to be beyond question.'

And I moved to walk at his side out of the Painted Chamber, my hand resting in his, which of course opened for me every door in the palace.

'Are you satisfied?' Richard whispered, the sibilants loud as we walked so that all must know that he exchanged confidences with me.

'Yes, Sire.'

'It gave me inordinate pleasure,' he chuckled, 'to stir the waters a little.'

And I nodded. We understood each other very well. He had put himself out to smooth my path, and done so with considerable skill. From that moment, no lady of the court who valued either her position or the King's goodwill for herself or her husband could afford to brush me aside.

'Well?' John asked when it was all done and we could escape to our rooms.

'Good,' I said. 'It was Richard who came to my rescue.'

'It was your own good sense.' John was at his most sardonic. 'And I know you have enough of it not to trust our mischievous king too much. He is guided purely by his own wishes. Today it pleased him to twitch the tails of the tabbies. Tomorrow—who knows?'

I cared not. My acceptance was assured, my role at court for the welcoming of the little queen made plain. I stared into my mirror, admiring the jewelled net that anchored my hair, thoroughly enjoying the prospect of my future role. I would travel to France and welcome the child bride. Joan would accompany me and might find a position in the royal household. John too had taken his rightful place at Richard's side. None of my fears had been realised.

'Why are you smiling?' John asked.

'Because I have persuaded Richard to take down the Halidon Hill tapestry from the new bride's chambers.'

'I always liked that one.'

'You were never a six-year-old girl. At this moment a pretty scene of a lady with flowers and a hawk on her fist is being hung.'

'Is that important?'

'Not to me. It might be to his little wife who would have nightmares if faced nightly with scenes of death and mutilation. But Richard paid attention to me.'

'Now what?' For I had laughed.

'It's even more important that you pay attention to me.'

'About what?'

'This.' I cast my mirror onto the bed and kissed him. 'The Duchess of Lancaster demands your attention.'

He gave it willingly. And yet as I lay in his arms in the aftermath of our lovemaking I could not help but agree with the Duke's assessment. Why did I think that Richard was playing games with us all? And that he had not finished? It might be that he had not even started.

But that was a matter to be pushed aside as I fell into sleep, for John, in his ultimate wisdom, had promised me one final step in eradicating the transgressions of our past and awarding me glorious recognition as the Duchess of Lancaster.

'What of our children?' I had asked. 'Will their legitimacy always be questioned?'

'Certainly not,' he had replied.

Chapter Twenty-One

Pride filled my breast so strongly that I could barely take a breath. The antechamber at Westminster was broodingly cool and for once empty. Usually it seethed with hopeful petitioners but today it was ours, this Beaufort gathering that seemed to fill it from wall to wall. My Beaufort family was a force to be reckoned with, and today was our day. Today a final seal would be placed on my life with John, in this most public recognition of our children.

There we stood. John and I and the four children that I had born him out of wedlock, all clad in white and blue. Lancaster colours, for that was what they were, bastards no longer. Fair of colouring, dark of hair, with a red burnishing when lit by the sun, they were without question their father's children, and never had I see four young people so comfortably at ease with what life had handed them. Bastard or legitimate child, their confidence was a mirror image of John's. It never failed to astonish me. Perhaps it was the care and love I had lavished on them for their own sakes as well as that of their father. Perhaps it was that they had never had need to question their place in the world. John had been openhandedly generous to them, cherishing them since the day they were born, even when we two were estranged and I could not speak of him without heaping curses on his head. If ever a family had felt loved, here it was, fully legitimised since His Holiness had finally been persuaded to sanction our offspring. I had not asked if John's purse of gold had been necessary.

Today the final jewel was to be set in their combined diadem.

The official awaiting us at the door cleared his throat loudly. Joan smiled complacently. Young John—with all the dignity and importance of being a knight as well as a new husband to royally connected Margaret Holland—firmed his shoulders. Henry looked for a moment uncomfortable out of clerical garb, before grinning at me with a little shrug. Thomas was simply Thomas, irreverent and still growing into his limbs with all the adolescent grace of an autumn crane fly.

The pride in John's face echoed mine. He took my hand, bowed and led me forward.

The Lords, fully assembled in the Parliament chamber, were waiting for us, every seat occupied, the whole assembly gleaming with a patchwork of colour beneath the boldness of the arches. Forcing my fingers to lie lightly in John's hand, I inclined my head left and right, acknowledging the faces I knew. And there Thomas Arundel, the Archbishop of Canterbury, waited to receive us, ushering us into the centre of the chamber where we made our obeisance to the Lords. The silence of solemnity fell on us as four lords approached at a signal from the cleric, one of them holding the folds of a mantle over his arm.

'We are here this day to perform this heavy and age-old ceremony granting legitimacy to these mantle-children.'

The mantle, of white damask to signal purity, gold fringed and banded with ermine to speak of royal authority, was spread, a corner to be taken by each of the four lords, who lifted it high above our heads on gilded poles, until we were entirely covered by its shadow.

'Richard by the grace of God, King of England and France to our most dear cousins…'

John was looking at me. The Archbishop, his voice suitably sonorous, was using the words from the King's own Letter Patent. There would never be any doubting the authority of this ceremony. Our children would be fixed into the legal structure of England for all time.

'We think it proper and fit that we should enrich you…'

For here was the case. His Holiness's recognition ultimately in writing, might have removed the taint of bastardy from our Beaufort children, but that was insufficient to give them any position under the laws of inheritance. If they were ever to have the right to inherit land or title, to establish their own families with provision for their own children, they needed this ceremony under the spread of this mantle.

'We think it proper that we enrich you, our most dear cousins, who are begotten of royal blood, with the strength of our royal prerogative of favour and grace…'

We emerged into the same antechamber we had left only an hour before, newly resplendent with legitimacy. The sapphires stitched on my bodice glimmered as I drew in a breath of sheer delight at the sweeping away of all the shadowy illegalities of the past. My life with John had been given legal sanction and I could ask for nothing more. Unable to express my sense of ultimate fulfilment, I simply smiled at my children.

'You now legitimately exist as dear cousins to the king,' John remarked with not a little cynicism. 'And your mother is very happy.'

'I have always existed.' Young John did not recognise irony.

'And I doubt Richard is any more a dear cousin than he has ever been. He has a chancy temper,' Henry added, who did.

'What more do you want?' Joan asked. 'Letters Patent, a white and gold care-cloth and an Act of Parliament promised for tomorrow.'

The delight that bubbled within her was catching. Wedded, widowed and wedded again, even though only nineteen years old, mother of two tiny daughters and step-mother for the past year to the twelve children of Ralph Neville, Baron Raby, Joan had become a woman in her own right and I admired her composure. It took much to rattle my daughter's stalwart heart encased today in embroidered damask.

John and I looked at each other. We wanted nothing more. Not for us. We had all we needed in each other. But for this quartet of handsome Beauforts, born out of love and sin? There would be no obstacle for them now.

It was for me a ceremony of great joy.

'I'm hungry,' Thomas announced.

'Then we must eat,' John laughed. 'Are we not worthy of a celebration?'

It was a happy day. What would life hold for these Beaufort children? Not the crown, of course, for royal inheritance was barred to them, but what did that matter? The world of power and politics was theirs for the taking, and I could not have asked for more. John the soldier, Henry the cleric,

Joan the managing wife and Thomas—who knew what fate would hold for my youngest child?

How transitory is happiness. It would be the last time I was so free from anxieties, so caught up in my family's recognition. I did not know what lay in wait for me or for John. I thought we had been fully blessed, and could see no end to the blessings.

'John!' I leaned forward, elbows planted on the wall coping, narrowing my eyes at the road, which was obscured by morning haze. I was standing on the wall-walk at Kenilworth, looking out towards the south, leaving John to the detailed—and tedious—inspection of a section of crumbling stonework, deep in conversation with his Constable.

'John!'

I raised my voice, informal in sudden concern. I was not mistaken. There was a cloud of dust, heralding a fast-travelling retinue.

What was it that made me alert John? Some presentiment, perhaps, for it brought a strange sharp jolt to my heart. 'My lord,' I called out again, but there was no need. John and the Constable were at my shoulder, the expression on John's face indicating that he was already alert for trouble of some kind.

'It's the Earl of Derby, my lord.'

The Constable confirmed what we could now make out in the pennons and banners bearing Henry's deer and swans. Henry was travelling fast.

'Something's afoot.' John was already halfway down the steps before I hitched the fullness of my skirts and followed him.

We met Henry in the Great Hall. Eyes still wide with bafflement despite the hours spent in the saddle, voice raw with patent disbelief, he had not even taken the time to divest himself of hat, gloves or weapons, but stood there in the centre of the vast room, feet planted, spine braced, one hand clenched on his sword hilt. Making no attempt to mute his voice, he brought every servant within range to a halt.

'There's a plot, father. Murder. And it's Richard.'

'A plot to murder the King?' I asked, astounded. Voices might be raised in criticism of Richard's use of power, but this uncontrolled announcement presaged treason.

'No!' Henry dragged in a breath to make sense of what held no sense for any of us. 'There's a plot to destroy Lancaster.' He flung out his hand to encompass the three of us. 'A massacre, by the Rood! You, sir. Me—you too, my lady— and probably my sons if he can get his hands on them. It's to happen on the road to Windsor, when we go there in the New Year.'

The moment of silence in that vast space disintegrated into impassioned response.

'No!' I heard myself breathe as my belly clenched.

'On what grounds would he plan this?' John snapped. I noted that he did not ask the owner of the hand behind this outrage.

'He accuses us of treason,' Henry responded. 'But there'll be no arraignment before a court, sir. He'll kill first and question later.'

Nor did John question this interpretation. 'Who told you this?'

'Thomas Mowbray. I'd not cast aside his warning lightly,' Henry replied.

Thomas Mowbray, the powerful Duke of Norfolk, together with Henry, was of the dangerous coterie of Lords Appellant with Robert de Vere, Earl of Oxford and royal favourite, in their sights. Was Mowbray to be believed? Henry thought so, but I looked to John, to test my own reaction. It had caused him to frown, but he was not a man given to foolish rumour. Perhaps it was nought but a piece of mischief, to stir up more strife between John and the King.

'Do you believe it?' I asked Henry now that he had recovered some of his equanimity along with his breath.

'*Mowbray* believed it. He stopped me on the road to Windsor to tell me. To warn me.' Shaking his head, Henry, gloves now cast onto a bench with his hat and sword, stretched out his hands palm up, as if he might divine the truth there, before he clenched them into fists. 'What do we do?'

John studied the floor at his feet. Then: 'Come. We'll talk about this in private.'

And when the door of an inner chamber was closed.

'We tell Richard what you've heard,' John stated.

Henry's grunt of dissent was answer enough. 'If Richard's hand is on it…'

'*If* it is.' As he gripped his son's arm I saw that the bones of John's face were stark beneath his skin, despite the authority in his decision. 'If Richard thinks to turn against his own flesh and blood, the fact that we know his plan might give him pause. We offer him a chance to see sense and draw back. I think Richard's courage is a finite thing and unpredictable. Given the incentive, he might enjoy the opportunity to turn about, to dispense royal justice with an easy hand and win goodwill all round, including that of Lancaster. He might pronounce that he knows nothing of it. And that could be the end of the matter. If he knows that we are forewarned and so forearmed, it might conceivably force him to realise that to declare war on his own family will raise a storm that he cannot ultimately control. And might conceivably damage him.'

It seemed to me to be good sense, but I could see the

troubled working of Henry's mind. It flitted like shadows over his features.

'Would he back down? I wouldn't wager my life against it. Richard puts no value on family loyalty if he sees it as a threat to his own power, or a chance to pay back past grudges. He had my uncle of Gloucester murdered quick enough.'

'For which I blame myself with every breath I take,' John growled, sinking back into a chair, the sudden expression of grief in his face so tangible that I had to resist moving to stand behind him, my hand on his shoulder. Then I did not resist at all. How could I? The muscles in his shoulder taut, John looked up at me with a glimmer of a smile but the re-gret was still there in his words and I knew the guilt would always lie on his heart. 'I should have done something to stop it and instead I turned my back and hoped it was just Richard demanding attention, as he does. And I was wrong. My brother paid with his life for my inaction. You are not telling me anything I do not know, Henry.'

It had been a time of simmering danger, Richard claiming that Gloucester was plotting against him and begging John for advice. John had tried to pour oil on troubled waters with stern words: Gloucester would never harm either the King or the little Queen Isabella of France. But Richard had had the suspected plotters, Gloucester together with Warwick and Arundel, arrested, and his uncle of Gloucester done to death, smothered in his bed in Calais.

'Do you believe the evidence that Gloucester was plotting against Richard?' Henry demanded, taking a seat opposite.

'No,' John responded softly. 'I think it a ruse by Richard to be avenged. Because my brother Gloucester was one of the Lords Appellant.'

Henry raised his eyes to John's face.

'So was I one of the Lords Appellant.'

And I felt the muscle in John's shoulder tense further, and in that tension, which he made no attempt to disguise, I learned the depth of John's fear for Henry, for all of us.

'I know you were involved. Why do you think I played the diplomat—or some would say the coward—and made little comment on Gloucester's death? Why do you think I tread carefully now? Every day I await the next step in Richard's plotting to rid himself of every man in the kingdom who has the blood and the strength to challenge his power. And most of all I fear that Richard has his next arrow trained on you, my son. He'll never forgive you for what happened at Radcot Bridge.'

This was Richard, who smiled on the Beauforts, who granted land and an Earldom to my son, John, approved a new and most valuable jointure for me for the term of my life so that I should never suffer hardship, who gave office to Henry as Chancellor of Oxford and recognition to Thomas who was retained for life by the King himself. All of this with one generous hand, whilst vicious and spiteful retribution was enacted with the other. Richard, God's anointed King, who abandoned all compassion, all loyalty, out of revenge on those who had dared to stand against him. Those who had rid him of his fawning and much-loved favourite Robert de Vere in the hope of restoring good government to England.

And one of these Lords Appellant, appealing to Richard to restore good government, taking a stand against their King, which some might construe as treason, was Henry who had joined up with the lords of York, Nottingham, Warwick and Arundel to push the issue by raising an army. At Radcot Bridge de Vere had been defeated and forced into banishment.

Richard's wrath was stirred to a new level, and so was his desire for revenge. Richard declared war against Henry, and against John, the one man in the kingdom who had guided and guarded him from childhood.

Now John's words were like the tolling of a bell to signal a death as his hands fisted to match those of his son. When John moved under my hand, I found that my fingers were digging hard into the cloth, into the flesh beneath. I flexed them, but I would not break the contact. All we had built together, of love and family, was suddenly in danger from Richard's revenge. Even our lives.

'You are in no danger,' John said, looking up at me. 'I'll not let you come to harm.'

My own response leaped into life.

But how can I save you?

How would I live out my days if I lost him now, after so little time together? My heart thudded hard. John might hope for Richard's good sense, but the conviction in his earlier words did not balance against the worry I now read in his eyes. We were threatened with death on the road, to all intents at the hands of some enterprising footpads, in truth paid for by the King.

'I am so sorry…' was all I managed at John's ruthlessly painful evaluation of his family's veracity. Of Plantagenet unity and loyalty.

His shoulder lifted under my renewed grip. 'It is a burden I must bear.'

'That *we* must bear…'

Which prompted him to close his hand over mine and press it hard against his chest where his heart beat with a steady rhythm. His gaze was wide and level, calming my rising panic. When he smiled with complete understanding, I found myself responding, the terror in my heart less fierce. We had an understanding, a link that would hold firm under all tribulation. Nothing would destroy that. I would not allow it.

But a murderer's dagger might—

Henry interrupted my thoughts, a little gesture of impatience. 'I came here for your advice. What do I do, my lord?' In his anxiety he became increasingly formal.

John stood. 'We call his bluff. We tell the King what we have heard, and deny that there could be any possible truth in it. We convince the King that we have utmost trust in his love for his family. We will not, God forgive us, make mention of my brother Gloucester.'

He looked down at me. 'Do you agree?'

He so rarely asked my opinion. It was a mark of his concern, despite his reassurance.

'Yes, I do,' I responded. I could think of no other way forward out of this lethal mire.

'Do you travel to London? Or shall I?' Henry was already on his way to the door with energetic strides. Since Mary's death I thought he had aged, no longer the young boy I had known. Still young in years, his capacity for clear thought and prompt action was impressive.

John's smile was wry. 'I think the old lion has had his day. You go, my son. I have confidence in you.' They embraced. 'But keep your temper.'

So Henry went to Windsor to disrupt the so-called plot, John brooded behind a wall of silence and I cursed Richard to the fires of hell for his destruction of our happiness.

'Take care,' I whispered in Henry's ear as he prepared to mount. 'Come back to us.'

For I knew that if his beloved son came to harm, John would be broken. I would have to be strong for both of us.

I would never forgive Richard. I would despise Richard until the day of my death.

September 1398: Gosford Green, Coventry

Holy Mother, I prayed silently, my palm hard around the coral beads restored to my belt. *Cast your divine protection over these two men. If Henry dies on this field, it will surely break John's heart. I cannot bear the anguish for him. And my own...*

If I was to act, it must be now.

Seated on the dais, clad in the white and blue of the heavy damask gown I had worn for our mantle ceremony when we had rejoiced in the favour of God and the lords of England, I absorbed the magnificent scene that Richard had created for this day. No one could fault his imagination, or his sense of the dramatic. Or the quality of mischief that rendered him dangerous to the existence of Henry of Derby.

I was close enough to touch Richard's ermined robe, if I stretched out my arm, and wondered momentarily if he could sense my thoughts. What John's were I had no idea behind his harsh features. Richard's were pure malevolence disguised by the benign smile.

I tensed my muscles to obey me.

We were hemmed in by flags and pennons, stamped with the heraldic devices of the aristocracy of England, all over-laid with a wealth of royal symbolism and Richard's own smoothly smug, gold-coroneted white hart. The canopy over my head fluttered with Plantagenet leopards and Valois fleur-de-lis, casting mottled shadows over my veils and on those of Richard's French child bride, resplendent in a gown she was clearly delighted in. Her little hands smoothed her velvet skirts in pleasure. Mine clenched, white-knuckled, until I remembered and stretched them, hot palmed against the stiffly embroidered cloth.

At my side, between me and Richard, was John, darkly formal, bejewelled yet austere, every inch King's counsellor, royal uncle and Duke of Lancaster and Aquitaine. He would not dishonour his dignity or his name by a show of emotion on this terrible day. We were here to witness the quality of royal justice, with fear in our hearts. Richard's justice could not be trusted. I shivered in the heat, for who could determine the outcome of what we would witness today? I could not. This was to be no formal jousting to entertain the court, no ritualised sword against sword to exhibit the skill of the two combatants. This would be a contest unto death, and it might be that the one to perish was John's beloved son, Henry of Derby.

How had it come to this? Everything had fallen perfectly into Richard's hands when Henry and Mowbray had faced each other. Presented with the knowledge that Henry had leaked his confidence to the King, Mowbray in a fit of self-preservation, had promptly accused Henry of treason. Henry had retaliated in kind. A ferocious stand-off ensued which Richard leaped on like a hunting cat. Our puissant king had pronounced that Henry and Mowbray would meet in trial by combat at Coventry, before the whole court. Trial to the death to apportion guilt. Death for one, banishment for the other. Two Lords Appellant obliterated at one blow, to Richard's seething delight.

So here we sat to witness the culmination of Richard's plotting.

The two combatants were introduced. Henry and Thomas Mowbray, Duke of Norfolk, the highest and best of England's blood, each man furnished with a lance. Despite the warmth of the day, I felt the blood drain from my skin, so much that I thought my face must be white with fear. No whiter than John's whose expression was carved from granite.

If I was to act it must be now. If John would not petition for mercy for his son, then I must.

'Will you not appeal to Richard?' I had asked.

'No, I will not.' John had been adamant. 'I will not impugn my son's honour, or mine. I will not grovel in the dust when we are innocent of the charges laid against us. Plantagenets do not bend the knee in supplication when the King overrides the law.'

So I must do it.

There, on the dais, skirts billowing, I stood.

Only to find a hand around my wrist, hard and relentless.

'No.' John's denial might reach no one's ears but mine, but it was formidable.

'Someone must.' I would not sit.

'No.' How bleak his tone. 'I know why you wear this today—but it will not serve.'

He touched the solid gold livery collar that lay impressively on the damask, not my own of red and gold, not John's blue and silver, but Richard's own, displaying Richard's white hart on my breast, given to me by the King as a symbol of his high regard, to wear at his wedding to the French girl who sat at his side with such innocent enjoyment when all around her was unbearable tension.

'It might.'

'No.'

Still I stood.

'Katherine. You will not.' It was the regal command he never used to me, implacable despite the low timbre. 'You don't know what predator you might unleash.'

Predator? It was a curious choice of word. 'I might harness it.'

'Or set it ablaze with fury.'

The strength in his arm was irresistible, as was the silent message in his gaze that warned me suddenly of things I knew nothing of. And I sat at last. Defiant, disturbed, but defeated by a knowledge greater than mine.

If Richard had noticed, he gave no sign, his eyes narrowed on the men on whom he would be revenged for all past slights. They had taken up their positions at opposite ends of the field. Such inconsequential details I noticed: the stiff wind whipped the flags, tangling their fringes; the plumes on Henry's helm frisked and bucked. I anchored my veiling with a heavy hand against my neck. John's eyes were fixed on his son. Richard was smiling.

The lances were not blunt, neither were the swords. This was no court entertainment. One would die. Or be so badly hurt that…

Henry is an expert swordsman, a champion jouster. He will take no hurt.

I could hear John's breathing, light and shallow, as he sat as controlled as if going into battle himself. And there was the sun glinting from the surface of Henry's armour, from the burnished coat of his white stallion, one of John's own with experience in the field, caparisoned in blue and green velvet embroidered with Henry's deer and swans. Pray God Abrax would carry Henry with all the swiftness and mighty strength of a swan this day.

I looked across at Mowbray in crimson velvet, his sturdy form a splash of brightness, like blood, on the scene. I could not wish him ill, for he was as much a victim of Richard's vengeance as was Henry.

A blast from the herald's trumpet signalled to make ready.

Henry gathered his reins into one hand, couching his lance against his body with the other. A mighty silence settled on the field, the only sound the snap of fabric. I held my breath, hands once again cramped in my lap in the blue and white folds. In the distance it was impossible to see the muscles bunch in Abrax's haunches, but I saw them tighten in John's hand, pressed hard against his thigh. Then began the thunder of hooves, increasing as the great destriers gathered speed.

I felt rather than saw Richard move.

He stepped towards the front of the dais, leaned and snatched the baton from his herald, hurling it onto the ground where it lay and glinted in the dust. Startled, fumbling, the herald caught his wits and blew a shattering blast.

And the combatants reined in, hauling their mounts to a reluctant stand as an expectant silence fell on the field.

'Approach.' Richard's order carried clearly. 'Kneel, my lords.'

'He will pardon them,' I murmured, and grasped John's sleeve as a tiny seed of hope began to live in my heart, even though the tendons in John's throat were prominent as he swallowed. 'He has realised his mistake.'

But John's mouth clamped like a vice, and seeing it I accepted the truth. There would be no royal goodwill here today, and whatever it was that John feared would come to pass. Today I would learn what it was. I removed my hand. This was his tragedy to face alone, as he would wish.

Richard was speaking. 'I will have no more of it, my lords. Your disloyalty is an affront to me and a threat to the peace of my kingdom. Here is my decision.'

He paused. When he spoke again his voice was as clear as his herald's trumpet.

'For your own past demeanours against my royal person you will depart this land of your birth and live in exile.

My lord of Norfolk—I arraign you for life. It is not for you to return except on pain of death. And you, my cousin of Derby—from whom I would have expected honour and loyalty—because of our shared blood and for the affection I bear towards your father, I will soften my judgement: I condemn you to exile for ten years.'

A strange singing tension stretched out around me, as if no one could believe what they had heard. I had been right to be afraid.

'Before God!' I heard John murmur.

'Sire,' Henry said, his eyes on his father's masklike face.

'There is no appeal, my lords. Is not my judgement clear?'

Ten years.

Fury roiled in my belly as I saw the plotting behind this. For here was the glittering prize, the treasure that Richard had always intended to grasp for himself. Ten years. Ten years, with the Lancaster heir and only son exiled. What an opportunity for King Richard to seize the wealth and estates of Lancaster for himself. If John's health should fail.

For there was my own worry that kept sleep at bay. John's health was compromised.

Richard's motives went far beyond punishment of Henry and Mowbray as Lords Appellant. Richard had his eye on a far greater treasure, as John had always known and had kept from me. On John's death, the heir in exile, Richard would claim the great inheritance as his own. It was as cruel a move as I could envisage. I had not realised, but John had.

John was standing, facing Richard, with no hint of the inner turmoil that shook me in the severity of his expression. His control was superb, marvellous in its courtesy, for all the past goodwill between uncle and nephew, all the care John had lavished on Richard, had been obliterated in that one pronouncement. John faced it with majestic simplicity.

'My lord, I advise you to reconsider.'

'What's that, Uncle? Advice in a matter of treachery? Would you have me be more lenient, for crimes against my person?'

'I would ask you to show the mercy appropriate to a great king. There has been no charge against my son or my lord of Norfolk. Nor has proof of guilt been shown. It would be an injustice to pass so harsh a judgement.'

'I know who I can trust, sir.' Richard was as unpleasantly smooth as a baked custard too long in the eating.

'Ten years, or a lifetime, is a questionable sentence for a matter unproven.' John continued to press his argument. 'It would be ill-advised for the King to show disrespect for the law.'

Richard leaned to clasp John's shoulder and I saw the gleam in his eye.

'Is death leaning on your shoulder, Uncle?' A little smile, disgracefully mimicking compassion. 'I forget that age creeps up on you, as on us all. So be it. I am of a mind to be lenient, for your sake. Are you not blood of my blood? I will reduce the terms of your son's banishment.'

'My thanks, Sire—'

'To six years.' Richard all but crowed. 'Any further requests of my generosity, my lord uncle?'

John bowed gravely, despite his ashen face. 'I can only express my gratitude for your compassion, Sire.'

I knew his fear, for was it not my own? Six years was as much a life-sentence as ten for John. He might never see his son again. I bore it in my own heart as Richard handed Isabella down from the dais, and as complacent satisfaction cloaked him, I could have stuck his smiling face.

'He has destroyed me,' said John, with no inflexion at all, as we walked from the field.

I could not deny it. I feared that that was exactly what Richard had done. Wretchedness kept step with me, a close companion.

After his parting with Henry at Waltham, conducted with stark self-command on both sides, a spectacularly awe-inspiring lack of emotion when the future for John and his son loomed so ominously, John shut himself away in his room at Leicester. Even from me. I wept for him, as I had refused to weep at Henry's banishment and leave-taking, and then hovered outside his door with growing fury. It remained barred to me as if he could not tolerate my company. One of John's squires, nameless to me in my emotional turmoil, made his apologies with a set face.

The parting had been raw. It was not to be spoken of, the silent anguish that hung in the air as John embraced his son, the lingering fear in the lines on his face, in the words that were not spoken. This might, as we all feared, be the final meeting between them.

'Go to Paris,' John advised. 'Travel is easy if Richard summons you back.'

Richard's malevolence loomed like a black raven, wings spread over us all. We knew he would never rescind Henry's banishment.

'He would not let me help him,' I raged in Agnes's initially sympathetic ear. 'I would have petitioned Richard. It may have done no good but...'

For in a final wilful, gleeful gesture, Henry of Monmouth, John's grandson, still young and vulnerable at ten years, had been summoned to live in Richard's household as hostage for his father Henry of Derby's good behaviour in exile. The chains about the House of Lancaster were being tightened to a stranglehold with every day that passed.

'Petitioning King Richard was more like to cause harm,' Agnes admonished. The years might strip colour from her hair and bend her back, her fingers might be less nimble, but Agnes's mind retained an uncomfortable needle-sharpness. 'The Duke saw it. Why did you not?'

'Saw what?' I rubbed hard at my temples, which ached.

'Would you trust the King?' Agnes asked. 'If Richard grew weary of the petitioning, might he not forget the debt he owed to the Duke and reimpose the full ten years? Or even longer? Best to take what's given, I'd say. You could have done so much damage, Katherine.'

I had not seen it in that light. All I had thought to do was to ease John's pain. I sank onto a stool, closing my eyes, acknowledging that in matters of high policy, and in knowledge of the King, John was more astute than I. Without doubt, Richard had his eye on the Lancaster land and wealth.

'I was wrong.'

'Not for the first time. And probably not the last.'

Her bracing words brought me back to my senses.

'But now he won't see me or talk to me.'

'Any clever woman can find a way round that. Come with me.'

I spent a profitable and enlightening hour in the stillroom with Agnes whose swollen fingers could still concoct a powerful remedy. Then, cup in hand, I walked to John's chamber and lifted a hand to rap smartly on the door, which belied the contrition in my heart. I had an apology to offer.

The door opened before I made contact.

'It is my wish to speak with—' I was already stepping forward, intent on forcing an entry.

It was no apologetic squire or uncomfortable body servant, but John who stood on the threshold, groomed and impressively clad in a damask houppelande despite the excessive pallor. It made me conscious of my own dishevelled state after an hour of pounding and stirring.

'Katherine. Did you want me?' The grief of Henry's leave-taking was absent and his smile was all welcome.

'I always want you. I was about to enter with or without leave,' I admitted.

'I have an apology to make,' he said gently.

'Yes. So have I.'

Relief at seeing him restored to his old authority was a balm to my soul, as I followed him back into his chamber, which was as fastidiously neat and thoroughly organised as it ever was. The bed curtains hung in good order, the disposition of the coffer, the chair, the prie-dieu, the open book of what looked like poetry, offered no evidence of the personal anguish of a powerful man that those four walls had witnessed. But it was written on his face for all time.

'I forgive you, whatever it is,' I said. 'Drink this.' I proffered the cup.

'A penance?'

'You might say that. It's hot and biting,' I warned.

He drank off the tincture in warm wine, shuddering with a grimace. 'Should I ask what it will do for me?'

'It's oil of black mustard. It strengthens the heart.'

'By God, it needs strengthening.' His smile warmed my own heart.

'And wards off poison,' I added for good measure.

We sat together in a sunny window embrasure. I made reparation in a kiss for my wilful behaviour at the tournament. He expressed his regret that he had closed his door against me.

'You were right,' I said. 'Richard is a predator and we have no redress.' Then, when he was silent: 'Are we at one?' I asked.

His fingers laced with mine. 'What can divide us?' And then as an afterthought: 'Richard must never be allowed to stand between us.'

'He will not. But don't shut me out again.'

'I will not. I have need of you as never before.'

I recognised it for what it was: the final rejection of Plantagenet arrogance, the ultimate acceptance of my position in his life. After all the years, some turbulent, some exquisitely happy, John knew that he needed me, and would allow me into his mind as he never truly had before. He would not hide the pattern of his thoughts, his desires or his fears from me again, and I would bear them. The naïve, youthful Katherine de Swynford could never have envisaged how powerful that first attraction to the old allure could become. John's glamour still stirred me, but the depth of our love had the power to shake me. Now I stood beside him and faced the world, bearing silent witness to his cares. I would nurture and succour him, adding no burden of my own. I would be a beacon for him against a dark sky. My love would be a strength and a salvation.

And John would love me and instinctively know my joys and woes. It was all I asked.

Silently, I rejoiced for this measure of closeness we had achieved, even as I grieved his great loss and the shortening of our days together.

Chapter Twenty-Two

October 1398: Leicester Castle

'What are you doing?'

What I had seen when I stepped into the Great Hall and manoeuvred around the haphazard piles of baggage and equipment appropriate for a long journey had chilled my blood. There in the middle of it all was one of the great travelling beds.

No! He could not!

I had turned on my heel to run him to ground in the steward's room, where I became coated with ice from head to foot that for a moment robbed me of what would have been hot words. How weary he looked, his eyelids dark and fine drawn. His skin almost translucent, his nose as fine as a blade. But there was nothing amiss with his spirit or his temper.

'I am, as you see, organising a journey.' There was the old undercurrent of impatience that I recognised.

'Is it imminent?'

He sighed. 'Not so imminent that I cannot give you a moment of my time.'

He gestured for the steward to leave us. The steward beat a fast retreat, sped on his way by the expression on my face.

'And is this a good idea?' At least I tempered my tone.

'Probably not.'

The slant of light delineated the increasingly sharp line of his cheekbones, yet it was not caused by the unseasonal cold, the days of cloud and rain. To my mind the culprit was Richard. His banishing of Henry had drained the blood from John's heart but although grief and loss held him prisoner, still our marriage held. Our love was as strong as it had ever been. As we had vowed, not even Richard could shake that.

Musing lightly as I poured a cup of wine from the engraved silver vessel at his left hand, I held to the belief that John would rally as he had before, if Richard allowed him to rest. John had found a need to retire to Lilleshall Abbey with me, at the end of the Shrewsbury Parliament in September, but had not his spirits been restored there? Had not prayer and a period of calm dispersed the fever that shook his limbs and bathed his face with perspiration, however cool the day?

But was he indeed restored? Cold reality on some days forced its way into my thoughts, making me acknowledge the inevitable. This was one of those days.

'Why are you doing this?' I asked, pushing the cup towards him, attempting to preserve an outward calm when fear of what was clearly a major expedition gripped me, and all I wished to do was shriek at him that he must not go. He was in no fit state to go on any journey. I suspected Richard's hand again.

'Because I am to go to Scotland, in October, at the request of the King.'

I knew it had been mooted. A diplomatic mission to which John was most suited. If anyone could talk the Scots into an alliance, it was he. And perhaps Richard saw an opportunity not to be missed to remove his uncle from the centre of government. It was in both our minds, but the King's will was the King's will.

I said no more, letting John return to his lists. We knew it would never come to fruition. The mighty Duke of Lancaster no longer had the energy to pursue such a venture. The following week the piles of baggage were removed and unpacked, the bed restored to storage. I ordered it and John, in a state of extreme lassitude, was unable to stand against me. Some days it took all his strength to raise his knife to his meat, a cup to his lips.

'God's Blood! It's a poor way to celebrate the Coming of the Christ Child!' he announced as the days of the celebration drew near and his listlessness, aggravated by poor appetite, failed to respond to the tincture of sorrel I pressed on him.

'We will still celebrate. We do not have to dance,' I said.

His eyes gleamed. 'I can still dance with you in my mind, my dear love.'

'Then that is what we will do.'

I would not let it become a house of mourning. Not yet.

These were the days of respite when we sat together, sharing a cup of wine. Memories were allowed to return, but only the good ones we might enjoy together. This was not the time to stray into the far reaches of bitterness and recrimination, and indeed there were no such memories to catch us out. Time and suffering had brought us closer, even when the limit of our intimacy might be hands enclasped, lips soft and gentle in chaste salute. The days of our physical coupling were long gone but my body accepted it. Had I not had many years to practice abstinence? It stood me in good stead. Instead, as John held me in his arms I relished the closeness of spirit.

'Shall I tell Henry?' I asked.

Proof, at last, of the depth of my despair. It was the first time that either of us had spoken of the absence of John's heir, or alluded to his own creeping death. Now we could turn our thoughts from it no longer.

But: 'It will do no good. Why worry him for no reason?' John replied. 'Read to me.' With his free hand he pushed the open Book of Hours across the bed towards me. 'Read to me from the psalm...'

It was Psalm 38, not one that came easily to my mind. I began.

'"O lord, rebuke me not in thy wrath, neither chasten me in thy hot displeasure. For thine arrows stick fast in me and thy hand presseth me sore. There is no soundness in my flesh because of thy anger. Neither is there any rest in my bones because of my sin..."'

I stopped, aghast.

'John...no!'

'Go on. I have to face my death. I know why I am suffering. My physician says it is God's judgement for my breaking of holy law. I need God's forgiveness.'

So I read on, hating it, but it was what he wanted.

'"I am feeble and sore broken. My heart panteth, my strength faileth me. As for the light of my eyes, it is also gone from me..."'

I could read no more. For the first time in his presence in these weeks I could not prevent tears gathering, falling. As I closed the book and laid it down beside me, we exchanged a long look, which spoke of everything we could not say.

'Not so,' he said at last, his smile a blessing. 'The light of my eyes is not gone from me. You are the light of my eyes. You are the bright sun in my firmament. You are with me always.'

'And I will be until the end,' I acknowledged.

We sat quietly together. Our minds were in tune. And so I abandoned the physical despair of the psalmist and sang instead of love and hope and an assurance for our future together:

> *'Your love and my love keep each other company—*
> *That is why I am so joyful.*
> *That your heart is constant in its love for mine*
> *Is a solace beyond compare.*
> *Yours in the clasp that hold my loyalty,*
> *You dismiss all my heart's sorrow.*
> *And yours is a devotion that does not bend or alter—*
> *Your love and my love shall be steadfast in their loyalty*
> *And never drift apart.'*

All would be well, I assured myself. Henry would return from exile. John's body would mend and become as strong as his mind. I would not release him. I would not give him leave to go from me. This was what I had wanted all my life, the right to be with him. I refused to accept our parting.

I held tight to his hand. I would not give him up. I would not.

His mind was as astute as ever, his will as firm. How could death claim him?

On the second day of the new month of February I entered John's room, knowing that his physician and body servant had left, only to discover that there was a clerk with him, and John was dictating, steadily, while the clerk wrote.

John acknowledged me with a glance, but did not stop his instructions. When he raised his hand to summon me closer, I saw that he could barely lift it. I stood beside him until he was finished, my eyes fixed on his face throughout, absorbing every nuance.

'What's all this?' I asked at last, for as I sank to the edge of his bed I realised that I was sharing it with an array of uncomfortable bullion. I shuffled, after sitting awkwardly on a girdle set with cabochon rubies, and made to clear it away.

'No. Leave it for a moment. It will be packed it into a coffer. I have bequeathed it all to Richard.'

I looked at the treasure, startled into a laugh when I saw the gold cup I had given to John at the New Year gift-giving. Next to it a great jewel set as a pin to hold a cloak. A gold dish, engraved with the garter motif, its cover flamboyant with a dove, its wings spread wide.

'My cup?' I could still smile. 'You've only had it a month!'

'But it's the best I have.'

'To persuade Richard to be lenient.'

'Yes.'

'Can he be persuaded?'

It was a beautiful cup. I begrudged it holding pride of place in Richard's treasury, but I would not deny John's right to give it.

'The gold means nothing to me,' he murmured. 'How strange that once I saw its value and collected such items with joy. Now, dearest Katherine, you are my treasure. A pearl beyond price.' He took my hand and raised it to his lips as he used to do in the days of love's glory. 'To you, I give you the gift I can give to no one else. I give you the most precious thing I have. Myself, firm in faith and love, steady in desire, never changeable. No matter how close death comes with silent feet.'

I sat with him, not speaking. I had no words to say.

I was warned. Had I not known it? Had I not seen death stalking us, no matter how often I would deny it? My careful dosing with black mustard or wild valerian could be efficacious, but it could not prolong life beyond its allotted span. The dying of the year had pre-empted the final days of a great prince.

Now his strength was fading fast. We both knew it. We did not speak of it but let the events unfold as they would.

My lord, my lover, slipped into death, at the end as gently as into sleep, while I sat at his side and watched his beloved face. He had asked me in his final breaths to play the lute for him. His soul departed as the plangent chords filled the spaces in the room. Without struggle. Without pain in the end. It was as if his flesh recognised the appointed hour and allowed his soul to depart without contest.

I sat for a long time in that room, sumptuously appointed as for the living, my hand hard on the lute strings to silence any vibration. So my lord, my love, was still and silent. But whereas I could make the lute speak softly again, or sing out in fervent joy, as the mood took me, my love would never more speak to me. The majestic polyphony of our lives together was dead.

I too was lost and alone and silent.

The depth of my anguish could not be expressed.

Epilogue

February 1399: Leicester Castle

I kneel in the chapel, beside the bier where my lord, my lover, my husband, lies cold in death. I keep vigil, as a good wife should, and as my heart dictates, but tomorrow we will begin the slow journey south from Leicester to London. And there, in London, I will lose him for ever.

The February day is short; already the night encroaches so that the pillars and arches fade from my sight. In my widow's weeds I am barely a shadow amongst so many others.

I work my way through the beads of my rosary—the first gift he ever gave me when I was still determinedly withstanding his impossible glamour—lips moving soundlessly, offering up prayers for John's soul, for my own strength to withstand the coming ordeal. My mind is quite clear but my heart is as uncompromisingly bleak as a Lenten fast. As coldly unresponsive as his, even though mine still beats, and his is still for ever. I cannot contemplate my life as it must now be.

I sit back on my heels, lips still but a little pursed, my stare decidedly judgemental.

'Behold me in full widow's weeds again,' I say. 'You don't like them, but you leave me with no choice in the matter, unless you wish me to become an object of gossip again.' I force myself to imagine life without him after all. 'I will have to keep a cage of singing birds for company. Do you recall how Margaret loved them? I remember you throwing a cover over them to shut them up. Now there will be no one to complain.'

His magnificence outshines me, even now, making me a shabby crow in contrast to a showy peacock. He had always loved me, as his Duchess, to wear jewel-colours. Emerald and sapphire blue, blood-red crimson or rich vermilion, all overlaid with cloth-of-gold.

'You might have condemned me to this for the rest of my days, but look.' I turn back the heavy folds of black cloth, to reveal a shift of red silk, the hem worked with gold thread in the golden wheels of St Katherine. 'I will not forgo my heraldic magnificence. I know you will approve.'

Pleating the black silk to my knees so that the red and gold continues to blaze in defiance, I reach up and smooth my fingers over the intricate stitching on John's tunic. As I outline one of the fleur-de-lis in silver on blue, stroking the svelte back of a golden Plantagenet leopard, there is complaint in my voice.

'I see you've demanded to be buried beside Blanche in St Paul's.' My voice echoes strangely amongst the dislocated arches that I can no longer see. Briefly I glance over my shoulder to ensure I have no priestly audience. But then, why should a wife not converse with her husband? 'Why could you not be buried in Lincoln, so that I might join you when my time comes?'

A petty complaint, but understandable, I think. I sigh, and reach out my fingertips again to touch the gleamingly embroidered silks. It is so cold, the heavy fabric as slick as ice.

'I never doubt your love for me, John, even if you leave me your two second best brooches, deeming the King more worthy of your best one. Although you did give me the gold chalice that Richard gave you. A shame that it has more ostentation than beauty.'

For a moment I lean my forehead against the edge of the bier, then despite the cold and the dust, and because my knees complain at my long cold kneeling, I sink down onto the floor beside him, disposing my skirts to my comfort, and draw towards me the little cypress casket he has left me. He has given me so much, his superb generosity slapping at my senses. As well as the gold chalices and brooches, there are ermine mantles, a circlet and collar that he loved to wear. I am a wealthy widow. I can afford to sit on the floor in the dust in black silk and spend my time with idle hands.

'I will never have to beg for my next meal,' I say. 'I will never have to kneel before some noble lord to petition for his charity, as I did to you. I was terrified that you would refuse me a place in your household and send me back to Kettlethorpe empty-handed.' My face lights momentarily with the memory. 'And then I ran away after all, so that you had to summon me back.'

I take the key, which he always kept in his purse at his belt, and work it into the casket's lock, smiling as I do so. John has left me our bed complete with all its sumptuous furnishings. Not only that but the whole collection of his travelling beds.

'Where will I be travelling, now that I am alone?' I ask him. I laugh a little, a genuine if watery smile. 'How like you, to leave me the beds.'

If his intent is to draw attention to the physical desire that brought us together and kept us so for more years than I can count, then he has achieved it superbly.

My laughter dies as I ponder his gifts to me. The air is still around me.

'I wonder if I was worth the two thousand pounds you have left me.'

It is a vast sum. Yet I would give it all away, together with every bed, every jewel, every chalice. I would sleep on these cold stones and drink water from a pottery cup for the rest of my days to have him back with me.

I cover my face with my hands.

It will never be.

With my sleeve I wipe away the tears and turn the key, lifting the lid. I have not had time to investigate this little treasury. Perhaps it does not seem important against the enormity of John's death, even though I know the casket was very personal to him. Now I stare at the contents.

'Oh, John. My love, my love…' The tears fall faster, leaving dark patches on the black silk.

So personal, so intimate a collection, this jumble of contents provides no less than a map of our life together. I stir them with my finger. These precious items mean more to me than the land or Richard's cup or the second best brooches.

Mistress Saxby's pinchbeck pilgrim's badge that I had pinned to John's tunic in Lincoln, dull now with age, barely glimmers amongst the jewels. I rub it on my sleeve, remembering how I had pinned it lightly, so not to arouse the sleeping dragon of John's desire. When we had been together again, yet not together.

'I did not know you had kept this.'

I replace it, to take up a silver funerary badge from the

Prince's burial, when John had mourned the loss of his much-loved brother.

'I was not allowed to stand with you that day. We were still very discreet, were we not?'

There is a diamond and ruby brooch that I recognise: from John's mother, Queen Philippa. I hold it up to allow what little glow there is from the candles to light fires in its depths.

'I thought you would have given this to Henry, your heir—perhaps I will give it for you. He should have it—to pin to the bodice of his new wife when he remarries. It might be all the inheritance he gets now that Richard has his avaricious hands on the rest.'

For Richard has fulfilled all our fears. The Lancaster inheritance is securely in royal hands.

And there at the bottom, beneath all the rest is a piece of parchment, folded close. Carefully—for it is brittle—I smooth out the folds to discover a mass of dry flakes, which crumble even further into dust as I open them to the air.

'What is this?' I poke at it.

And I know. It is the remains of the rose I picked at The Savoy when I stepped across the line from dutiful widow to scandalous mistress. After my night of contemplation with the *Roman de la Rose*.

'You kept it. You kept it all these years.'

Suddenly it is too painful. My heart is awash with tears, and I close the lid.

'Not today,' I say. 'Today my heart is too sore for this.'

Some other time when I am stronger and can see the past with pleasure rather than grief, I will open it again and pick apart the memories. Cradling the little box I sit and look blindly at the altar where the silver crucifix glimmers with heavy mystery.

There is a movement, making me hold my breath, but it

is just a pigeon flying blindly, trying to find some means of escape.

Regrets?

I have some now, in my loneliness. The years—too many of them—when I was no better than a harlot in the eyes of the court and I resented the judgement even though it was an honest one. The years that we were apart, through hurt and bitterness that John had forsaken me for God and returned to Constanza, a woman he did not love, and who did not love him.

Life is too transitory. I would undo those years in the wilderness, defying Walsingham and all he stood for, if I could.

'Forgive me,' I whisper. 'Forgive me for the times I wounded you.'

The pigeon's wings seem to reply.

I do. I do. I know I wounded you too.

Yes, he had, but only to restore my dignity and my reputation at the end. How strong love can be, to bind us fast through all vicissitudes.

The pigeon flutters: *I love you. Death will not destroy what was ours. Such love will outlive the years. The echo of my devotion will remain a constant presence in your thoughts. I swear it.*

'I know,' I reply. 'I will remain true until my death and beyond.' Words he had once said to me, and I had never forgotten. 'I know now that love outlives death.'

At last I stand, my limbs stiff, and reorder my mourning black. My vigil is at an end and the pigeon seems to have found an escape or settled to roost. I touch John's hand, cold with that strange quality of dead flesh. I kiss his cheek one last time and then his lips. The embalming has restored his beauty in some strange manner, leaving his face severe and fine-boned, the elements of the final suffering obliterated.

He is the finest man I have ever known. The most beautiful.

'Will you remarry?' someone had asked. My son Henry, I think, who has come now to escort me to London. He is not insensitive, merely practical.

'Never,' I say. 'Never. How can I find a better man than my lord of Lancaster?'

But nor will I sink into lethargy. It is not in my nature and John would not want such a barren life for me. I will go back to Lincoln, and there I will try to pick up some of the pieces of friends and associates. And there are our children, and their children, to demand my affection.

'My love. My dearest love. Walk with me, you used to say.' My words are anguished as I close my hand over his for the final time.

Walk with me, the echo comes back to me from wall and pillar. *Walk with me for ever*.

I lift my head, as if waiting, but now here is Henry come to find me.

I close the latch of the little coffer, on our life together, turn the key and let tears run unchecked down my cheeks. As I walk from the chapel towards my waiting son who is pretending that he has not seen the inappropriate glory of my shift, now suitably hidden, I feel a flutter of awareness around me, moths' wings, doves' wings.

Walk with me...

I swear he is with me still.

* * * * *

ACKNOWLEDGEMENTS

All my thanks to my agent, Jane Judd, whose love of history is as strong as my own. Her support and encouragement for me and the courageous women of the Middle Ages continues to be invaluable.

To Sally Williamson at MIRA whose empathy with what I wish to say about my characters is beyond price. To her and to all the staff at MIRA, without whose advice and professional commitment the real Katherine Swynford would never have emerged from the mists of the past.

To Helen Bowden and all at Orphans Press, without whom my website would not exist and who create professional masterpieces out of the rough drafts of genealogy and maps I push in their direction.

AUTHOR NOTE

Katherine Swynford is a name known to every reader of historical fiction as the mistress of John, Duke of Lancaster, known to history as John of Gaunt. Other than that, historically, we know very little about her or their life together. We have no portraits, no descriptions of Katherine. She left no letters or useful diary records. Although the Duke recorded the gifts he made to members of his household in his detailed registers, Katherine's name rarely appears.

So what do we know about her?

History provides us with a skeleton of Katherine's life. Katherine de Roet, a young woman in the household of Blanche of Lancaster, was married to Sir Hugh Swynford and was widowed when Hugh died in Aquitaine. Katherine became mistress of John of Lancaster for twenty-five years, before he married her and made her Duchess of Lancaster. She had children with both her husbands. Her sister Philippa was wife to Geoffrey Chaucer. Katherine died in 1403 in Lincoln.

Other than that, the detail of Katherine's life is sketchy, even the exact year in which she was born is open to debate, as is the year in which she began her liaison with the Duke. We know that she was *magistra* to the Lancaster children and as such must have spent considerable time in the ducal household, but her movements during her years as John's mistress are not always clear. It is not even on record where Katherine took refuge during the terrible months of the Peasants Revolt; all we know is that she disappeared from the turbulent scene for a short time. We cannot even pinpoint the year in which the couple renewed their relationship after the issue of the quitclaim.

For a writer of an historical novel, this is both frustrating and at the same time fascinating. It is a matter of obtaining a 'best fit' picture of their life together from the facts that we have, making use of what was—and equally what was not—recorded about the scandalous affair.

Once again, it is a task of reading between the lines and joining the dots. Thus my novel of Katherine Swynford is firmly based on factual evidence. Where we simply 'don't know' I have, unapologetically, used historical licence. Where we do know, I have used the events to dramatic effect to create in *The Scandalous Duchess* a credible and awe-inspiring account of Katherine's place in history.

I am always delighted to keep in touch with my readers who are interested in my writing, both the process and the content. I enjoy receiving feedback and readers' thoughts and insights into my heroines.

You can keep up to date with events and signings on my website and contact me at: www.anneobrienbooks.com.

Why not visit me on my Facebook page: www.facebook.com/anneobrienbooks or follow me on Twitter: @anne_obrien.

I also have my own blog, where I write about history in general and what I am investigating in particular. Or anything historical that takes my interest. I will certainly be blogging about the world of Katherine Swynford and John of Lancaster. www.anneobrienbooks.com/blog.

INSPIRATION FOR *THE SCANDALOUS DUCHESS*

I was inspired to write the story of Katherine Swynford for two reasons.

Katherine's love affair with John of Lancaster was matter of great scandal, earning her vicious censure as a she-devil and enchantress, yet, despite all the pressures on them to end their liaison, their love did not die under attack. It would have been so easy for them to part and live separate lives, but they didn't.

What sort of love was it that bound them together, that could survive so many vicissitudes without destroying itself in guilt and despair? I was interested in exploring such a remarkable depth of emotion.

My second reason was based on what we know of the characters of John and Katherine.

Katherine was, on the evidence, strongly religious. A respectable widow, highly principled, raised under the influence of Queen Philippa of Hainault, who was known for her staunch beliefs, Katherine would seem to have been the last woman to ignore her conscience and take up a role that would destroy her reputation and bring her under the dire judgement of God.

John was equally known to hold to strong religious views, with a powerful sense of duty and a reputation for high chivalry despite his affairs outside marriage.

And yet both were prepared to abandon all moral integrity, all sense of responsibility, all thoughts of God's grace, when embarking on an adulterous affair that lasted on and off for twenty-five years, producing four illegitimate children as evidence of their sin. John was perfectly willing to place Katherine in the ducal household, in effect forcing his wife Constanza to accept his mistress. This was flaunting Katherine under Constanza's nose, an action that defies most attempts to explain or forgive.

Why did they take such a scandalous step? Was this just a love affair? I think not. I think it was far more powerful, in effect a Grand Passion. Remorseless, relentless, it was not at all a light-hearted romance but an emotion beyond their control, sweeping all before it, all sense of right or wrong. I consider it to be a tale of compulsive desire and need, so much stronger than love.

And, as I came to know them, the breathtaking enormity of what Katherine and John did took over to drive my writing and engage my own emotions.

I hope I have got to the heart of this most famous pair of medieval lovers in *The Scandalous Duchess*.

FOLLOWING IN KATHERINE SWYNFORD'S FOOTSTEPS

Tempted to travel? Feel an urge to follow in the footsteps of Katherine Swynford and John of Lancaster, even if it's only through the internet or travel guides, from the comfort of your armchair? Here are some of the best locations associated with them, and I have added website addresses, but of course there are others.

Kenilworth Castle

The jewel in the crown for Katherine and John. We think of Kenilworth in connection with Elizabeth I and Robert Dudley, when much building was undertaken, but much of the pre-Tudor construction was planned by John of Lancaster. Visit his Great Hall and dream…

www.english-heritage.org.uk/daysout/properties/kenilworth-castle

Lincoln Cathedral

A magnificent church in its own right, but also the site of the tomb of Katherine and her daughter Joan Beaufort. An essential place of pilgrimage for those following in Katherine's footsteps.

The cathedral close is where Katherine rented property and lived for many years in the Duke's absence and in her final years as a widow.

lincolncathedral.com

Pontefract Castle

The most important Lancastrian stronghold in the north of England. Much ruined today, but still with a sense of the past when John of Lancaster used it as his base of northern power.

And of course where Katherine probably took refuge…

www.wakefield.gov.uk/CultureAndLeisure/
Castlesandmuseums/Castles/PontefractCastle/default.htm

Also a very attractive and useful Facebook page:

www.facebook.com/Pontefractcastle

Tutbury Castle
Much ruined, but one of Duchess Constanza's favourite places. Katherine must certainly have spent time there with her sister Philippa and the Lancaster household.

www.tutburycastle.com

Hertford Castle
Only the gatehouse survives of the original castle where Constanza spent much time.

www.hertford.net/history/castle

The Savoy Palace
Sadly destroyed and with nothing extant to see. But the Savoy Hotel is built on the site and, viewed from the Thames, it gives a superb idea of the extent and dominance of this incredible building that was completely laid waste. One of the finest palaces in Europe with a wealth of valuable items collected by the Duke, it remains a matter of great regret that it is lost to us along with all its treasures.

en.wikipedia.org/wiki/Savoy_Palace

Kettlethorpe
There is little left of the manor that Katherine would have known, but the gateway arch to the present Kettlethorpe Hall, an eighteenth-century building, is certainly fourteenth century and so probably constructed by Katherine. There are also the remnants of a deer park that Katherine acquired.

The church was much rebuilt in the fifteenth and nineteenth centuries and sadly has no Swynford memorials.

www.britainexpress.com/counties/lincs/churches/Kettlethorpe.htm

Loved this book?

Visit Anne O'Brien's fantastic website
at **www.anneobrienbooks.com** for
information about Anne, her latest books,
news, interviews, offers, competitions,
reading group extras and much more…

Follow Anne on Twitter **@anne_obrien**

www.anneobrienbooks.com

London, 1938.
Meet Daisy Driscoll, the
working class orphan whose
luck may be about to change…

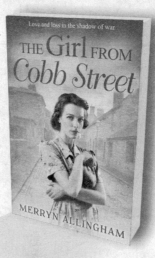

The war has just begun when Daisy meets and falls
madly in love with Gerald Mortimer. But when
Gerald returns to serve in India as a cavalry subaltern,
Daisy is left alone once more and, unbeknownst
to Gerald, pregnant with his child…

Wed by duty, Daisy struggles to adjust to life with her
new husband and soon discovers that Gerald is
in debt, and tragedy is about to strike…

*'Stephanie Laurens' heroines are
a marvellous tribute to
Georgette Heyer'*
—Cathy Kelly

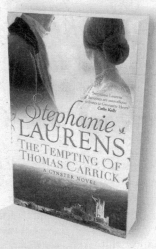

Strong-willed and passionate Lucilla Cynster is
the last woman Thomas Carrick wants to ask for
help, but when events take a disturbing turn on his
family's estate, he is faced with no choice but to do
exactly that. Will he be able to ignore the bond
that seethes between them?

HARLEQUIN MIRA®
www.mirabooks.co.uk

COMING SOON

**A dramatic new tale of desire and devotion
in book three of the new Cynster trilogy by**

Stephanie
LAURENS

A Match For Marcus Cynster

Marcus Cynster is waiting for Fate to come
calling. He knows his destiny lies near his home
in Scotland, but what will it be? Who is his fated
bride? One fact seems certain: his future won't lie
with Niniver Carrick, a young lady who attracts
him mightily and whom he feels compelled
to protect—even from himself.